Faction Paradox

ERASING SHERLOCK

by Kelly *Hale*

mad norwegian press | des moines

Also available from Mad Norwegian Press...

Faction Paradox Novels: The Complete Series
Stand-alone novel series based on characters and concepts
created by Lawrence Miles

Faction Paradox: The Book of the War [#0] by Lawrence Miles, et. al.
Faction Paradox: This Town Will Never Let Us Go [#1] by Lawrence Miles
Faction Paradox: Of the City of the Saved... [#2] by Philip Purser-Hallard
Faction Paradox: Warlords of Utopia [#3] by Lance Parkin
Faction Paradox: Warring States [#4] by Mags L. Halliday
Faction Paradox: Erasing Sherlock [#5] by Kelly Hale
Dead Romance [related novel] by Lawrence Miles

Sci-Fi Reference Guides
Redeemed: The Unauthorized Guide to Angel
by Lars Pearson and Christa Dickson

Dusted: The Unauthorized Guide to Buffy the Vampire Slayer
by Lawrence Miles, Lars Pearson and Christa Dickson

Doctor Who: The Completely Unauthorized Encyclopedia
by Chris Howarth and Steve Lyons

About Time: The Unauthorized Guide to Doctor Who
six-volume series by Lawrence Miles and Tat Wood

*AHistory: An Unauthorized History
of the Doctor Who Universe* by Lance Parkin (and Lars Pearson)

I, Who: The Unauthorized Guides to Doctor Who Novels and Audios
three-volume series by Lars Pearson

*Prime Targets: The Unauthorized Guide to Transformers, Beast Wars
and Beast Machines* by Lars Pearson

Now You Know: The Unauthorized Guide to G.I. Joe TV and Comics
by Lars Pearson

All rights reserved. No part of this book may be reproduced or transmitted in any form or by any means, electronic or mechanical, including photography, recording or any information storage and retrieval system, without express written permission from the publisher. Faction Paradox created and owned by Lawrence Miles, licensed to Mad Norwegian Press.

Copyright © 2006 Mad Norwegian Press, www.madnorwegian.com
Cover art by Sandy Gardner, www.sandygardner.co.uk
Jacket & interior design by Christa Dickson.

ISBN: 0-9759446-8-1
Printed in Illinois. First Edition: November 2006.

PART ONE

Chapter 1

Wednesday was my half-day and, as luck would have it, he went out.

I had everything arranged well in advance, awaiting only time and opportunity. But the man had been most uncooperative. Suffering the trademark ennui. *Avoir le cafard.* Classic bipolar. He indulged it wholeheartedly, and I think he rather enjoyed the image of world-weary malaise he presented to the casual onlooker. Me, for instance.

I came to clear after tea and found him lying with a newspaper draped over his face, one arm languishing off the edge of the sofa, fingers twitching now and again as if to signal that he was alive, if anyone were interested. I think he watched me from beneath the tented paper, and sometimes felt his eyes like cattle-prods urging me to hurry my tasks and be gone. My industrious presence disrupted the slow pulse of his lethargy, and quite took the joy out of it, I believe.

I counted myself fortunate, since I could leave the sitting room when I'd finished cleaning. His roommate didn't always have that option. There's nothing worse than having to share one's public space with a vegetating body that hasn't had a wash in several days.

'If I were your physician,' I overheard the doctor say, 'I would prescribe a brisk walk in the fresh air.'

'It's well that you are not my physician then,' came the hoarse reply.

Thankfully, the situation changed on Wednesday.

There I was, on my hands and knees with skirt pinned up, bucket of soapy water and brushes at the ready. I was dreaming of taking my guitar to Regent's Park and busking for the strollers, nary a thought to the man upstairs and my purpose; that's how deep-cover I'd gone. Then the hansom pulled up in front of the house. A lady stepped out. A *client.* The first one he'd had since I'd started working at the house over a month ago.

She had neither gloves nor hat, and wore a man's Ulster over an evening gown of midnight-blue velvet. Brown hair frothed over her shoulders in a boudoir tumble. On her narrow face was the dazed and puffy expression of someone for whom the previous evening's fun had lost all its charm.

Her appearance quite scandalised Mrs Hudson, who refused to be in the same room with such a creature. I was sent with the tea and naturally took a moment for a close, surreptitious inspection of the lady which merely confirmed what I'd seen when she'd arrived; French-cut gown, very décolletage, taken off and then put back on without the help of a maid. The third finger of her left hand showed a band of pale flesh where there'd been a ring, and her blue eyes blinked out a panicked semaphore of: "Help Me. Help Me. Help Me."

Sitting across from her was the young detective; spanking clean, smelling yummy, and fully dressed for a change, as if he'd risen from his stupor that morning knowing something interesting would walk through his door.

He dismissed me as soon as I set the cups on the saucers, so I had no excuse to stick around. Nor did I linger outside the door, since he would have known that.

Around eleven, the doctor was enlisted to hail a cab for the lady and escorted her off somewhere. I tried to hear where they were going, thinking I might catch them up later when I was free, but couldn't without it being obvious.

So imagine my delight when - at about noon, as I was finishing sweeping those other steps, the seventeen steps - the detective himself stuck his head out and asked me if I'd seen what's-her-name, little whoozzit-this-week, the girl who'd taken his boots to be polished. I said, 'I'll get her for you, sir,' and he said he really just wanted his boots as he was going out. Zippity do da, I said to myself, and me just finishing my work and ready for an afternoon of grand adventure.

I found little whozzit-this-week, Liza by name, and kept her from the requested errand by first sending her to fetch my hat, jacket, and guitar. I then washed up in the kitchen, told Mrs Hudson I'd done with my work, and asked leave to go.

As the streets were always crowded with lads in cast-off clothing, I figured I'd blend well enough in my dirt-coloured jacket and moleskin trousers, with my hair pinned tight beneath a cloth cap. I had to wear three pairs of socks to get the boots to fit: Such a fine pair of boots too, nicely distressed by a summer rain before I'd rescued them from a rubbish heap. With coal dust on my face and hands, and a wool muffler to hide my exuberance, I stepped from the alley onto Marylebone just as he was reaching the block of shops across the street.

He strolled in a leisurely manner, gazing into windows and swinging his walking-stick absently, endangering the unprotected knees of passers-by and the lumpy heads of children. The man was in a new mood and looking quite natty, I must say. He had a lean, loose-limbed grace, which reminded me of Fred Astaire in those black-and-white classics with skimpy plots and plenty of excuses for breaking into song. Not every man wearing a top hat and swinging a stick could carry it off, even in 1882 when it was *de rigueur*. He looked so sure of himself as he bounded down the steps to the Baker Street Underground that I felt my initial excitement start to wane. Not only was this the first time I'd actually tailed someone; I was tailing a self-proclaimed master of the art.

I assumed he was headed for the West End. The West End had the class restaurants with plush-appointed "cabinets particuliers", where a wealthy woman could be discreetly felt up between courses. I thought maybe he'd make a few inquiries at the hotel where the lovers did their little samba between the sheets, then head off to Simpson's for the stuffed sole. Of course, he could have walked to the West End from Baker Street faster, but that didn't occur to me until he got off at Bishopsgate and we passed from heaven to hell in just a few short steps.

It was in the people-packed, flea-market mess of Petticoat Lane that I saw Sherlock Holmes pick a man's pocket.

I couldn't say I actually saw him lift the purse, because he was quite good at it, but I saw him walking behind the old gent and move in swiftly as the crowd surged together through a narrow funnel of carts and barrows. Then the purse in his hand, and the smile on his lips just before he gave it back; a coy, triumphant grin. And wasn't he the sly-boots?

Tap on the shoulder. 'Excuse me sir, I believe you dropped this.'

'Bless you, sir. An honest gentlemen!' The man opened the little clasp tentatively, to offer a reward he hoped wouldn't be accepted.

'No sir, that won't be necessary, but I caution you to take care. These street Arabs are quite ruthless.'

'Yes sir, thank you, sir. Oh Lord, what the missus would say if she knew I'd lost the church fund for the new hymnals!' His victim scurried away, trying to clutch all his pockets at once.

'Silly old fart,' the young detective said. He bought a glass of beer. Downed it quickly.

Why was he here, amongst purveyors of pawned underwear and mended cravats? His next stop gave me a clue.

An old man with a withered arm leaned against a wall, tray full of trinkets and penny-toys suspended around his neck. Holmes picked through the offerings on the tray. Subtle body language in both buyer and seller indicated that their conversation had only a superficial relationship to the brightly-coloured objects being sold.

An informant. Excellent!

I moved in closer. Holmes held up a man-shaped figure, three or four inches high; a tiny warrior made of gutta percha, the nineteenth-century version of a cartoon action-figure.

Penny-toys were amongst the many oddities that littered his bedroom. I'd itched to pocket one of the whimsies, but invariably lost the nerve.

The detective pressed a coin into the toy-seller's hand, pocketed his prize, and moved on.

He led me into deep territory then; darker worlds that twisted round like filthy water down a drain-hole. Banks and brokerage firms on one side, sweatshops and slaughterhouses on the other. An incestuous union of haves and have-nots.

Technically, I knew the streets as well as he did. They were encoded in my memory, and I only had to call up the mnemonic trigger, like flicking a switch. I could see the streets of Spitalfields vividly, a haphazard grid of narrow thoroughfares and dangerous dead-ends wedged between Whitechapel, Bethnal Green, and the broad back of the City. But having a map of the streets in my head and actually *knowing* them were two very different things. I closed my eyes, mentally turning the map around and around. When I opened them I realised that in this jungle, Holmes was Viet Cong and I was the dumb American bastard from the Midwest.

Tenements loomed and teetered and squatted amidst scary little public houses that smelled exactly like the vomit from mixing beer and gin. Layered over it was the pervasive aroma of fried fish and dry rot, wet dogs, unwashed human bodies, and industrial-strength coal fumes.

In this picturesque part of town, the detective visited two pawnbrokers in quick succession, whatever business he had with them swift and to the point. At the third similar establishment, he reached for the bell over the grimy transom, only to dart suddenly into a passage barely wide enough for the breadth of his shoulders and covered by a corrugated tin roof that must have been six inches lower than he was tall.

I walked past the pawnshop, past the pleas of beggars, past the gossip of haggard women, past kids who offered to blow my non-existent dick for a penny, and hustled round the corner, down to the end of the street to wait. I gave it five minutes without any sign of him, then inched my way along the bricks to look for an egress from the passageway. There wasn't one. So I jogged to the next lane over, and found myself peering down a narrow, cobbled crevice to hell.

An open gate at the end of the lane exposed a Gustav Dore etching of single-story, soot-smeared cottages set in a horseshoe ring. Tiny windows on either side of the doors made the cottages look like something an abused child would draw; ugly scrawls of houses with eyes, a nose, and no mouth. Here and there, heroic attempts to make them homey - curtains in one, spindly geraniums in a rusty pail at another - just added a poignant touch of colour to something uncompromisingly squalid. I could see the dull glint of the corrugated-roofed passageway against the taller building behind them.

The courtyard was currently serving as a communal laundry for the mostly Jewish inhabitants, all women and small children. Regardless of the ambience, it was a strangely cheerful, gossipy group that greeted my eyes; singing, laughing, and passing judgment on others in Yiddish. I waited and wondered where the hell he'd gone to ground, fearing that at any moment he might appear behind me, or across from me, or right in front of my face. Yet, I wasn't surprised when he emerged from one of the cottage doors, scraping it across the dirt on saggy hinges.

Sherlock Holmes was dressed for rabbinical studies - yes, that's right - in spectacles, prayer shawl and soft-billed cap. He carried books, I assumed of the Hebrew variety. His clothes were drab and dusty, his shoes well-worn. Bill of his cap over his eyes, he threaded his way through women up to their armpits in steaming tubs, and lines strung with never-quite-clean underwear.

I pressed my back to the crumbling stone-and-daub wall, and slid back, back, to a recessed stairwell of brick and iron railing several yards behind me.

I heard the women greet the detective enthusiastically, as if they knew him, and his reply, delivered with just the right touch of youthful embarrassment and in passing fair Yiddish.

It was such a daring bit of deception on his part. Smooth. Flawless. Just this side of *mushuganah*. I knew he was gifted, but this had me repressing a squeal of delight.

The good wishes and farewells of the women followed him out the gate, and he set off down the street, passing my hiding-place. I counted seven footfalls, eight, ten, and was just about to lift my head over the railing when I heard him stop. A low whistle sounded, then the soft crunch of his feet in the gravel as he retraced his steps.

'Interesting,' he said. Another step, and another -

I groped awkwardly for the handle of the door. Five or six more steps and he'd be at the railing, looking down. Then, suddenly, he stopped and let out a laugh instead; a laugh of pure, uninhibited joy.

'Oh, but this is wonderful!' he exclaimed to no-one in particular. 'What nerve! What devilish nerve.' A pause, then: 'Hullo! I'm currently on my way to Hanbury Street if you'd care to follow.'

Shit. Shitshitshit. The handle of the door dropped down with a groan. I held my breath, pushed back ever so slightly. The door didn't open.

'Come out, come out, wherever you are!' A pause, then the sound of his shoes in the gravel again. 'Don't be shy.'

A few more steps and it'd be all over. Not even two months in the field, and I'd already screwed up. But instead of the quick pounce and grab by the throat I anticipated, he shouted, he challenged. That was his mistake. The cocky little bastard blew his opportunity.

'Really, it's been jolly good fun,' he cried. 'Come out from there and we'll have a nice chat over a pint and pie.'

A baby gave a high-pitched wail from a tenement across the narrow lane, and a window was thrown open with more force than its frayed wooden sashes could tolerate.

'Oi! You down there!' A woman's voice, rough-lunged and angry. 'Jew-boy! You want to take it somewheres else? You woke the babe took me a day's end to get to sleep, you bloody mumper!'

'Sorry,' he said, but his laugh rendered it an insincere apology.

Three very tanked-up Irishmen chose that moment to come out of the pub on the corner. They heard a baby screaming, must have seen the woman leaning out of the window, apparently put-upon and with a Jew laughing at her. They couldn't see me nestled in my dark little recess, but they did see a wonderful opportunity to beat the crap out of someone for a vaguely justifiable reason.

'Look, lads,' one of them said. 'Tere's a bloody kike makin' sport of a lady.'

The woman said 'Jeh-sus,' because it was obvious she wouldn't be getting her baby back to sleep anytime soon, and the window came down with a bang that should have shattered it.

Sherlock Holmes, being the clever young man that he was, did not take those few more steps that would have given him a view of his stalker hiding in a stairwell just scant yards away. The World's First Consulting Detective chose, very wisely I might add, to run like hell. I heard the clatter of footfalls echoing into the distance and the shouting of men who would never catch him.

My feet were rubbed raw inside the boots, and I was limping by the time I made it back to the alley behind the house on Baker Street. I stripped and buried the disguise under the coals. After washing down in the pail of water I'd left for the purpose, I smoothed my hair, buttoned the basque jacket of my poor-girl's best, grabbed my guitar, and was out of the cellar door in a wink. I took the laundry off the line and picked some summer savoury to add to the soup. I was such a good girl, Mrs Hudson said, she'd never had a better girl to work for her. I played my guitar and sang Negro spirituals while she cooked. They're uncommonly fond of Negro spirituals, the English.

He wasn't back for supper. Nearly midnight and not back yet. And what had I learned besides the fact that overlarge footwear cause blisters just as painful as shoes that were too tight?

He had a bolt-hole somewhere in Spitalfields. He spoke a smattering of Yiddish. He wasn't stupid enough to take the pugilist's approach when outnumbered and in a hurry to get somewhere else. And of course, he was a genius with the deceptively simple disguise.

I'd learned what I already knew: he was a clever lad. Oh, my goodness, yes. He nearly had me collared on my first time out.

Chapter 2

At elevenses today, I got to bring tea to the charming Inspector Lestrade. He *did* rather resemble a rat in a suit; a rat who'd rather be sitting around in his vest and drawers, reading the paper.

I was supposed to be sweeping the carpets but couldn't, since the gentlemen were taking a meeting. So I bustled about, picking up the dirty glasses, the apple-cores that never quite made it into the dustbins, that kind of thing. Holmes was sitting in his usual chair, none the worse for wear, apparently. His legs were crossed, elbows resting on the antimacassars, fingers steepled. Watson was on the sofa with a copy of the *Lancet* and his cup of tea. Lestrade sat in the basket chair, liberally dosing his own tea with something from a flask he carried inside his coat. He left the saucer on the table when he picked up the cup. Accustomed to drinking from a mug, I could see.

Holmes smiled obligingly. 'And what auspicious occasion can we thank for your presence with us today, Inspector?'

'No doubt, Mr Holmes, you've kept up on the burglaries that've been causing such a fuss hereabouts -'

Holmes held up one finger, saying, '*Pas devant les domestiques,* Inspector,' which Lestrade didn't understand immediately, though I did.

The burglaries were the sort that frightened and also stimulated the imaginations of female domestic servants. We met at gates, in the squares or the mews to discuss the potential horrors and secret delights of having a man slipping into the tiny windows of our uppermost bedrooms en route to the moneyboxes of our masters and mistresses. It was said he'd been known to take the most outrageous liberties with sleeping housemaids, kissing them upon their lips before leaving by the same said window, out to the roof and the shrouded expanse of the London nightline.

Naturally, I wanted to stay and watch Mr Holmes interact with his favourite local constabulary and judge for myself which was the most condescending to the other. I ignored the painful rubbing of the blisters at my heels and tried to look terribly busy; oh, don't mind me gentlemen, just the maid, thought I'd trim the lamp wicks while I'm here. But they remained steadfastly silent, waiting for me to leave. Well, I wasn't about to leave, not until they picked me up and threw me out.

Arms full of their dirty shirts and linens, I went over to one of the windows to adjust the shade, ostensibly because they needed more light in the room, but mostly just to annoy them. As I reached for the cord, a stocking tumbled to the floor. I casually swooped to snatch it up, one of those ballet moves that's supposed to quick and graceful, leaning from the waist, one leg out for balance -

Another wadded-up stocking went rolling across the floor. It was bad physical comedy as well as embarrassing, because men's underwear kept tumbling from my arms in untidy heaps. As soon as I'd pick up one thing, another would fall out of the bundle.

There was a sound from behind me, a cross between a shudder, a moan, and a snicker. Rather than the faceless servant that disappeared their dirt, I'd become a clumsy spectacle for their amusement. But when I turned around, it seemed the gentlemen had been elbowing each other and taking the opportunity to eye my backside, amply displayed as it was.

Caught out, Watson reddened and cleared his throat, eyes quick upon his medical journal. Lestrade gave me a lopsided grin and winked. He winked! I didn't know anyone actually did that. And Mr Holmes... well, Mr Holmes was busy examining the burning tip of his fancy Egyptian cigarette while hissing a little tune between his teeth.

I clutched the laundry tightly to my chest, completely flummoxed. I forgot to curtsy, or ask if they'd be requiring anything else. I just closed my mouth and hurried my backside out of there. Before I'd even shut the door behind me, I heard Lestrade say: 'Cor... that's a nice bit o' biscuit, that is.'

Curiously, I could find no appropriate reaction to being ogled by men who considered me a nice bit of biscuit. Up to that point I thought I'd been the ideal servant, a barely noticed automaton: quiet, efficient and unobtrusive. It had certainly paid off in small ways. I knew what bills Holmes hadn't paid and how much money he had in his bank account (somewhere between a little and not much). I knew his tailor was in Bond Street, where in some distant future would be a club advertising lap-dancing and "Girls! Girls! Girls!" in flashing neon.

The problem with the whole housemaid shtick was that there was no downtime, no idle time whatsoever, in which to analyse and codify data. One thing never mentioned or even hinted at in Dr Watson's writings were the two other lodgers in Mrs Hudson's house. I suppose the existence of these lodgers had little bearing on the cases he documented, but their presence certainly put a hardship on me.

Holmes and Watson had a suite of rooms on the first floor. Not huge. Two bedrooms and a sitting room that also served as dining room, study, smoking parlour and chemistry lab. Full of the usual Victorian excess, the sitting room was made even more cluttered by the fact that Holmes, though generally particular about clean underwear, was a slob. Watson's staked share of public space was in constant danger of encroachment from mountains of newspapers, towers of books and boxes, and a trail of crumpled bits of paper that fell from the detective's pockets whenever he reached for his pen or his watch. I'd been warned not to throw any papers away, so I collected these notes regularly and placed them in a bowl on the sideboard. "McMurdo, Alison's Rooms" and "G. T. shoved the queer 8th of Aug" were among these intriguing missives. They were usually gone from the bowl when I next tidied the room.

Though they had the most spacious apartment, Holmes and Watson were required to share the water closet and bathroom with the other two gentlemen. I cleaned those rooms as well and believe me, men are men when it comes to hitting a certain target consistently.

Gerard Cavendish had a small room on the first floor right next to the WC, which wasn't much of a perk, reliable plumbing being in its infancy and all. Cavendish was a Bible-thumper who worked at a branch bank in Oxford Street. Though he never complained about the proximity of his room to the john, he did complain about Holmes playing violin so late at night. Most of the detective's compositions were actually really good, and he played a wicked Paganini, but Cavendish didn't like anything passionate that wasn't related to Hell and how we're all going there.

The other lodger was the spotty, myopic, stammering Thomas Peerson Corkle. Some sort of assistant curator at the British Museum, he had the second-worst room in the house, mine being the worst in the garret at the very top. To complicate things further, Mrs Hudson's son, Jack, was sleeping on a sofa in the parlour. Like the tweeny Liza, he was kind of a tweeny himself, being perpetually 'tween jobs. Fancied himself quite the charmer in spite of it.

I knew I'd be living the life of a maidservant. I'd done the research, trained in an authentic restoration of a Victorian mansion. I'd polished copper pots with sand and swept the carpets with old tealeaves. Quaint, novel fun. Not this crawling up the final steps to my room after sixteen-hour days, arms so sore I could barely pull the night-dress over my head. I was using muscle groups I didn't even know I had. Something so ordinary as slicing bread would suddenly stun me with the fact of its necessity. Bread-slicing was a daily order of business. But musing over it only brought a cuff from Mrs Hudson. 'Mind how thick you slice it, Rose! Och, not fit for toast, that! Where's your head, girl?'

At the end of each day, I'd spend an hour or more organising my notes and recording everything of consequence that I'd witnessed or heard, minutiae ruthlessly thrust upon me by mnemonic enhancements. Then I'd collapse. Sometimes I'd play my guitar before I'd collapse.

The routine had definitely taken its toll on my looks. Cuteness had been my curse professionally, but now vanity was suffering a crisis of faith. I hadn't washed my hair in two weeks. My eyes were ringed with dark shadows. Oh well. Apparently, Victorian men didn't look at my face anyway. And what did it matter, really? Who was there to charm? It was a world of clearly-defined classes, and I had no interest in those that were technically of mine. Poor, pitiful me.

No-one with whom to commiserate in the narrow comfort of my lonely bed. I wouldn't have dared, even if there *had* been someone. Mrs Hudson was firm on that subject. So I had only my guitar for company, and when I wasn't fingering that I was miserably fingering myself, remembering former lovers with a fondness they didn't deserve.

***

I finally hit pay-dirt. An actual conversation between the doctor and the consulting detective, heard in full as I was cleaning up after the chimney-sweep and his underfed little apprentice.

The flues were open, the fireplaces empty. With my head in the parlour hearth, I could hear everything they said.

It began with Watson extolling the virtues of keeping the *membrum virile* in sound working order. At least once a month, so my local sources informed me, the good doctor was off to spend a few happy hours at a certain house run by a certain Mrs Sterling, in the company of one Maddie Collins or one Abigail Hewitt. And let me just say, Watson was a gorgeous piece of man-flesh. In my time, he'd *never* have to pay for sex. But, as he had paid for it on numerous occasions, I was privileged to hear him waxing scientific on the subject.

Apparently, a man was at risk of contracting a kind of glandular toxicity in which the seminal fluid (for lack of anything better to do) invaded the tissues of the brain and caused numerous problems, not the least of which was a cumulative debilitation of the mental faculties. Watson was quite adamant in his insistence that Holmes was doing serious damage to his mental faculties by not tending to his needs 'as a man, my dear chap, as a man'. I envisioned some serious doctorly pose as he asserted that the young detective risked not only damaging 'vital organs' but also the brain itself.

Holmes ceased making strange and lazy noises on his violin, and pulled the bow up the strings in a screech. 'Watson, if I ever think myself in danger of poisoning my brain in such a dreadful manner, I am perfectly capable of averting disaster by use of my own hand and a French picture-postcard.'

There followed a long moment of silence, and then Watson said in voice hoarse with what I can only assume to be shock: 'There is a sound medical reason that it's called self-abuse, you know.'

'Pity, that. And I had the solution right at my fingertips.'

'This is no joking matter!' Watson sputtered.

There was a beat of silence, and then they both burst into laughter.

'I'm sorry, dear chap,' Watson said in that weak, high voice that follows a fit of the giggles. 'But I don't see you as the sort who would find a naughty French postcard remotely stimulating.'

'Indeed, I would not. Now, if the postcard had a caption declaring that the scantily-clad *demimondaine* was in fact a thief who'd stolen a priceless Greek amphora from the British Museum and had it secreted somewhere on her person... *that* I might find stimulating.'

'That is, I believe, my very point,' Watson said. 'Seriously, Holmes, I am concerned for you. It isn't healthy. You're a young man -'

'How is abstinence worse than exposing oneself to the social diseases that plague the whole of London? You are in far more danger than I.'

The doctor declared that it was a very respectable establishment he was recommending.

'Oh?' said Holmes. 'I must've misunderstood. It *is* a brothel, is it not? *Le maison close?* A house of joy -'

'Yes! Yes, but Mrs Sterling operates one of the cleanest houses of the kind. And I am not the only man of my profession to make use of it.'

'Oh, well, that definitely puts the medical seal of approval on the whole matter, doesn't it?'

'I am not suggesting you engage a harlot off the Ratcliff Highway. These are women from decent backgrounds.'

I heard the twang of the strings as Holmes set the fiddle on the floor, his voice fading and rising in pitch with his agitated pacing. 'Good God, Watson! Listen to yourself. Women from decent backgrounds? What makes them so? Why should a woman like that rise in our estimation while a hard-working girl like Rose Donnelly is called a slut simply because she makes an honest living as a housemaid?'

I started at the sound of my name.

'I have never in my life referred to a maid as a slut,' Watson replied coldly. 'When I said decent backgrounds, I meant just that. You know how it is for some of these young women. Dismissed governesses or ladies' companions, forced to the streets through no fault of their own. In Mrs Sterling's establishment they have clean lodgings and a fair income -'

'With a substantial percentage taken by Mrs Sterling herself, no doubt. At the very least, Watson, she has used their misfortune to line her pockets.' There was an unspoken judgement as well, that Watson himself was taking advantage of their misfortunate. Holmes returned to his position at the fireplace, and I could hear the tense thud-thud as he packed a cigarette. He struck a match, puffed. 'Let me ask you this, then: Do any of these professional associates of yours have wives? Yes? Forgive the foolish questions of one not in the medical profession, but aside from the danger these liaisons present to his wife, it seems to me that a married man with access to his own marital bed would have no need of the services of a whore, no matter how decent her background.'

'I regret having brought the matter up at all,' Watson muttered.

'But I was so counting on the wisdom of your vast experience to sort these matters out, due to my rapidly diminishing mental faculties.'

The detective exhaled loudly, and the fumes of his Egyptian cigarette filled the flue before drifting upwards. I heard footsteps moving away from the hearth. On hands and knees, I waited to see if the conversation would escalate or move on to subjects less volatile, but the tense silence between them seemed to go on forever, punctuated only by the distant burble and hiss of the gasogene. I guessed Watson was brewing himself a drink. Finally, Holmes ventured: 'Er, Watson?

You do take the necessary precautions with these women, I trust?'

The doctor groaned. 'I'm not an idiot, despite my being a hypocrite in your estimation.'

'Have I not freely admitted the flesh has its temptations? But the mind is the ruler of the carnal realms, Watson, or that is how it should be. It is so for me.'

'I see,' Watson said, returning to the vicinity of the fireplace. I shivered. He had a very sexy voice. 'May I ask then, who is this Rose Donnelly?'

'The maid.' A pause. 'Oh. Shrewd, Watson. Very cunning. Wrong, of course.'

The doctor chuckled. 'She's quite pretty.'

'Your transparency would be laughable were it not so offensive. She's a common wench from Yorkshire. And though she clearly aspires to improve herself in both speech and manner, she has neither the breeding nor the mental sophistication to interest me, thank you very much.'

Fat lot he knew about it. But, oh well. We are who we pretend to be.

'That goes without saying,' Watson assured him, then added thoughtfully: 'Still, she has the most delightful dimples.'

'I think they make her look a trifle sly.'

'Pretty ankles, too.'

'Watson, do shut up.'

Delightfully frank subject matter aside, the conversation revealed that Holmes had made more than a rudimentary study of his housemaid. Perhaps I flattered myself there. Rose Donnelly would be a simple, almost automatic exercise in observation for a man like him. That he'd seen what he was supposed to see meant I was playing my role effectively. Rose was indeed from Yorkshire, as the undercurrent of dialect would have indicated to him. And though I'd love to believe I was chosen for my brilliance, my mother happens to have come from Yorkshire, a fact certainly taken into consideration when I was recruited.

Still, I'd have tread more carefully. Much ill could befall a woman in the nineteenth century if a man took an uninvited interest in her.

I told the Professor we ought to have at least discolored my teeth.

Chapter 3

Autumn decided to put in an appearance with gusts of wind and rain, and a decided turn for the chilly. I was in the sitting room, getting up the fire before supper. Luckily both Holmes and Watson were ignoring me, but for the usual reasons that all masters ignore servants. Who wants to watch someone working, right? You might get a guilty urge to help her out, and then the entire fabric of society would unravel. So I was laying down brand-new coals in the thrifty manner prescribed by my employer, being careful not to crush any of the cigars that were (for reasons known only to Holmes) stored in the scuttle, when he casually informed Watson that someone followed him when he went out Wednesday.

OK. No reason to panic. Why should he suspect a dirty wench with her head in the fireplace? Still, it was all terribly déjà vu, or unpleasantly coincidental, seeing as I'd had my head in a fireplace when they'd spoken of whores. And *me*.

'Good lord!' the doctor exclaimed. 'By whom? Did you see?'

I struck a match. It flickered and died. I struck another and noticed my hands were shaking.

'Not a good look. And, er, circumstances prevented me from collaring the devil.'

'But why, do you suppose? For what purpose?'

'I've no idea. It seems unlikely to be the same villain who robbed my client. He assumed she wouldn't go the police, and rightly so. Therefore, he has no reason to suspect anyone is after him.' From the corner of my eye, I saw him take a cigarette from the case in the pocket of his dressing gown. 'He was no seasoned veteran in the art of skulking, that much is certain. And the boots worn for the task were definitely too large for the person wearing them. There was something in the pressure of the foot that made the print...'

The second match died. I put my head inside the hearth, trying to look up the chimney to see what the problem was.

'Having trouble, Rose?'

I jumped at the sound and turned to find myself looking right into his eyes; eyes that might have been almost blue, on a sunny afternoon in the south of France. He had one hand on the surround as he leaned over.

'There's a strong wind come down the chimney. Sir.'

'Perhaps if you adjusted the flue,' he said, reaching for the device to do just that. I cursed myself for an idiot. He then squatted next to me and lighted a vesta, leaning across me with the flame cupped between his hands. Those hands moved past my shoulders and my bowed head, and held the match to the tinder for what seemed like my entire life. I could smell him; bay rum and the waxy odour of the vesta, the scent of starch in his shirt, the wool of his dressing gown with its cling of stale tobacco, the faint and musky aroma of armpits, the acrid fumes from the coal. This face with its defiant chin and infamous nose, blowing gently on the chunk of coal he'd ignited, while a thick lock of his hair, black as the coal itself, flopped down from his forehead in a curve across one brow. The coal began to glow, teased into it by his breath. He put the cigarette to his lips, touched it to the glowing edge, and puffed until the tip burned evenly.

He could have lighted his cigarette with another match, but no, all this to unnerve me. And I was unnerved. Here was the god made manifest, breathing right next to me, close enough for me to touch the pores of his smooth, freshly-shaved cheek.

He darted a glance, the coolest flick of a gaze, intent upon some puzzle he'd fixed on me. *What is it about you that has put this itch in my brain?*

A diversionary tactic was definitely called for. I was forced to channel my inner Eliza Dolittle.

Ooh, master's taken a fancy to me. What am I t'do? If I refuse 'im, I'll be turned out, forced to sell me virtue. Oh, please, sir, don't look at me so. I'm a good girl, I am.

I made certain he could read this internal dialogue in my trembling lips and heaving bosom. His eyes widened in alarm, and he stood abruptly, bumping his head on the edge of the mantel in the process. I turned away and bit down on a giggle. Partly relief, partly hysteria.

Straightening to his full imperious height, the detective reached tentatively to the potential lump at the back of his head, then thought better of it. He aimed his blush at a bland landscape in oil hanging above the fireplace.

'You know the most curious thing about the young man that followed me, Watson? The curious thing is not so much the fact that he was following, but rather that he was wearing my own boots to do it.'

Oh Christ. I pumped the bellows madly, feeling the detective's eyes boring holes between my shoulder-blades.

'Your own boots?' The doctor laughed. 'I'm assuming not the boots which are currently on your feet.'

'Naturally not. An old pair I'd consigned to the dustbin several weeks ago.'

'Ah. *Those* boots. No doubt the young rascal snatched them before the dustman hauled away the rubbish. They were perfectly good boots, Holmes, I told you that at the time. For a man with a sporadic income you're not very thrifty -'

'Rose,' Holmes said suddenly. 'Are you quite through?'

'Yes, sir.' The fire, if anything, was too hot now. I set the bellows aside and backed out of the aperture as gracefully as possible. Resisting the urge to rub the itchy black dust on my nose, I ventured a humble: 'Shall I inform Mrs Hudson you'll be wantin' your supper sir?'

'Yes, but fetch me an apple from the sideboard before you go. I'm near faint with hunger all of a sudden.'

This capricious demand was so very typical of the master / servant relationship that I didn't question it, even in the face of Watson's startled expression. I went to the sideboard and reached for an apple in the bowl -

'Are your shoes troubling you, Rose?'

Instantly, I was aware of the sticking-plasters curled into painful wads at the backs of my heels.

The bastard. The smarmy prick.

I turned. 'Sir?'

'You were limping just then, and I wondered if your shoes were troubling you.'

I opened my mouth, a dozen ready lies to choose from, but the angel of cold reason saved me from a foolish course. A lie could be followed, proved as false. A lie would only give him cause to look at me more closely. I chose something approximating the truth.

'I'm on my feet all day, sir. They swell a little come evening.'

The stem of his pipe jerked like a divining rod toward the toes of my sturdy oxfords. 'Your shoes seem well-chosen for hard work. They can't be pinching your toes or rubbing your heels much, even if your feet are swollen...' His eyes shot up, and I do believe I gasped.

It was as if a switch had been flipped in his brain. Facts slipped into their slots; patterns unfolded like a Chinese puzzle-box. The pupils were pinpricks of black circled by granite, and they said *en garde*.

Watson rose from his chair, sensing this sudden charge in the atmosphere. 'Holmes...?'

There's a moment of grace between the predator and its prey, a kind of divine equanimity. Just a moment of grace, when it could still go either way.

Be the maid.

This was a man whose dirty linens passed through my hands.

'These apples are badly bruised, sir,' I said, holding one out to him. 'Is there somethin' else I can fetch so's you don't faint dead away?'

Watson made a small choking sound of laughter, and Holmes's hawk-like gaze lost its grip. 'No,' he said tersely. 'You may go.'

I dipped a curtsy, flew to the door and freedom. As soon as I'd shut it behind me, I heard the doctor exclaim in a rush: 'What the devil was that all about?'

Holmes shushed him. I knew he was listening for the sound of my footsteps retreating, so I thought it best to oblige loudly and with purpose. At the service stairs I slipped out of my shoes and crept back, a risky and heart-pounding manoeuvre.

'I'm not suggesting it was she,' Holmes was saying, rather defensively. 'I was merely struck by the idea that it might have been a woman.'

'Why in the name of all that's holy would a woman want to follow you?'

'My word, Watson. True, I am not blessed with your *beau ideal*, but really, you cut me to the bone -'

'Do forgive me, Holmes. I didn't mean to suggest...' Watson began, then sputtered irritably. 'Oh, just answer the question, will you?'

Holmes laughed. 'I am as perplexed as you. I've had no cases since June, and it seems odd that I should find myself followed on the very day my fortunes changed, does it not?'

'It does. But, really, Holmes, a woman wearing your old boots? It stretches credibility... what? What is it now, for pity's sake?'

A creak in the floorboards had me bolting for the back stairs. I snatched up my shoes and was halfway to the kitchen before he'd flung open the door.

I was spared having to wait at their table, thank God. Liza had leave to go early on Saturday nights because she spent Sundays with her folks in Whitechapel, so Mrs Hudson took the gentlemen their supper while I cleaned up the mess she'd made preparing it. Afterwards, she retired to the parlour to spend the dwindling evening hours in the company of her son, Jack. Shortly after, Holmes and Watson went out. I took a lantern to the cellar.

There seemed nothing remarkable about the boots at first glance. It wasn't until I turned them over that I saw the pattern of the nails in the soles, which proved on close inspection to be his own initials. ESH. The nail-heads were pretty worn down, but he could hardly have missed the imprint I'd left in the muck to read; a signature in slop and filth, and probably some particular clay he could distinguish from any other in the whole stinking city.

My first impulse was to burn the lot, but leather, wool, and linen had telltale odours and distinctive ash. He'd know, or suspect.

I considered burying the items, or tossing them into the river, but paranoia was the curse of common sense. I was sure that no matter where I sought to rid myself of the incriminating evidence, it'd return to haunt me. So I wrapped the lot in brown paper, tied it with string, and decided to ship them out of the country at the soonest opportunity. New York seemed far enough away. With any luck the package would remain unclaimed forever. In the meantime, it'd hide under the bed like Poe's telltale heart.

I played my guitar for a while, melodies that restlessly wandered in and out of melancholy. Then I went to bed. I dreamed I'd pawned the boots, but when I went to claim them, Holmes was behind the counter eating an apple.

Chapter 4

The very next night, Mrs Hudson took to her bed early with aches and chills, and by morning she was sneezing, coughing, and dripping snot all over the breakfast preparations. Over her protests, I sent her back to bed with a cup of rosehip tea, an arrangement that would have worked out fine if Liza had shown up. I cursed her for a lazy little bitch and got breakfast ready all by myself.

Mr Corkle and Mr Cavendish were required to come to table for meals, serving-times being set and never varied. As they had their jobs to go to, and paid to have their bellies filled, I cooked up rashers of bacon, fried bread, porridge, and sliced oranges, with the addition of boiled eggs for the men in "B".

Jack Hudson hung around the kitchen while I did this, taking advantage of his mother's infirmity to chat me up. Charming without being particularly bright or witty, Jack still had that malleable quality of youth, suitable for training if a woman had a mind for it. The fact that he didn't have a job, and spent most of his time idling about the parlour pretending to look for one in the papers, rather put the kibosh on that idea. Too many ex-boyfriends with the same qualities.

He asked me if I'd sneak out to the Oxford Music Hall with him this coming Sunday instead of going to church.

Although I did go to Holy Cross Church in St Pancras most Sundays, it was *not* for my spiritual well-being. It was there that I met with my informant, one who knew me as the Widow Tory. I declined Jack's generous offer: I wouldn't feel right about it, didn't think his mum would approve.

Undaunted, Jack took the opportunity to follow me into the dry pantry to, you know, 'help me out'. And he accidentally tripped over a sack of flour and oh, imagine my surprise when his hand came in contact with my right breast as he was trying to brace his fall. Boyish embarrassment turned sappy serious in an instant, and I knew he was going to try to kiss me.

I was not in the mood to tolerate this with any patience. I hauled off and slapped young master Jack so hard that his head bounced off the wall. Then I shoved him without waiting to see where he fell, grabbed the big pot of coffee off the fire, and went into the dining room. After a few minutes he slunk in after me.

Mr Cavendish, permanent scowl on his narrow, pinched, I-haven't-taken-a-shit-in-weeks face, said, 'If my pay is docked for lateness, you may tell Mrs

Hudson I shall adjust my rent accordingly.' Whatever, I thought, just stuff your bloody gullet and get out. But I said, 'Yes, sir. Dreadful sorry, sir. It won't happen again, sir.'

Mr Corkle merely smiled, his eyes magnified to saucers behind the spectacles, and told me how everything looked scrumptious, which was what he always said.

By the time I was headed upstairs with the tray, I was ready for a fight. One word from Mr Sherlock Holmes, one sly inference, and I was prepared to grab him by the balls and twist until he screamed for mercy. I was fantasising about doing it for no reason at all when I heard the back door open, then bang shut. Someone came sprinting up the stairs, two at a time.

I was balancing this huge, heavy tray, taking each step with the mindful caution of one who wore skirts to her ankles. Spitefully, I slowed down to an even more methodical plod. Unable to get past me (the service stair being somewhat narrower), Holmes was forced to rein in those long legs to accommodate *me*.

To my annoyance, he didn't seem bothered. When I got to the landing, he dodged around me, frock coat flapping about his thighs. Gallantly opened the door with a sweeping gesture and a tip of his hat.

Watson was seated at the dining table like some bleary-eyed lord of the manor, with the mess from a late-night snack littering the surface. Holmes discarded the newspaper, half-read, onto the sideboard. I set the tray on top of it with a loud bang and pulled the tea-towel from my apron ties, sweeping the crumbs from the table, careless of where they flew; I'd be cleaning them up later anyway. Holmes danced aside, like a matador evading the bull's horns, as bits of cheese and sunflower seeds flew past his shoes.

'Mrs Hudson is feelin' poorly, doctor.' I snapped the tablecloth open and spread it out. 'If you'd be good enough to look in on her later, I'd be most grateful, sir.'

He winced as a plate came skidding across the cloth toward his lap. 'Of course. I'd be happy to do so.'

Another plate in front of Holmes. Napkin. Napkin. Knifeforkspoon. Knifeforkspoon. Cups, saucers. Coffee service -

'I have him, Watson,' the detective said, beating an exuberant tattoo on the edge of the table. China rattled.

Watson started and groaned. It seemed he'd had a bit to drink last night.

'He has taken the bait,' Holmes continued, not noticing his friend's discomfort at the sound of his voice. 'Master Edward LaCroix, Esquire. Ha! Known to his friends as "Handsome Eddie".' Here he removed a notebook from his breast pocket and flipped the pages. 'One of the many names he goes by. But, ah, what have we here? One Herschel O'Malley. Born on the 18th of June, 1851, to a Princess O'Malley - her actual name, mind you - and Father Unknown. I think we can guess that Pa was a Jew, and that Princess knew him fairly well to bestow upon her son a name like Herschel. Can this Herschel be our own "Handsome Eddie"? Why yes, I do believe he can. ' He slapped his hand on the table again.

Watson flinched and rubbed his eyes. 'You've taken him this morning? What time is it?'

'Oh, I've not got him yet. But I intend to this very afternoon.' Holmes sugared his porridge and took some bacon. 'I knew he would have to piece the items out, you see. That necklace is much too hot to sell of a whole. And the emerald in the wedding ring would be difficult to get rid of in the best of circumstances. Unusual in cut, extravagant in size. It was only a matter of time. A bit quicker than I'd thought.' He gave a little shrug, as if disappointed by his own speedy efficiency. Eyed the fried bread in mild disdain. Oh, right. He only liked toast, no butter, gooey egg spread all over it. Too bad, Mister Man, you can just trot down and toast your own damned bread.

Watson happily lifted two slices onto his plate. 'I don't understand why she wore all those jewels in the first place,' he commented, adding a dollop of butter to a square of saturated fat.

'Because she's a vain idiot,' Holmes said, lopping off the top of his boiled egg with a knife. 'Doubtless he encouraged her vanity. The sapphire colour of her eyes, the rubies in her lips... the usual nonsense women like.'

I piled the remnants of last night's repast onto the tray, while dwelling on a *Venus in Furs* scenario in which I whipped Holmes to madness with science beyond his feeble comprehension, crying "deduce this, arsehole".

Smiling to myself, I lifted the burdened tray for my journey to the scullery, and that's when it caught my eye; the newspaper Holmes had placed on the sideboard. I bent closer, squinting over the annoying font.

The partially clothed body of a young girl, identified as Liza Murray of 57 Leman Street, Whitechapel, was found Sunday morning at the London Dock, floating between the ties and a

The rest of the words were cut off by the fold in the paper, but I knew it was Liza, my employer's thrifty nod to the labour-intensive care and feeding of men. The poor little girl never made it home to her three siblings and ailing father.

I must have made a sound, anguish I suppose. I heard the scrape of a chair, and suddenly Holmes was beside me, catching up the tray before all the dirty dishes clattered to the floor. He set it carefully to the side of the paper. I picked up the *Times* with trembling hands and held it out to him.

'She didn't show this morning,' I said, as he peered into my eyes. If he sought a hint to my true self, then I was too shocked to hide it at that moment.

In spite of the world in which I grew up, I'd never actually known someone who'd been murdered. An acquaintance had committed suicide, two friends of my mother's had died of AIDS in the early '90s... and my father's death reared its ugly head, although I stuffed it down as indicative of a cultural phenomenon far-removed from the nineteenth century. But the murder of someone I actually knew, worked with and bitched about occasionally was a wholly unfamiliar sensation.

Gently, Holmes pried the paper from my fingers. With a flick of his wrist he unfolded it, and we read it standing side-by-side, sudden equals.

She'd been raped and strangled, although the rape was euphemistically rendered as "interfered with", as if being strangled wasn't interference enough. Her hair had been hacked off.

'Jesus,' I whispered.

'Here, what's happened?' Watson said, starting to rise from the table. Holmes walked slowly back to him, handing over the page and pointing at the tiny box wherein Liza Murray's death was summed up and summarily dismissed with the ubiquitous "Scotland Yard is looking into the matter".

Holmes poured himself some coffee and sat looking thoughtfully into the middle-distance, the tongs poised over the sugar bowl.

'Fourth one this year,' he said.

Watson started. 'What? What do you mean?'

'There have been three other murders of that type this year,' Holmes repeated, enunciating each word carefully, as if the doctor were an elderly gentleman hard of hearing.

'Three others? But I've seen nothing in any of the papers -'

'No, you'll not have seen much about those, I'll wager. This is the first to make the honours of the police page.'

'But Holmes, the murders of young girls...'

'Well, what of it?' Holmes snapped, causing Watson and me to jump. 'The bodies of infants and children are found in floating in the Thames on a regular basis, Watson. The fact of a girl's body being plucked from the piers at the London Docks is nothing.' Oblivious to the doctor's shock, he dropped another lump of sugar into his coffee. 'Which is what makes the report of it so very intriguing.'

'That assessment seems very cold-hearted to me, Holmes.'

'Haven't you said as much yourself? Really, Watson, the only reason you find this at all horrifying is that the emaciated Liza has only this moment ceased to be an abstraction to you.'

It was a vicious thing to say, and I saw he regretted it as soon as it left his mouth. He stood abruptly, toppling his chair, and began to pace.

Watson watched him with wary eyes, his mouth tight. He said nothing. Nor did I. We didn't dare. Some dangerous combustible aura quivered around Holmes, like the fumes from gasoline. We waited it out, mouse-quiet and a little pissed off about it.

'It's not simply the murder which is disturbing, nor the violation of a young girl, for such occurrences are a daily order of business in parts of this city. So I can claim with some certainty that this particular murder is of interest because of what it has in common with the others. Each girl was found floating at the London Docks in close vicinity to the previous victim. They were all strangled with a piece of cloth, possibly a sash or tie from their own frocks. After the first murder, the shorn hair was believed to have been the result of a fever sometime prior to death. But, the second and the third? One can safely assume a pattern. The murderer needs a small remembrance of the experience. The fact that they all had red hair lends credence to this theory.' He pointed at the *Times*, still in front of Watson. 'What it does not reveal in the paper is that the victims have been killed first, then removed to a hiding place where the murderer can finish his deeds at leisure, after which he disposes of the bodies.'

'Are you saying...? You're saying the murderer has... has *congress* with these girls after... after they're...' The good doctor, and I do mean good, looked stricken, unable to finish his question.

Holmes gazed at his friend with sudden, genuine fondness. His voice was gently chiding.

'Sexual congress would, by definition, imply mutual consent, and as they were dead they could hardly have consented.' His expression was one of both revulsion and fascination, and in that moment I caught a glimpse of the man hinted at in the doctor's chronicles, with the glint of mania dancing in his eyes.

'How do you know all this if it's not been in the papers?' Watson asked.

'I've a source at the morgue. He brought it to my attention, knowing my interest in such things. These murders are terribly outré, don't you find?'

'If what you describe is true, than I must say I find it disgusting, vile -'

'Oh, most definitely that. Yet a curious reversal of a common, although vicious, act. The violation of a young girl I can understand on some level; she is small, innocent, without the coarseness or insincerity of her older counterparts...' He broke off suddenly. 'Oh, good lord, Watson, do remove that expression from your face. I am merely constructing a model here. It is logical, in a bestial sort of way, for a man to rape first and murder second, if merely to prevent himself from being discovered, yes?'

'It is not logical at all in *any* sort of way,' the doctor said, emphatically.

'Quite right, quite right. Logical is perhaps not the word I mean.' He waved his hand about, erasing the word from the air. 'Still, it is an interesting switch when one considers it. Where is the pleasure?'

Watson stared at him, his mouth agape. 'What?'

'Well, the girl is dead, isn't she? Stone dead. The eyes open and staring -' He gave a small theatrical shudder, then pointed at Watson. 'As a doctor, you know eyes remain open, and after strangulation... think of it. What sort of creature would find that stimulating?' He paused, chin in hand, fingers drumming against his cheek. 'But no, he'd have plenty of time. Hours before rigor mortis set in. The body would still be quite malleable. It could be manipulated into any compliant position one can imagine...'

His eyes jerked in the sockets, watching whatever horror was being played out behind them. Oblivious to us, he began plucking the images out of his head, colouring in the details with his strange, soft voice. 'Yes. She lies open before you, and you imagine a kind of loving submission in her posture. So perfect and so tiny and so very... pale. She waits for you, lips parted, as if about to speak. And you imagine a "yes", don't you? She is the cold embodiment of an affirmative. The very soul of "yes".' One hand trembled before his lips. 'Of course. Of course. Perfection. She cannot squirm, or scratch, or beg you to stop. Will she bleed? Will she bleed when you -'

'For God's sake!' Watson cried. 'Have you no decency at all?'

I'd covered my own mouth to keep from screaming. Watson pushed himself away from the table, but couldn't seem to get out of the chair.

Holmes stood blinking insensibly, still transfixed by the spell of his own words. Then his chest expanded, a huge deep breath let out in a long sigh. 'Dear me.' He ran a hand back over his hair. 'My apologies. I go too far. In future I shall keep such ravings to myself, lest you see fit to have me committed.'

Watson held up his hand, a hair's breadth between thumb and forefinger. *That close*, the gesture said.

Even if my own stomach had protested at the way Holmes had insinuated himself into the mind of a murdering paedophile, I still marvelled at his ability to do it. That he could turn so quickly from berating Watson for treating London's poor as abstractions, to the creation by an abstract process of a killer who could only know sexual intimacy with the cold, dead bodies of little girls... this was a true window into his genius. And he didn't bandy euphemisms about for the sake of propriety.

But even as I had this thought about propriety, he shot me a look, a sudden realisation that I'd been witness to all of it. One did not use words like "rape" in mixed company, and a true gentleman certainly, *certainly* didn't give voice to the idea of popping a girl's cherry - let alone a dead girl's - in the presence of a woman, domestic servant or otherwise.

'What are you going to do about it?' Watson asked.

Holmes flinched slightly and turned back to him. 'Nothing.'

'Nothing at all?'

The detective shrugged. 'No-one at the Yard has approached me concerning these murders, nor are they likely to do so.'

'This is quite unlike you, Holmes.'

'To most of the constabulary I am merely a pretentious upstart who should have taken an office in a court row off Fleet Street, like the rest of my ilk. They will not be kindly disposed to any interference from me.'

'Lestrade seems to respect you.'

'He likes me. He uses me. He does not respect me.' A breath rattled out of him. 'Anyway, I'm certain the Yard would prefer to keep the whole business out of the public eye.'

'Why?' I asked.

Both men started, uncomfortably reminded of my presence yet again. When Holmes spoke, his manner was subdued, his tone almost respectful.

'The police are sitting on a powder-keg. There are certain factions... anti-royalists, Fenians and the like... who see violence as an expedient to social reform -'

'Nihilists,' Watson spat.

'I'm merely pointing out that there are those who do. What better excuse to blow up another monument to the peerage than the grisly murders of little girls from the East End?'

I knew that in a few short years *another* serial killer would draw a great deal of attention to the East End, but my foreknowledge was meaningless. Liza Murray was dead, murdered, her body abused and tossed into the river like garbage.

'Some ambitious newshound must have been on the scene when they recovered the body,' he continued, 'most likely before the police arrived, or we would not be reading of her murder today.' He gnawed a thumbnail. 'I suppose I could have a chat with the fellow, go to the scene myself and take a look around. It would be useless, of course. All the evidence will have been crushed and trampled by now. Bah! I cannot think on this, I simply cannot. I need to catch a different rat today, and if I don't hurry he'll have chewed his way out of the trap.'

With that he disappeared into his bedroom, leaving Watson to stare at the food on the table, which I knew he wouldn't be able to eat.

I picked up my tray, and left to begin a grueling day of work alone.

Chapter 5

It rained hard all night on Tuesday and showed no signs of letting up, even by two o'clock on Wednesday when I was finally free of my duties. I wasn't looking forward to going out, but there seemed no getting around it. I felt compelled to mail a pair of boots to New York City.

As a further precaution, I decided to purchase a pair of cheap, girly shoes - shoes that pinched - to justify the blisters. New shoes meant new blisters, but it was a small price to pay for peace of mind.

The post office in Baker Street was too close for comfort. What if *he* was watching out of the window? What if he saw me looking over my shoulder to *see* if he was watching out the window?

I needed to put as much distance between me and those windows as possible, so I trudged through dreary London, resenting my own anxiety and the burden under my arm. My umbrella kept catching in gusts of wind and threatened to drag me into the path of whip-wielding cab-drivers. My skirt pressed against my legs, spattered with rain and mud. A counterpane in dull colours, enlivened only by the occasional yellowing leaf from a tree which plastered itself to the damp wool.

The pall of Liza's murder hung over me, and the entire city. London was, like my skirt, stained beyond repair. I saw it full of ugly people, with ugly lives, and mean, ugly little faces. I hated all of them.

Okay. I was having my period. I just wanted to stay in bed and read a book.

I bought my new boots at Harvey's. Except for the fact that they were technically leather, they closely resembled the footwear one could find at Best Value in the late twentieth century; "the look and feel of real leather at an affordable price". The uppers were scalloped around the eyelets, and in that startling shade known as "electric blue". Trashy, slutty shoes, just the sort a stupid country girl might consider chic. And, as the rain had eased into a light drizzle, I wore them to the post office.

I waited in a queue for nearly twenty minutes, clothes and temper steaming. Finally, I pushed the damp parcel across the counter and said: 'I should like to send this parcel to New York City, please.'

The clerk, wearing that look reserved by ill-paid employees for those making less pittance than themselves, eyed the package over his spectacles. 'It's wet,' he told me. 'We'll have to charge for wrapping it over.'

'Fine,' I said, tapping my fingers impatiently.

'The name of the recipient, if you please?'

I stared at him blankly, which he assumed meant I didn't understand the word.

'The person for whom the package is intended, Miss. The recipient.'

Arsehole. 'Er, Petra. First initial, G.' Why not? It might be fun to see if I could track it down when I got back.

He weighed it. 'General delivery?'

'Yes, sir.'

'Six shillings, eight pence, Miss.'

My mouth dropped open. 'What?'

'Six shillings and -'

'Isn't that rather a lot for general delivery?'

'There's the charge for the box and the wrapping -'

'What're you wrapping it in? The Dead Sea Scrolls?'

Obviously he didn't know what that meant, but it didn't stop him pushing the parcel across the counter with one finger. 'You can take it to a shipping agent, if you prefer.'

Muttering under my breath, I counted the change in my purse and found it wanting. It appeared that the cheap leather of my trashy shoes was not only altering the shape of my toes but my best laid plans as well.

My other persona, the young widow Mrs Tory, had more than enough to cover the expense. Unfortunately, to get to her funds I had to go through her late husband's solicitor. But I had neither the time nor the inclination to schlep all the way to her rooms, put on the widow's weeds, and then try to make it back to the solicitor's office. It was impossible to do it on foot in the allotted business hours left to me, and nearly impossible with the public transport system. I left the post office with my damp parcel, a nearly empty purse, and a box from Harvey's containing my sensible shoes.

It wasn't until I stopped for a cup of tea near Portman Square that I noticed the big man in the brown waterproof and black bowler standing under the awning at a newsvendor's stand. He'd been waiting in the queue at the post office too, hadn't he? He'd also been lurking near the shirt-collars when I'd been buying the shoes. He was as tall the detective, padded around the middle, and had a blotchy, puffed-out kind of face, made puffier still by the thick brown muttonchops that furred his jaw line.

So, Sherlock Holmes had donned a costume in my honor. Instead of fear, I was struck by how ridiculous, annoying and rather pathetic it made him. Had he nothing better to do with his time? His little charade could easily render my research null and void, but he'd never learn the truth. He'd never be able to comprehend it even if he did.

You're out of your depths with me today, mister. I'm on my period, my feet hurt, and now I'm pissed off.

I finished my tea and returned the cup to the proprietor. Making my way to the covered stall I located the latest edition of *The Queen*, touted as the "Lady's Newspaper". Reaching for a copy, I managed to drop my packages in the process, and as I bent to retrieve them I accidentally-on-purpose hit the gent in a sensitive area with the pointy part of my umbrella. Maybe just a teensy bit harder than I intended.

'Oh, dear me!' I cried, as he doubled over with a grunt. 'Goodness gracious! I'm so terribly sorry, sir!'

Gasping, he self-consciously cradled his groin with one hand while the other waved aside my offer of assistance.

It was not Holmes. No amount of clever makeup could alter the colour of a person's eyes, not in 1882. This man's eyes were brown, squeezed between epicanthic folds that gave a kind of Sumo-wrestler look to his homely occidental face. Cavernous, dirty pores pitted the end of his nose, and he hissed in pain from between stained and crooked teeth.

Genuinely embarrassed, I began sputtering sincere apologies. The newsvendor offered his stool to 'rest up, as it were.' Another gentleman suggested the possibility of 'ice for that' in the butcher's shop round the corner. Clammy-faced and clearly in pain, the injured man's expression was nevertheless an oddly guilty one for having been hit in the testicles with an umbrella. It occurred to me he might be one of those bustle-pinchers I'd heard about.

I decided I was being overly cautious. In a city of millions, a pair of decent boots and some serviceable (if somewhat grubby) clothes would find a needy recipient quickly. I tossed the package that had caused me so much worry onto a pile of refuse in an alley. Hopefully, it would make some indigent very happy.

***

Sunday morning, Shinwell Johnson was waiting in our usual pew at the very back. He patted the empty space on the bench beside him. I sidled past people in their Sunday finery to sit next to him, awash in the calm of morning service in the Anglican Church.

I liked coming to Holy Cross. On Sundays, most everyone smelled clean. Soap and starch and lemon verbena, mixing with the scent of wood-polish and leather Bibles. It was the only clean day of the week for most people.

Earlier, as Rose Donnelly, I'd crept up the back stairs of Mrs Tory's lodgings, shrouded in my cloak. An hour and a half later, I'd emerged, bathed and dressed in a sombre black gown, shrouded now by crepe veiling.

The service was long and pleasantly dull. Afterwards we sat in a teashop, and he gave me all the knowledge he'd gathered over the course of a month.

Shinwell Johnson brokered information, mostly for the bookmakers and gangsters, the extortionists, cracksmen, and confidence runners. He'd been a involved in every sort of criminal activity that thrived in a bustling metropolis such as London, but his remarkable memory for facts, numbers, and other people's business made him a natural when there was information sought or for sale. He had a network far superior to that of my subject of study, at least at this point in the detective's career. And, for all that he dealt with unsavoury sorts, Shinwell was a lively human being, with an infectious sense of humour, intelligent eyes like little jet buttons poked into his jowly face, and a very, very sharp mind. I'd caused more than one scandalous aside from eavesdroppers by laughing heartily at his quips. I was supposed to be deep in mourning, you see.

At the end of our meal he handed me a packet of papers, tied with a red ribbon. 'That's what I got from Yorkshire, Mrs Tory, where he grew up,' he said. 'Everythin' the old servants remember 'bout when he was a lad. It's all in there, the whole family history, such as it is. Hain't all sweetness and light, o' course. But I've seen some worse.'

He clearly couldn't understand why I might be interested, but he didn't ask. He grinned at me, the folds in his chin stretching out. 'Servants are like them magic fishes at the bottom of the well. Once you hook 'em, they give you everythin' and then some. I wouldn't care to be a master, no, I don't think so. Who would buy my little secrets if they could get 'em free from the girl who does m' shirts?'

'Well, I thank you for your efforts just the same. You've collected your fee, I take it?'

'I have indeed, ma'am, and most generous it was, too.' He stood, and I offered my hand, which he graced with a gallant's cool salutation, his thick lips pressed to my gloved fingertips. His eyes narrowed thoughtfully as he let go of my hand. 'One more thing, Mrs Tory. While I was seekin' knowledge from those fishes in the well, I came 'cross a bit of information you might could pass on for me, if you've a mind?'

'I shall do what I can, sir.'

'If you should happen to meet up with a lass name of Rose Donnelly, would you kindly tell her that Mr Sherlock Holmes has been inquirin' about her in the Yorkshire village of her birth? He's sent a few telegrams to the local authorities in Aberford. I think she'll appreciate knowin'.'

He winked and gave me a little pat on the hand before donning his bowler. I watched in numb silence as he strolled out the door and into the grey afternoon.

I suppose it was foolish to expect that Shinwell Johnson wouldn't have made the effort to investigate the young Widow Tory and discover her other identity. But as long as he and I had a mutually beneficial arrangement, his knowledge wouldn't present a problem. Sherlock Holmes, on the other hand, was a very big problem indeed.

According to the information I received from Johnson, Holmes caught the villainous Handsome Eddie the very afternoon he claimed he would. Eddie LaCroix, alias Herchel O'Malley, was well-known in Shinwell's circle. The detective trapped his mark by impersonating a gem-broker from Belgium who had a buyer for the stolen goods. Eddie fell for the scam and was caught out, plain and simple. As he couldn't be taken to the police, for the sake of the lady's reputation, he and Holmes came to an arrangement. Master O'Mally left for America shortly thereafter and would, no doubt, do a booming business in that rich land of opportunity. Holmes had handled the entire matter with discretion and aplomb.

Mrs Merriam must have paid him accordingly, because he retrieved a lot of stuff from a pawnbroker off Tottenham Court Road. Among these items were a pearl tie-pin, and a rapier with a very handsome grip and guard. He also purchased a new toothbrush, crisp new collars, a couple of nice bottles of wine, a box of fancy Egyptian cigarettes, and many packets of smelly chemicals. The stack of bills stabbed to the mantelpiece with a jack-knife had shrunk considerably.

As to the murder of young Liza Murray, I read in the papers that the police had arrested the girl's own father, a suspected Irish extremist. Holmes scoffed at this, seeing in the arrest an obvious ploy by the police to make it look as if they were on the case whilst sending a harsh message to anti-royalists. Lacking anything more stimulating, he'd apparently turned his attention to me. Consequently, I took to hiding Johnson's sheaf of papers next to my skin.

The personal history contained in those papers offered a few interesting titbits, but was surprisingly scanty. There was the stuff I'd already learned: He'd been born in late February of '57, and not January of '54. His first name was Edmund, not William. He liked horseradish with his beef.

One bit of trivia came from a former maid who'd travelled with the family abroad: Little Sherlock was nursed at his own mother's breast until well after the time he should have been weaned. The woman still seemed quite shocked by this. 'If a child can walk up to his marm, tug on the apron and demand her give him a suck, he's a bit too old to be needin' one,' she was quoted as saying.

The big surprise came at the end of the document. The detective had a sister, ten years younger than himself. There'd never been a single mention of a sister in the history. But then, Watson hadn't even known about Holmes' brother until he'd been friends with the detective for seven or eight years. Sister Genevieve was born brain-damaged as a result of the birth trauma which had killed their mother, what we in the twenty-first century would politely refer to as "mentally challenged". She lived in perpetual childhood in a big house in the country, spoiled by her father and brothers, and cared for by an elderly nurse. She was more fortunate than many of her kind. But the fact of her existence lent a humanising vulnerability to Sherlock that I wasn't entirely ready to grant him.

I'd fancied myself a kind of Jane Goodall or Dian Fossey, observing the lower primates in their natural habitat, taking precise notes. My position in the house was to be my camouflage. But he'd caught a whiff of the real me while I'd been hiding in the piles of laundry, dirty dishes and buckets of coal. I imagine it was a curious, unfamiliar scent that instead of driving him away, drew him closer.

Chapter 6

The son-of-a-bitch searched my room.

It happened on my half-day, naturally. The air was unusually crisp and clear for London in November, and everyone was out taking advantage of the weather. I chanced to see him as he was coming through the park. Couldn't help but see him really, he was cutting such a swathe through the ordinary denizens on that extraordinary day.

Sherlock Holmes was not a conventionally handsome man, not by any stretch of the imagination, but when I saw him that afternoon it was one of those breathtaking moments when a person's soul shines through and animates the features in such a way as to make him almost beautiful. The greys of his costume shimmered in the light of a November sun. Mr Holmes, in his top hat, seemed to tower above everyone. "I am ever-so-brilliant," his walk said. "And I'm young, and I'm going far in this world."

He didn't pretend not to see me, as would many a gentleman upon recognising a girl employed by their landlady playing guitar for coins in the park, but boldly took a seat on the bench across from me, leaning one elbow on the backrest, the other hand on the silver knob of his walking stick. He crossed his long legs, foot bouncing in absent-minded time to the music.

I finished my flamenco with a flourish. Holmes lobbed a shilling into the waiting receptacle, where it collided with half-pennies and farthings.

Such a large donation required me to ask: 'Have you a favourite I could play for you, sir?'

'Thank you, no. I have... a previous engagement.' He rose, dusted himself off perfunctorily, and picked up his overcoat from the bench. 'You demonstrate remarkable passion and skill, Miss Donnelly. Really, most delightful. Perhaps in the future we might endeavour to play together? I have some small talent with the fiddle and a good ear for improvisation. Might I suggest later this afternoon, if you are not otherwise engaged?'

What the hell? To cover my consternation, I glanced into the guitar-case at the scattering of coins. I would have been foolish to stop in such fine weather if I were, in fact, the person I pretended to be. 'I thought I might play another hour or so, sir. Perhaps if you're still of a mind after tea?'

When under duress, my dimpled smile could be most effective in restoring a sense of balance. I looked up and gave him both barrels.

The malacca stick slipped from his fingers, though he caught it before it hit the ground. He blinked a couple of times, swallowed a couple of times, took a deep breath and shook himself straight.

'Splendid,' he said, touching the brim of his hat. 'I look forward to it.' Then he bestowed upon me a deep bow, almost as if I were a real lady.

Oh my God, the chivalrous gall of the man! The entire exchange was merely a ruse to find out how long I'd be away.

A very professional job of searching he did, too. I probably would have missed it but for the Bible on the bedside table. I had the Lord's Prayer book-marked with a clipping of a sentimental poem about precious babes cradled in the arms of Jesus. The clipping had mysteriously slipped into the Gospels of St Paul.

After that I noticed other small signs. The bedstead had been moved out and back again; the dust on the floor beneath hastily smudged over. I assumed he'd located the hidey-hole beneath the floorboards, though he would have found little of value there. I'd taken my notes and journals with me, secure between songbooks in my satchel, an instinctive precaution I hadn't questioned at the time. They were written in code, but it would have made him suspicious just the same. The only items left in the hole were what I had left of my wages and what little I earned playing guitar in the park. The sum total of my estate.

I'm sure he examined my new boots, duly noting the wear on the soles and the stains inside from broken blisters.

The casual replacement of the poem between the wrong pages in the Bible seemed incredibly stupid, and at first I couldn't credit that Holmes would make such a mistake. Jack Hudson had been pestering me again, and I considered briefly that it might have been he who'd gone through my things. But the Gospels of St Paul, with all its acrimonious misogyny, seemed a pointed message, by chance or design. "Consider yourself warned, woman," it said.

Holmes avoided me that evening. I knocked on his door at five and Watson answered, blinking in puzzlement at my request.

'Mr Holmes has left for the evening, Rose,' he said, and I stood at the door with my guitar in hand, mortified by his expression, and later by Mrs Hudson's suspicious disapproval.

Because of the search of my room and those inquiring telegrams to the town of Aberford in Yorkshire, Rose Donnelly - maid-of-all-work - was forced to take the doctor into her confidence. Thursday morning I caught Watson before he went out for his daily constitutional. We stepped into the relative privacy of the side-yard, and stood near the wall, while laundry snapped in the cold wind.

He looked put-upon and slightly apprehensive, perhaps fearing that I was seeking free medical advice. The subject of Holmes quite threw him off-guard. I began by asking what Mr Holmes had against me, did he know? And could he please ask Mr Holmes to stop bothering me?

At Watson's expression of alarm, I became genuinely flustered. 'Oh, no sir, I don't mean that. It's just, well, sir, I think he's been in my room, looked into my personal, private things.'

'Surely not, Rose! You must be mistaken.'

'There was things out o' order, sir, not how I left 'em. I can't think who else t'would be, given how his business is pryin' into others' business and all.' I looked down, my lips trembling a bit. 'This mornin' I gets a letter from m'sister back home, sayin' as how someone's been askin' on me. Telegrams to the constable, to the county records office, the vicar, and more.'

The doctor pinched at the skin between his brows, muttering, 'Good heavens.'

I blinked up a few tears. 'I've had some trouble, sir, which you bein' a doctor might understand, but it's nothin' to concern him. And if he starts all them people 'round there talkin' again, it's me family what'll suffer for it, sir. Me sisters and me dad.'

I could see that he was already guessing the gist of my tale. 'You don't have to tell me -'

'But I want to, sir, so you can tell him, and he won't be askin' no more about it. It'll break me father's heart if it all comes out again, what with m'sister to be married next month. Please, sir.'

I told him Rose's sad story. Her fall from grace at the tender age of fourteen with a married man, the death of the child from that union two days after it was born, which 'though God might punish me for thinking so, was a blessing for the both of us.'

'I went into service with a kindly woman and t'were she give me good character when I came to London. Her sister-in-law - that'd be Mrs Hudson, sir - was lookin' for a hard-workin' honest girl. You can ask her if that's the truth. And I pray for my babe in the arms of our Heavenly Father every night.' Here I broke down. 'I don't ask for m'self, 'cos I don't much deserve it, but please, sir, for the sake of my family, can you not speak to him?'

Dr Watson said he would do so at the first opportunity.

At ten I brought the early post with me as I came in to do the beds. Holmes took it, bestowing upon me the famous hooded, bird-of-prey look. He knew I'd thumbed through the correspondence. I knew he'd received another letter from his father.

He used to open these letters with furtive, expectant, I-hope-to-God-there's-money-in-here expediency. But recently he didn't open them at all, just stabbed them to the mantelpiece. Eventually he burned them. I'd had only one opportunity to go through this correspondence after cleaning the ashes from the grate, on the first of September. He'd been angry, and the letter had been thrown in while still folded, so the text in the centre had been legible.

"If your mother's brother wishes to support" and something about "pursuing this folly" and "I cannot in good conscience" something, something, and then a reference to his brother, Mycroft, and a clerk's position at Whitehall. Well, it was easy enough to fill in the blanks.

As the money issue was no longer pressing, he pulled the knife from his pile of unanswered mail, and placed this letter on top.

Stab. Ha. Don't need you, Pa.

Keeping my expression neutral, I carried the linens to his room and began to strip the bed, trying to ignore him as he followed and stood in the doorway. I had a sudden unreasonable thrill that he was going to step in and close the door.

I didn't think he'd buy the Eliza Dolittle routine again, so a variation on theme was in order.

'Fancy a bit of a ride while the linen's dirty?'

His mouth fell open.

'No?' I said, shaking a pillow out of its casing. 'Just as well. I'm afraid the Captain's at home this week.'

He crossed his arms over his chest and rallied a nasty grin. He wouldn't be cowed be me, a mere woman, and a slavey at that. 'My goodness, Donnelly. You are quite the clever pugilist. Left jab, invitation to frolic. Right hook, the monthly courses. Punches guaranteed to floor most any man.' He gave his head a small shake. 'But it won't do. The "Captain" can reside with you permanently for all I care.'

'That so?' I rolled up the sheets and tossed them onto a pile of books at the foot of the bed. 'Yet here you are favourin' me with your attention. Between you and Jack Hudson -'

'Jack?' The presentation of this new player on the board clearly confused him.

'Either you or him been sneakin' about my room whilst I was out.'

Master Holmes kept himself cool with a bit of business, taking a cigarette from his case and lighting it. 'Why would I have cause to be in your room, under those circumstances, Rose?' He exhaled a stream of smoke. 'Or young Master Hudson for that matter?'

'Jack wants the usual, which I won't give him, so maybe he's lookin' for somethin' he might hold over me to get what he wants.'

'And you think the same applies to me?' I could tell he was amused by the thought.

'Well, it don't appear to be from our mutual love of music, sir.' I went to turn the bed and glanced up at him, giving my patented half-smile, one dimple like Diogenes' lantern. 'Was it you then, sir?'

He took a drag from the cigarette and smoke came out with his words. 'Not unless you are in the habit of following gentlemen about the city dressed as a boy.'

'A strange habit for a housemaid, sir.'

'Very strange.' The ash fell onto the carpet and he caught my wry amusement at his carelessness. He twisted the toe of his shoe over it, cool grey eyes fixed on me. 'Why are you here, Rose Donnelly?'

I matched his cool. 'I'm here to turn your bed and change the linens.'

'I am not asking why the maid is here. I am asking why *you* are here.'

'Well, sir, clearly you have some thoughts on the matter you're dying to share.' My dialect was going completely out the window, but as I was muscling his bed around and had my jaw clenched, he might not have noticed.

'My only thought is that servants make perfect spies,' he said.

In the middle of strong-arming his mattress, I started to laugh. It was true, if not in the way he thought, and I wasn't pretending to be a housemaid. I *was* a housemaid, and it was bloody hard work. *And all so I can observe you, Mr Holmes - the World's First Consulting Detective - standing there watching me do it without moving a muscle to assist.*

'You've found me out, sir. I'm just now workin' my secret cipher on your bedsheets. My spy friends will know by the way I hang the sheets on the line whether you're smokin' the cherrywood pipe or the clay.'

'And if I'm smoking the clay?' he asked dryly.

'Jesus!' I put my hands on my hips and stared at him. 'Can you honestly think you're so fascinatin' that there's people as want to spy on you?'

'No,' he replied quietly, 'but I think that you do.'

I remember closing my mouth, though not how long it hung open. There was something so poignant in his statement, both a certainty in what he perceived and an embarrassment at how arrogant it made him seem -

'Holmes?' the doctor called from the far side of the sitting room. 'With whom are you being so chatty at this ungodly hour?'

'With Ro... with the maid,' he called back over his shoulder.

There followed a short brooding silence, easy enough for me to read, full of disapproval.

'Has the post come?' Watson asked.

'It's on the table.'

'Why don't you come away and leave the girl to finish her work?'

Holmes turned suddenly, bouncing his body from the doorframe and spinning to face the other man in one easy motion. I couldn't see the doctor from where I stood in the bedroom, so I had no idea what his body language was saying at that moment, only that Holmes responded by walking toward him, saying, 'What? What is it?'

They spoke in hushed tones, rising and falling with the level of emotion; the doctor's voice angry and vaguely apologetic, the detective's voice embarrassed yet self-aggrandising. I finished making the bed, smoothing the counterpane and fluffing the pillows. When I entered the sitting room, arms full of bed-sheets, the conversation stopped dead. Watson turned away, but I saw his face was flushed. The detective's chin was sunk almost to the level of his chest, and the butt of his cigarette smouldered in the ashtray on the table. He looked at me, eyes narrowed dangerously. I dumped the dirty sheets in the basket, demonstrating what I thought of his suspicions. He had no recourse but to storm off to his bedroom and slam the door. On the cluttered table where he did his experiments, retorts and beakers rattled in the wake of his fury.

As I stepped toward the doctor's room, he said: 'Rose? A moment, if you please.'

'Sir?'

'I think it would be best if you did not wait upon us in future.'

My brain went into a spasm. Shit. Goddamn it. This wouldn't do. This wouldn't do at all. 'Have I done somethin' I oughtn't, sir?'

'No. It's just, well, you see...' He gave a loud sigh replete with frustration and embarrassment. 'This is rather difficult to explain. Mr Holmes seems to be under the impression... that is, he believes that you are, er, spying upon him for some unfathomable reason.'

'What am I to tell Mrs Hudson, sir? That I can't do as she bids me because I'm accused of bein' a spy?'

'I'll speak to Mrs Hudson -' he began.

'Oh, for heaven's sake, Watson,' Holmes said, coming out of his room again. He took up his hat and overcoat. 'If you speak to Mrs Hudson, the girl will likely lose her position. I doubt she'll be so fortunate in finding another as the ladies at Mrs Sterling's.'

'Holmes -' Watson warned.

'Just leave off,' the detective said. 'I promise to behave myself.' He put on the hat and adjusted it with a sharp tap of his cane. 'I'm going out. I shall not return before supper. Good day, Rose, and my humblest apologies to you.' With his coat over his arm, he flung open the door, and thumped down the stairs.

I wasn't sure what Holmes was going to do next, but I was pretty sure "behaving" was not part of his plan.

His inquiries to Aberford, where Rose Donnelly was born and raised, could only have uncovered what was already known about her life from the preliminary research. If Holmes decided to go to Yorkshire to investigate in person, it'd be more of a problem. Descriptions of me might not coincide with the real Rose Donnelly; height, eye colour, and other things, like the guitar. Rose played, but not as well as I did. I doubted he'd make the journey merely to satisfy his curiosity. For one thing, it cost a hell of a lot more than sending a few telegrams, and for another, his father still lived in Yorkshire and *any* part of the county was too close to Pa for comfort.

The real Rose had died in early August, just before I arrived. She'd come to London to work at the house in Baker Street with a good character reference from Mrs Hudson's sister-in-law. But she'd met a devious, sweet-talking man at the train station who'd convinced her she could do better in a different profession. A week later she'd been found beaten to death in a court row near Hanover Street. Nine months and six long days from now, Rose Donnelly would again be officially dead with only a slight alteration to her actual history.

Jack Hudson asked if I'd go to the Oxford Music Hall with him Wednesday night. I said yes, if he took me to Previtali's afterwards. Figured I might as well get calamari and a big bottle of pinot grigio out of the deal. Besides, a night on the town with someone else footing the bill was just the sort of chance a girl like Rose Donnelly would jump on.

That'd show Mr Sherlock Holmes, wouldn't it?

Chapter 7

Before I started work at the house in Baker Street, I spent a week wandering London; soaking up the nineteenth century like a tourist, buying things I'd never be able to use in my guises as grieving widow or maid-of-all-work. One of those things was a blue silk gown from Neekham and O'Leary's dressmaker's shop off Stephen Street. It was a deceptively simple and extremely sexy frock, sporting a deep square neckline and small standing ruff known in fashion circles as *di'Medici*. The problem with the dress was that a corset needed to be laced tight to make it fit properly, and the narrow cut of the skirt meant that my lumpy country-girl petticoats and drawers wouldn't fit under it. With just shift, corset, and stockings beneath, my ribs protested and my legs were chilly, but I fancied I looked very fine indeed. Vanity led me to wear the cursed electric-blue boots, because the color went with the dress. Sort of.

With finery hidden beneath my wool cloak, I sneaked out of the house and was in front of the Oxford Music Hall promptly at a quarter to seven on Wednesday night.

Jack was shocked, to say the least, and intimidated, for he'd dressed in a tweed suit and bowler, having assumed I would be wearing something a little more in keeping with my station. He made a solemn pledge, delivered to my breasts, that he'd treat me to a cab ride to the restaurant.

After two-and-a-half hours of the silliest entertainment imaginable, we took a hansom to Previtali's in Covent Garden. We were seated right next to the kitchen door, not a good sign, considering we had a reservation. So when the waiter came to our table with just a hint of attitude, I asked Jack ever so sweetly if he'd allow me to order as I spoke a bit of Italian. I didn't give him the opportunity to protest. To the delight of the waiter, I ordered our meal in his own language. Bruschetta with goat's cheese and peppers; something called Calamari All'Inferno - which was, as the name implied, hot and spicy, made with whole squids the size of my thumb - and gnocchi. That was just for me. For the gentlemen, a traditional antipasti platter and a lovely linguini with smoked mussels in cream. I ordered *for* the gentleman, a terrible social faux pas, but I didn't care. He'd already embarrassed me by asking for gin.

Over the course of the evening I became very "gay" as the 1882 concept went, emitting throaty laughter in response to the amusing witticisms and vaguely improper advances from our servers. "Gay" was also a euphemism for harlot, but that distinction escaped me by the second bottle of wine. The corset limited the amount of food I could fit into my stomach but not, apparently, the amount of alcohol.

Outside the restaurant, Jack stood with his hands in his pockets. There were cabs lined up in Arundel Place, and I restrained myself from hailing one. Man's supposed to do that. But he didn't. The light rain that had fallen on our journey to the restaurant had stopped, and a fog was creeping in. He took a deep breath, watching me sway under the street-lamps. I couldn't quite read the look, save for the fact that his eyes stayed pretty much at the level of my cleavage, so I assumed he was still calculating how to get me into bed.

A hansom rolled up for a couple coming out of the restaurant behind us, splashing Jack's trouser-legs. He muttered a sharp curse, effectively shaking me out of my reverie.

Brushing at spots of mud, he asked: 'You up for walking it off a bit, Rose?'

'Oooh... I need to be getting home soon, Jack. Work starts blessed early for me.' I belched and covered my mouth, then leaned into him. 'Do let's take a cab.' The words came out in a sickening, flirtatious whine.

'Don't have the money for a cab, Rose, not after that meal.'

'I've got money,' I said, and then spent a few seconds trying to get the cords of my reticule untangled from my wrist. I was still spinning it in frustration when he said: 'I won't take money from a woman, Rose.'

'Don't be such a git, Jack. You take money from your mother all the time –'

He grabbed my arm and pulled me roughly to the other side of the street, gazing about to see if anyone had overheard. 'You leave my mother out of this. I'm not taking money from you, Rose. Don't know how you got that money, do I?'

'I got it playing guitar in the park,' I said, before it dawned on me. 'Oi! Just what are you implyin', Master Hudson?'

'Not implying anything, Rosie girl, 'cept that you're flying a might high and need to walk it off before we get back to the house.'

All the time we *were* walking, or rather he was walking and I was being dragged jerkily along after him. My boots were killing me already. I dug in with the wobbly heels and pulled out of his grasp, stumbling backwards into a wall. He made a grab for my arm again.

'You just hold up there, mate,' I growled. 'Hold your horses. I do not like being man-handled. I won't have it, d'you hear? If you are nice I shall likewise be nice. If not, you and I will be company... will be *parting* company here and now!' I stamped my foot, then handed him my cloak. 'Hold this, will you? I have to pee.'

And I walked into a narrow, dark alley. Just like that.

Though dotted here and there with piles of refuse, none of them moved, so I steeled myself with the lunatic bravado of a drunk and inched my way along one slimy wall. We were still in the Strand, I was pretty sure, and I had supreme confidence in the effectiveness of the police in areas where people with money chose to entertain themselves. When I emerged from the passage, mission accomplished, I could see Jack picking his way down the alley in search of me. The thin light of the moon and the hazy drift of gaslights leaking through the fog made him look like a frightened little boy. Suddenly my foot turned, the heel of my right shoe catching on some loose stone from the paving, and the sucker broke right off, just as he reached me.

It was straight out of a romance novel - not a very good one - as I fell into his waiting arms. I was still laughing about it when he shoved me up against the wall. The force of my head banging into it killed the laughter instantly.

His body was pressed against me, pinning me to the slimy damp of the bricks. 'What the fuck?' I wheezed.

Jack pulled his head back, staring at me in shock for a moment. Then his eyes narrowed, unreasonably excited. Before I could get a less evocative word out, like "stop" or "no", his mouth banged into my teeth.

'Say it again, Rose,' he slobbered into my ear. 'Say fuck. Say fuck, Rose -'

'Get off.' I tried to yell it, but he was pressed against me so hard it just came out as a squeak. Between Jack's body and the lung-crushing corset, I seemed quite unable to take a breath. I started to panic. I was panicking over the corset, oddly enough, and in a moment of mortification - like an accident victim in dirty underwear - I remembered I wasn't wearing any. My vanity would now make it simple for him, an open invitation to easy virtue. I struggled, I whimpered, the strength in my arms poisoned by a toxic level of alcohol.

Survival desperation gave me enough air to make an attempt. I appealed to comfort.

'Jack,' I whispered, and this little scared baby voice came out of me. 'Let's go back to my room. Your mum'll never hear us...' Too much sob in the voice, not convincing. He towelled my privates with his fingers. Fabric tore as he pried my thighs apart and manoeuvred his prick into position. The son-of-a-bitch had it out now. He was really going to do it. Jesus. Jesus Christ. Jesus.

I drew in a sharp, shallow breath, going nowhere, filling nothing -

Then the pressure of his body was gone. I slid down the wall, my legs at a curious angle to the rest of me, and sat there, half-aware of some activity in the gloom; muted thuds, like the carcass of an animal flopped onto a kitchen table.

Thwomp. Someone was beating the carcass with a stick.

After a bit, minutes or mere seconds, I felt the cords of my reticule being jerked open, still attached to my wrist. Ammonia was thrust under my nose. My head went back and hit the wall again. Ah, smelling salts, my own little vial, which no woman in a corset should be without.

A man was leaning over me, sporting a billycock hat, mutton-chop whiskers and a big, thick moustache. I shrunk back. 'No! Get away from me! Get away!'

'Calm yourself, Rose. It is I, Sherlock Holmes.'

The way he said it: 'It is I,' properly grammatical, delivered in a reassuring manner and yet muffled or garbled somehow. I focused on his face and the preposterously altered shape of it.

He rose and stood over me, shoulders hunched. One hand was still curled around a thick, brass-knobbed cane. He pulled some of the wadding out of his cheeks, made an *ack* sound and then, *bleah*, before asking: 'Are you hurt? Can you walk?'

What? Of course I can walk. If I could just breathe.

'Do you have a knife?' I whispered. He stared at me for a moment, then began patting his pockets.

'I hope you do not intend to kill yourself,' he said, unfolding the short blade of a pen-knife, 'because it's getting rather late, and it will take forever with this.'

I took the knife and began to unfasten my bodice.

'What are you doing?' His voice was tinged with panic, suspecting his joke had just turned deadly serious.

I hooked the blade through the long ends of the corset-strings, which, in my over-enthusiasm, I'd looped around to the front and hopelessly knotted. His face relaxed, the thin lips stretched into amusement beneath the fake moustache. He didn't do the gentlemanly thing and turn around, but watched me sawing at the cords until they snapped. I loosened my stays, expanded my ribs and tortured lungs, communing with precious, precious oxygen before clawing my way up the wall. He reached out to assist me, but I pushed his hands away. When both feet were under me, I found the wobbly sensation didn't abate but seemed to grow in intensity. I attributed this to the broken heel of my shoe, until my stomach lurched and I turned my head in time to aim the chunky conglomeration of fine Italian dining, white wine and stomach acids at the wall instead of his trouser-legs. It was a tremendous relief, despite my mortification at having done it.

In a pile of refuse, Jack Hudson was likewise retching. Holmes took a couple of long strides over to him and jerked him to his feet.

'Listen to me carefully, Jack Hudson.' He gave the boy a hard, teeth-rattling shake. 'Can you hear me? Good. Button your trousers and pay attention. No, the trousers first, Jack. Still listening? Splendid. Here's what you're going to do. You will return to the house and pack a bag. You will then compose a lovely little note to your mother - pay attention! - a note to your mother explaining that you've found employment on a tramp steamer bound for Australia. You must leave right away if you are to take advantage of the opportunity. Tell her you'll be sending money every month. It will be the truth -

'No! Don't argue! Do not *dare* to protest, or I shall whistle for the constable and tell what I've witnessed. The lady's appearance alone should condemn you.' He forced Jack to stand upright, and proceeded to brush him off a bit, as if trying to make a naughty boy presentable.

'Leave my mother out of this!' Jack cried. He leaned over again, dribbling blood from a split lip or a lost tooth onto the paving. 'Who are you to be telling me anything? I don't know you from Adam.'

'I'm the man that thrashed you,' Holmes said, holding up the cane. He began to peel away his facial hair, wincing a little as he changed from a gentleman of merchant industry into a young gentleman of more unusual enterprises. He put the false hair into his jacket pocket and scratched at the bits of gum-adhesive over his lip with a fingernail. 'As you can see, we are acquainted.'

Jack looked at me then at Holmes, a sneer crawling across his handsome, bloodied face. 'You should have said you had a man in before me, Rose. I never would have gone sniffing up another bloke's bitch.'

'Shut up, Jack,' Holmes snapped. 'You can only worsen your situation with such stupidity.'

'You got no right to be following me!'

Holmes laughed softly. 'I wasn't following *you*. The point is not what I was doing, but what you were about to do before I stopped you.'

'She had it coming. No better than she should be, that one.'

Though I had no moral objections to prostitutes per se, being called one in that passive-aggressive manner really ticked me off, for some reason.

I threw myself at him, snarling.

Holmes grabbed me and pulled me back, whisking the knife from my hand before I realised I was going to use it. There was no judgement implied in his gesture, just common sense and caution. His grasp on my arm was reassuring. He wouldn't let me fall down or kill anyone. That was good. But it left me

Holmes gave Jack a look, difficult to read in the wet gloom of the alley, but the thick cane he brandished was easy enough to understand. 'Do you agree to my terms, or shall I call for the police? A constable should be strolling by on his rounds any minute now.'

Jack considered for a moment and, embarrassingly enough, sank into the filth and began to cry.

'How can I leave my mum? I'm all she has left!'

'It's high time you were weaned from the teat, Master Hudson,' Holmes said. 'Stop that blubbering or I'll thrash you again.'

Obligingly, Jack sucked in a breath full of snot and utter misery. He drew a sleeve across his eyes. Holmes released my arm carefully, one hand out in case I toppled like a vase from a crooked table. He removed a stubby bit of pencil and an envelope from his breast pocket and scribbled something. 'I will have your passage arranged by morning. When you've done packing and writing your letter, go to this address, and give this note to the man I've named here.'

Still sniffing, Jack reached for the note and turned it back and forth, his eyes straining to make out his future writ on a bit of envelope. 'Australia!' He looked up, stricken. 'Sweet Christ, no! I can't. I can't. It's so far away.'

'If you are not on that vessel tomorrow I will send you to hell. Prison, Jack. A place where the warders do things to pretty young whelps like you that would make what you intended for Rose here seem a frolic in the park.'

Part of my brain tracked this dialogue with scientific precision. The history of sexual domination in nineteenth century prisons. There were hardly any personal accounts of such things on record; sure, a lot about the beatings, the enforced silence, the Sisyphean torture of the treadmill, but only guarded hints at those things considered worse by Victorian standards. I could get a dandy little paper out of it -

Another part of my brain said, "wait a moment". I picked up my cloak, damp and muck-covered, and drew it around my shivering shoulders. 'Have I no say in this? I'm the one that was...' I swallowed. 'It was me that was...'

Holmes turned to me, but I couldn't make out his face.

'Do you wish to have him arrested?' he asked.

He knew as well as I did that the charges wouldn't stick. A housemaid putting on fancy airs and getting herself drunk on a man's money deserved what she got.

Losing my job was not an option.

'He goes to Australia,' I said, then turned and started limping really fast towards the street.

I suppose I was still disoriented, possibly in shock. I heard someone running up behind me, the quickening staccato of boot heels on the street, like the sound of gunfire from an automatic weapon; oddly comforting, the familiar sounds of home. I knew it was Holmes, yet I whirled, my fists curled into tight balls, ready to pummel him if he came any closer. He stopped, hands held out, fingers splayed.

I seem to recall pulling the cloak over my head and curling up against the side of a building.

'Wait here,' he said. And, more emphatically: 'Don't move.' He took off running.

Then, quite unexpectedly, I really wanted him to come back. I was terrified that he wouldn't.

I peeked out and realised I had no idea where I was. The place had an ominous similarity to every other street in London, cast in shades of burnt cork, smoke and ash. The sounds of horse-shoes and metal-rimmed wheels stirred my panic to fever-pitch, and I sprang up in a dead run, heedless of my broken heel, heedless even of my direction.

'Rose!' I heard him shout over the clamour of the hooves. 'Rose, stop!'

He'd fetched a cab. I'd barely stopped running when the four-wheeler caught up with me, Holmes hanging by an arm and a leg from the open door. He leapt down, prepared to sweep me manfully into the warm, dry interior. I staggered back from him.

'Get into the cab, Rose. I'll take you home.'

The jarvey gazed down on me, the sight of this wild-haired woman with her bodice unhooked, gown spattered with mud and refuse, clearly alarming him. He looked suspiciously at the man who'd hired his services.

'The lady's had a bit of a fall,' Holmes explained tersely.

Chapter 8

For a few minutes I simply watched the light from the cab's lanterns swing over the street; short flashes that illuminated creatures in doorways like big-eyed nocturnal animals from another planet. But they were just the beggars and the luckless whores with no place else to go.

He broke the silence. 'If you've need of a doctor, Watson is very discreet.'

'No,' I croaked, then cleared my throat. 'No. I'll be all right. I'm not... I mean, he didn't actually...'

'I know he didn't *actually*, Rose,' he said. 'I was watching. Although I will admit, it took me a few moments to realise you weren't enjoying his attention.'

A number of coarsely-phrased responses came to mind, but I thought it best not to share them. In a desperate attempt to recover the pretence of my housemaid role, I put my face in my hands and wailed: 'Oh lord, sir, what you must think o' me, tryin' to make m'self out better than I am -'

He laughed. 'Brava! Now, try the same lines in Italian.'

My head shot up. That man sitting alone near the fireplace, glass of Chianti in one hand and a book in the other...

'You were at Previtali's.'

'And at the music-hall.' He settled into the seat and leaned his head back, tipping his hat forward over his brow with disconcerting jauntiness. He smiled, had rolling gently with the rhythm of the coach.

'I promised myself this would be the last effort I made to determine who and what you are. If you chose, for instance, to succumb to the wiles of Jack Hudson, as might any country wench beguiled by strong wine and the dubious charms of a handsome face... then I would leave well alone, truly and forever, amen. But I saw your expression at the Oxford. Watching the entertainment the way a missionary in Africa might watch natives cavorting about a fire in some heathen, ritualistic dance. Needless to say, I was sufficiently intrigued to follow you and your swain.'

He laughed, and the sound of it sent an autonomous quiver through my legs. Evidently, my body was long past the "fight" stage and making ready to flee. I adjusted the cloak over my knees, rubbing them a little.

'By God, you were a joy to watch!' he continued. 'A riveting performance. Your fluency in Italian had the waiters in a frenzy of speculation. "Madonna Bellisima", the mysterious lady whose cloak decried her lack of means, yet whose gown and manner were so far above their own Saffron Hill. Yet they all agreed on one thing.' He paused. I gazed at him coldly. 'Poor Jack was out his element.'

My face burned. 'Yes. Poor Jack. Poor pathetic little rapist.'

'Rose, forgive me, but what did you expect? It was clear to every man in the room that you've barely a stitch on beneath that gown. The lad was understandably confused by your appearance and behaviour. You ignored him, insulted him, yet also gave the impression you would be amenable to his advances.'

'I most certainly did not!'

'Yes, you did. I had a clear head as I watched. Please keep that in mind.' My hands tightened into fists in my lap. I made a concerted effort to unfold them as he went on. 'Naturally, he misinterpreted when you fell against him.'

'Oh, right, of course. Men will "misinterpret", won't they? After all, a woman who allows herself to get drunk in the company of a man has no right to expect him to behave in a civilised manner.'

He had the sense to look discomfited. 'I did not say that -'

'You're saying I nearly got what I deserved -'

'What was that gesture you made?' he asked suddenly. 'Curling your fingers, thus? Quotation marks, was it?'

'I... yes.'

'You held up two fingers on each hand.' Gulp. How American of me. He gave himself a little shake, dismissing the oddity to address my statement. 'No woman deserves such treatment, but you must admit, there are those who invite it. You walked into that alley with the young man following. What was I to think?'

Really. What was he to think? What had *I* been thinking?

'I was drunk,' I said. 'Oh my God, I'm still drunk.' I rocked forward with a moan, the full implications of my folly hitting me hard. Fearing another spew of stomach contents, Holmes drew his legs in and wedged himself close to the door. 'I knew what Jack was after. I just... I thought... Jesus, this is so humiliating.'

His voice drifted towards me through the shadows of the cab, and in it was the impossible hope that he could illuminate the mysteries of womankind with one simple question. 'If you knew of his intentions, why did you step out with him?'

I opened my mouth to respond, but the reasons were all jumbled in my head and what came out was a desire almost too stupid to be verbalised. I did it anyway.

'Calamari,' I said.

'I beg your pardon?'

'I wanted calamari.'

Holmes burst out laughing. 'Well, I'm fond of the calamari there myself, but I don't think I'd...'

His amusement withered as the shocks of the evening finally washed over me. Sobbing, I fumbled to extract the handkerchief from my bag, but after fighting with the cords I sullenly snatched the one he offered.

'What *are* you doing here, Rose?' he asked, after my tears had abated somewhat.

I blew my nose. 'Do you want me to say I'm spying on you, Sherlock Holmes? Will that make you happy?'

'Happy? No. Though it would give me a small measure of satisfaction to hear it confirmed. You are no more a housemaid by nature than I am a bank clerk.'

'Women enter domestic service out of necessity, Mr Holmes. Nature has nothing to do with it.' I wiped the square of linen beneath my eyes and did a mop-up job on my nostrils. I handed it back to him, but at his look of dismay I tucked it into my sleeve instead. 'It's the only work most women can get.'

'Then you have proved my conjectures to be correct. You do not work at the house in Baker Street because you can get no other position. You are clearly intelligent, educated, and talented as well. What, then, could be the attraction to such a thankless position but the opportunity to observe the people who live there - and do forgive my seeming vanity - myself in particular? I can only hope it isn't something dull, such as trying to get the goods on me for blackmail.'

'Why?' I shot back. 'Do you have the sort of secrets that would make it worth my while?'

'I certainly don't have the money to pay for your silence if I do.'

'I'm not a blackmailer. Nor do I work for one.'

He pounced on this. 'But you are working for someone? The Fenians, perhaps?'

I sighed feebly. 'Have you done something to damage the cause of the Irish extremists, Mr Holmes?'

'Not thus far.'

'Then that's a stupid speculation on your part, isn't it?' He tensed at this mental slap in the face, followed by a tremor of embarrassment and a brief flash of anger at my having called attention to it.

Several adolescent boys, dressed in shreds, burst from an alley and raced in front of our carriage. Vermin-infested, pitiful creatures that thieved, schemed, scraped and fought their way through each miserable day of their lives. Through the opposite window I watched as their blackened bare feet slapped through glittering puddles to the opposite side of the street. High, rough voices shouted encouragement and obscenities. Their arms were full of writhing burlap bags. Rats, maybe, or cats.

Here was Henry Mayhew's cultural study of the London Poor *live and in the flesh*, but for me there was only a gut-punch of disgust and then the need not to see them. The Age of Victoria had swallowed me whole, and I now resided in the belly of the whale.

The voice of Sherlock Holmes startled me with its reasonable tone. He'd seen all this a hundred times before. His concerns were, quite properly, for himself. 'What, then, do you hope to gain from your observations?'

I turned to him again, my voice dead flat. 'Perhaps I intend to start my own consulting detective business.'

He threw back his head and laughed, again.

'You think I can't?' I asked.

'Irrelevant. I think you are lying.'

'I'm merely seeking knowledge.'

'About me, for me, or against me?'

'I assure you, sir, I intend you no harm.'

'Intentions and results are not always the same thing.'

I swallowed that truth like an overlarge pill. It was time to change tactics. 'Did you search my room, Mr Holmes?'

He leaned back once more and crossed his legs. The toe of his shoe brushed the silk of my gown, making it crackle. 'Have you searched through *my* belongings, Miss Donnelly?'

'To some extent. One can cover a multitude of sins with a little haphazard dusting.'

'And what did you find of interest?'

'You first.'

'Unlike you, I have admitted to nothing.'

'And I know you found nothing!' I cried. I'd already betrayed myself by acknowledging his suspicions, but I had to know. 'Why did you persist? Why did you follow me?'

'I should think you might be glad I did.'

'All right, I'm forever in your debt. But that hardly answers my question.'

'Well, in truth, it was the absence of crucial evidence that piqued my suspicions. I noted long ago, long before you trailed after me in my own boots, that you did a great deal of writing. I assumed personal journals, letters, even musical notation... the callus on the third finger of your right hand, Rose, pressure from holding a writing instrument. Sometimes you had traces of pencil-lead on your fingers, sometimes ink. Yet, when I searched your room, I found only pen and ink. No diaries, no papers. I concluded you had all of those articles with you at the park. Why take your correspondence with you, but for fear of its being discovered? And there were other points of interest...' He let the words trail off, glancing out of the window. I looked out as well. We were on Baker Street, nearing the house.

He threw back the shutter. 'Driver!'

'Yes, sir?'

'The lady is in need of hospital. St. Mary's, if you please.'

He settled back into his seat. I stared at him in growing panic. 'I don't need hospital.'

'It won't help us if we arrive while Jack is still at the house. We can walk from St. Mary's.'

'Not in these boots, I can't.' I pressed my thumbs into my eyelids. Tired and thirsty. 'I don't suppose you'd consider returning to the pretence of a master-and-servant relationship?'

'Consider it? By God, Rose. I'm counting on it!'

A shiver started in my toes and came shuddering out of the top of my poor, besotted head. In a voice both cunning in its modulation and thrilling in tone, he added: 'How else might we continue this delightful game?'

Chapter 9

The next evening, while I was still reeling from the blows of my experience and suffering a sizeable hangover into the bargain, Sherlock Holmes invited me to play music with him the coming Sunday.

'Will I show up and look the fool again?' I asked.

'I am completely sincere in my invitation, Rose,' he replied. He met my eyes, in order that I should see how completely sincere he was.

I was suspicious, but said I'd see if it could be arranged. I knew he hoped to trip me up, but as I'd be doing the same thing, what did I have to lose? And music was an area in which I felt supremely confident, more than his equal. But music had a way of superseding logic, a fact that somehow slipped my mind.

Mrs Hudson was adjusting to the blow of her son's sudden departure by retreating into the solace of the church, and that Sunday left only porridge for the lodgers, in a warming-dish on the sideboard downstairs. I found a note in the kitchen, saying she was staying for every service and wouldn't be back until later that evening. I took the opportunity to return to my bed, but found myself floating between sleep and odd masturbatory fantasies. I indulged myself quietly until nine.

By ten, the porridge had congealed to a hardened lump. I left it on the sideboard, choosing to wash and dress carefully in my Sunday best instead of dumping the lump and scrubbing the dish. At eleven, I appeared at the gentlemen's door with a coffee service on a small trolley, and my guitar-case in hand. With what I hoped was a dazzling smile, I entered the sitting room at the invitation of Mr Sherlock Holmes.

Dr Watson reacted to this unconventional arrangement with tremendous discomfort. Not only was he confused as to what I was doing there with my instrument, he was also confused by the absence of tea, and aware of an indefinable something deeper; something improper, which the coffee represented and my presence exacerbated. A female servant had brought the wrong beverage and was now seating herself comfortably in a chair, while Holmes calmly removed his violin from its case.

We proceeded with tuning. Holmes rosined the bow, then adjusted the instrument on his shoulder and fitted it under his chin. I took a deep and calming breath.

At first, we were just testing each other's knowledge. What do you know? What does this say about you?

He hurried through Mendelssohn. I did a little Rodrigo, not as well as I would have liked.

'Do you read?' he asked, flipping through a book on the music stand. 'Music, I mean?'

'Of course,' I replied.

'Do you have to read, or can you play from memory?'

'That depends on the piece, sir.'

'Paganini's Cantabile for guitar and violin?'

'I know that one,' I said smugly.

He set the stand aside. 'Good. We've no one competent to turn the pages anyway.' Watson rattled his newspaper by way of comment.

We screwed up the first time through. Then we did it again, *perfectly*.

Holmes proposed we improvise on one of his own works.

Watson said, 'Oh, Lord, no, please...'

Ignoring him, we began speaking excitedly in that musician's patois so irritating to outsiders; about augmented fifths, half-steps, countering at the intervals, down two at the bridge, modulate a bit, then back up to the -

'What key?' I asked suddenly.

Embarrassed and vaguely apologetic, he said, 'E minor.'

I smirked. The most emotional key in the business.

He smirked back. 'Just stop when you can't follow along, and pick it up again if you can.'

Good advice, because it was a scary little number that moved into an intense and almost impossible 7/8 time signature. But I kept up. It was thrilling, and by the end of the piece we broke off, exhilarated, sweaty, and laughing breathlessly.

'That was remarkable.'

We both started, having forgotten Watson was there. He was smiling, but there was tension behind the smile. 'I don't think I've ever heard its like.'

'You've heard that piece before,' Holmes said, dabbing his forehead with a handkerchief.

'Not like -' Watson waved at the two of us, '- *that*.'

Holmes shrugged. But the hand around the bow curled and flexed, convulsively. His nonchalance was all sham. There was something in the room with us now, something we all felt and endeavoured to ignore. And this elephant-in-the-lounge might have stayed formless and eventually faded away, were it not for that bloody E-minor.

I mumbled my excuses, packed my guitar and fled.

Not that it made a bit of difference later that night, when he was on his way up and I was on my way down. I'm not sure where I was going, except that I wanted to run hard and fast until I'd run off the inexplicable sensations of the past few days. Where *he* was going, I may never know.

In darkness on the servant's stairs, just after midnight, we met with a shock of surprise, then understanding. We didn't speak, only the sound of breaths in and out before we glommed onto each other with our mouths. We kissed for a long, dizzying time, until we were swaying dangerously, about to tumble and break necks or promises we'd secretly made to ourselves. Instead, I pulled him into the linen cupboard, and I will never inhale the fragrance of lavender and laundered sheets in quite the same way again.

'This isn't... we shouldn't...' I stifled his protests with my lips. Any further objections left him with a gasp and a shudder as I reached for the buttons on his trousers.

It was the first open doorway to the flesh, and that was how we proceeded, exposing only what was necessary for quick, impassioned and terribly furtive coupling. A nipple here, a taut bit of belly there, until maddened by slick tongues and hot fingers, he grabbed me up and perched me on the edge of a shelf, sliding my skirts over the landscape of thick stockings and the bumpy ruffles of garters, to the bare flesh above my knees and up farther still. A wriggle on my part, a push on his, and then that melting, encompassing 'aahh' before we got down to business.

All in all, this spectacular *tour de force* couldn't have taken more than fifteen minutes, from the kissing on the stairs to the climactic finish. His orgasm was accompanied by a cry of pure astonishment, quickly muffled into my hair. Mine, accompanied by the usual "yes-yes"es and invocations of deity.

We found ourselves on the floor afterwards, my legs still wrapped around his back, his bony knees like tent-poles beneath the fabric of his trousers. We leaned against each other that way, hypnotised by the sounds of our synchronised breathing.

Then came embarrassment, apologies, your classic Victorian shame, coupled with the perfectly normal concerns that any intelligent man would experience after having unprotected sex in a linen cupboard with a woman he hardly knew.

'We must never do this again,' he said stoically.

'Yes. I know.'

He pulled his head back and tried to fix me with a look through the fuzzy darkness, the better to demonstrate some firm resolve directed more at himself than at me. 'It could only lead to misfortune for the both of us.'

Ah. Misfortune. The code-name for pregnancy and ruin. 'You mustn't worry about that,' I told him.

'I would be a fool not to, Rose.'

'It's all right. I can't get pregnant.'

He heard this matter-of-fact statement, and I could tell he was dubious. But more than that, he was intrigued, mind racing around a track of possibilities. 'How can you be sure of that?'

I sighed, the fairy-tale fatedness of our encounter undeniably over. I thought of a lie but couldn't bring myself to use it. 'Please don't worry about it. It's risky enough for other reasons.' I shifted uncomfortably. 'I'm afraid we've made rather a mess of your trousers.'

'That's why God made cleaning solvent,' he said.

We parted with promises never to meet again, in a linen cupboard or anywhere else.

But we did. Of course we did. In his bed chamber two nights later. Watson was at his club. Holmes had rung for more coal at around nine-thirty, and I'd brought it up on the way to my own room, my own bed.

He was seated at the messy chemical table in his shirtsleeves, no waistcoat, silky black braces bisecting his narrow back and making his shirt puff out on either side like the elytron of some mutant beetle. Dr Jeckyl meets Franz Kafka. He seemed absorbed in his work.

'The coal's for my room, Rose,' he said, over his shoulder.

'Shall I take it in, then?'

'If you would, please.'

A minute later he followed me in, closed the door and locked it.

He did not apologise. If he were ashamed of himself, he didn't show it. Prone beneath me, he idly twirled a corkscrew strand of my hair around a finger, while his other hand caressed the skin under a cheek of my bum. It was surreal, to say the least. I pushed back from his chest and gazed at him in wonder. I had a girlish urge to ring up all my friends and squeal about whom I'd just shagged on the floor of his bedroom.

The glow of the hearth softened the angles of his face, and his eyelashes cast long shadows across his cheekbones as he watched me from beneath sleepy lids. His black hair was sweaty, curling across a vaguely furrowed brow and giving him the look of a puzzled child. He reached out, touched the hollow of my throat and dragged a fingertip down between my breasts and all the way to my belly-button.

'What's this little scar here?' he asked. For a moment I didn't know what he was looking at.

Oh. Oh, yeah. That piercing I'd got at the age of eighteen. I hadn't worn a ring in it for at least five years. How did he even see it?

I said nothing, merely kissed him, dressed and left him to ponder the meaning of the hole through my belly-button.

We maintained an unspoken agreement to play our parts when in the presence of others: Watson's initial suspicions dissipated into the reassuring certainty of daily routine. We went on like this for a giddy fortnight, never caught because we were both so goddamned clever. But every time we met, Holmes appeared to glean a little more about me in the thoughtful silence that followed his pleasure. He said things like: 'Your hands are not long accustomed to this harsh life, are they?' Or: 'What remarkable teeth you have. Not a single sign of decay.' Sometimes a compliment would slip out about my soft skin, the way I smelled, the incomparable joys of being inside me. Once he said: 'By God, girl, you'll wear me to the bone if we go on like this!' But he was skin and bones already.

Perhaps he merely intended to expose me through this process, peeling away a layer at a time. Or perhaps, like most human beings, intention became muddled when sexual pleasure was involved. I convinced myself I'd found an elegant way to salvage my compromised research. Eventually, I reasoned, he'd be compelled to present me with a completed picture of who and what he thought I was. It would be wrong, but well-thought-out given the available data and his frame of reference. I'd then document his methods with myself as the subject to which he applied his genius. It was a fascinating spin on the research, one that I felt certain would land me offers from the history departments of any number of prestigious universities. I was totally self-deluded, of course. I wouldn't be able to publish my work until the year 2018, according to the binding contract I'd signed. I could hardly defend my thesis before then, not without revealing my sources or the technology that had made them possible.

The truth was, I didn't want to stop. The sex was surprisingly good, and the novelty of the circumstances made it even better.

One night, he fell asleep in my bed, a place where he should never have been. With my research notes under a floorboard beneath us, I let him sleep, comforted and terrified by the deep, sated sound of his breathing. Earlier that night, we'd giggled at the thought of the rooftop burglar climbing through my window, and what a surprise the devil would have had. But as I lay there, jerked awake by every hiss through the gas pipes or yowl of a cat, I felt only the restless dread of discovery. In an hour I'd be getting up to begin my workday, and still he slept.

I touched his arm. I shook his shoulder gently. No response. I rolled close, my mouth next to his ear. 'Sherlock,' I said. It was such an awkward name, but when you whispered it, ah, much different. It was the very soul of *sotto voce*, that name. He stirred. I said his name again and his hand came up to his ear, as if to brush away an insect.

'You have to leave,' I whispered. He moaned and threw an arm over me, pulling me to him like a fierce infant searching for the breast. 'It's nearly four.'

His eyes flashed open, and he rose on one elbow, reaching over me to grope for his watch amongst discarded clothing on the tiny chair beside the bed. He found the chain and pulled the cold, heavy watchcase across my back.

In my own time we would doubtless spend tremendous energy on copulation for its own sake. Weekends screwing our brains out, then examining each other's brains over long philosophical debates and the occasional afternoon breakfast. Eventually we'd fight and make up for the sake of the sex, and fight again, and then break up because, after all, one cannot base an entire relationship upon sex.

Of course, we weren't there in my world, my time. Love may be a grand, expansive thing that moves mountains, but "in love" just makes people stupid. I'm not saying I was in love, but I was stupid to let this man sleep in my bed. I could be turned out, and, very possibly, so could he. Historically speaking, that would not be good. Who could say he'd be the same man without the address? The misfortune he'd predicted that first night was on a potentially much grander scale for him than getting a servant pregnant.

'Sherlock, you have to leave. *Now.*'

'I have not yet heard the cock crow,' he muttered.

'Your cock has crowed plenty enough.' I gave him a little shove. 'The rest of the house will be rising soon. The longer you stay, the riskier it becomes.'

'It will be less risky the longer I stay, Rose. The others will have gone to wherever it is they slave away, and I can sleep here in the damp sheets of our love until you return.'

'You are not spending the day in my bed, you lazy shit!' I hissed.

He propped himself on an elbow and brushed a thick tendril of hair from my shoulder, as it was also obscuring the breast he wished to fondle. 'An interesting turn of a phrase. I wonder, could I alter your opinion and somehow become an industrious shit?'

'Leave now. Please, before you're seen doing it.'

'I'm quite skilled at getting in and out of places with appropriate finesse, Rose, as I'm sure you've noticed.'

I scoffed at this, at the arrogance of brainy dweebs who think they're good at everything. 'Yes, well, it's not your position that's at risk, is it, sir?' His body tensed, fingers ceasing their lazy brush across my nipple. 'You've 'ad what you come fer. If the missus should find you 'ere, I'll be dismissed without me character.'

'Don't do that,' he said irritably.

"Ave I displeased, sir? Dreadful sorry fer it if I 'ave done.'

He flung himself onto his back with an explosive sigh that shook the bed. We lay next to each other that way; time, gender-roles, and the ever-present social order crowding the space between us. I'd degraded him by bringing our disparate social standings into the picture. He'd failed to respect my requests for the very same reason.

After a long, chilly moment, he rose. I heard him dressing, but I kept my face turned away. He slipped down the attic stairs, shoes in hand, with the stealth of an experienced burglar. The door at the bottom opened then closed quietly. I could hear the soft tread of his feet through the corridor below only because I was listening for it -

Another door was flung open, with a suddenness that stopped my heart.

Men's voices, exchanging hushed words: Mr Corkle's, anxious and slightly high-pitched; Holmes', low, with the smarmy tone of a con-artist. The floorboards groaned as one of them moved down the hall to the staircase. After a moment, the door closed again.

Thomas Peerson Corkle had seen Sherlock Holmes carrying his shoes as he stole down the hallway from my door, which is what I told him would happen, the bastard.

Chapter 10

The rest of the morning was spent cleaning up after my own clumsy exhaustion, with Mrs Hudson's exasperated bitching following me everywhere I went. But no rest for the wicked, it seemed. When Corkle caught me in the hall that night, I could barely stay on my feet.

'R-Rose, may I... may I speak with you a moment?' He blushed and gave a little jerk of his head, indicating his own door. 'Privately. That is, i-i-if you don't mind terribly?'

I looked longingly at the door that led up to my room. 'Can it wait 'til morning, sir?'

'Well, it's-it's rather delicate. That is, I-I shouldn't think you'd want Mrs Hudson chancing upon us discussing such ah, ah, a delicate matter.' He gestured to his door again and I stared at him, forcing him to stammer his way to the point. 'I just, well, I-I-I feel it's more proper than were I to enter your... your... chamber, you see.'

I knew what it was about, but I was hoping that if I looked clueless, he'd let me go. No such luck.

He opened his door and gestured me in.

It was same room I entered on Monday mornings to change the linens and gather his laundry. Some of the books that littered his room were rare volumes even in 1882. But as there were hundreds of them stacked against the walls, doubled up on the bookshelf and scattered at the foot of his writing-desk like offerings at a shrine, I would have been surprised if he'd known which.

His bed was still unmade of course, because I didn't come in every day to make it. His night-shirt and cap hung from an iron post, as grey and wrinkled as the sheets. On the hand-wash stand, the basin was full of water, with bits of bristle and soap scum floating at the top.

In one corner was a massive steamer trunk. It was locked. I knew because I'd checked. In another corner was the stove, sooty pipe piercing the ceiling, dented copper kettle steaming away on top.

The combination of clutter and Spartan minimalism declared his occupation and obsession in classic fashion. Here lived an untidy, ill-groomed academic, myopically focused on his work. I'd seen all this a dozen times, but suddenly and for no reason I could understand, the room became a red flag. It was too perfect somehow.

When I turned to face him again, he'd just locked the door and was placing the key in his trouser pocket. Countless possibilities went whizzing through my mind. None of them were nice.

Thomas Peerson Corkle removed his spectacles and slipped them inside his frock coat. He rubbed at his temples, and said, wearily: 'Have a seat, Gillian. I'll brew some tea.'

For a moment, I couldn't respond to the sound of my own name. I hadn't heard it for so long.

'Who the hell are you?'

'A friend of Jimmy's.'

'Jimmy Moriarty?'

'Is there another?' He smiled, and it was the cold, utterly false cheer that finally forced me to sit.

'So,' he began, pulling a wooden chair from the desk to sit facing me. Knees inches from my own, smile still on his fat, wet lips. 'It appears you've broken what should be a cardinal rule for this sort of research. Would you care to justify that?'

I was still holding my breath, and let it out heavily, a couple of emotions vying for attention. Shame was one, paranoid caution another.

'You're my operative, is that it?'

'More like the pilot, navigator and flight engineer, all rolled into one.'

'Huh. That would make me mission specialist then, wouldn't it?'

His mouth twitched. 'Specializing in shagging the subject, are we?' My stomach cramped. He fixed me with a cool gaze. 'Does Holmes know?'

'Know?'

'Well, obviously he knows in the biblical sense. Does he know what you're doing here?'

'Of course not.' It wasn't exactly a lie. 'We share an interest in music.'

'Ah, yes. I heard the two of you making music together in the wee hours this morning. Very primal.' He giggled. 'I must say, it amuses me to think of the great detective sneaking down hallways in order to get a little poontang -'

'You're a bit of a pig, aren't you?'

'It's the nature of the times in which we have immersed ourselves.'

I stood up, crossed my arms over my chest. 'I see. Well, now that we've established that, you can unlock the goddamned door, Mr... I'm sorry, Mr...?'

'Oh, I'm afraid Corkle is my real name. I didn't have to be insinuated into my position by the timely death of another. You see, Miss Petra - sorry, *Ms* Petra - I've been here nearly two years, setting this up for you. Establishing the bank accounts from which we pay our local sources, making sure Rose's sister gets cheerful, newsy letters on a regular basis. Keeping the Widow Tory's landlady from asking too many questions. Who did you think took care of all that?'

'I was told I wouldn't be meeting you until I boarded ship in June.'

'And I was told you were well-trained, with a cool head and professional ethics. Imagine my surprise.' He got up to tend the kettle. 'Surely you didn't think you were on your own until the send-forward? That the locals would continue doing what they're asked to do without someone dangling bank-notes in front of them?'

'I've been dangling the bank-notes.'

'I've been making sure you have them to dangle. I can't say it doesn't have its rewards. And I do actually work at the British Museum. I'm in the lower levels most of the time, cataloguing archaeological treasures, most of which will be destroyed for the sake of public morals. Right now I'm going through a cigar-box full of Roman brothel-tokens. They're deliciously explicit, got 'em recorded on disc.'

'What?' I whispered.

Corkle dug a fist into a coat pocket and brought out a digital camcorder. 'Just minimal equipment. I have to confess, I went a bit mad when I first arrived. Shot everything, simply everything I saw.' He withdrew a couple of discs from another pocket and clicked them together like castanets. The sound of plastic against plastic was a sound like no other. But I was both shocked and unreasonably envious.

'The methods of observation were to be kept strictly within the confines of the period. That's what *I* was told.'

'Well, it would hardly do for you to get caught with such a thing.' It was like a fat little gun, with his forefinger over the trigger. He put it back in his pocket, along with the discs. 'You're under a different sort of scrutiny. Even Mrs Hudson would be hard-pressed to figure out what a girl with two dresses to her name would be doing with a pretty little thing like this.' He patted the pocket. 'And Holmes... God 'a mercy, that'd be no good at all. Still, I'm safe enough. He takes no notice of me. You, however, you're a bit of a problem now.'

Something in the way he said it tweaked my subconscious, like the buzzing of a noisy travel alarm clock. This was a bigger situation than I could fathom.

Bigger than invalidating my own research, that was for damn sure, but I couldn't seem to wake myself up to *how* big. I blurted out the first anxiety that came to my mind.

'I won't be sent forward sooner because of this.'

My face flushed as soon as the words left my lips. He snorted in derision. 'Jesus, Gillian! Didn't you read any of the specs when you got 'em?'

'Yes, but -'

'Well, then. Unless you and I should miraculously split the atom by lashing it to the front of a locomotive and, oh, I don't know, running it into a brick wall or something, we're pretty much on our own until the big blow on August the 26th. We'll have to fly by the seat of our trousers 'til then. Make the most of a bad situation.'

'Why don't you just tell me what's going to happen now, so I can get some sleep, all right?'

He began spooning tea into the oddly dainty teapot. 'Well, first of all, I'm going to have to ask you to turn your notes over to me. For safekeeping, Gillian. It wouldn't do for him to see them, now would it?'

'I'm not giving you my research.'

'Yes you are. I have authority to act in the best interests of the project.' I gnawed my lip and looked at the floor. 'Relax. I'm not here to steal your thunder, love. Keep doing what you're doing if it gets you what you want.' He poured the water into the pot and swirled it around. 'Just don't get caught, because if Rose Donnelly is dismissed for doing the nasty with the master, then Gillian Petra will find herself on the streets of some godforsaken backwater until the send-forward.'

'I'm perfectly willing to do whatever's necessary to remedy the situation. But the vague threats are just pissing me off. I've got other options besides begging or prostitution.'

'I'm not threatening you, Gillian. I'm being logical. That's a characteristic you admire in a man, isn't it?' I snarled. Corkle shrugged. 'Personally, I think Sherlock Holmes is an arrogant prick. But I doubt he'd be comfortable letting you take all the blame if you're dismissed. At the very least, he'd need to know what becomes of the girl he ruined. In which case, you couldn't very well slip into Mrs Tory's widow's weeds and expect him not to notice.'

He was right. Damn it.

'My advice is to stop,' he said, pouring me a cup. 'Fear of pregnancy or something. Or you could push the marriage bit. That's guaranteed to stop a man dead in his tracks.'

I took the offered cup. Milk and one sugar, just the way I liked it. I swallowed hard and heard it echo inside my head. 'That may not be necessary. As soon as he gets another case, he'll have no further interest in me.'

'You think? I do hope you're not undervaluing the tempting allure of unlimited sex with a willing woman.'

'It's like morphine to him. Temporary euphoria to relieve boredom.'

My cool manner must have seemed strained. I could tell he wasn't convinced.

'And what's it like for you?'

I rallied the hardened bitch within and said: 'An exciting research opportunity.'

A slow grin, full of ugly appreciation, spread across his face. 'Ah. But what truly useful data have you gleaned as a result? Scars? Ticklish spots? Not the real meat of a man like him.'

'Naked or not, I can't get inside the man's head. That was never a possibility in the best of circumstances.'

'Noooo,' Corkle said quietly. 'But you can still get inside the sitting room.'

He looked at me over his cup, blue eyes glittering in the light of the lamp.

'What are you proposing, Mr Corkle?'

'I have in my possession some charming devices which will enable us to put a technological spin on the whole business.'

My eyes flicked to the steamer trunk. 'Surveillance equipment?'

He nodded. 'Audio transmitters. Video would be lovely, but a little too risky for my comfort.'

'This is not what I signed up for.'

'No. It's easier.' At my expression of disgust, he leaned forward, trying to infect me with his enthusiasm. 'Think of it, Gillian. You'll get to hear every interview with every client. Every insult to Watson's intelligence. That means spending a lot of hours with me. But you can handle it.' He patted me on the knee. 'You're a trooper.'

I looked at my cup, poised on its journey to my lips, and remembered once upon a time...

My Master's thesis, a clever little book entitled *The Magic Feather Duster: A Brief History of Domestic Service in Victoria's England*, is placed on the shelf of a university library to gather dust with all the other clever theses. Unexpectedly, it catches the attention of a corporate wizard named Jimmy Moriarty, who needs a social historian to help him with some research.

'Are you familiar with the work of Sherlock Holmes?' he asks.

He obviously knows about my proposed doctoral thesis. Sherlock Holmes, Bertillon, Pinkerton. Premiere detectives when criminal investigation was in its infancy. They created something new, made art where previously there'd been none.

'Would you like the chance to meet him?'

'Well, yeah,' I reply. 'But it would kind of involve a physical impossibility, wouldn't it?'

What had I been thinking back then? That a project of such magnitude, surrounded by secrecy and costing billions, was designed so I could make a big splash in the academic community? Apparently, my ego was more inflated than that of Sherlock.

I was aware of Corkle still waiting for an answer. I took a slow swallow of tea.

'I don't have copies of my notes,' I said. 'I wouldn't want them to be lost.'

'They'll be in a safe-deposit box. I'll keep the key, of course.'

'Of course.'

In my room, I moved the bed as noiselessly as possible, and lifted the board that hid my treasures. Corkle was hugging himself. 'Bloody cold up here, isn't it? What, the old bat can't provide a little stove?'

In our time, Mrs Hudson - in her forties - would hardly be an old bat. She'd dye her grey hair back to its natural colour, and be managing the housewares section of a big retail department store. 'The comfort of a maid-of-all-work isn't at the top of anyone's list,' I said.

He eyed the thick sheaf of papers I handed him. 'Is this all of it?'

'At the moment.'

'What about the little notebook you carry?'

'I need that. It's in code, no-one can read it anyway.'

'You'll have to copy it out and turn those notes over to me as well.'

'Fine,' I said, moving the bed back into position. The watch-chain came slithering out from beneath the pillow. He reached for it, but I snatched it up first.

'He left a little token of his esteem, I see. Not very discreet of him.' Corkle shook his head in mock-wonder. 'Deary me, you must be quite the shag to make that man forget to remove all traces of his presence.' Still hugging himself, he pointed with his chin at the satchel next to the guitar-case. 'What's in that?'

'Sheet music. A couple of songbooks.'

His eyes perused my features, and I managed to meet his gaze without flinching. 'Nothing out of period, I trust?'

'Jesus Christ!' I said, going to the satchel and starting to unbuckle it.

'Oh, don't trouble yourself, darling. I believe you. All right then, Rose Donnelly, I'll be going about my business and leave you to yours. Pleasant dreams.'

He pointed to the stairs and put a finger to his lips, then began to tiptoe in a burlesque fashion down the steps.

'Mr Corkle?'

'Yes?'

'Don't come up here again.'

I heard him chuckling quietly as he closed the door.

After I had satisfied myself that he was safely in his own room, I opened the satchel and took out my journals. I spent the next two hours filling in addenda and annotations from my stolen material.

Chapter 11

Two days later, neither rested nor refreshed, I was once again at the door of the sitting room. I had two of Mr Corkle's listening-devices in my apron pocket.

I'd told him I wouldn't plant any in the bedrooms, which he thought was funny. I just thought these men should have some privacy, even if Corkle and I were the only ones who knew they had any at all. I hadn't even decided whether I'd go through with it. Nevertheless, they were in my pocket; one for the fireplace, and one to be placed near or around the side-table, between the sofa and the two most commonly-used chairs. I was painfully aware of how I was being used, both by the implications of the tiny devices in one pocket and the device in my *other* pocket.

I pressed my hand over the watch and chain, knocked, and entered. I was to sweep the carpets and dust the room.

Holmes sat cross-legged on the floor, still in his dressing-gown, surrounded by newspaper clippings and with a big, loose-bound scrapbook in front of him.

Watson nodded my direction as he reached for his hat. 'Well, I'm off to meet my cousin at the station.'

'You've been saying that for the past twenty minutes,' Holmes muttered.

'You're not getting out of this, you know,' the doctor replied, drawing on his overcoat.

Holmes growled. 'Henry Irving is much too old to be playing Romeo.'

'You can tell him to his face after the performance.' And with that, Watson went on his merry way. I could hear him whistling down the steps.

We were completely alone, but Holmes pointedly ignored me. He scowled at his clippings and scrapbook, like a child trying to figure out what Teacher wanted him to do with all this stuff.

'I'm to sweep the carpets,' I announced.

He glanced up at me darkly. 'Don't you dare.'

'I'll just dust then.'

'If you work up a whirlwind with it, I shall have to throttle you.'

'Fine. How about I sit on my arse and do nothing,' I said, and plopped onto the sofa, the duster dangling between my knees.

'I would prefer it if you were to go away. I'm very busy at the moment.'

'And when will the gentleman be through playing with his paste and scissors?'

His eyes focused on me; cold, hard-edged shards of ice. 'Don't use that tone with me again, girl. I'll take a strap to you.'

A shock of laughter froze on its way out. 'You'll do what?'

He met my incredulity without so much as blinking. 'You seem to be forgetting your position here. You are a domestic servant. I am the master you are supposed to be serving. You would do well to remember that when next you open your mouth, or I shall beat it indelibly into your memory.' He kept his eyes on me for a long, vicious moment, and if it seemed a ludicrous threat, there was nothing of the ludicrous in the way he said it. Just absolute certainty. 'You may go.'

I felt my face tighten in mute shock, and then my whole body followed. A hard knot of humiliation and rage formed in the region of my solar plexus.

'Yes, sir,' I said, rising from the sofa, my voice flat. I smoothed my apron. 'I'll inform Mrs Hudson you don't wish to be disturbed. Sir.'

I moved to the door, fingers trembling as they closed around the handle.

'I shall be wanting tea in half an hour.'

I'd been playing at maid all this time, and now I knew what it actually meant to be one.

Still, as I stood there shaking, it occurred to me what a calculating bastard he was. Take a strap to me? I felt certain he'd do nothing of the sort, and yet, by his tone, I was put firmly in my place. I knew what he was trying to do and I wasn't going to let him get away with it.

'If you're hoping I'll show my hand, Mr Holmes, just because you've used and rejected me, then you're gambling with the wrong woman.'

His expression was one I hadn't seen in a long while. Cool and impervious, a void without any indication of what motivated him. 'I never indulge in that vice, Rose.'

'Gambling? Oh, I think you do. You've taken an awful big chance with me.'

'Have I? But I could prove you to be a liar against any accusations you make. I could accuse you of stealing and not be entirely wrong.'

The weight of his watch became very heavy indeed. He casually allowed his eyes to return to the project surrounding him. Maid dismissed.

That evening, Holmes, Dr Watson and his cousin Violet went to the Lyceum to see *Romeo and Juliet* starring - blast of trumpets, please - the great Henry Irving and the great Ellen Terry. The good doctor was trying to set Holmes up with the hapless Violet. At least, he said something to that effect as he handed over their eveningwear for me to sponge, brush and press. The twinge of jealously I experienced at this was followed by a sharp-edged sympathy. The detective's mood hadn't altered during the course of the day, and I suspected Violet was in for an unpleasant evening.

I'd metabolised my rage like a vitamin, which gave me the energy and focus to do the dirty work I'd decided to do.

I placed one of the transmitters on the underside of the occasional table. It was a flat, flexible little wafer about the size of a man's thumbnail, and made of a microchip-bonded polymer. The plastic neatly mimicked the colour and grain of the wood. You'd have to know it was there to see it, and even then it'd be hard to find. The other one was more difficult to situate, since it needed to be near the fireplace.

I debated placing it on the ornate frame around the painting he didn't like, but since he could take that down at any moment and toss it in the lumber room, I opted for the cornice on the mantelpiece. The device was supposed to perform its function even in extreme temperatures. Corkle and I would soon find out if this were true.

The transmitters were voice-activated. I said hello to Watson's portrait of General Gordon. Sound-check for later. The portrait was a cheap print in a cheaper frame, which Holmes tolerated only as a compensation for his own gruesome collection of the likenesses of murderers, all of them represented hanging by their necks. He had these small posters tacked haphazardly to the wall over his desk. I suppose they weren't much different from the Marilyn Manson poster I had over my bed when I was thirteen. I'd been challenging my mother's Grateful Dead spiritualism by openly embracing the dark side. Of course, I was thirteen at the time. What was *his* excuse?

I looked more closely at the pictures, and realised that they were all basically the same etching with different names attached. Florid descriptions of crimes committed were emblazoned beneath each depiction of the same dangling feet. I had to laugh. Either he'd been ripped off by street-patterers like an ordinary idiot, or these were a tribute to his quirky sense of humour. I said "hello" to the images. Then I said goodbye.

Goodbye to the pipes and the Persian slipper. Goodbye to the violin, which wasn't a Stradivarius, not yet. Goodbye to the knife in the mantelpiece, and the creaky basket-chair. Goodbye, and sod off.

I went to the tantalus with the broken lock and took the cork from a bottle of gin. Yes, they had the drink of the unwashed masses in their liquor cabinet, only a much better quality. I gulped down four huge swallows in hurried succession, lest I taste it too well, then added water to the bottle. Holmes would notice, but since he hardly ever drank hard liquor and certainly not the gin, I didn't worry about it too much.

One final thing to take care of before I departed that messy male bastion with no regrets. I went into his bedroom and dropped the watch on the bed. It was a lovely parting shot, and covered a multitude of sins should he detect any lingering presence of me-ness in his rooms. The return of his watch showed me to be the honourable sort, whereas he was clearly an arsehole.

If Corkle had made his presence known earlier, I could have been listening in on valuable information without ever having to chase Holmes through the rookeries in his big old boots. Even that camaraderie with Corkle, hunched over the receiver in his shabby little room, would have been preferable to what I'd put myself through for the sake of an associate professorship in history. I could have played the simple housemaid by day, compiled the data by night, and Holmes never would have been the wiser. He would have gone chattering on, telling people where they'd been and what they'd been doing; being rude to Watson; being surly with me; looking at my ankles and wondering what it would be like to run his fingers along the lump of bone and up the calf to the mysteries beneath my petticoats, resenting my dull presence for having brought the thoughts into his head and distracting him from more important ones.

Here I was, living the absolute be-all end-all *dream* of research in the field, reduced to a pathetic Cinderella wishing the Prince of Abstruse had taken her to the ball instead of Violet. I began to wonder if I wasn't genetically hard-wired for self-sabotage.

I had travelled through *time itself*, the most incredible technological achievement known to humankind, and yet managed to sleep with the one of the biggest jerks the nineteenth-century ever produced.

A testament to genius if ever there was one.

PART TWO

Chapter 12

Christmas was not the Dickens snow-globe filled with jingle-bells and velvet Victoriana I'd hoped for. For one thing, there was no snow. And for another, Christmas goose, boughs of holly and holiday well-wishers meant more work.

Mrs Hudson wept into the batter of her Christmas pudding. She wept over the sweater she was still knitting for Jack. She wept while looking out the window onto the dreary grey of another day. She'd yet to hear from him, the little shit.

As for the lodgers, well, Mr Cavendish was scamming some widow he'd met at a church function and was hardly ever home. Maybe "scamming" is a bit strong. Suffice it to say, he was in the market for a wife, and a woman with a nice annuity was worthy of pursuit.

Corkle, on the other hand, was a carol-singing, Tiny-Tim-impersonating annoyance to everyone. I overheard Holmes say that if Corkle sang the "was-sailing" song one more time, he was going stuff the man's body in a wassail bowl and offer the bloody cordial to the next group of carollers that came to the door.

Watson's attempts to keep the spirit of the season fell flat in the face of Holmes's mood swings. Worse than a woman, I swear. Either a listless brooding lump on the couch, or biting someone's head off. The new tweeny, Margaret, was terrified of him.

I was lucky. He barely spoke to me at all.

After my workday was through, I spent two or three hours in Corkle's room reviewing the data gathered by the transmitters.

He had a nice little set-up in his steamer trunk: computer, receiver, digital master, disc burner, ear-buds... the works. Clearly, the sneaky bastard had hoped to use the transmitters all along, although how he'd intended to plant them without my help was open for speculation. He didn't know the layout of the sitting room in 221-B. He'd never been in it, apparently. I rather got the impression he longed for the camaraderie of brandy and cigars with gentlemen of good breeding, but the role he played didn't allow for it. And truth was, Watson and Holmes thought he was a total wanker. They'd actually said words to that effect. We had it on record.

But we had precious little reward for all our efforts. Examples of highlights follow:

9th December, 1882. 01:41.

'Your rudeness was unforgivable, Holmes! Violet merely asked what you thought of the play.'

'No, Watson, she asked me what I was thinking. Until that moment, she was tolerable company.'

'Unlike yourself.'

'It was none of her business what I was thinking!'

13th December, 1882. 11:33.

'Where's the *Times*?'

'Er...'

'You've cut it up! I hadn't even looked at it yet!'

'Sorry. I thought you had.'

A sigh. 'I'm going to my club.'

'Yes, you're sure to find an intact copy there.'

'Holmes, you are the most -' Another sigh. 'Never mind. Good day.' Door slamming.

Mid-January I met with Shinwell Johnson. He gave me a report on the murders of the four little girls.

Liza Murray was from Whitechapel, but two others had lived close to each other - Fagin's own Field Lane in Saffron Hill - and the fourth had been born and raised in Cheapside. She'd been only eight years old, the daughter of a charwoman.

Johnson rifled through his stack of notes, licking his fat thumb occasionally, black eyes scanning the documents. 'Now it appears that last week, a lean and hungry-lookin' bloke kitted out like a costermonger was askin' 'bout some pieman name o' Francis Black, who was plyin' his trade outside a public house Cheapside in July. Seems this pieman, 'stead of offerin' his pies for a ha'penny toss to the boys, was givin' 'em free to certain little girls for certain little favours.' He chuckled, jowls shaking. 'That poor fool didn't know what he was lettin' hisself in for. Word got out quick, and 'fore he knew what hit, he was overrun with offers from the child beggars. He's not been seen in them parts since.'

Johnson believed the "lean and hungry-looking bloke" might have been Holmes, but he admitted the possibility that it could just as well have been a policeman under cover. If Liza's murder plagued Holmes enough to investigate it on his own, he never gave voice to it in the sitting room.

I burned the report Johnson gave me. Call it childish. Call it a hunch. I didn't want to give Corkle any more than I absolutely had to.

Finally, in late January, things started to get lively again.

25th January, 1883. 21:10.

Lestrade's voice. 'And I thought this daredevil climbing through windows and kissing all the slaveys would be just in your line, Mr Holmes. But it seems we fellows at the Yard are a bit quicker than you on this one.'

'Yes,' Holmes replied. 'I read that you'd arrested someone. A chap who replaces roof-tiles for a living, I believe.'

'That's right. It was good work from the lads, piecing that together.'

'Of course, they're completely wrong.'

Lestrade scoffed. 'Sour grapes, Mr Holmes.'

Holmes's voice assumed the tone he reserved for police inspectors and other idiots. 'It states in the paper that the man is five-foot-eight and weighs fourteen stone. How do your clever lads at the Yard suppose he climbed in through those tiny little windows in the dead of winter?'

'Well, now, we figure he'll make that known once he confesses.'

'Did I mention that the burglar would probably have been in the circus? High-wire. Trapeze artist, possibly.'

'I don't count that for much. Our man can climb like a monkey, for all that he weighs fourteen stone.'

'I'll give you another hint. The person you're looking for is not a man.'

'A boy! You're saying a boy could plan these robberies and pull 'em off? Bloody unlikely. He'd have to be a damn clever little boy now, wouldn't he?'

Holmes sighed. 'Inspector. Let's play a little game of association, shall we? I say "black", for instance, and the first word that springs to mind is...?'

'White. But what has that got to do with the price of oranges?'

'Bear with me. I say "black", you say "white". I say "man", you say...?'

'Woman.' A pause from Lestrade. He laughed. 'You've lost you're mind now, sir. A woman? And how'd she... oh, you think it's a woman dressed as a man?'

'It's done all the time, Inspector. Trouser roles in the theatre.' A pause. 'Opera?' A longer pause. 'Shakespeare, Lestrade!'

'Look here, Mr Holmes. You're off the tracks, if you'll pardon my saying so. The servant-girls have all said this devil takes liberties, unbuttons their night-clothes, kisses their throats and such. Why would a woman be doing the likes of...' Lestrade thoughts were nearly as loud as his voice. 'Bloody hell! One of those?'

'Isn't it delicious?' Holmes said.

'How's it done, d'you suppose?'

'She shimmies through the windows.'

'Well, yes, I know that, don't I? I mean the other. You know... two women? They've not got the tools for doing the job proper, have they?'

'Rather puts a shiver up one's spine just thinking on the possibilities, doesn't it, Inspector?'

'Not exactly up my spine.'

'All right, all right, enough of this sort of talk if you please, gentlemen. *Gentlemen.*' Watson again. 'I've nothing personally against you, Lestrade, but often I find that in your presence we seem to fall into a certain mode of thinking which is best suited to the gutter.'

'Begging your pardon, Dr Watson, but this tidbit didn't come from my imagination. And quite an imagination it is too, Mr Holmes. Circus girls sneaking through windows to kiss and...' He cleared his throat again. 'Damme, sir, but you've put some wicked thoughts into my head.'

'You know what amazes me most about you, Inspector?' Holmes laughed. 'That your imagination roams freely over the titillating possibilities of Sapphic love, and yet cannot embrace the idea that this same winsome nymph is skipping across rooftops in order to steal.'

'And do you know what amazes me most about you, Holmes?' Watson asked.

'A goodly number of things,' said the detective.

'Oh, yes. Ha ha ha. No, it is this: that you should imagine a winsome nymph rather than a coarse-faced, narrow-hipped female with cropped hair and scraggly little whiskers on her chin. Isn't it more likely she's merely a guttersnipe who molests those housemaids simply to confuse and misdirect the police? Or as the Inspector suggested, only a girl rather than a boy who's working for someone else.'

'But that's so dull.'

'Not everything put upon this Earth is here to amuse you, Holmes.'

'Which is a pity,' Holmes said. 'The world would be a far more interesting place.'

'Even so, Mr Holmes, I agree with the doctor. If it's a girl as you say, some little trick from the circus, she'd most like to be working for somebody else, like a- a hurdy-gurdy man's monkey. Getting into places where he can't. There's knowledge of the floor plans to consider -'

'All the buildings have been essentially the same, Inspector. Houses with attics and basements, designed along the same lines to serve the same functions. Not much of a brain demanded, if one happens to be a maidservant...'

'Oh, and now she's a slavey as well as a Sapphist and a circus performer!' Lestrade declared.

'Sounds pretty farfetched to me,' Watson said.

'Of course it does to you, Watson, your mind being incapable of focusing on more than one thing at a time. But some of us are cursed with the ability to be and do any number of things, all at once. At this moment, I am not only talking to the two of you, but also composing chamber music in my head and writing a monograph on social colonial hymenopterous insects.'

'Blimey!'

'He's being facetious, Inspector,' Watson admonished.

'Inspector Lestrade,' Holmes said. 'I urge you to consider the items on your list of stolen goods that have not turned up with pawnbrokers, or with any of your known fences. A number of those items would lend credence to what I'm telling you...' He made a sudden sound of disgust. 'Why am I bothering? Clearly you have your man. Now, if you've quite finished gloating over your triumph with the use of my good cigars and very respectable port, I would consider it a kindness if you would scurry off. Have a laugh with the lads on me.'

'All right, Mr Holmes, I take your point. As usual, it's been highly educational. And I'll keep in mind what you've said.'

'That's more than I deserve, I'm certain. Goodnight.'

'Goodnight, gentlemen.'

Sounds of the door opening and closing, and then Lestrade's distinctive tread fading down the steps.

'Oh, dear God, Holmes. You're not going into a sulk over this, are you?'

'I'm right, Watson.'

'Of course, you are. How could I have forgotten you're always right?'

'I happen to know who she is.'

'What! Why didn't you tell him?'

'I practically handed him her head on a platter, dear chap. But she still has in her possession - what was it? - a CB from Her Majesty, Most Honorable Order of the Bath, made up in cheap gold wash and enamel. Why ever would she keep that, except for some perverse, private reason of her own? In a month or two, she'll have enough rope to hang herself without any help from us.'

'Well, who is it then? What's your nymph's name?'

'Oh, no. You'd be motivated by conscience to reveal it.'

'Whereas you clearly have no such motivations whatsoever,' Watson muttered.

For a moment there was only the sound of Holmes lighting a match, the soft slough of the pipe. 'I do have a conscience, Watson.'

'And a somewhat high-handed, autocratic sense of justice to go with it,' the doctor replied. Holmes made a small sound, a genuine emotional reaction to this evaluation of his character. Watson sighed. 'Do forgive me, Holmes. I'm tired. I meant only that your conscience is... differently motivated to that of the normal individual.'

'No,' Holmes said, thoughtfully. 'I... think you were right the first time.'

Watson yawned noisily. 'Me for my bed.'

'Will it bother you if I play a while?' Holmes asked. 'Very softly.'

'Something suitable for dreaming, if you please.'

'Ah. Brahms it is.'

***

Click.

I was startled from dreamy Brahms back to the stuffy little world of Corkle's room.

He leaned back, stretching and yawning. 'It's just him playing until he goes to bed. Two freaking hours of it.'

I removed the buds from my buzzing ears. Listening to Holmes's voice rubbed my insecurities raw. Not that I would've let the bastard back into my bed even if he came there to die, but it did seem a terrible betrayal of whatever intimacy we'd shared so briefly. This was actual spying I was doing here. Not surreptitious observation under the cover of a feather duster.

I dug my fists into tired eyeballs. 'I wish I'd had access to this stuff in the beginning. I could have done this research from my rooms in Midhope Street and not have to get up at five o'clock every fucking morning. God! I could murder a pizza about now.'

Corkle laughed, and strangely enough, I needed him to laugh. He wasn't shocked by my language, or by my manner. I didn't have explain any anachronistic references, nor guard myself against uttering them.

Frappuccinos. Action-figures. Tattoo grannies. Game cubes. CGI. DVD. CSI.

SUV. I could say all these things out loud and he'd never bat an eyelash.

'Pizza in nineteenth century London. Mastercard priceless.'

And I laughed.

Chapter 13

Sunday afternoon, the eighteenth of February, a hand-delivered letter was presented to Mr Sherlock Holmes. After reading it he was the most cheerful of men. He even inquired after my health that evening, bestowing upon me a stunning smile, the sort that made my heart race and my knees shaky.

The actual case arrived the following morning in the form a sleek, closed carriage, the kind that announces nobility travelling incognito: too good to be hired transportation, but with neither coat of arms nor discreet insignia to indicate which little piggy was out and about.

I was standing with the calling-card in my hand when Mrs Hudson came rushing to the door and snatched it from me. With an imperious command that I should escort our guests into the parlour and see to their needs, she went up to inform Mr Holmes that he had visitors.

The lady was dressed in widow's black, but with a subdued elegance of line and materials which indicated substantial wealth, old money that didn't need to flaunt itself. The veils of her hat were thrown back, revealing a face that had once been truly beautiful, but never soft or pretty. Her eyes were greyish-blue, much like my detective's, and just as sharp. A lorgnette attached to a gold chain allowed her to examine the middle-class googaws and ornate necessities cluttering the parlour whilst maintaining her distance from them.

The man was less interesting. A solicitor, I guessed, from his high, stiff collar and black bowler. Definitely a senior partner in his firm, his deferential attitude toward the lady demonstrating just how important a client she was.

That night, Corkle and I listened as Holmes, in one long, breathless monologue, told her exactly who she was and what she was doing in his sitting room. I don't think he was showing off; he was just really excited. It was kind of cute.

19th February, 1883. 10:03.

'Lady Holbrook. It is an honour to meet you. And this must be Mr Lucius Maitland of Maitland, Pearsall, and Abernathy. I was once privileged to work for another client of yours, a Victor Trevor of Norfolk. Perhaps you remember him? Oh, well, one of the junior members of your firm must handle his affairs, then. I trust your journey was not too distressing, ma'am? Still, you did not come straight from the station, as I would have assumed, your business being so urgent. Oh, forgive me. Do come in.'

'Madam!' This was the voice of the solicitor, Maitland. 'I swear to you, I have revealed nothing of this to anyone -'

'That is true, Lady Holbrook,' Holmes said. 'It was only when I saw the card... a charming ruse. Mrs Darcy Bennett come to call. Plucked straight from the pages of Austen, and on a card apparently printed for this occasion. The ink is still a little damp. You see how it's smudged here? And that odour. Fellowes and Sons on Mortimer Street, if I'm not mistaken. "Quick Work, Printed to Order". Though why you took the detour from Paddington station all the way to Mortimer Street simply to obtain this one card... oh, I see. You intended to represent yourself as your own agent. Really, completely unnecessary. You can rely on my discretion, I assure you.'

'Young man, after you have recovered your manners sufficiently to offer me a chair –' Holmes made some bumpkin sound of anguish, and there was a flurry of activity in which I assumed he fell over himself to show her to one, '– who is this gentleman, if you please? I am certain it was made clear that this was to be a private interview, as the matter is extremely delicate in nature.'

'This is my... associate, Dr John Watson. He is the very soul of discretion, and has been invaluable to me on a number of cases.'

That was a bit of lie. The doctor had not assisted Holmes on many cases at all. There was the Jefferson Hope case in '82, and that was about it. The rest of the time he simply tagged along when invited, if he hadn't anything better to do.

'A doctor, you say?'

'Yes, ma'am,' Watson said, 'that is, your ladyship, er, ma'am.'

'That may prove useful. Please be seated. I am old, and gazing up at you is giving me a crick in the neck.' There was a pause while they seated themselves. She continued. 'Before we begin I must have your word, as gentlemen, that what I say will be held in the strictest confidence.' Beside me, Corkle chuckled softly. 'Mr Maitland will witness your signatures. Note the time and date, Mr Maitland, and have them both sign.'

A long pause.

'Madam,' Holmes began carefully. 'I need no witness to my own conscience nor, I think, does my friend. This must be sufficient, or I am afraid I can be of no service to you at all.'

I squirmed in my chair, feeling dirty, listening to secrets which had already left the sitting room without his even knowing.

'Very well,' Lady Holbrook finally replied. 'Your word in the presence of legal representation will be acceptable. Now then, Mr Sherlock Holmes. Do you care for women, sir?'

Corkle glanced at me, shit-eating grin on his face.

'Ma'am?' Holmes croaked.

'Do you care for women?'

'I'm afraid I... I don't, er...'

'It is a simple question requiring only a yes or a no.'

'Not entirely simple,' he corrected her, 'as it is clear that my answer will determine how this interview proceeds.'

The lady's voice was strident. 'Mr Holmes, there are many subjects of which, as a woman, I am presumed to have no knowledge. But as a woman who has lived sixty-eight years, I am not wholly ignorant of these subjects. For example, I might assume, based on your living arrangements, that this gentleman is something more to you than a business associate.'

There was only a brief pause before Holmes said: 'We maintain separate bed chambers, Lady Holbrook.' A cry of outrage from the doctor was followed by: 'No, Watson, let it go. It isn't worth your rancour. We share these rooms for practical reasons, perhaps difficult for your ladyship to understand, being but mundane matters of finance.'

'I have the same concerns as you, young man. It is only in scale and degree that they differ.'

'Ah, yes. The marriage between your grandson, Lord Merrill, and the former Miss Henrietta Barstow. A financially agreeable match, I should imagine, her father being one of the wealthiest men in America.'

Lady Holbrook's voice took on a decidedly chilly tone. 'Yes. Of course, I was not entirely aware of Merrill's predilections until after his marriage to Henrietta. It is always women who bear the burden of men's dissolute ways, and yet men strive to keep us ever in darkness.'

Palpable discomfort on the part of the men present.

'Your letter indicated that a situation has been brought to light which has the potential for scandal. Might I presume blackmail?'

'We have been approached.'

'If I may, your ladyship?' Maitland interjected. 'We received a letter. The person or persons offered no evidence, or witnesses with any authority. But they claim to have the means to produce proof -'

Lady Holbrook broke in. 'And they claim that Henrietta is the most telling proof of all.'

'May I see the letter?' Holmes asked.

'Unfortunately no,' Maitland said. 'Lord Holbrook, Madam's eldest son, saw fit to burn it.' Holmes hissed in annoyance. 'But I was the first to read it, Mr Holmes. It was sent to our offices, addressed to me. The text was cut and pasted from parts of the newspapers.'

'Could you recognise the fonts if you saw them again?'

'I could try.'

'Excellent, Mr Maitland! I will also ask you to write down for me, as closely as you can recall, the precise wording of the letter. Madam? Do you know of any situation which might implicate Lord Merrill's wife as other than innocent of her husband's activities?'

Lady Holbrook gave a short, humourless laugh. 'Her innocence is the very thing they intend to offer as proof, Mr Holmes. She and Merrill have been married nine months, and she is still as "innocent" as when she came into this world. My grandson has not bothered to perform that simple duty which is required of him. She is a lovely girl. It can hardly be odious, even to one such as he.'

'There are those of his... persuasion who might find it well nigh impossible, your ladyship,' Holmes said. 'And it seems ruthless indeed to lock the young lady into such an unhappy arrangement simply to avoid returning the considerable dowry she brought to the union.'

'But the monies from the pre-nuptial arrangement have already been spent -' Maitland began.

'Lucius!'

'Madam. There is no question of returning the dowry. Most of it is tied up in investments, and her properties have been sold to maintain your family's estate.'

'Even so, the money was never my main concern. Merrill is the only grandchild yet living. He must produce heirs. As to your accusations of ruthlessness, Mr Holmes, Henrietta would have children of her own to comfort her. It is a woman's most noble calling.'

'I see. What, exactly, do you want me to do?'

'I want you to find him. He may have gone to the Continent. Paris or Venice, most likely. He's not drawn any funds from our accounts here in well over a fortnight. You have three months in which to accomplish this task.'

'The blackmailers have given you three months? That seems terribly generous of them.'

'In three months the marriage will be annulled,' Mr Maitland offered wearily.

'Oh. So the blackmail is not your true concern.'

'I will be frank with you, Mr Holmes,' Lady Holbrook began. Holmes gave a yelp of laughter. After another pause, in which I imagined she put him in his place with a stern look, she continued. 'I was shocked to learn how flagrantly remiss was the girl's own mother in her maternal advice. Henrietta had no idea what to expect in her life as a married woman, and yet this same negligent mother so distressed the poor child over her failure to conceive that she went, of her accord and quite in secret, to a physician, supposedly an expert from Austria. It was this doctor who determined that she was still... that she was unaware of the intimate nature of married life. He did not tell her what the difficulty was, but took it upon himself to contact her father.'

'And have you contacted this doctor?'

'We have endeavoured to do so,' Mr Maitland said, 'but we can find no record of him. No such physician is listed in any of the directories, nor at any of the hospitals, sanatoriums or teaching facilities in Vienna. He is either a charlatan or using an assumed name.'

'How came he to be recommended to Lady Henrietta?'

'Her companion, *an American*,' Maitland said, as if this explained everything, 'is engaged to a student at London Hospital. The young man had seen the doctor's card posted, which declared him to be a specialist in matters of infertility, and brought it to her attention. She gave the card to Lady Henrietta.'

'I should like to speak with the maid and her fiancé.'

'She has been dismissed, of course,' said Lady Holbrook.

'Of course,' Holmes said. 'He has posted no other cards or notices?'

'Not to our knowledge,' Maitland replied.

'Wonderful,' my detective murmured in hushed delight. 'More and more wonderful.'

Then someone (and I'm sure it was Lady Holbrook) clapped sharply, like a governess demanding the attention of unruly charges. 'Mr Holmes! I see nothing wonderful in the situation, nothing at all!'

'I'm sorry,' Holmes drawled. 'Perhaps I should have said "intriguing".'

'Such impertinence speaks to the lack of a firm hand in your youth, Mr Holmes. Merrill suffers from that lack as well.'

'I was whipped on quite a regular basis when I was a boy, Madam. The fear of punishment only serves to make some of us better at not getting caught.'

'That is hardly a recommendation that will gain my trust. I need to know - to *know*, sir - that the society Merrill keeps is not one you would find tempting. Such men easily lose their way.'

'That can also be said of those who "care" for women overmuch, Madam,' Holmes said smartly. 'The name of the physician, if you please, Mr Maitland?'

The solicitor must have written it down and handed it to him, because it was Holmes who said the name, savouring it slowly. 'Dr Jacob Armitroy. Armitroy? That's an odd sort of name for an Austrian.'

'Mr Holmes,' the lady said, drawing the proper focus back to herself, 'will you undertake this task or won't you?'

'And when I have found your wayward boy, Lady Holbrook, what do you propose I do with him?'

'Can you find him?'

'Yes.' The quiet certainty in his voice gave me shivers.

'When you find him, you will contact Mr Maitland, and he will handle the rest.'

'As you wish.'

'I shall leave the business arrangements to him as well. No, you needn't see me out. I'll be waiting in the carriage, Lucius. Good day, Mr Holmes. Doctor...' She must have forgotten his name, because she just repeated 'Doctor', and left them to the dirty business of money.

A real, live case! It was as if I'd captured Sasquatch digging through my dumpster on home video. Corkle was more blasé. He sat back, his fingers laced across his belly. 'So, deductive reasoning or lucky guesses?'

'Which?'

'You know, all that stuff about the names and the card and the train.'

'Extrapolation from perceivable data!' I declared. He was soooo trying to rain on my parade.

'I'd like to see him pull data out of his arse like that in the twenty-first.' He laughed at the thought. 'I wonder if he realises how deep he'll have to go to find Lord Merrill? You did catch the not-so-subtle nuance, didn't you? If Sherlock Holmes wants the boys to talk, he'll have to cruise them. Maybe even put out.'

I snorted. 'I doubt that. He's very good at getting information without giving anything.'

'Is he?' I willed myself not to look away. Corkle turned his attention to his teacup. 'Doesn't it make you a wee bit nervous, though? As the woman hinted, it's easy to get lost in that world.'

'Personal experience?'

'Oh, I never get lost down there. I know the difference between a peg and a hole.'

'How romantic.'

He pinched my cheek hard. 'You are so cute.'

'Fuck off,' I said, and went to my room and my bed.

I dreamed that Holmes and I were in high school together. We were ditching Mrs Hurley's History of Western Civilization, smoking cigarettes in the park. He was trying to talk me into going to a rave, which was, in the logic of dreams, happening in the basement of a doss house in Spitalfields. And I kept saying I couldn't because I had all this homework to do.

Chapter 14

I let the young man back into my bed.

I will confess to a certain satisfaction that he came to me, a heady combination of anxiety and excitement, because I couldn't be sure of the reason. Not entirely. But it happened that Corkle was away, tending to the dull business of money and contacts that kept our little operation running smoothly. Holmes would never have been so bold otherwise.

I'd been playing my guitar, an eerie waltz for the late hour. How long he waited in the corridor below, deciding whether or not to intrude upon my music and my life, I'm not sure. But as soon as I realised that someone was listening and that the someone was Holmes, I made the decision for him.

Dressed for bed, he travelled wordlessly up the steps behind me. From the centre of the attic room (the only place he could stand upright without his head brushing the slope of the ceiling), he made a quick, sweeping glance, taking in the shadowy monsters of my furnishings. I'd been playing by the illumination of the street-lamps below, something he often did himself. After a moment, he went to the bed and sat yogi fashion, slippered feet tucked under his dressing gown. The man had no shame.

'Yes, well, make yourself at home,' I said, lighting the lamp on the desk. My journal was there, not open. A cheap, commonplace book. I shook out the match and turned back to see his eye shift casually, as if he hadn't been looking at the journal and had only been looking at me.

The flame was low, but I could see him well enough. The glow of the lamp warmed his normal pallor, dulled the brilliantine black of his hair. His narrow hawkish nose seemed even more pronounced in the shadows, the eyes above it mostly pupil, ringed by an indiscernible colour as he watched me watching him.

I tacked the tattered quilt back over the window and moved to retrieve my shawl. A soft breath escaped him. He wasn't looking at my face anymore, but at my body, which he could see through my nightgown, back-lit by the lamp.

Ashamed, he gazed hard at his hands, forcing them to stay still. 'I have gravely compromised my ethics, Rose.'

'What ethics are those now?' The words came out icy, more so than I intended, I think. I drew the shawl about my shoulders and clenched it over my chest.

He took a deep breath and conscientiously looked me in the eye instead of elsewhere. 'I have a fondness for the game - the challenge and the chase - which

I fear will fade once the puzzle of you has been pieced together. I have taken the most egregious, most despicable advantage of you that a man can take of a woman. It is craven of me to want you the way I do, when I know I will not once you cease to be a mystery to me.'

I drew one hand dramatically across my brow. 'You have no affection for me? *Mon Dieu*. I shall die.' His mouth pursed in annoyance. 'If this is supposed to be an apology,' I said, 'it's a piss-poor one.'

He sighed. 'Please... move. The light is most distracting.'

I stretched languorously, feeling powerful and petty. The shawl dropped to the floor. 'I'm tired,' I said. 'I need my bed.'

Taking this as a dismissal, he unfolded his legs and placed his feet on the braided rug next to the bed. But he didn't stand up. Instead, he hung his head pitifully, his hands locked together between his knees, unwilling to move despite his attack of conscience. He wanted to go. He wanted to stay. He wanted me again, but didn't want to want me, and so he sat, motor running, unable to shift out of neutral.

I went to him and stood with my belly at the level of his bowed head, testing his resolve, his conviction, his ethics. I threaded my fingers through his hair. It was inspired cruelty.

He grunted a soft acknowledgement - of failure, or possibly of success - and clasped me by the hips, fingers pressing into my flesh all the way to the bone.

'Don't ever threaten me again,' I said.

'Or what, Rose?' he asked, excited by this caveat.

'I don't know.' My arms went around his back. 'Something.'

With a breathy sound, close to derision, but not quite, he began inching up my gown until his cool hands made contact with my naked thighs, my buttocks. And then, to my amazement, he was on his knees and kissing the rose of Rose like a supplicant, imploring with his tongue, yet lacking the appropriate humility. He didn't know how to be humble, but he *did* know how to do this. Even as I admired the masterful way in which he manoeuvred me onto the bed to save the strain on his neck muscles, even as I directed his efforts with sighs and moans and squeaks of pleasure... I wondered where he'd learned this, my young Victorian gentleman, known for shaving twice a day and a fastidious attention to clean underwear.

We made love in earnest, hard passion, just this side of violence. Caution to the wind and all that, difficult to justify, impossible to explain, dangerous and completely mad. A power-struggle, I think.

I was fully present, more present than I've ever been in my life, aware of every sound and sensation. The scrape of the bedposts against the wall, the rhythmic creaking of the floor beneath, breath beating the air like a rattlesnake's warning.

I wanted him to shake me to the bones, wrench the truth from me, so that the mystery would dissolve and he'd never feel compelled to return. So I took him in, impossibly deep it must have seemed, because he gasped at the sensation, a combination of awe and panic. He held himself there, suspended above me like an avenging angel, self-control of the most excruciating sort. His body wanted to thrust and thrust and thrust, but his arms trembled with the effort to stay absolutely still, and all so that this rare opportunity to see who I really was wouldn't be lost to him.

'Look at me, Rose,' he whispered. I kept my eyes closed, turning my head to get away from his voice. His voice seemed to get inside all the places his body couldn't. 'Look me in the eye.'

I had never liked looking into the eyes of a man under those circumstances, and for that reason: because he could see too much and it was none of his business. But I wanted him to see me. I wanted him to know *me*. I opened my eyes and became a bare-naked psyche at Judgement Day.

The hard angles of his face softened, a fleeting compassion, and something else, something unreadable. Arms shaking, legs shaking, he moved inside me, and again, and again, changing the rhythms, watching my reactions with the fascination of a scientist probing the glistening, jewel-like organs of a newly-discovered species. Finally, when I'd given him everything in me a dozen times over, when I was begging, begging, please, please, please, his eyes closed, his head arched back, and a sound escaped his throat, '*aaahhh...*', as if the entire cosmos had just been poured into his brain.

Afterwards, I cried. I hate it when I do that, but it happens sometimes. And it didn't mean anything. That is to say, it meant something, but not... what he thought it meant.

'Are you hurt? Did I hurt you, *ma fille*? Oh, *bijou*, I'm so sorry.' Kissing me all over my face, my ears, my throat, my damp eyelashes. 'You should have said if I were hurting you.'

Not a supernatural being. Not clairvoyant. Just a man. I clung to him all the more because of it.

My youthful appearance was supposed to allow me to play the part of a girl of twenty, whilst maintaining the distance of the social scientist. But I could just as well have *been* twenty lying there, cradled in the arms of a man who murmured endearments to me in French. Did he really think he'd hurt me with his vigorous lovemaking? Or did he think this some typically female reaction beyond his ken, or even his interest? He stroked my body idly, mind already elsewhere, perhaps pondering an unfinished experiment, or his current case, or correlating data I'd revealed in the throes of passion. He was sated. His whispered words were like petting a dog.

'Poor girl, poor *chere*,' he murmured. 'Lost and alone with no-one to help her.'

Or... I'd underestimated him, and he knew I was weeping because I was floundering, no longer able to navigate these murky waters. I dragged my fingers over my wet face. 'Don't be silly. I cry sometimes for happy reasons.' I wrapped my arms and legs around his slender body and squeezed. 'I'm just... I mean, I'm totally... oh my God, that was so good!'

He seemed pleased with this answer, but shy and a little sceptical. He allowed the vice-grip hug of my limbs for a few moments before squirming out of it, and then we lay next to each other, vaguely aware of everything and nothing at all.

Finally, the physical reasserted itself. He got up to relieve himself and wash up. Then I did the same. This casual intimacy was the result of mere hours. It had never existed before.

From my boot cupboard, I retrieved a pickling-jar full of beer I'd stolen from the kitchen. I downed half of it, then handed it to him while he held the blankets up, inviting me back into the warmth of the bed. He leaned against the wall with his back propped on my pillow, one arm around me, fingers paddling my flesh absently as he gulped the beer.

'Rose?'

'Yes?'

'What is your real name?'

I sighed, but that was the only hesitation. 'Gillian Petra. Gillian *Rose* Petra. But... you mustn't call me by that name.'

'No, I suppose I mustn't.' I busied my fingers and he shifted uncomfortably. 'I will not be distracted, so do stop trying.'

'Distracted from what?'

'Putting the new information into perspective.'

'My name? What can you do with that?'

'Find out who you are,' he said, surprised. 'Where you're from, of course.'

'Don't think so. Sorry.'

'I have more than your name to go on.'

'No, you don't. You're just messing with my head.'

'A very evocative example. As if I could plunge my fingers into your skull and dabble in your grey matter. I must say, the idea of squeezing your brain like a sponge has tremendous appeal.'

'It won't help you.'

He moved his hand from my shoulder to my head, and started wriggling his fingers in my hair. 'Let us see what the grey matter reveals. Hhhmn, yes, your use of the English language is quite telling. "Shall" and "will" are used interchangeably with the, er, wilfulness, shall we say, of an American woman, though you are undeniably English.' I giggled at this, and he insisted, almost petulantly. 'You *are* English. Ah, English *and* American.'

'Now you're just guessing, Sherlock.'

'I never guess.' He took a long, thoughtful swallow of beer. 'When you are thoroughly relaxed, the syntactic of your speech, though not unpleasant, is odd. Verbal contractions, likewise. And the occasional coarseness of your language, stimulating as I may find it under certain circumstances, seems inappropriate in a woman with your obvious higher education.'

'Why obvious? I could be a self-educated harlot for all you know.'

'More likely the daughter of a college don. I have established a certain, erm...casual erudition that speaks of a university education. I might venture to say Cambridge, were that not impossible -'

'Hah!'

'Are you saying it is possible?'

'How could it be?'

He eyed me obliquely. 'Precisely my point. There are no universities, here or even in America, which allow women to take advanced degrees.'

My breath stopped of its own accord for a moment. 'What makes you think I have a degree in anything?'

He smiled, declining to elucidate on that. 'I can say that the subjects you studied were rather esoteric. I dismiss music as a possibility. You could have studied that anywhere. Theoretical mathematics, perhaps. Or physics. Possibly anthropology.'

'Total conjecture, Sherlock. I've given no indication of knowledge concerning theoretical mathematics, nor any branch of physics related to it.'

'Aha! But you knew precisely to what I referred just now, did you not? I doubt Watson knows there *is* a specialised field of learning such as theoretical mathematics.'

'Of course he does. He's not an idiot. You don't give him nearly enough credit.'

'He likes books about the *sea*, Rose. Sailing men and their battles with nature. If he knew half of what went on below decks -'

'He's a very good person.'

'Yes. And a good doctor. That story about the child you bore would never have passed muster with him had he examined you.'

'Ooh,' I said, wriggling beside him. 'I've fantasised about that on more than one occasion.'

There was a long silence, in which he seemed to be running an internal dialogue and rejecting all responses that would make him look foolish or, worse, jealous.

'He thinks you're pretty, but your complexion is a trifle too... dark for his tastes.' He swallowed the last of the beer and placed the empty jar on the edge of the bedside table. 'Tastes I do not share. I'm very fond of honey and molasses.' He kissed the dimple at the edge of my mouth and moved down, sliding his tongue over my nipple, while his long fingers traversed the landscape of my belly to worm their way between my thighs. Lips to my lips once again, he murmured, 'More honey, please.'

We kissed forever. I sank into the sensation, forgetting anything else, including that Holmes could easily focus on several things simultaneously. Our lips parted with a noisy smack. He withdrew his fingers from their lubricious hiding place, and returned immediately to the point.

'He's not a fool in the medical department, you know. You've not a mark on you, no scars from the skin stretching.'

I blinked several times to recover from this cunning sorcery. 'I was fourteen. The skin is much more elastic then.'

'That was... what? Ten, fifteen years ago?' He jiggled my breasts experimentally, which showed some slight weight of my years. I pushed his hand away in annoyance. 'There are probably other indications which would be more familiar to a doctor.'

'Well, then, he'd have to be making a very thorough examination, wouldn't he?'

'I don't think I care for the direction this discussion is taking.'

'Anyway,' I said. 'That's just evidence that I lied. It isn't any sort of evidence about who I am.'

'I have more.'

'Do tell,' I murmured, mouth inching its way down his bony chest to his navel. The crispy hair began just below it.

'Ah, ahhh... I'm not sure this is... I mean I'm sure it isn't nice for your mouth to be there.'

'You did it to me,' I said, lifting my head.

'Yes, well, you needn't feel obligated to reciprocate. I'm only a quarter French.'

'Never had this before, have you?'

'Not -' he began. 'No. But I do recall imagining it in great, though rather imprecise, detail. I remember a sixth-former at Harrow regaling his youthful audience with the tale of himself and a field girl during the summer holiday. He claimed she "played his rod like a flute". Even then, my logical little-boy mind was fairly certain the activity would be more akin to smoking a cigar than playing a wind instrument.'

I laughed softly, resting my head on his stomach, listening to the healthy burble of his bowels. 'You're not supposed to be like this, you know.'

Hard muscles tightened beneath my cheek, his cunning prickled, mind on red-alert. 'How am I supposed to be?'

'Different,' I whispered.

He blew out a noisy sigh. 'You're so very good at this game, Rose. You drop the apples, and I stop to pick them up. Just like Atalanta.'

Weary of his suspicions and sick of the games, I pulled away. Alarmed, he reached for me. 'No, no. Where are you going? Come back.' He wiggled down quickly to lie flat upon the bed, opting to be satisfied in some other way. 'I believe I've conquered my shyness.'

I looked at him from under my lashes. 'Do you trust me?' And oh, wasn't that the wickedest question?

'I trust you not to bite,' he said. But he twisted his fingers in my curls, just in case, and watched as his cock thickened under the wisdom of my tongue. Watched, until he couldn't watch and feel at the same time.

Later, he pulled me over his body until our noses touched.

'Merciless woman,' he whispered, '*ma belle dame sans merci.*'

That would have been such a nice place to leave it. But he didn't. He couldn't, I suppose.

In an all too fragile state of tenderness, I snuggled in under his arm, contented, expecting nothing from him. His next words were not the nothing I expected.

'Are you with me now because someone else requires you to be?'

Every muscle in my body seized up.

He held me tighter and swallowed hard. 'I may be stewing in conventional morality at the moment, I'll grant you, but I've serious misgivings as to why a beautiful woman is doting such affections on a man who, although admittedly brilliant, is also ill-humoured, often broke, and rather ugly.'

Oh. Insecurity. Ah. OK. 'You're not ugly, Sherlock. Beethoven was ugly. He had lots of women.'

'Well, I haven't.'

I shifted beside him, excited by the alternative I was about to offer. 'You know, there's a far simpler explanation as to why I'm doting these affections on you. It could be the simplest one of all. I could just be in love with -'

'No!' he said, trying to cover my mouth before the words came out. 'No, Rose, don't say it. Please. It won't do.'

'Why?' My voice was quiet, a tiny whisper. My heart beat loud and fast.

He gave a short laugh, as if it were the most stupid question in the world. 'Because, my dear Rose or Gillian or whoever you are... it's unsporting of you. It places me in a terribly awkward position. A man may love a lie - many have - but only if he does not know it to be one. Although I am quite fond of your golden apples, you can hardly expect me to reciprocate any deeper affection under the circumstances.'

Oh God, oh God, oh God. There was nothing like the humiliation of unrequited love. My humiliation filled the room to the rafters. His hand reached out - sympathy, compassion - I didn't know and it didn't matter. I shot out of the bed.

'Time for you go now,' I said. My voice was soft, airy, much too cheerful. It scared me.

He blinked at me a moment, numbed by my dismissal, then began fumbling on the floor for his underwear.

The lamp on the table sputtered, flame leaping and dying repeatedly, just like my heart. Ow. Ow. Ow. Hadn't I heard him say, scarcely two hours before, that once the mystery was solved he'd feel nothing for me at all?

Fine. Solve this.

'I came here to study you.'

He looked up sharply, one hand clutching his drawers. 'I know that much. From where and why?'

My laugh was brittle and hurt my chest. 'Farther than you can imagine. To observe and document your methods at the inception of their development.' Fear gripped his features momentarily, then dived beneath the surface of his eyes. Acknowledging the path I was on, implicated by my choice of words and what he'd discerned from them, I took a deep breath and went for broke. 'It's for my doctoral thesis.'

He looked like he was waiting for me to spontaneously combust. 'I see. From what university will you receive a doctorate?'

My lips stretched into a smile. 'A fairly good one.'

'All from studying me? How my head swells.' He shoved his feet into the legs of his woollen long-johns, slightly off-balance. His hands were shaking. 'Perhaps if I go to my old Cambridge dons and explain what an important subject of study I am, they will give me a doctorate without my having to attend any tedious lectures.'

'My thesis has to do with the social-economic changes that create a crucible for the evolution of the criminal mind. An evolution that's brought about your field of study. Without this evolution, there'd be no need for a man like you to exist.'

It was part of a dissertation I'd rehearsed dozens of times, though not for this audience, and certainly not in a nineteenth-century attic bedroom with my nipples standing at attention.

'Interesting,' he said, buttoning up with quick, tense little movements. 'I think perhaps you're oversimplifying, not that I don't agree with the basic concept.'

'Well, one must begin with a theory and build on that.'

'I allow the facts to lead me to hypotheses, not the other way around.'

'I have some experience with the formulation of theory based on observable data, Sherlock. This...' I waved at the room, the bed, the miasma of sexual activity that permeated the air. 'This is just for fun. Because I like it. Because I'm that kind of woman.'

He lowered his head. 'Rose -' he began. I had no idea what he was going to say, only that I didn't want to hear it.

'No, no, no. It's all right. Really.' I spotted my nightgown and snatched it up. 'You've made your position clear. You need to go now.' My voice was too loud, and he began to hurry in earnest.

He pulled his arms into his dressing gown inside out, started to take it off again, then paused, staring at me, his eyes huge. 'Dear God,' he whispered. 'Did I - ?'

I followed the trail of his gaze to the trickle of blood running down the inside of my thigh.

Great. How much more could I possibly humiliate myself this night?

'Congratulations,' I said. 'You are *not* going to be a father.'

A split-second of incomprehension crossed his features. He paled and his hand went to his mouth, then he gave a panicked look down at himself.

'Contrary to popular wisdom,' I said, 'it won't fall off.'

Though embarrassed by his own reaction, anger followed quickly. 'I was under the impression I had no reason to concern myself with getting a child on you.'

'Well, now you have proof.' I held the nightgown over my bleeding vulnerability. 'Look, I'm probably going to have a good girlish cry, followed by sleep. I don't think you'll learn anything of further use to you tonight.'

'But I've learned nothing.' There was a fragile, desperate quality to his voice. He was staring at the floor, the tips of his fingers pressed into his temples as if he were trying to keep his skull from bursting at the seams. I shuddered, and not from the cold. His gaze shot up and sent a shock through me.

'What I'm thinking is madness,' he whispered.

It was more than fear of madness I saw in him. It was something soul-deep. Something that made the gods of reason and logic tremble.

'Please go away, Sherlock,' I begged.

Chapter 15

I hit bottom. Hard.

I cried myself to sleep that night, something I don't think I'd ever done in my whole life, and I let it be about the drama of unrequited love, because I couldn't look at anything else. The pillow in which I'd buried my sorrow still smelled of him, and the next morning that really annoyed me. This enabled me to take stock of the other things I had to cry about.

It's very easy to mistake physical intimacy for love when a person has nothing else. The absence of people who knew me, knew Gillian Petra and could validate my existence as that person, was suddenly, completely devastating. How essential other people's memories of me became. All my memories of those people were memories not yet born. My mother had sported a purple mohawk the day she'd given birth to me. I'd seen the snapshots. My father, whose band The Petranauts had burned brightly and briefly in the VH1 heavens, had died when I was fourteen. I could barely remember his face on a good day. Was it any wonder I'd formed an attachment to the one *living* person who'd stroked me in a moment of tenderness and called me *bijou*?

Once thing was certain: I was not a very good spy.

I knew I should go to Corkle, confess all and get out. Lingering, amorphous fear urged me to caution. I'd flagrantly disregarded research protocol, possibly invalidated years of work - much of it Corkle's own - and I had no idea how he would react. He gave me nothing of himself but surfaces. Therefore, the wisest course of action was to keep my stupidity to myself.

In the days that followed, it became clear that whatever effects I'd expected my revelation to have on the entire fabric of the universe were unwarranted. As I swept and dusted, polished and scrubbed, I began to feel merely foolish. It was hardly the first time I'd been convinced I was in love just because I'd had a really great orgasm. If he thought I was crazy, so be it. Mystery solved. I could live with that.

To my relief, Corkle was spending long hours at the museum and had to beg off our regular meetings several times. Holmes was out of the house often, and when he wasn't out, he was sleeping. I saw him maybe twice that week. We skirted the danger-zones of eye-contact and physical proximity.

Then, about a week after the best sex of my life and the resulting fall-out, Corkle and I were sitting in his room in front of the receiver. The rustling sounds on the recording, combined with Watson's occasional cries of 'the nerve!' or 'what utter rubbish!', lulled me into a kind of automatic writing: doodles and scribbles as I pretended to glean insights from a man reading the paper. Corkle skipped forward a couple of times in search of anything more interesting, when suddenly we hit the jackpot.

In looking back, I can see that this was *the moment* - one of those moments you only recognise in looking back - when everything came apart and fell into place at the same time.

***

3rd March, 1883. 10:15.

'Aha!'

A startled cry, then: 'Damn it, Watson!' The door slammed. 'Don't do that!'

'Do what?'

'Lie in wait for me like some evil little child on Guy Fawkes Day.'

'You've been out all night, I perceive.'

'By Jove, Watson, you are good. Could this brilliant feat of deduction have something to do with the fact that I'm still in my evening clothes at ten in the morning?'

'You look as if you've slept in them.'

A grunt from Holmes.

'I hesitate to put this forward,' Watson said, 'but if I didn't know better, I'd say you've been seeing a woman.' Rude noise from Holmes. 'It's the third night in a row you've been out. Twice until nearly three in the morning, and, well, not home at all last night.'

'I am often out all night.'

'But you usually don't drag yourself back reeking of alcohol, with rouge on your shirtfront.'

'What? Dear God. Is it on my face?'

'Mmmm... I don't see any. No.'

'I need to bathe.'

Watson chuckled. 'Definitely a woman.'

'Definitely, eh?' Holmes's voice had taken on a lighter tone and faded as he'd gone into his bedroom. I could hear him shouting his amusement from there. 'How do you determine this? The facts, Watson. What is it about my person that leads you to the definite?'

'Aside from your appearance this morning?' Watson shouted back. 'For one, you pay rather more attention to your toilet then usual.' His voice resumed normal pitch, as Holmes apparently returned to the sitting room. 'I found you shaving at nine in the evening just last week.'

'What does that prove?'

'Nothing, in and of itself. It was the, er, nail-trimming that caught my attention.'

A squeal of outrage left my mouth. He'd had every hope of getting laid the night he came up to my room to "explain", the son-of-a-bitch. Corkle shot a glance at me. I shut my mouth quickly.

'You don't recall whether I went anywhere that evening, I presume?' Holmes asked smoothly.

'I had a head cold, remember?' Watson replied. 'I was in bed shortly after.'

'Your evidence is inconclusive. I have always been fastidious in matters of grooming.'

'Ah! I have also noticed a decidedly new spring to your step. One with which I am intimately familiar.'

'My dear chap. You usually limp home from that brothel you frequent. You do not spring.'

'A new limp to your step, then.'

'There isn't!'

'It is the limp of a sated man.'

'Rubbish.'

'Holmes, you are not refuting my observations. You're simply denying them.'

'I am not in the habit of engaging prostitutes, Watson, and other than that, I don't know where you think I could be getting this limp.'

'Perhaps you're keeping a mistress.'

'On my income? Let us hope she has other friends on the side.'

'Then where the devil have you been?'

'For God's sake, Watson, you sound like a suspicious wife!'

'If I were your wife, Holmes, I would have hit you over the head with a poker by now.'

The detective laughed, and gave a sigh of surrender. 'Very well. I attended a bacchanal. Fondled and flirted with by the most rapacious, predatory creatures in the world.'

'Actresses!' Watson cried gleefully.

'Some may aspire, but they shall never attain that goal. Watson? Tell me, do I appear effeminate in your opinion?'

'Er... why do you ask?'

'Do I?'

'Well, occasionally your mannerisms do seem rather... affected.'

'I was referring to this particular moment and not your general impression.'

'Oh. Oh! But I would never mistake you for... for one of *those*, Holmes. Really, I never intended to imply -'

'No. By all means imply, for in this instance you would be correct.'

The silence that followed was so rife with horror that both Corkle and I burst out laughing. We could actually hear Watson swallowing.

'You're joking with me. Aren't you? You *are*!'

'John, dearest. There's something I've been meaning to tell you...'

Apparently, Watson's reaction prompted Holmes into an evil chuckle.

'This isn't funny, Holmes!'

'But it is. You assume I've been with a woman. For once, I wish to God it were true.' 'This has something to do with Merrill Holbrook. Please tell me this has something to do with the case.'

'Of course it does,' Holmes said. I could envision the roll of his eyes and dismissive sneer that accompanied it. 'Lord Merrill hasn't been seen in his usual society for nearly a month. Nor has he kept correspondence with anyone. Two of his gentlemen friends were quite annoyed with this snubbing, and another was deeply concerned. Rumour has it he's run off with a new boy, but quite frankly, I'm beginning to suspect foul play.'

'Murder?'

'I haven't enough information to draw that conclusion. I have uncovered the mysterious disappearances of at least three other young men of that persuasion. One of them - "a simply gorgeous Italian youth" - was Lord Merrill's *amour de voyage* to Venice, if one can believe these invidious friends of his. Venice is so dreary this time of year. I would have gone to the south of France, I think. At any rate, if Merrill *did* leave the country, he's most likely used an assumed name. I've had no luck tracing his itinerary. And no luck tracing that Austrian doctor, either. Have you?'

'No. None of my associates have heard of him. If he is a specialist in matters of infertility, then he's not published anything. I've been through all the back issues of the *Lancet* for the past five years.'

'Oh, well. I shall have to be content with the progress I made last evening parading about like a harlot. Blessed little to show for it really. Rouge on my shirtfront, and a few cards from gentlemen wishing to encourage a closer friendship. Look here. An invitation to the Monico at six this evening from a Mr Ralph Pritchart. He would like me to wear a brown hat or some such... no, wait. Never mind. That's a nasty one. Straight into the bin with you.' I listened to the *thwip* of a card hitting the trash receptacle, and looked forward to reading the nasty invitation on the morrow. 'Ah. This looks much more promising: A Shamus Tiramory wishes to make my acquaintance at the Long Bar, also this evening. Seven o'clock. He's a photographer.'

'I don't even want to imagine what he photographs.' Watson muttered.

Suddenly, Holmes drew in a sharp breath, and repeated the name slowly. 'Shamus Tiramory. That's... that's odd.'

'Irish, obviously,' Watson said. Then: 'What?'

'Nothing. Probably nothing. I definitely would have remembered being introduced to a fellow with such a name. It's too coincidental.' He laughed. 'It's almost ridiculous.'

'What do you mean?'

'Hmm...? Oh. It's nothing to concern you. I'll sort the matter out when I see him.'

'But Holmes... damn it, man! Not the Long Bar, I beg you. Everyone I know goes there. What if you're seen with this person? There could be serious ramifications...'

'Ramifications,' Holmes repeated, then started to giggle. Giddy, not-enough-sleep sort of giggling.

'I don't see the humour in it.'

'You don't? The word evokes a host of associations for me. Ram, ramming, reaming... come on, it's rather funny, don't you think?' More laughter. 'Oh lord, I *am* losing my mind. Temporarily, Watson. I'm sure to find it again after I've slept. Be a dear, would you, and ring for the girl to light the fire in the bathroom? I need to cleanse Sodom from my pores before I rest.'

'I'd appreciate it if you would not refer to me as "dear" for the duration, Holmes.'

'Not even privately, my dove?'

'I mean it. I have my revolver at the ready, and I am prepared to use it on you.'

Watson's voice came from a distant part of the room, near the bell pull most likely. 'Did you see the papers? Your robber-girl took a house in Manchester Street last week.'

'She is not *my* robber-girl!' Holmes declared.

A door opened and shut again, and that was the end of the conversation.

I recalled sending Margaret to light the fire in the bathroom and how she'd whimpered on the way up about "mean Mr Bones". Watson had been gone for most of the day. Holmes had slept till five, had been out of the house by six.

Corkle covered the equipment and locked the trunk. Inside the monstrous piece of luggage, the small receiver continued to function in quiet readiness like a tick in a tree, while he sat tapping his pencil on the brass trim. Even in his contemplative moments, he grated on my nerves. His celluloid collar was unfastened and stood straight out on either side of his dirty neck. Dandruff littered his shoulders. The shiny, worn knees of his trousers bagged. He had his part down well, but it repulsed me nonetheless. Holmes always smelled clean, at least: even in his vest and drawers, he had more style than this man did fully-clothed. I quickly shoved down the annoying and complicated sensations that accompanied thoughts of Holmes. Corkle's words came at me like a blow.

'Christ, Gillian. Even Watson can tell the man's been getting laid on a regular basis. Sipped the nectar from the gillyflower recently, has he?'

My mouth hung open in stunned panic for a second, but then, for some reason, I just blew. 'It's none of your goddamned business!'

'Keep your voice down.'

'No! Fuck you!' I leapt from the chair, knocking it over. 'I'm doing exactly what you wanted me to do from the very start.' I pounded on the top of the trunk. 'This equipment was brought back to be used in precisely the way we're using it. You had every intention of getting me to plant the transmitters.'

'Strictly back-up, darling -'

'Can the crap, OK? You think I can't see you're planning to benefit from all this, somehow? You and Jimmy Moriarty and all those corporate bastards?'

'As do you. I mean, really, how useful is your research to the average twenty-first century guy? What bearing does it have on anything at all, except your associate professorship?' He cocked his head slightly, eyes catching the light of the lamp.

We maintained an uneasy silence for a moment. 'OK. Why are *you* here, Tom?'

'Same as you. Opportunity of a lifetime.'

'I guess I meant, what are your actual credentials?'

'You think to ask that now?' He laughed. 'I took a degree in criminal psychology, if that impresses you. I do have a professional interest in the work we're doing. Ah, but I'm a dabbler. Don't have nearly the handle on research in the field that you do. Oh, don't look at me like that, Gillian. I know how hard you've had it. Pioneers on a new frontier, aren't we? No idea how it'd affect us to walk amongst living, breathing antecedents. Besides, for a "skinny wanker", Holmes has lots of charisma. Could've charmed the pants off me if he'd had half a mind.'

Truth was, *my* pants had never been in that kind of danger. I'd dragged Holmes into that linen cupboard before he'd even known what was happening to him.

I took a ragged breath. 'So, have I completely blown it, or can something be salvaged?'

'Oh, I don't think it's bad as all that. Besides, we've all blown our share, haven't we?' On the verge of a giggle, he seemed to think better of it and scratched behind his ear instead. 'We could both use a good night's rest, don't you think?'

And that was the end of our discussion.

Later that night, on the edge of sleep, a thought startled me out of any hopes of it.

Sipping the nectar of the gillyflower. The look in his eye when commiserating over how *hard* I'd had it 'We've all blown our share, darling'... nudge nudge, wink wink.

He knew what had transpired between Holmes and me in my attic room. Everything I'd said and done. He knew because he'd heard it all in intimate detail.

Panicking, I started to search my room, running my hands along every likely surface - the walls, the eaves, under the table, the bedstead - until I was drenched in icy sweat and overwhelmed by the impossibility of the task. Unless I knew where to look, finding a hidden transmitter made of a self-camouflaging plastic would be next to impossible.

And something else struck me. Something my mind would have caught right away if I hadn't been stupidly preoccupied. "Armitroy". "Tiramory". Holmes had immediately noticed that they were anagrams of each other. It was so obvious, it had made him laugh. Jacob and Shamus were derivatives of "James" -

There were probably thousands of people with the surname Moriarty walking around in nineteenth-century London. But the name and the situation together? Not a coincidence. Jimmy wouldn't have risked the journey himself without testing the technology on others first, but his own scrambled name smack-dab in the middle of what was supposed to be a genuine, previously undocumented case for Sherlock Holmes was no accident. It was an intentional flag, a century-spanning marker proving that his people had made it here and back.

Even so, someone must have insinuated the names and characters into the case of Lord Merrill's disappearance. Or, more disturbingly, someone might have orchestrated the case itself.

There was only one someone it could have been.

Unable to consider sleep, I went down to the kitchen and dipped out a cup of beer. Downed it in one long draught.

If Corkle was interfering in the detective's life, it was with Moriarty's approval and for reasons I could only guess at. Better to find proof and then demand explanations. But the only time I had access to Corkle's room without his say-so was on Mondays, when Mrs Hudson let me have the passkey.

I spied the pale droop of her apron, suspended from a peg on the door. The ring of keys was in the pocket. I made a wax impression of the passkey - an act I'd only seen once in a movie - and returned to my room. I wrapped the wax glob in a handkerchief and hid it in my boot cupboard until I could have a copy made. I had no idea where one could get a key made from a wax impression, but I was certain that Shinwell Johnson would. I was meeting with him a week from Sunday at Holy Cross Church.

Chapter 16

I fully intended to do a bit of preliminary scouting with Mrs Hudson's original key when I went to tidy the room on Monday. Unfortunately, Corkle didn't go to the museum.

He was on his way back from the loo, a sour chemical cling to him that reminded me of hospitals. 'I'm really in the shits,' he said, pushing past me. 'Fetch up some toast and tea, will you?'

Back in the kitchen, I handed Mrs Hudson the key, mentioning Corkle's illness and request.

'Well, I suppose I'll have to tend to that, though my ankles swell up something awful when I climb them stairs.' She set the kettle over the flame. 'Margaret has got herself hired over to the Milton's, so the slops'll need tending.'

'Great,' I muttered.

'Are you giving me lip, girl?'

'No, ma'am.'

I fetched the slops bucket and went from room to room, dumping scummy basin water and full chamber-pots into the bucket. As the rain was heavy that morning, I grabbed the umbrella from the mud porch on my way out of the back door. A kind of "Singin' in the Rain" act commenced, only with rat-dodging instead of puddle-jumping, and not a lot of singing. Flinging the contents of the bucket in the vicinity of the sewer grate, I glanced up, and who should I see dragging his sorry ass home in the hopes of slipping unnoticed through the back door? None other than the Great Detective himself, a drenched opera cape over his clothes, trousers soaked to the knees. Water pooled in the brim of his top hat and poured occasional floods down the front of his shirt. He'd either had a very successful night, or a very miserable one. He didn't look up, and proceeded to walk past me without a word.

But in the process of lifting the latch on the gate, he stopped suddenly and turned. He tipped his head back and looked at me from beneath his brim. A waterfall cascaded down his back.

'Hullo,' he said. His face was grey from lack of sleep, his voice flat.

With a grudging sigh, I stepped closer and lifted the umbrella high so that it shielded both of us. 'Hullo, yourself,' I said.

'How've you been, Gillian Petra?'

'Don't call me that. Ever again.'

'Are you well, *Rose*?'

I shrugged. 'Fair to middling.'

'And has your friend gone yet?' he asked.

'I don't believe I have any friends in London presently,' I replied.

He laughed. Some of the strain in his face fell away. 'I'm sorry to hear that, but I was actually talking about your "monthly" friend.'

'Oh. *That.* Yes. Elvis has left the building.'

'Elvis...? Never mind. I don't think I want to know.'

'It's none of your business anyway,' I said.

He cleared his throat. 'Quite so. I only asked because... well, I was wondering if...' I tensed. He looked at his feet. 'That is, I wished to know if perhaps you were free Wednesday afternoon.'

Hello! Not the question I thought it would be. 'We could get into a philosophical debate on that subject,' I began carefully. 'The concept of freedom as an inalienable right. Is any man truly free? Certainly no woman is free. Is there any freedom without responsibility...?'

'Have you noticed how very wet and cold I am, Rose?'

'Yes.'

He sighed and cleared his throat. 'I should like to take you on a tour of the city, if you have no pressing engagements on Wednesday.'

OK. Apparently Sherlock Holmes was asking me out. I was stunned into forgetting my recent paranoia for the simple girlish thrill of the invitation. 'You're... asking me to step out with you?'

'Strictly in a professional sense. This will be a tour of the fashionably illicit; that which can be seen in the West End. It would require that you dress as a lady. Can you manage that?'

I thought about Mrs Tory's widow's garb. Without the veils, it was perfectly appropriate.

'The costume would need some hint of colour,' he added. 'Red would be preferable, or a bright yellow.' My eyes narrowed and he looked at me innocently. 'A hat in the appropriate hue. Indulge me. I'll treat you to luncheon.'

'Simpson's?' I suggested hopefully.

He made a face. 'Somewhere a bit more discreet, perhaps. Will you or not?'

Deciding I'd punished him enough, I said yes.

In the kitchen, Mrs Hudson was grinding up bits of animal flesh with a tense fury I hadn't observed in her before. She acknowledged Mr Holmes's greeting with what could only be described as 'harrumph'. He scraped his shoes dutifully, not seeming to notice her mood as he dripped water up the back stairs.

I thought it best not to interfere with someone grinding meat in such a manner, and tried to slip nonchalantly past her.

'Rose,' she said, her voice modulated for the lecture. I turned. She wiped her hands on her apron and placed them resolutely on her ample hips. 'I'm telling you just the once and I won't be telling you again, so mind you listen. You're not to hang on the gate talking and laughing with a man, *especially* one of my lodgers. There'll be none of that in my house, d'ye hear me, girl?'

'Yes, ma'am,' I said. I was still elevated from the remarkable invitation. 'I meant nuthin' by it, ma'am. He was wet and cold, and I felt sorry for him.'

Her stern look softened slightly. 'Well, it don't look proper to the neighbours. Now, go and fetch your wrap. I've some errands for you.'

Typical of my class, I did the errands in record time and took the rest of the morning for myself; a little detour to that dress shop off Tottenham Court Road. I was only looking for a hat, and a scarf in the required colour, but I saw this fabulous coatdress: red serge with jet buttons. I gave the ladies a deposit for it, jotted off a note to the Widow Tory's solicitor to send a cheque for the balance, and promised the ladies I'd pick it up Wednesday morning.

Holmes wanted red. I'd give him red and then some.

By Tuesday the rain became an ice storm. I received no message to the contrary, so I assumed the plans with Holmes were still go. I went to Corkle's room at nine as usual. He still looked terrible.

'Anything juicy about that Irishman at the Long Bar?' I asked.

He drew his fingernails through the bristles on his face, sunken eyes shifting from me to the steamer trunk. 'I haven't gone over it yet.' He gazed at me again. 'Look, can we beg off this tonight? I don't feel at all well.'

'Yeah, all right.' *I'm just fine with that, Thomas P.*

My half-day dawned clear and bitingly cold. Thick patches of ice clung to the sidewalks in places, though in the streets most of it had melted under the unrelenting traffic. Cocooned in my cloak, I took an omnibus to Tottenham Court Road, and slipped and slid my way on Stephen Street to the little court lane of the dress shop. By twelve-thirty I was standing in front of a mirror having my corset pulled tight by an expert, once again a slave to fashion.

Which completely cleaned me out, except for bus fare. But one good thing about the nineteenth century was that a lady could always expect the gentleman to pay. I left my poor girl's best in the backroom, intending to return at five-thirty. Another bus got me to Portman Square only a few minutes late.

Holmes was standing at the same news-stand where the man who'd followed me had stood when I'd crippled him with my umbrella. I took a deep breath, patted my hair and hat, and then noted with alarm that Sherlock was dressed for the weather: sensibly, in other words. I looped my new fur stole around my neck to make it seem practical, and cleared my throat loudly.

He turned, took one look at me and gave a startled laugh. 'You look like a holly berry!'

Not the reaction I'd hoped for. 'It makes me look fat?'

He blinked like a dullard a couple of times. 'No. Not fat... exactly. Er, delightfully round. And very red.'

I gazed about in anxiety, certain that everyone passing was making note of the size of my hips. 'Great. That's it. I'm not going.'

'What? Why not?'

'A delightfully round holly berry rolling across London? I think not.' I spun on my heels and started walking away.

'But you must,' he insisted, grabbing me by the arm.

A great deal depended on my going, it would appear. I looked at his hand, then at him. He let go immediately. I lifted my brows, waiting.

He drew his hands over his face in frustration, then threaded his fingers together in a little gesture of supplication, to me, or God. 'Let me start again. Miss Donnelly. My, my, don't you look fetching. That colour quite brings out the roses in your cheeks.'

'Really?'

'Yes. You have exceeded my expectations.' He gave me a cautious once-over, touching the feather on my hat. 'Will Scarlett to my Robin Hood. Although I doubt a merry man would tolerate being so hobbled about the lower limbs.'

Despite my being a holly berry in a Robin Hood hat, it was clear from the appreciative looks I received from other men that I was, apparently, one hot, sexy babe in a tight dress. As Holmes became aware of this, a change came over him, a kind of "in your face, losers" attitude that made up nicely for the "delightfully round" business.

As we walked, he pointed out the sights. 'There lives the finest gentleman cracksman in the business. Wanted to be a mechanical engineer, I understand, but his family are members of the peerage. Wouldn't allow it. Someday, I'll undoubtedly be the cause of his arrest.' Two blocks later: 'You see that chemist's shop there? Specialist in exotic poisons from South America. I used his expertise to solve a case last year. His wife performs abortions out of her kitchen. They put on a splendid tea. Jolly couple really, considering how many die as a result of their work.'

Sherlock Holmes was totally adorable when speaking of murder and mayhem.

We strolled through the shopping arcades, idled in art galleries, passed glorious theatres, elegant hotels and restaurants. Most of the crime on these higher-class areas revolved around forbidden sexual encounters, extortion, or professional rivalry. Crimes of passion didn't interest Holmes overmuch, and he spoke of adultery and blackmail with a yawning boredom.

I noticed a number of cafés and shops with discreet signs in the windows, advertising simply "beds". 'Many a luncheon ends in a tryst,' Holmes explained, unnecessarily. But, sadly, he did not offer that option to me.

Feet freezing and aching, I begged a rest stop, demonstrating my seriousness by coming to a dead halt before an expanse of storefront windows. A clerk was wiping off condensation on the inside, and I noted, half-consciously, that I was looking at jewellery. But what caught me more was the sight of an attractive woman in red. I didn't see the resemblance for scant seconds, and when I did, my attitude immediately reverted to the old insecurities that only a distorted reflection of oneself in a storefront window could elicit. I *did* look like a holly berry, a mutated one, linked in the middle by a corset. I tugged at the dress, trying to smooth it over what now appeared to be rolls of fat around my waist.

I caught his reflection examining my own, his arms folded, smoke curling up from the cigarette between his teeth.

'What?' I said, fussing with my hat as I turned around.

He took my chin in hand, touching one earlobe matter-of-factly. 'You need ear-bobs.'

'Isn't that something they do to dogs?'

'Earrings, goose.' He tossed the cigarette aside, his eyes continuing to appraise me. 'Garnets would be perfect, or carnelian, but coral might do.'

I thrust my gloved hands into the muff, unaccountably angry. 'Well, you see, I've spent quite a bit of money on this ensemble, so I won't be adding even coral -' Then it occurred to me. I shot a glance at the baubles in the window. 'Oh. You have an urge to buy me something pretty, is that it?'

Caught by a sudden impulse, aware of everything this impulse implied, he reddened and began to stutter excuses, backpedaling furiously.

I patted his chest. 'I'll settle for luncheon at the Café Royal.'

Holmes groaned. 'I could never afford to keep a mistress.'

We were seated quickly at the restaurant, but not at one of the best tables in the house, in spite of my pretensions at quality, in spite of the fact that I was with a man who spoke perfectly elegant English and looked every inch the polished gentleman. They were busy here, and we were but one couple among many who looked just as pretty. Our table was against the wall between the main seating and the kitchen. It was also within earshot of a private dining room full of noisy bohemian types. The curtain to the room was closed, but smoke still managed to drift in our general direction, along with the accompanying miasma of alcohol and the very loud voices of men.

We had already ordered, but Holmes seemed anxious about something: that nervous, vibrating anxiousness that could have been about anything at all; his boredom with the general atmosphere or his suspicion that one of the patrons was about to drop dead face-first into the soup tureen. Holmes had just raised his arm to gesture to the wait-captain when a squeal of delight and enthusiasm cut through the cacophony of drunken voices from the private room, and hailed in our direction.

'Good grief! If it isn't Sherlock Holmes in the flesh!'

I looked at Holmes, who closed his eyes and grimaced, then at the young man extricating himself with difficulty from the swag of heavy curtains that separated us from his sanctum. I could feel my companion's knee bouncing up and down under the table, causing little tremors in the floor beneath my shoes. Above the table, he gave the fellow the palest imitation of a smile, which was greeted as if it were the embrace of a long-lost brother.

'Sherlock m'dear, haven't seen you in simply ages! You're looking quite dapper.'

'Harry,' Holmes said in a voice as dry as talc. 'What a surprise.'

'And you with a woman. More surprising still.'

If Holmes occasionally resembled a fag in the closet, Harry Hughes fairly glowed with the aura of one who was unabashedly out.

I glanced at Holmes, who smoothly introduced me as his cousin, 'Mademoiselle Vernet, recently arrived from Paris.'

'Enchanté, Mam'selle. Harry Hughes at your service. A dear friend of your cousin's.' He touched his lips to my offered fingertips.

'Cher cousin, de quoi est-ce quil parle?'

As he'd started it, he had no choice but to follow along. 'My cousin speaks very little English, I'm afraid.'

'Really. Oh, dear. And I am so out of practice with my French,' Harry said. 'I was always pitiful with the foreign tongues, not like you a'tall. Though I'm well-versed in the tongues of foreigners.' He waggled his brows suggestively, and Holmes gave him a cold, hard stare. Harry ignored it. 'This works out wonderfully well. I was actually going to call on you. Private business to discuss. Just in your line, I should think.' He gestured with an airy wave at the room behind us. 'Would you and your cousin care to join me?'

'Hardly a fitting place for a lady, Harry, do you think?'

'Oh, pooh, a lady's perfectly safe in there. It's bound to be better than sitting at this table.' He gazed around the room, nose crinkling. Holmes's expression was stubbornly resolute. Harry sighed dramatically, but kept his voice low. 'Fine. I'll send my little monkeys away. We can discuss the matter without the nasty sods making eyes at you, yes? Not that they would, you know. You're not that pretty.'

I pressed my lips together to keep from smiling and pretended to look about the room, since I didn't understand a bit of what they were saying, being French and all. This was a fascinating development. Master Hughes was clearly in with the homosexual scene, and yet he didn't know Holmes had been traversing it regularly.

Harry sent his drunken sodomites about their merry way, in search of another accommodating establishment. A couple of them eyed Holmes, a flash of recognition as they passed our table. One leaned close to whisper in the other's ear, whereupon they fell into conspiratorial chuckles before stumbling out of the front door.

It stank in the private dining room, of sweaty men in wool who drank too much and tried to cover it with various scented oils. It stank of cheroots and half-eaten food and the waxy effluvium of candles. It also stank of the musky aroma of male-on-male sexuality, which can't be fully appreciated until one has accidentally walked into any club devoted to such things.

Holmes's reaction to the room was more acute than my own, and quite at odds with any desire to shock me. It was becoming clear from his unremitting grasp on my elbow - tighter and more painful by the moment - that I would not be allowed to sit among the remnants of a bacchanal. This struck me as odd, since in some other circumstance he might have required me to clean it up.

Harry breached the wall of Holmes's revulsion with a cry. 'Grief! Who'd've thought five Marys could make such a god-awful mess!' He called for a boy to clear the mess away.

When I was finally permitted to sit down, I watched Harry pour himself a tot of pale green liquor from a crystal decanter. 'Absinthe?' he offered.

Holmes pushed my hand from the offered glass. 'No, thank you.'

I protested in the sweetest French you ever heard, and he replied that he'd ordered a perfectly good wine, so would I just shut up.

Harry observed the exchange, comprehending only a few of the words but most of the sentiments. 'A tiny bit of absinthe couldn't hurt the girl, Sherlock.

She *is* French after all. I say! That means you're French as well! Jolly clever of you to be French, Holmes. It justifies your boorishness by lending a certain continental allure.'

Holmes scowled. 'Weren't you living in Glasgow or something?'

'Edinburgh. But my London auntie finally died and left me her house and all her money. Rather a lot of it. I only arrived in town the day before yesterday.' The young man cocked his head thoughtfully as he looked at me. 'That hat just cries out for ear-bobs, don't you think?'

Sherlock shot me a smug look from the corner of his eye, though why he should be smug about having the unerring fashion sense of a homosexual was beyond me. 'Get on with it, Harry. What is this business you wish to run past me?'

'Forthright as ever. Can't believe we survived the same public school, considering, well, you know... everything.'

I could feel my brows rising. *More, more, more, Harry Hughes, keep talking, I adore you.*

'Is this what you called me in here for? Reminiscing?'

'Lord, no! Who wants to remember *that*? Of course, I wouldn't be what I am today if it weren't for those long hours fagging for Arthur Templethwaite. He's a barrister now, did you know?'

'Don't care.'

'Whose slave were you again?'

The detective froze for a fraction of a moment. 'I don't remember.'

'Nasty chap as I recall. Oh, oh, let me think... was it Dodd or Griffith?'

'I don't remember, Harry. I prefer not to clutter up the already-crowded attic of my brain with memories that serve no useful purpose to my life now.'

Happily for him, the conversation was interrupted by our meal. Beautiful food, and a lot of it. The waiter decanted a Montrachet and left us to our own devices. Holmes picked up his glass in one hand, forked his salad with the other, and said: 'What is it you want?'

The detective's forthrightness seemed somewhat less amusing to Harry the second time around. 'I want you to find a young friend of mine.'

'Is he lost, or merely disenchanted with you?'

'He's gone missing.'

Holmes paused, fork mid-shovel to his mouth, his eyes betraying a tremor of interest. 'How do you know?'

'He hasn't been seen in nearly a month. Not anywhere, by anyone.'

'By "anyone", I take it to mean your particular circle of associates?'

'Yes, mostly.'

'Perhaps he's just found another friend and is too occupied to tell you.'

'That's what I thought at first, but then Stewie's mother contacted me... Stewart Ronaldson, the aforementioned friend...'

Holmes choked slightly, and placed his glass carefully on the table. 'Does his father own a lead factory in Newcastle-upon-Tyne?'

Harry started. 'Yes. Do you know him?'

'No. Pray, continue.'

'Well, he'd been having some trouble. I guess Pater disowned the poor chap, then supposedly they made it up all right on account of his Ma's ill-health. Those forgive-and-forgets never last, though, do they? Anyroad, Stew's mum asked if I, or any of the other chaps, had heard from him, from Stew, because he hadn't shown up on the day of appointed reconciliation. All right, I thought to m'self, he's probably found a proper old brown-hat that's keeping him well and truly in poggies, and they're holed up somewhere doing the -'

Holmes snarled over his soup. Harry shot a glance at me, blushed, then straightened in his chair like a schoolboy conjugating Latin. 'No-one has seen him, Sherlock. No-one. Not since the night before he was to leave. There was a party at the Belvedere, and everyone was there - well, save m'self and Oscar - he has yet to return from that tour of America.' He took sudden notice of my expression and tried to include me by careful enunciation. 'A-me-ri-ca?'

'*Oui*,' I nodded.

'He's getting married, if you can believe that,' Harry said. 'Anyway, I remembered Oscar telling me you'd taken on this investigating business quite keenly. He said he thought you terribly clever at this sort of thing.'

Holmes paled visibly. 'Did he?'

'Yes. He claimed your talents were almost supernatural.'

'I'm sure he never did.'

'Oh, but he did! He said your brain was like a pair of sharp little nail scissors. Snip, snip, and a fellow's mental trimmings would be in your pocket. He actually remembers you quite fondly.'

Holmes sat back in his chair and looked at the young man with a combination of rueful disbelief and horror. 'If he remembers me at all then he does so while laughing up his sleeve. Seven years ago I attended one of Oscar's impromptu *salon d'artistes* at Magdalen, and much, *much* later awakened in a strange bed to discover I was bereft of my trousers. I've spent these many years trying not to dwell on the possibilities. So please,' he leaned across the table with quiet intensity, '*please*, don't tell me he remembers me fondly, or I shall most assuredly vomit.'

Harry's hand flew up, trying to stuff the laughter back in his gaping mouth.

'That was you! You were the inflated young fellow who dared to call his poetry derivative?'

'Hardly the last.'

'Oh, this is too delightful! But... you poor dear. You're not his type at all. Your lips are much too... well, let's just say you've not enough mouth for him.'

A strange little sound slipped out from between my own lips, and Holmes whirled on me, glaring furiously.

'*Pardon moi*,' I said, dabbing daintily with a napkin.

'You were drinking, I'm told,' Harry continued, 'and pulling off the hookah quite a bit. Too much liquor and hashish, old chap. They set you up with a town girl. A *girl*, Sherlock.'

The detective's relief was instant and obvious, but outrage soon followed. 'I could have been expelled!'

'Well, you weren't, were you?'

'And my trousers? I only had three pair to my name, and they were the best I had.'

'The Jane copped 'em. It was part of the joke, I'm afraid. To prove you'd done the deed with her so she could get her money.' Harry reached over and clasped Holmes by the arm, a genuinely compassionate gesture, but Holmes only flinched. 'Nothing happened, Sherlock.'

'As I cannot remember, I must take your word for it.'

'Well,' said Harry with an embarrassed grin, 'I have it on good authority. It seems the pranksters were watching from a little peephole in the next room.'

'Bastards,' Holmes muttered.

Harry laughed. 'I don't know why I'm coming to you for help if you couldn't even find what became of your trousers after seven long years... oh, dash it all! Is that the time?'

I heard the echo of a bell chime, fading into the busy traffic sounds outside. Holmes took out his watch. It was three o'clock.

'I must run, m'dear. Can I call 'round your digs at eight? Give you the details?' Holmes nodded. Harry grabbed his overcoat from the rack and rushed from the room, crying: '*Bon jour, Mam'selle.*'

In the silence that followed Harry's whirlwind departure, the detective took another spoonful or two of his soup, then pushed it away. He pulled out his pipe and tobacco, and started loading the bowl.

'If Master Hughes appears this evening, you must not wait upon us. I don't care how you manage it, only that you refrain from being seen.'

'All right.' I took a thoughtful sip of wine. 'You were rather cruel to him about his missing friend.'

'He has so many friends, I'm surprised he noticed one missing.'

'He seemed to count you among them.'

'I don't associate with his kind for the most part.'

I almost started to laugh, knowing where he'd been going this past week. 'I thought you *were* one of his kind when I first came to the house.'

He drew back in mild alarm. 'On what would you base such an assumption?'

'Well. You love stylish clothes. You're rather effeminate in manner sometimes. You wash yourself more than average -'

'I don't see what cleanliness has to do with... oh, God. I see it now. You have, in effect, stolen my trousers. Now you can return to wherever it is you're from and run them up the flagpole. Proof positive. I am a man.' He held up his arm, listlessly displaying a biceps.

'I didn't come all this way just to shag the great Sherlock Holmes.'

I could see the words echoing in his head. *All this way from where? From where, Gillian?* His lips curled, sardonically. 'Great, am I? My sexual prowess precedes me. Or does it *proceed* me? A subtle but significant distinction, would you not say, Mam'selle Vernet?' He pointedly drained the bottle into my glass. 'You're looking rather pale, my dear. Have more wine.'

'Are you trying to get me drunk, sir?' I asked, leaning across the table with a forced flirtiness.

'You hardly need my assistance, as I recall. And I cannot imagine such inducements are necessary. You're always so willing.' There was a nasty undertone that I didn't much care for. 'Anyway, I've never had you when you were drunk.'

Strange, how the Victorian slant on sexuality could so surprise me. The "take" and "have" of it.

'Nor will you,' I said between clenched teeth, 'if you continue being such an utter bastard.' Holmes jerked his chair sideways and leaned back in it, arms and legs crossed. I suddenly felt myself a very tiny, insignificant thing. 'But it seems, Miss Petra, that you will only reveal your true self when you are drunk. Or naked. *I* will not give myself up so easily. Do I make myself clear?'

'As a bell,' I replied. I set my glass on the table carefully. 'I've finished my lovely lunch, and I thank you.' I gathered my muff and stole, and stood up.

He scrambled to get to his feet, knocking the table with his knees. 'You can't go yet.' The glass toppled and rolled into the lamp as he reached for my hand. 'We've still Soho -'

I looked at his distraught expression and laughed. 'I'm going to the loo.'

'Oh.'

By the time I'd returned from wrestling with my layers of garments, Holmes had paid our bill and was waiting near the door, coat and hat in hand. He was peering intently through the glass and didn't hear me approach. When I touched his arm, he jumped.

'My goodness,' I laughed. 'What's got you so spooked?'

He shot a glance out the window, and looked back at me again. I saw something in his eyes, something tender, but fierce. Not love, but something very like it. It confused the hell out of me.

'I thought you might have shinned out,' he said. And I knew he was lying.

Outside the traffic rattled by, spattering globs of manure and ice onto the walks. Newsboys hawked their papers. Indigents paraded back and forth with sandwich-boards advertising various good and services. Carts, carriages, cabs and omnibuses. People, parcels, slush, and horses. Lifting the skirts of my pretty-princess gown, I gained a solid understanding of the heavy canvas dust-ruffle fitted under the hems of all m'lady's frocks. I had no protection for my shoes though, and I mentioned this to my escort.

He took it as a complaint. 'How else would you have us get about?'

I pointed out that there were these things called cabs with jarvey chaps directing horses to desired destinations. He turned out a pocket and presented me with a crown, a couple of shillings, and some lesser change. 'This is the sum total of my wealth until Monday next. I have other expenses between now and then. If you would care to use your own money, however, I'd be quite happy to -'

His eyes flicked to something over my shoulder, and I turned to follow his gaze.

A large, vaguely familiar-looking man darted into St Alban's Street. It was so fast, this dark image in a flickering tableau of black, brown and grey, that I wondered if I'd seen it at all. I looked questioningly at Holmes. His mouth was twisted in irritation, overlaid by another emotion. Worry, I think.

He folded my hand into the crook of his arm, and did an about-face toward Piccadilly. 'I'll make a concession for the sake of your feet,' he offered. Then he took me into a shop and bought me a pair of galoshes.

Chapter 17

I gimped along in the galoshes and tight dress, my bustled backside like a swaying red target. I was so angry about it that I refused to speak to him, which would have been very effective if he'd actually been talking to me.

We were being followed and he'd known it from the beginning, no doubt suspected we would be when he'd asked me to accompany him. What kind of a man could be so ruthlessly secretive? Was he being followed or was I? Or was it because we were together?

As we wandered with touristy aimlessness through Soho, he squeezed my hand where it rested on his arm, arrogantly reassuring me that he had everything under control. I begrudged him the comfort he offered because he had no right to offer it. He hadn't let me in on the plan. It was so typical of him, this arrogance. And yet, at the same time, his hand lain over mine felt good, and steady, and absolutely necessary to my continued well-being.

Finally, we turned with some purpose into a lane, at the far end of which was a small courtyard with a coffee shop. We stopped at the door next to it, the shingle advertising "Georgio L. Santelli, Art Photography and Photographic Portraiture".

'I fancy a portrait of you,' Holmes said brightly. 'Something artistic.'

I eyed him suspiciously, but my hand went automatically to my hair. 'It'll cost something more than what you've got left, won't it?'

'Oh, I doubt it. We're under no obligation to retrieve the finished product.'

At the ring of the bell, Mr Santelli himself bounded down the stairs to greet us; a spry, attractive man in his early forties, oozing charm to the point of obsequiousness. Lighting upon me, his eyes narrowed fractionally, full of the quick, cunning assessment of the practised sexual predator. "Art Photography" my arse.

He escorted us up to his waiting room / studio, quite the Victorian bordello in its delusions of opulence. Velvet draperies covered everything, not merely the windows. Threadbare velvet, faded to a sultry dark pink and ornamented with gold fringe and tasselled swags. The walls displayed portraits in ornate gilt frames. Women in their very finest gowns rendered in shades of sepia, posed next to military men with moustaches waxed to sharp points and plumed hats tucked under their arms. A few sombre-eyed, frightened, or defiant children - none of them smiling - occupied scattered places on the wall.

'You wish to have a sitting, you and your lady?' the photographer said as, he began pulling down and rejecting backdrops with a professional zeal that made me take a step back toward the stairs.

'Not precisely,' Holmes said. His voice had taken on the subtle nasal quality of old money. 'I shall be travelling to the continent on business of my father's. As my dear little friend' - me, apparently - 'will not be able to accompany me, I should like to have a personal token to carry whilst I am abroad. I had heard from a certain royal personage in my acquaintance that you have made a speciality of such portraiture. Is this true, Mr Santelli?'

Santelli froze, and a backdrop of rose-entwined trellises scrolled upwards with a snap.

'I saw the photograph of his latest,' Holmes continued. 'That young actress at the Palace. Oh, what was her name? Darling, do you remember?' I shook my head. 'Mrs Torrance, or Trevor, was it?'

'Talbot?' Santelli offered.

'That's it! Damme, but she's a pretty creature. And the portrait... so like Lorenzo Lotto's *Venus and Cupid*, same style, same subtlety of hue. Without the colors, of course. Really quite charming.'

Mr Santelli flushed with pleasure, and the accompanying gleam in his eye stripped me naked. 'You wish something similar of your friend?'

The detective squeezed my hand painfully, cautioning me to silence. 'I should wish to see your portfolio, of course.'

Santelli begged our indulgence and disappeared behind a hang of drapes that separated his studio from his living quarters. Holmes went to the window, peering into the street below. We weren't there to get a picture of me naked, I was fairly certain, but I wasn't sure how far he intended to take the charade in order to get what he was really after. He let the curtains drop over the window and turned, flashing a smile of pure dazzle, a showman's bravado and tease. Oh, he could be such a charmer when he'd a mind! I couldn't help it: I laughed, experiencing a giddy rush, like I was fifteen again, sneaking out my window to do something stupid and illegal.

Mr Santelli returned with a large portfolio. He turned up the lamp on the tea-table and began laying out photographs.

A woman posed in a magnificent mink-lined robe, framing huge, pendulous tits; another doing a Salome thing, down to her last veil; another posed with an obviously phoney snake. With their corset-deformed ribcages and big dimpled bottoms, they had all the current ideals of feminine sex appeal. Most of them were young. Some were very young, judging from the perkiness of their attributes, and were likely domestic servants looking to make a few bucks on the side.

Holmes took out a cigarette and lit it carefully. 'Is this all?' he asked. His matter-of-factness startled me.

'This is the type of portrait you requested, is it not, sir?'

'Actually, I was thinking of something without quite so much draping. I suppose I expected, oh, I don't know...' He inhaled thoughtfully, eyes still on the photographs. 'A bit more quim.' The naughty little word came out of his mouth without a stumble. 'Would you have any with men and women together? Or those charming lesbian duos I've heard about?'

'Or just boys,' I added. Holmes shot me a look of astonishment, then grinned.

Mr Santelli's avarice went on red alert. We were a kinky couple. Maybe here merely to feed our voyeurism. Would we pay?

'Ah, such are for limited viewing, sir, very, very private. Some of these... works are not even my own. The prints I make for another photographer of my acquaintance, for reasons of discretion, you understand?'

My companion removed a five pound note from his wallet, and I stifled an outcry. Here I was wearing these stupid, ugly galoshes, and all this time we could have been riding in cabs.

He smiled at Mr Santelli, the smile of the perpetually bored. 'Just for a look. Of course, I'm willing to pay the going rate for a truly striking portrait of my mistress. How do you feel about posing with a snake, my pet?'

'Ooh, I'm ever so good wif snakes.'

Santelli's body of work was considerable, and it took a while for Holmes to sift through the stack to what he was looking for: pornographic pictures of men and boys. The photographer sat at a small table, with a scenic backdrop of Italian mountains behind him and a cup of tea in front. He read a magazine while keeping an eye on us, the banknote in his pocket.

Holmes was diligent about flipping the photographs over as he discarded them, I suppose out of some urge to protect my delicate sensibilities. There were notations on the backs indicating the date and the number of prints in the series, the photographer's initials, and in some instances the name of the model or title of the piece. His own perusal was necessarily matter-of-fact - attention focused not on what the young men were doing, but on who they were - and each time he turned a picture over, his eyes took note of the writing, recording the information with a quick blink. I picked through the discards gingerly, as if I were doing so to maintain the pretence of our perversion.

Due to the long exposures involved, the pictures all had a quality of infixion rather than of having captured a moment: molecules pinned to cardboard like a dead bug collection, bugs that remained in that state of vital penetration for eternity. Up close, the stillness of the images ensnared me. Knowing that I held a teaming mass of constantly-moving particles in my hand did nothing to alter the sense that I was becoming two-dimensional through the very act of looking at them.

When the ceaseless flip-flip-flip of paper halted next to me, the spell was broken and a picture dropped from my hand onto a messy pile of others. I was so relieved that I fell against Holmes with a quiet cry of joy, poignant even to my own ears. His right hand moved to cover mine in what I foolishly took to be sympathy, before he casually slipped a photograph up his coat sleeve. He patted my hand, squeezed it over his forearm and, through that action, managed to curl the stiff cardboard beneath the fabric of his jacket so that it wouldn't be too noticeable when we made our departure.

We set an appointment for me to pose with a snake the following week. Mr Santelli unlocked the door and bid us good day, whereupon we vaulted to the cafe to sit and quietly revel in our daring adventure over coffee.

Holmes took the photograph from his sleeve and placed it in his breast pocket. He didn't show it to me, and I didn't ask to see it.

'I feel I should apologise for that,' he said. But you won't, I thought. 'What made you think of inquiring about photographs of boys?'

I shrugged. 'It seemed the next logical step.'

'It was inspired. I wasn't sure how I was going to broach the subject.'

'You're welcome,' I said. No thank-yous. No apologies. Typical.

A young couple were just leaving, wrapped in their woollens and their obvious affection for each other. I thought, ah, wouldn't that be nice? Filled with a profound spiritual ache, I sighed heavily. Me, cast adrift in my little boat christened "Lonely Girl".

'What is it?' he asked.

'Oh, nothing.' He eyed me questioningly. I shook my head, embarrassed. 'No, really. I just thought... nothing.'

'You thought nothing? I find that hard to believe. Your mind is always very busy, it seems to me. A whirling dervish of a mind.'

'That's hardly flattering. It means you think I can't be precise and am merely spinning about in the hopes of altering my perception of reality.'

Holmes propped his chin in his hand and grinned. 'What a marvellous twist on my metaphor. Women are usually so dull or devious in the expression of their thoughts.'

'You haven't known many women, have you, Sherlock?'

He looked at his hands, some private embarrassment causing the colour to rise in his face. 'Enough to bore me. You do not bore me.'

'*Yet*. I feel like that Salome in the photograph. I only have a couple of veils left to go.'

'Whose head do you want as a reward for my pleasure?'

'Whose ever it is that's following us.' He drew in a sharp little breath, but otherwise didn't move from his casual position. 'Many men are blind to the colour red, you know,' I said.

He jerked his shoulders in a shrug. 'A chance worth taking. Men in that line of work have a tendency to make mistakes when the target is easy to spot. They become lazy. Ah, you see? Here comes our fellow now.'

Through the pebbled-glass windows, I saw the figure of a man approach, then hesitate before reaching for the door.

'I imagine he thought we'd taken one of the beds upstairs,' Holmes said quietly. 'Thought he'd come in to warm himself while we romped.' The little bell over the door rang. 'Good. He's going to brazen it out.'

'But *why* is he –?' I started to ask. Holmes shushed me.

The man entered, collar turned up, hat pulled low, and went to a table on the far side of the long, narrow room. He didn't look in our direction.

Holmes had his back to the man, and the man had his back to me, yet I couldn't shake the feeling that I should know him. He hung his coat and muffler on a hook, then off came the hat. He smoothed his greasy hair back, hung the hat over the coat and turned. I stifled a gasp.

'You recognise him?' Holmes asked, under his breath.

The mottled skin. Epicanthic folds over a wide, pitted nose. The furtiveness which tried not to seem furtive. The furry side-whiskers were gone, but it was the man I'd once mistaken for Sherlock in disguise, the man I'd assaulted with the umbrella back in October.

I didn't understand any of this. Why should I be followed? And why for so long? Even if Corkle had been bugging my room from the beginning, it wasn't as if I'd dictated my notes to a computer. He didn't even get hold of my written research until early December. Before Holmes and I became lovers, I'd done nothing to justify such a thing. But who else would have me followed?

'Gillian? Do you recognise him?'

I looked away. I looked at the counter with its steaming pots and sticky pastries. I fiddled with the items in my fur muff. I adjusted my hatpin. Then, for reasons I'm not sure of even to this day, I said: 'No.'

His fist came down on the tabletop, causing the plain little cups to leap from the saucers. Automatically, I began dabbing at the spilled coffee with a serviette.

'Why do you persist in these lies?' he said, in that scary, quiet voice that made stronger people than me wet themselves. 'Why?'

Afraid that the scary, quiet voice wasn't quiet enough, I put my elbow on the table and shaded my face with my hand. 'Hush. He's looking over here.'

Holmes spun about, glaring at the man. 'Is there something in a private conversation between a man and his wife that interests you, sir?'

The man started at the sudden attention and smiled a vague apology. 'Naw, sir. Just wonderin' what ye ha' agin the table to bang it so.'

'Kindly mind your own business!'

Two older women seated behind us began to gather their parcels in a hurry. The proprietor eyed Holmes nervously.

My stalker looked at the slateboard above the counter, coolly dismissive, as he perused the list of offered beverages.

Voice modulated to the barely audible, Holmes said: 'The next time he looks at you, make me aware of it. I'll create a diversion, and you will leave by yourself. Return to the house. I intend to see where he goes after that.' My face betrayed my alarm. 'I shall be close on your heels. I'll not let anything happen to you.'

I sipped from my cup and shifted my gaze carefully, watching as the man ordered tea in a coffee shop, to the annoyance of the proprietor. He was brought an assortment of biscuits, bit into one thoughtfully, then darted a glance at me. I looked back. He grinned, showing a mouthful of crooked, discoloured teeth. My cheeks burned automatically.

At this cue, Holmes thrust back and stood. The ladies, on their way out the door, squealed and fumbled for the handle, bustles creaking as they darted outside.

'You are displaying a rudeness which is unforgivable, sir,' Holmes declared. His "angry husband" mode was greatly enhanced by the fact that he was actually really mad. 'My wife does not appreciate your attentions, and you would do well to keep your eyes to yourself!'

The man's hands clenched around the cup. Holmes took two steps toward him. 'Do you hear me, sir?'

'Husband,' I said, cringing with an embarrassment not as fake as it was supposed to be. 'You are mistaken.'

He stopped, looked back at me. 'Am I?' he said, eyes narrowing suspiciously, darting from me, to the man, and back to me again. 'Do you find something appealing in this oaf? Is that it?'

The other man stood up. 'Mister, ye're skatin' on thin ice.'

Sherlock Holmes growled. 'Let's see who falls in first, shall we?'

In comparison, the two bodies were painfully dissimilar. Holmes, the taller of the two, nevertheless looked no match for the beefy man in the brown suit. But a crazy, jealous husband was a fearsome creature, and one couldn't count on relative size to keep from being grievously injured.

Holmes held his ground in the centre of the room, urging the other man to move closer with one of those "you want a piece of me?" hand gestures that I found so ridiculous.

'Are you mad?' I cried, rising abruptly. 'Stop this at once!'

The squat little proprietor inched his way from behind the bar, prepared to make a run for the back door. 'Sir,' he cautioned, in a voice high and loud. 'I'd listen to the lady if I were you. I'll not tolerate brawling in my establishment -'

'This brute has insulted me!'

'He's done nothing of the sort!' I said.

'Caught you making eyes at a common ruffian. Gentlemen too good for you now, are they?'

I picked up my gloves and muff from the table, suddenly aware that I was not equipped with a wedding ring. I thrust my left hand into the depths of the fur. 'There would seem to be a decided lack of gentlemen in the room at present,' I said, and with suitably dignified outrage, threw open the door and marched out of the establishment into the cold, dark, late afternoon.

I walked as quickly as the gown would allow - anxious to be out of that alley, any alley, especially a dark one - driven by adrenaline and the spirit of my pretend-fury at my pretend-husband. I soon realised I was headed in the wrong direction and, feeling like an idiot, turned and made my way towards Oxford Street. I still had to get back to the dress shop and retrieve my other clothes.

The skirt of my gown was bedraggled, damp and stained with mud. My feet were numb. If Holmes expected me to schlep all the way back to Baker Street from the dress shop just to make it easier for him to follow the man, he could forget it. As soon as I was back in my dry, comfortable housemaid's clothes, I was hopping the first bus I saw. I turned into the lane headed for the passage wherein the shop of Neekham and O'Leary, Ladies' Furnishings and Habiliment, was located.

A strange panic prickled the hairs at the back of my neck. I quickened my pace. Unexpectedly, my feet decided to take a little walk in thin air...

A lack of foot-traffic had conspired to preserve a stubborn, nearly-invisible patch of black ice. My bustle collapsed awkwardly into my spine and I arched back, my head hitting the pavement *hard*. For a moment I felt nothing but that rush of flashing light behind my eyes, then the murmuring of voices, getting louder, anxiously inquiring about my health.

'Are you all right, Miss?' A woman's voice, but a man's grip took me under one arm and pulled me to my feet.

'Yes,' I replied, my voice seeming to come from somewhere behind me.

'You took a nasty fall there, Miss.' A man. Deep and gravelly. 'Steady now.'

'I'm all right. Thank you.' I reached back to stop whoever was pulling my hair, only to discover my hat upside-down and flopping at the back of my head, still attached by the hatpin. I righted it, my hands shaking.

'Are you dizzy? Perhaps we should take her to the apothecary, my dear,' the woman said.

The man on my right looked at his watch. 'Yes, I suppose we've got time.'

'No, really, I'm fine. I need to get to the dress shop just a ways down.' I turned to the man on my left, whose firm grip was becoming uncomfortable. 'Thank you, sir. I shall be all ri -'

I looked up into the face of my stalker.

'I'll see the lady to the shop,' he told the other two.

'No.' I extracted my arm forcefully, stumbling backwards a little. 'I have no need of your assistance.'

'Come now, missus, yer *'usband*'d fret sumfin awful were I to abandon ye after a nasty fall like tha'.' The sparkles that danced in front of my eyes were now dancing in a rapidly darkening field. He caught me up by the arm again, tipped his hat at the helpful, worried-looking couple. 'I'll see 'er to the shop, get word to 'er man.' Then he began marching me into the passage, my feet barely touching the ground.

'Hey! I don't know this man!' I shouted. 'I don't -'

He clamped his hand over my mouth and nose, half-dragging, half-carrying me between the black buildings. I heard muffled cries behind me, and the trill of a cab whistle cutting through them. I could make out a conveyance at the other end of the passage, a delivery van with its doors open, a dark hole waiting to be filled with me.

I started to fight in deadly earnest then, but if he hadn't slipped on another patch of ice as he tried to hoist me over his shoulder, no fight from me would have made a bit of difference. He went down the way a big man will. I did an unintentional somersault over his shoulder and tried to come up running, but the dress had me hobbled like a horse. Instead, I found myself clawing the pebbles in an effort to propel the heavily-padded back half of me forward.

Desperately focused on my goal - a dress form in a window - I scrambled like a crab over the cobbles. Made it to the door, fumbled with the handle *forever* before managing to open the damn thing. I flung myself across the threshold, rolled, brought my rubber boots up, and kicked the door shut. The bell over the transom rang hysterically. Another struggle with voluminous draperies brought me up to my knees, where I threw the bolt, spun about and shoved my back against the door for good measure. Mrs Neekham and Mrs O'Leary were rooted to the floor, frozen in the act of hiding their moneybox.

'Lock the back door!' I cried. 'Lock the back door!'

Mrs O'Leary had started for the back when the door behind me rattled, that ominous jiggling handle which only happens in slasher films, then

- *bang bang bang*. The three of us screamed in unison.

'Gillian!' More pounding. 'Gillian! Open the door!'

Mrs O'Leary started praying. Mrs Neekham burst into tears.

'It's all right,' I assured them breathlessly. I drew back the bolt to admit Holmes.

He was winded, hatless, completely dishevelled. I could have kissed him. His eyes skimmed over me quickly. 'You're unharmed?' I nodded. 'Wait here,' he said, and disappeared into the darkness again.

The Good Samaritan couple peered in a few moments later to inform me that a constable was on his way. After ten minutes, Holmes came back. By that time I was huddled in the back room amongst paper patterns and pincushions, my shaking hands wrapped around a mug of hot tea.

'I told you to return to the house,' he snapped.

I shot a glance at the two women at the counter out front. 'I had to come here first.'

'What for?'

'To change my clothes, Sherlock,' I muttered out of the side of my mouth. 'I can't go back dressed like this.'

'You should have made that clear to me. The man obviously knew it and headed here while I was busy trying to get the jump on him four streets over in the opposite direction!'

'Well, I'm sorry! Next time I'll -'

'I'd pray to God there *is* no next time if I were you... ah, constable, at last. That the streets are not safe for a woman on her way to her dressmaker's is an issue the police should address with more vigour, don't you agree?'

Pow. A direct hit at the young bobby's failure to serve and protect before he'd even opened his mouth to say 'evenin', sir'.

For several minutes I watched in weary sympathy, as the officer tried to keep up with Holmes's rapid-fire recitation of the facts.

'- and a grey furniture van with the company's name painted over in a hue that doesn't quite match. One of the wheels has a new iron rim. One horse is a big roan with no markings and a bent nail in the shoe of the right foreleg. The driver is five feet eight inches, weighing approximately twelve stone. More accustomed to handling a dogcart than a larger rig, I should think. He's wearing a billed cap and a chequered muffler. The van emerged from this lane and headed east toward Charlotte Street, making for Goodge Street I'll warrant...' He broke off both his pacing and his patter. The constable had ceased his furious scribbling in his notepad to stare in amazement at the detective's wealth of information. Holmes jabbed a finger at the page. 'Bent nail, right foreleg.'

The man reddened. Holmes went over the information again very, very slowly until it was all the poor fellow could do to keep from telling him to sod off.

'If you think the lady sufficiently recovered from her fright, sir, it'd be most helpful if she'd come to the station to file a report.'

'Constable...' Holmes peered at the name on the man's badge.. '...McBride. Are you aware that there is a gang of white slavers operating in your district?'

McBride pulled back in alarm. 'You don't think 'tis that, sir?'

'I've been investigating this gang for some time now. Villains who snatch innocent young women off the streets and sell them to seraglios abroad.' Holmes leaned in with quiet intensity. 'Turks and God-knows-what worse.'

The young man's eyes got huge.

'At least my dear sister has been spared such a fate. But think of the countless other sisters who have not been.' He gave McBride his card. 'I have a personal stake in the matter, and would be very interested to hear what you discover about the van.'

Smooth, Holmes, very smooth.

After the policeman left us, pumped full of purpose, I pulled on my other clothes while the toe-tapping, finger-drumming detective waited in the main part of the shop. Mrs Neekham and Mrs O'Leary brushed as much of the mud from the hem of my fancy gown as they could, but Holmes refused to wait for it to dry.

'Just have them wrap it up and let's go,' he growled.

Easy for him to say. He hadn't paid five quid for it.

With the damp gown wrapped in paper and the hat in a box, we took the underground to Baker Street Station. I knew he was angry, mostly with himself, but it made for tiring company. He escorted me into the house, handed me over to Mrs Hudson with a short explanation about my having slipped - hit my head, might be concussed, needed watching, et cetera, et cetera - then went up to his rooms.

After examining the back of my head, Mrs Hudson asked: 'Did you buy a new hat, dear?'

I looked dully at the parcels clutched in my arms.

'A stupid waste of money,' I replied, and went up to confront Corkle. But the son-of-a-bitch was gone, his door locked up tight.

Chapter 18

Thursday morning Corkle was at breakfast, smiling as if everything was grand and he wasn't at all surprised to see me there pouring the coffee. Perhaps he wasn't. I had no evidence my room was bugged, could think of no reason he would have had me followed for so long. What if the van and the men *were* part of some white-slaver gang? But I had to dismiss that as ridiculous. My youthful appearance wasn't *that* youthful. The mode of operations for such gangs was the opportunistic, hit and run variety; the young women sold to local pimps and bawds. I'd been stalked for months by the big man with the Oriental eyes. The only thing that changed between October and yesterday was my relationship with Holmes.

It had to be Corkle's doing. There was no-one else.

My mind was still running circles around this poser when I went upstairs to deliver the breakfast tray just after nine. Trailing behind me up the steps was a boy with a telegram for Holmes. I made the boy wait in the hall. I was supposed to, it was the protocol.

Watson was temporarily indisposed in the WC with his newspaper, so *I* had to awaken the lion.

'What?' Holmes roared.

'There's a telegram for you, sir,' I replied. 'The boy's needin' you to sign for it.'

I heard him groan, then the creak of the bed as he rolled out of it.

Watson returned, whistling merrily, though a trifle on the sharp side. I laid out the breakfast while the detective stood at the door, yawning, scratching, and wincing at the doctor's trills.

He turned the envelope over and over as if seeking meaning from his own name and address. Finally noticing the lad waiting patiently for a gratuity, Holmes thrust a hand into the pocket of his dressing gown. Seeming surprised to find no coins in the depths, his bleary eyes scanned the tabletops, then, muttering incoherently, he went to the sofa and began to dig behind the pillows.

Watson watched this performance in mild annoyance, before resigning himself to the inevitable. 'Oh for Heaven's sake.' He tossed Holmes a penny. Holmes deftly caught it, handed it to the boy, and closed the door on his 'cheerio, guv'.

It was the sound he made after reading the telegram that caused both the doctor and I to turn in alarm. Not much of a sound, but a significant one, made more so by how long he stood by the door staring at the message.

'Is everything all right, Holmes?' Watson asked.

The detective looked up at Watson, not really seeing him. He moved his head, something between a nod and a shake. Biting his lower lip, he crumpled the paper in his fist and stuffed it into his pocket, then moved lethargically to his room without uttering a word. The door hadn't quite closed when he came out again, heading straight for the liquor cabinet. With a bottle of whiskey in one hand and a coffee cup in the other, he returned to his bedroom and very quietly shut the door behind him.

It was disturbing behaviour, even for him.

Later that morning he emerged, asked Mrs Hudson to send a telegram for him, and went back into his chamber where he remained for the rest of the day.

Watson, well accustomed to these bouts of incommunicative depression, went to his club to dine. Minutes after he left, Holmes's brother came to call.

Mycroft Holmes did not give me his name or send his calling card before him. He merely pushed me aside, saying 'out of my way, girl!', and dashed up the stairs, surprisingly nimble for a man of his girth. The family resemblance was obvious, particularly in the heat of anger, and Mycroft Holmes was exceedingly angry.

That evening Corkle welcomed me with hand-rubbing delight. 'Pull up a chair, and settle in for an episode of Dysfunctional Family Feud.'

He offered me no recordings from Wednesday night. If Harry Hughes had paid a call, I wasn't made aware of it. I was dished up this juicy steak instead, like something tossed to a vigilant guard dog.

10th March, 1883. 17:38.
'What is the meaning of this telegram?'
'Oh, hello, Mycroft. Can I offer you a whiskey?'
'As that appears to be gin, I shall decline.'
'Gin? So it is.' There were glug-glug sounds.
'Charming,' Mycroft said. 'The infant with his pabulum. Answer my question. What is the meaning of this telegram?'
'I meant to inform you that I am too much... much too busy to accompany you to Yorkshire.'
'This isn't a weekend in the country, Sherlock! Father has died. I believe you can take a week from your busy schedule to attend his funeral!'
'I cannot feign grief when I feel none. I've been trying all day. I had some hopes that the unpleasant after-effects might move me to tears in the morning -'
'Well, hang-dog or not, you will be on that train tomorrow morning at seven-thirty sharp if I have to drag you by the scruff of your neck! You've been spoiled and coddled all your life, Sherlock...'
'Oh, is that what it was? Here, my darling son, bend over and allow me to lavish my affections on your backside.'
Mycroft sighed heavily. 'Yes, yes, you're the only boy in the whole of England who was ever beaten with such cruelty. It's a wonder you survived, with your pony and your private tutors...'
'Ah. Here it comes, the litany of privileges denied the long-suffering eldest. Who, by the by, inherits everything.'
'Only the responsibilities, Sherlock. And one of those responsibilities is our sister.'
'I don't understand the problem,' Holmes said. 'Why can't Mrs Dougherty take care of her?'
'Mrs Dougherty is seventy years old and nearly blind. Jenny should be placed in an institution where she can be suitably cared for.'
'Mycroft! I've seen the vilest abuses in asylums. You can't put our sister in such a place!'
'I've had a very good private institution recommended to me.'
'How can you even consider it?'
'Have you a better idea?'
'She can live with one of us.'
'Let me guess which one.'
'*I'll* take her. I can find other lodgings -'
'Don't be an ass, Sherlock. You'd have to hire a nurse *and* a housekeeper. The out-of-pocket expenses would be crippling for you at this point in your career. '
'No asylums, Mycroft. Promise me that.'
'We can discuss it on the train -'
'Promise me that or I shall not be going.'

'Here is your ticket,' Mycroft said. 'Be there tomorrow or I'll have nothing further to do with you. Do you understand?' Silence. '*Do you understand?*'

'Perfectly.'

The next day Sherlock was gone. On the train to Yorkshire, I assumed, without his brother coming and dragging him by the scruff of his neck.

At four-thirty Sunday morning, I left the house through a service crawlspace used mostly by plumbers. I was afraid the more obvious exits might be watched. I wasn't wrong.

At the north end of the alley, the figure of a man leaned against the corner of the private hotel. Light from the street-lamp framed him as he shifted his feet and crossed his arms against the chill of the morning. He was dressed for the weather. Definitely not a vagabond. There were probably good reasons for a man to be lurking near an alley at four-thirty in the morning, but I couldn't think of any.

In my thick cloak, I crawled on my belly to the far side of the alley, pausing now and again to mimic a pile of refuse. It was the longest few yards I'd ever traversed. It took me another forty-five minutes of stealth to get to Mrs Tory's rooms.

I bathed and changed into my widow's gear, and was waiting for Mr Johnson at the back of the church much too early. Just me and the charwomen. I settled into my seat, bowed my head in sorrow and took a little snooze beneath my veils.

I was awakened by a gentle nudge. Evidently, I was the only person in church still sitting down. The gentleman next to me - not Shinwell - handed me a hymn book.

I gazed around, disoriented, wondering if I had somehow slept through the first service and was well into the second, but the light outside still showed early morning. I placed the hymnal on the bench and brushed past the parishioners to see if my contact was about.

A man in a tweed overcoat was standing in the vestibule. I pulled a hanky from my bag and began to weep quietly beneath my veils as I walked past. He glanced at me, then away. I continued to cry softly until I was past him, down a hall, and out through a side door. I'd just turned into the alley behind Argyle Street when I heard:

'Mrs Tory.' The words were low, spoken quickly, from somewhere to my left. I slowed, my eyes darting. In a recessed doorway, garish finery hidden beneath a huge astrakhan overcoat, Shinwell Johnson gestured to me. 'Quickly.'

I hurried toward him and he swept me inside.

He led me through a maze of corridors, up a flight of stairs and into a spacious private room. A full tester bed, heavily swagged in sunflower-coloured satin, occupied a central position. Curtains were drawn back, allowing light to spill over a highly-polished floor scattered with plain but very expensive rugs. Tea and dainty little sandwiches were already on the table.

'I hope you won't think ill of me bringin' to such a place, ma'am, but I could think of no other.'

Since I had only a vague suspicion of exactly what sort of place it was, I threw back my veils. 'I feared you had abandoned me altogether.'

He gazed at me thoughtfully then lowered his eyes. 'I'd considered it, but feared you'd be inquirin' as to my whereabouts, and that wouldn't do. Not under the circumstances.'

I took a deep breath. 'What are the circumstances, Mr Johnson?'

'Perhaps you should tell me, Mrs Tory.'

I held out my hand to him. 'Rose Donnelly.'

He stared at my offered hand and shook his head, wearing an odd, strained smile. For a moment, I thought it was the manliness of the gesture that caused his hesitation.

'Rose Donnelly is long dead,' he said. 'A nasty chap name of Tom Thornton dashed her brains out near White's Row a few months ago. I know, cuz Tommy was braggin' on it in one of the pubs 'round there, trying to keep his other girls in line. He was found dead in a pool of his own vomit a couple of days later. Peelers said he drowned in it, but the locals knew better.' He paused. 'You'd best sit, Mrs Tory. You've gone all pale on me.'

I sat stiffly in one of the gold chairs. 'What else do you know?'

'Well, for one, you're being followed by CID. And that does me no good at all.'

Oh God. The Criminal Investigation Department.

'Why?'

'Haven't the foggiest. Nor do you, apparently. Which hain't my problem, only I don't want to find m'self mixed up in their business as I'm sure you can understand.' My expression (and I can only imagine what I looked like at that moment) seemed to move him to a show of compassion. 'Let's have some tea and we'll try to sort it out. But, I have to tell you straight off, Mrs Tory -'

'Gillian,' I whispered. 'My name is Gillian.'

'Pretty name, that. Well, Gillian, I have to tell you that once you leave this room, I'll not be able to help you no further. I have my own affairs to consider, and those affairs overlap quite a few others who won't take kindly to being narked on.'

I looked up at him. 'A detective from the Yard wouldn't grab me off the street and try to throw me into the back of a furniture van, would he?'

He raised his brows, which barely managed to lift the fat folds of his face. 'Not bloody - beg pardon - likely, ma'am. When did this happen?'

'Wednesday.'

'Hmm. What did this fellow look like?'

I described the man as Johnson poured our tea. He seemed terribly impressed with my recall.

'Sounds a bit like a nobbler I know of, beats on those that don't pay. He goes by "China" Crow on account o' his eyes is like a Chinaman's. He's a Family Man. Gang nobility.' He shook his head in wonder. 'He's not the sort to be so delicate when he's got a job to do.'

'His touch was hardly delicate, Mr Johnson,' I said, as he handed me my cup and saucer.

He took a seat across from me, the massive armchair sighing from the weight of him. 'But, you see, ma'am, he's quite the artiste when it comes to blows. China can place a hit precisely, break whichever bone he chooses, or not break any at all if they's just supposed to suffer a fright. So, I'm wonderin' why he didn't give you a good clout over the head. Lucky you got away, Gillian, and I'm figurin' maybe the only reason you did is cuz them that's payin' China's fee didn't want you hurt.'

'How comforting.'

He shrugged, as if were neither here nor there to him. 'Well, it seems clear to me that someone don't like whatever it is you're doin' and wants you out of the way. Now, seein's how I don't know what you're doin' -' I looked at him sharply, and he held up his hand. 'And I don't want to know, believe me, but seein's how I don't, I can only speculate that whatever it is, it's become a threat. As to why Yard Bulls are skulkin' after you, you may need to seek clues from your mark on that subject.' I gazed at him blankly. 'Sherlock Holmes? He's your mark, right?'

Ah. I suppose it looked that way.

I remembered the wax impression I'd wrapped in a hanky, hopefully not melting, in my purse. I took it out. 'I need a key made, and I need it today, before I leave here.'

Sharp black eyes gazed at me. He nodded. 'Consider it done.'

'I have no money to give you at the moment, Mr Johnson.'

'Well, ma'am, I'd appreciate it if you'd repay me by forgettin' we ever met.'

'I have one more request.'

'You're strainin' the limits of my generosity, Gillian.'

'I'm sorry, but I must. There are two men, Dr Jacob Armitroy and Mr Shamus Tiramory. I need to know who they are, who they work for, and where they can be found.'

'I don't intend to meet with you again, Mrs Tory.'

'Send whatever you find to 221-B Baker Street, care of Sherlock Holmes.' I drew in a breath and blew it out real slow. 'Tell him it's from Gillian. He'll pay you for it.'

He searched my face for any hints of trickery and, seeing none, nodded.

Two hours later I left with a shiny new key in my handbag.

I was followed immediately after leaving Mrs Tory's rooms by the Bull in the tweed overcoat. Curiously, it made me feel safer. I even entertained the notion that Holmes had asked some of his chums at the Yard to keep an eye on me. But whatever the reason, I thought it best to pretend I didn't know he was there.

Chapter 19

Corkle's agenda was in his camcorder all along.

I wish to God I'd never found it. Everything that happened afterwards might have occurred in exactly the same way, but the pictures I saw wouldn't have been able to fill my mind the way they did in the days that followed, nor put the pall of evil over my role in the whole bloody business.

Monday morning, Mrs Hudson told me I needn't set a place at table for Mr Corkle. 'He's got a sick aunt in Chelsea, taken with influenza, poor dear. He left me a note, said he won't be back for a day or two. You can hold off on his room until tomorrow. If the weather holds, you'll have time to take the carpet up in the parlour and give it a good beating.'

Naturally I wondered what he was really up to, and as soon as I had a chance, I tried out my copy of the passkey to see if it worked. And because it did, I entered his room.

I was only looking for a place he might hide something he didn't want me to know about. I found that quickly, a single disc in a first edition of *Alice in Wonderland*. Glib and too obvious, I reasoned.

At the back of the bookshelf was a panel. Behind that, a hole in the plaster containing the camcorder and discs wrapped in oilskin. The images were remarkably clear, startling. My months in the nineteenth century had revived a sense of wonder at these technological marvels, and for a few moments I was spellbound by the thing I held in my hand.

A young man was dancing on the screen, something between a waltz and a strip-show strut. He seemed drugged or drunk. Possibly both. Corkle's voice provided the musical accompaniment, hushed and intimate, almost as if he were singing to me.

'You know what he wants to see, Stewart,' he murmured. 'Why don't you remove your vest?'

'Should I?' the boy asked. 'What if someone comes down?'

'We're safe here.'

The young man grinned slyly and began to unbutton the placket of his undershirt. His face was still soft around the edges, lips wet and pouty as a baby's. Long dark lashes batted slowly, unbearably slowly. But his body was a man's. The expanse of his chest revealed that fact as he removed his garments in sultry striptease, supposedly for the benefit of a third party.

I figured Corkle, the weasel, was filling his home DVD library with unusual Victoriana. The young man would end up sucking him off or something, and I sure as hell didn't want to see that. But I couldn't take my finger off the play button. Perhaps because the young man's name was Stewart, and that was the name of Harry Hughes's friend.

I pressed fast-forward until another image leapt out. For a second, I didn't realise I was still on fast-forward, because the picture looked almost like a still photograph. A body on a stone slab. Naked. Lanterns positioned on either side of his head, with shutters opened part-way, illuminating a drawn face, mouth open, eyes *wide* open, moving frantically in the sockets as if trying to see something just out of range, something moving in the darkness.

A hypodermic syringe, brown glass and scary-big needle, pierced the tender flesh of his left arm. This syringe was connected to a thin, black, rubber hose. The end of the hose was in a bucket on the floor. Blood dribbled into the pail.

I pressed "stop" and sat with that incongruous bit of technology in my hands, until muscles started to jerk, protesting at the tension of my grip. I picked up a disk at random and inserted it.

On makeshift table, draped with a white sheet, lay a little girl. Candles sputtered and hissed in a circle on the floor around her, a ritual space with a sacrificial altar in the centre. There were lanterns too, set on stacks of crates, shutters fully open, so that light spilled over her. It had all the trappings of a stage set for the theatre. The image shook and trembled as I watched it. I thought it was my own hands shaking, but it was the camera jiggling in the hand of its operator. A sound, the camera bumping against wood, being propped, steadied, and then Corkle's back came into view.

He went to the girl, and stepped into the ring of light, and the sacred space he'd created.

She had red hair, tangled, wet and dirty. Not Liza Murray. This one was younger. Maybe eight or nine. I could tell she was dead. Strange, that.

He circled her body, wineglass in hand, taking sips from it as he arranged her limbs, adjusted her filthy dress. He placed the glass on the table at the curve above her shoulder, then spread his fingers through the tangles of her hair and fanned it out, bright against the white sheet. He leaned over, cupping her small face between his palms, and kissed her forehead upside-down, gently pressing his thumbs over her eyelids as he did so, forcing them to close. When he removed his thumbs, the eyes popped open again, and he repeated the action, over and over. The skin at her temples was adored by his lips, then her mouth. He kissed the open mouth of a dead girl, squeezing the soft flesh of her cheeks and forcing her lips into mockeries of passion. I watched, listening to the smack of his lips, and his murmured words as if he were standing behind me, holding my head and propping my eyelids open.

Finally, he picked up his glass and moved slowly around the table, dragging his fingers along her body. Another swallow of wine, the glass set aside -

He threw up her skirt and thrust his hand between her legs. Tears burst from my eyes. I mean they *flew* out, as if I'd been slapped hard. Her little bottom came off the table and down again with a sound like a dead fish flopped onto the dock.

Then - oh, God - then he rolled his head and looked into my eyes as I watched. I felt the scream bubble up in my throat and get stuck there, as the camera slipped from my sweaty fingers, crashed against the edge of the bookshelf and tumbled to the floor.

For second I stood motionless, staring at it like some desiccated animal I'd tripped over in the street. Then I fell to my knees and started shoving things back into the hole. I hammered the panel into place with my fist, and arranged all the books and papers I'd pulled from the shelf, trying, desperately, to put them precisely where I'd found them. I couldn't think, couldn't remember anything, couldn't *see* anything but Corkle's eyes staring straight at me over the blue-white ankle of that little dead girl.

I ran down the hall, no idea where I was going, and was nearly out the back door before reason stopped me. I hadn't locked up his room again.

Rushing up the backstairs, I fumbled the key out of my pocket, dropped it, snatched it from the floor. The door swung in slightly. It was then that I began to recognise the other sounds I'd been hearing: Mrs Hudson's shrill protests, men's voices, clipped and officious.

Heavy-soled boots clattering up both sets of stairs -

I bolted for my own door and raced up the steps, trapping myself in the garret bedroom. A sheer panic reaction, but stupid, so stupid. It just made me look guilty to men who already thought I was.

'Stop right there, girl!'

Two young constables tripped over each other, bumping their helmets on the incline in their hurry to catch me. They were pumped on adrenaline and embarrassed about hitting their heads, so they took me with more force than was necessary, considering I had no place to run. Each grabbed one of my arms, and the key pinged to the floor at my feet.

'Sir,' one of them yelled, 'we've got her!'

Lestrade emerged at the top of the steps, looking pleased. When his eye caught mine there was a flash of wonder and curiosity. Then revulsion. He scooped up the key, tossed it high and caught it tight in his hand.

They found things searching my room, things that hadn't been there when I'd got up that morning. A lady's watch and fob. Love letters to a woman named Julia. Tickets. Travel-papers. Some highly inflammatory pamphlets printed by the Fenians. And a small bag of money and jewellery, the latest take from the robbery in Manchester Street. Even as I stood watching, transfixed and helpless, aware that every protest to ignorance I uttered sounded false, I was struck by the sheer amount of evidence. Everywhere I looked there was more.

I could hear Mrs Hudson's anxiety and outrage in the hall below, as the constables wreaked their havoc on my bedstead and my precious feather pillow. They'd started emptying the drawers and prying up the floorboards.

Watson muscled his way up the stairs, and stood breathless, looking around. I made a gesture of desperate confusion before Lestrade bounded over to him.

'Well, sir, much as I'm loathe to admit it,' he said, 'your friend had it right, and I'd like to thank him for putting me onto the idea.'

'Right?' Watson echoed.

'About the burglar being female. We figured he was investigating the girl himself. One of the lads from "G" division saw Holmes with her Wednesday last. We got an anonymous tip,' he said, elbowing Watson in the side and winking. 'She's quite a piece of work, isn't she?' His eyes fixed on me for a nasty moment. 'Where *is* Mr Holmes? Thought he'd want to be in on this.'

'He's... he's been called away,' Watson said, his voice flat, toneless. His eyes moved around the crowded room, watching the methodical, heedless search of my belongings. 'Oh!' He cried suddenly. 'Careful with that.'

I turned. A bobby was lifting my guitar from the case, trying to shake any hidden booty out of the soundboard. 'No, sir, please! There's nothing in it. Please!'

A decoration, Most Honourable Order of the Bath, in cheap gold wash and enamel, fell out.

Another man was pulling books from my satchel. Music books and songsheets. The journals were gone.

After ticking off a list of items, Lestrade tucked the notepad in his breast pocket and shifted the key from one hand to the other. 'This looks to be a master-key.'

Oh Christ. The duplicate.

'I believe Mrs Hudson allows her to use it on laundry days, Inspector,' Watson was saying. 'Really, we've had nothing stolen from us in this house.'

Lestrade handed the key to Watson. 'You'd best give this over to the landlady, then. Have her take stock just to make certain.'

'The girl was coming out of the room on the floor below, sir,' the policemen on my left arm said. Lestrade nodded and gave Watson a telling look, as if to say, "that's the place to start".

My knees buckled then, and after that, a blur. Watson throwing his own coat over my shoulders after they'd cuffed me. Being escorted from the house, flanked by policemen in full view of a growing crowd of neighbours and passers-by. Being pushed into the police van.

At the station, I submitted to a tentative search of my person by a man. There was no matron present, so he just sort of patted me down, embarrassed and angry at the wicked female who'd made it necessary for him to touch her so familiarly. He removed the sewing-kit from my apron pocket, the only thing I had that could be used to inflict bodily harm. After that I was pushed into a holding cell with three drunken "unfortunates" and two petty thieves.

Two hours later, I was interrogated by Lestrade and a Detective Inspector Clarke.

'Are you fond of persons of your own sex?' Clarke asked. As if that pertained to the crime at all.

I was moved to a new cell, which I had all to myself. After a few hours I stopped expecting a big, ugly bloke to come in and show me what he thought I'd been missing. Which left me with nothing to occupy my thoughts but the horror I'd viewed that morning, vivid images in living colour that wouldn't shut off no matter how hard I tried. Prison seemed safe compared to the suspense of waiting for Corkle to discover what I'd seen and what I knew about him.

Holmes was the only person, besides the rooftop robber herself, who knew who she really was. And he was gone. My arrest for this crime had been set in motion long before. By the time he returned from Yorkshire on Friday, I'd have entered my plea and would be stuck in a cell for months awaiting trial.

I sat on the cot, praying for escape to every name that God was known to use amongst mortal beings. Finally, I did what most people do in such situations. I cried like a baby.

***

The following morning, Tom Corkle came to see me, all dressed up in a nice suit. Round collar, black cravat, new felt bowler on his head. He was wearing his spectacles and looked so ordinary. 'Your solicitor, Mr Gray,' the warder announced, as he let a monster into the only sanctuary I had. The monster carried a leather satchel and a folding stool.

I rose the instant I saw him, but I had nowhere to run. My legs wouldn't hold me up and I found myself on the cot again, inching as far away from him as I could. Watson's thick overcoat suddenly became a magic suit of armour.

Corkle unfolded his stool and sat on it.

'Good morning, Rose. How was your night? Not too frightful?'

Not daring to speak, I focused on the toes of his shoes and shook my head.

'Not bad for a nineteenth-century jail cell,' he commented. 'I've seen far worse, believe me.'

The cell was a brick cubicle with an open-hole commode in the corner, a wash basin bolted to the wall, and a iron cot with canvas stretched across it. The only light came from the gas fixtures in the corridor outside. No rats. The blanket on the cot was clean. No fleas.

Corkle's feet shifted, disturbing the straw carpeting as he adjusted his butt on the stool. 'I've come to lay the facts before you, darling,' he said.

I knew I'd have to look up eventually, but I found that if I concentrated on his shoes then I could at least get sound to come from my throat. 'You set me up,' I croaked.

'Yes, well, thought that was a given. No need to belabour the point.'

He leaned forward suddenly. I pulled back, stuffing the edge of Watson's coat-sleeve into my mouth to stopper a cry.

'My goodness,' he said, sounding genuinely surprised. 'This has really shaken you up, hasn't it?'

I looked up at him, amazed at the wicked, presumptuous gall of the man. 'Yes!' I cried. 'It's shaken me up quite a bit, you evil little prick!'

He appeared chastened, his face reddening. 'It's not as bad as it seems, Gillian. I'm unclear as to how much you know, and that's my main concern at the moment, you understand?'

'Apparently, I know too much.'

He chuckled softly. 'I think you know very little. I do know you've spoken of matters you shouldn't have.'

I swiped the coat-sleeve roughly across my eyes and nose. 'I searched my room, but I couldn't find the bug.'

He clicked his tongue, a mockery of chagrin. 'I had to keep tabs on you. The problem here is that you've shown you can't be trusted to maintain your scientific objectivity. You've messed with the program, my dear, and that's caused me a lot of scrambling to get back on track again. There's an overarching purpose to all of this.'

'And that is?'

'What's your best guess?'

Keeping my eyes on my lap, and the comfort of the wool garment belonging to the only true gentleman I'd ever met, I said: 'Don't have one. But I think I might be going to prison just the same.' Corkle's voice took on a tone of vague annoyance. 'It's possible. Very likely, in fact. Substantial physical evidence, and a member of parliament victimised by your thieving ways. He'll put the pressure on, unless I say otherwise. As it stands, even if Holmes can clear you of these charges -'

'He knows who the thief really is, remember?'

'Poor Gillyflower, you really are quite in the dark, aren't you? I'm saying that even if he can get you off... and isn't it funny, haven't I overheard him doing just that? Anyway, it won't matter, because there'll be nothing left for you outside. No position to return to, no bank accounts to draw from...

'Don't look so frightened, darling. All is not lost. I have another proposal. Cut off any further contact with Holmes and the good doctor, and I'll see to it that you have plenty of funds, some really fabulous frocks, and a comfortable place to live until we go back.'

I stared at him. What trick was this? Why was he making this offer when we both knew it would only arouse Holmes's suspicions? How stupid did the man think I was? It'd be far easier for Corkle to arrange a convenient suicide for me in my cell.

Unless... he didn't know what I'd seen.

'Look,' he continued, 'I know you're fond of the chap, God only knows why. But honestly, if you engage him again then I can't guarantee you'll make the send-forward.'

Of course. My ticket back to the twenty-first. My friends, my family. I rocked forward with a low moan.

'You want to go home, don't you, darling?'

...and the son-of-a-bitch patted my knee.

I sprang from the cot, fists beating him anywhere they could. The stool toppled as he fell backwards. But he was only startled for a moment. He was up and on me, arms locked and pinning my own to my sides as he wrestled me down. He pushed my face to the floor. I twisted and writhed beneath him, scraping my cheek, jaw, mouth -

'Don't make me hurt you, Gillian.' His knee dug into my back. 'That would be very bad for both of us.' He stroked my hair, my neck. He was *touching* me, touching me with the same hands that he'd shoved between the dead girl's legs.

The jangle of metal and the scrape of the key in the lock brought him to his feet again. 'No, no, constable, all's well. I've not been injured. The poor creature is overwrought.'

The warder jerked me up, nearly pulling my shoulder from the socket as he raised his truncheon.

Corkle righted his spectacles, one hand out to stay the intended blows. 'There's no need for further violence. I've not been harmed.' His glasses were bent and sat lopsided on his nose. 'I think she's calming down a bit. Aren't you, dear?'

The warder let go. I sank onto the cot, fell sideways, and stayed that way.

'I'll be just outside, sir, if she's a mind for more trouble.' He grasped his truncheon with a pointed look and stepped just beyond the door. He didn't close it.

I could feel Corkle gazing at me, but I wouldn't look up.

'You should know,' he said, his voice like dry ice, 'that you're up before the magistrate the day after tomorrow. I suggest you consider my offer.'

Chapter 20

'Donnelly!'

I bolted up, anxiety twisting my gut.

The warder, whose name I'd learned was Mr Pitty (or as another woman on the ward had called him, Mr Pity-It's-So-Small), banged on the door with his truncheon / penis-extender and yelled my name again.

Oh God, oh God. Corkle was back. He knew what I'd seen. Brought poison, some lethal needle to jab into me when the warder's back was turned...

But it was Holmes, dressed in his superhero costume, Inverness cloak and deerstalker. He stepped into that cell as if it were some great mansion's drawing room and Mr Pitty the butler.

He hesitated a moment, elegant nostrils flaring at the smell. Seeing nowhere else to sit, he placed his parcels on the cot and perched his spare, lanky frame beside me; still managing - in a man's way - to take up most of the space. I knew I'd never be able to send him away. So I kept my head lowered, messy hair obscuring as much of my face as possible. When he took my hand and squeezed it, I couldn't help myself.

We gasped at the same time, and it was almost funny how our faces mirrored each other's, both in the emotions and the injuries. Before I could ask him what had happened to *his* face, he leapt from the cot to accost the constable as he dutifully attempted to lock the door.

'What in God's name have you done to her?'

The warder took a startled step back. 'Sir?'

'Her face, man!'

''Ere now! She done that to 'erself, tryin' to nobble 'er shyster.'

Holmes looked back at me. I jerked my shoulders in a shrug and whispered: 'I didn't like the look of him.'

He turned back to the warder. 'Fetch something to clean those wounds.'

Mr Pitty hitched up his trousers in an attempt to recover his dignity. 'Not obliged to take orders from you.'

Holmes handed the man a coin. '*Now*, if you please.'

Pitty made a face, rubbed his nose, then took the coin. The key turned in the lock, and we waited until the sound of his footsteps had faded.

'Have they treated you well otherwise?' Holmes asked. 'Because if they haven't... if any one of them has done anything improper or indecent...'

'No, Sherlock,' I interrupted. 'Other than occasional speculations about my gender preference, they've all been perfect gentlemen.'

He considered this statement, momentarily bemused. 'Oh. Lestrade's been talking. Don't let it trouble you.' He sat beside me again, and the left side of his face came into view.

'What happened to you?' I asked.

'I was nobbled by my doctor.'

'Watson?' I couldn't imagine Watson doing the fisticuffs bit. 'Why? What did you do?'

'Why do you assume...?' he began then gave a rueful laugh. 'It would be difficult to believe he struck without cause, I suppose.'

He offered me an orange and took one for himself, digging his thumb under the rind as he spoke. 'He told me what had happened as soon as I arrived this morning. He was quite angry that I hadn't bothered to inform him he'd been living with the rooftop burglar for months. When I told him how I knew you were not, he responded by punching me in the jaw and calling me a despicable rogue.' I started to laugh. It was the first time I'd laughed in days, it seemed. 'He's also under the mistaken impression that I seduced you, and refuses to believe what a wicked temptress you are.'

'Watson's such a darling man,' I said.

'He has the most adorable knuckles.' I traced the red swelling along his jaw and he pulled away, wincing. 'It looks much worse than it is. Anyway, Watson was right. *Peccavi*, "I have sinned". I should never have left London when I did...' He popped a orange section in his mouth. It was only there for a second before he was spitting it back into his hand. 'Damn,' he hissed between his teeth. He touched his jaw. 'Must've bit the inside of my cheek when he hit me.'

'Poor baby,' I clucked sympathetically.

He grunted, peering at the abrasions on my cheek. 'Why did you attack your solicitor, Gillian?'

I swallowed hard. 'He said I'm probably going to prison.'

'Rubbish! What kind of a solicitor is he? Give me the man's name and I shall thrash him for you.'

Our eyes met. He clearly knew I was holding back and I clearly knew he was trying to manipulate me into spilling my guts. He was motivated by the sincerest desire to help me, but I could tell him nothing, not if I entertained any hope of getting home. I looked down at my hands, still wrapped around the orange. A splash of hot tears fell on them.

Holmes sighed and lobbed the rest of the fruit into the commode. This was followed by the quick grin of triumph that all boys wear when making the basket on the first try. For some reason this made me cry more.

'Enough,' he said gently. 'You are not going to prison. You mustn't worry on that account. If worse comes to worst I shall offer myself as an alibi.'

Nice of him to offer, but it was pretty obvious he hoped he wouldn't have to. 'Think of the scandal,' I said. 'Your career might never recover.'

He laughed softly. 'Such a sacrifice will hardly be necessary. I've more than enough evidence to prove your innocence in these matters.' I wiped my face on my apron. 'Oh, I nearly forgot.' He withdrew an envelope from his cloak. 'Watson found this. Well, he stepped on it actually.' He emptied the contents onto his lap. 'I wonder if you might know what it is?'

I stared at the broken compact disc, unable to connect the broken pieces with the place, the cell, the man holding them. The room began to spin, and I leapt up to outrun disaster. The pan of porridge I hadn't finished that morning banged into a corner from the mad scrabble of my feet, and I tore my nails clawing at the bricks before turning around to face calamity. I sank down the wall, both hands pressed over my mouth.

Holmes had taken his cue from my reaction, and now stood with his back pressed to the cell door, staring at the broken disc as if it were a poisonous snake, or a bomb about to go off. Which, in a very real way, it was.

I'd left a disc on the floor of Corkle's room. Watson had stepped on it. If he'd spoken of it to Holmes, if Corkle had heard them...

I gathered the pieces off the floor, and stuffed them back into the envelope. At the jangle of the warder's keys, I grabbed Holmes by the coat, and jerked him to me, shoving the envelope into his coat pocket.

'Don't show this to anyone else - *anyone* - do you understand?' He nodded, eyes wide, clenching his fist over the pocket. I pressed my fingers over his hand. 'And for God's sake, don't talk about it to anyone, especially in the sitting room. It's not safe. He can -'

The door opened, and I snapped my mouth shut. The warder had brought a basin of water, a bottle of something antiseptic, and a flannel. He looked at the closeness of our bodies and attributed the charge in the atmosphere to something else.

If he noticed how the young detective's hands were shaking as they dabbed the scrapes on my face, he never said a word.

***

Corkle didn't show the next day, which only served to fuel my creeping terror.

I refused the food and watery beer they brought me, choosing instead the sure safety of Holmes's oranges. Not that Corkle couldn't manage to kill me with something other than poison, but I clung fast to the talisman of the oranges. They were from Holmes, and therefore imbued with magical properties.

But on Thursday afternoon, instead of being hustled off to the Marylebone County Court, the arresting officers sent for me.

Dressed in the clean clothing Holmes had brought me, I stood before Inspectors Lestrade and Clarke from Scotland Yard. With them was Chief Constable Morrison, a pinched and weary man who'd long ago chosen the three-strand comb-over method to announce his baldness to the world. They sat at a long table cluttered with stacks of papers and cardboard boxes. Sherlock Holmes sat with them. All of them were facing me.

The scent of my own nervous perspiration seemed rank in spite of the clean clothes, and I found myself lowering my eyes in their presence. I wasn't offered a chair, but rather made to stand like the bad girl they thought I was.

Without preamble, Morrison said: 'Miss Donnelly. Mr Holmes here seems to think he can prove your innocence in the matters of these robberies, about which you claim to have no knowledge. He has managed to convince the magistrate that we must be very certain of the validity of your arrest.' Morrison was clearly miffed that this youngster had the temerity to go over his head. 'Mr Holmes? Get on with it.'

Holmes scraped his chair back from the table and jumped to his feet. 'Right then. We'll begin with the obvious fact that the letters were planted in Miss Donnelly's room to serve as an indictment against her.'

'And how do you figure that, Mr Holmes?' Lestrade growled.

'Is it obvious only to myself? The letters were addressed to a Julia. Why would she have letters which she had presumably sent to Julia in her possession, and not those addressed to herself?'

'Perhaps the name is an alias,' Lestrade commented, 'or hadn't you thought of that?'

'The Julia of the letters is a person apart from Miss Donnelly, as I will show.'

'Then isn't it likely this Julia person thought better of the whole sordid business and returned the letters?' Clarke asked.

Holmes arched a brow. 'Have you read the letters, Inspector? Yes, I can see by your blushes that you have. The correspondence dates over a three-year period, the last from only two weeks ago. There is every indication that this relationship was an ongoing one.' He flipped the lid off of one of the cardboard boxes and withdrew a letter. Entirely at random and, I suspected, mostly for effect. 'The author and recipient had made plans to run away to Paris together. They'd booked passage separately so as not to arouse suspicion.'

'Evidence we found in this girl's room, by the by.'

'*Planted* evidence, as is the booty you discovered in Miss Donnelly's room. The robbery in Manchester Street was over a fortnight ago, yet the take included everything on the list and then some. None of it had been turned into cash. Now, part of the modus operandi of the burglar was the unusually quick disposal of the take. She had reliable contacts and made good use of them.'

'That proves nothing,' Clarke said. 'Perhaps she hadn't the time or opportunity -'

'She was planning a trip to the continent, sir! She'd need to spend a bit of it, don't you think? Yet, it was fully accounted for, to the penny.'

'You said "had",' Morrison interjected, 'she "had" reliable contacts. You have reason to believe she no longer has?'

'I have reason to believe she's dead,' Holmes said quietly.

My chest tightened. Another horror piled on top of so many others. I knew that foolish girl, with her foolish daring and her foolish love, had gone the way of Liza Murray and Stewart Ronaldson.

'Her name is, or *was* rather, Carolina Lopenski,' Holmes continued. 'Her parents were Czechoslovakian aerialists - circus people, Lestrade - who died during a performance in this country, leaving her an orphan, forced to make her way as so many other girls before her; in domestic service. She was taken into the house of Sir Felix Upton, who happens to have a daughter named Julia, and from whose household Carolina has been missing for a fortnight. Miss Julia Upton is in Paris. Miss Lopenski was your rooftop robber, Inspector Lestrade, and had I but told you this when I knew it to be so, she might still be alive and learning a hard lesson in prison.'

There was silence for a moment. Then Morrison spoke. 'You understand that this confession may lead to you being brought up on charges of misprision of felony?'

Holmes swallowed hard. He bowed his head, in genuine contrition. 'Yes, sir.'

'Why would anyone go to such trouble to implicate Miss Donnelly in these crimes?'

'That is something I intend to discover, sir.'

I looked quickly at my feet. Worse and worse. If he got me off, I'd have to go into hiding. As if *that* would be possible, given the two men I'd be hiding from.

'We can hardly release the woman based on your say-so. The goods were still found hidden in the floorboards beneath her bedstead.'

Holmes tugged on his earlobe, a casual gesture that disguised his irritation with the man. 'Well, the proof is in the pudding, Inspector.'

He reached beneath the table and withdrew a window-frame from a gunnysack, complete with pane of glass, latch, everything save the building from which it came. Lestrade threw up his hands and rolled his eyes heavenward. Holmes carried this prop around the table to the centre of the room.

'Miss Donnelly? Would you come here, please?'

I shot him a look of wary trepidation as I moved to join him.

'The dimensions are exactly the same as those of the attic windows at the house in Manchester Street, and also of two other burgled houses. As you can see, the latching mechanism is a standard one.' He demonstrated this to the gentleman, opening the framed glass on its hinges. 'There are three of these windows in the attic at the Manchester Street house. We will assume that Miss Donnelly was able to jimmy the latches from the outside while clinging to rain-slicked ledges.' He pried the pins loose from the hinges and removed the paned shutter. 'I will now ask Miss Donnelly to fit through just the casement itself.'

The window was long, but very narrow, maybe fourteen inches wide. The gentlemen were already having doubts as their eyes flicked from my hips, to the frame, and back to my hips again.

'Must we?' I said tersely.

'I believe we need to prove this beyond a shade of doubt, Rose.'

I raised my arms above my head like a southern belle being helped into her crinoline. Turning the frame sideways, the way it'd look if I were slipping through it, the prop moved over my arms, past my head, past my shoulders. Over my torso to my hips, and with effort, farther down, coming to an abrupt halt over the mounds of flesh that Lestrade had, once-upon-a-time, found so biscuit-y.

I squirmed and twisted within the confines of the wooden aperture, but short of splintering the wood, the frame wouldn't budge. Though I was happy to have my innocence proven, I couldn't help but feel a bit irritated that I stood before three Victorian police officers with a window-frame stuck on my arse.

It took two hours to negotiate the paperwork for my release. And then I was free. Whatever that meant. Outside were the signs of spring returning - birds, crocuses, trees in timid bud - hopeful signs, cruelly flaunted.

We returned to the house on Baker Street immediately upon leaving the Marylebone police court. Holmes was naively surprised when Mrs Hudson refused to let me in, even to retrieve my belongings.'

'But I have proved her innocent.'

'That's as may be, sir. But what with all the neighbours gossiping and pointing at me, I can barely hold my head up when I walk out. My reputation is besmirched, Mr Holmes.'

'By taking her back into your employ, you will prove them to be the foolish dolts they are.'

'I've lost two lodgers because of this, sir. Mr Cavendish has gone to stay with his sister in Lambeth rather than live in my house. And Mr Corkle was most distressed. Two hired men came and took away his goods -'

'Corkle is gone?' I choked out. 'When?'

'Last night. Not that it's your business to know, my girl.'

'Do you know where he went?' I persisted. Holmes shot a glance at me, which I ignored.

'He left no forwarding address. Mr Corkle was most distressed, as I've said, Mr Holmes. What with the constables in my house, stomping about, accusing me of harbouring criminals.' Her lower lip began to tremble, and she bit it stoically, saying: 'He was a good gentleman. Quiet, and he paid his rent on time. I shan't find lodgers as respectable as them two. Not now.'

'Then you would not care to lose another, Mrs Hudson, I'm sure,' Holmes said, between clenched teeth.

She looked at him, twisting her apron. 'You'd not make me choose, sir, knowing the truth of the matter as you do.'

She was on the verge of tears. I touched Holmes's arm. 'Leave it. It's not worth the bother.'

I decided to check out Widow Tory's lodgings in St Pancras right away. I had money in a lock-box there, not much, but enough to get me out of Dodge for a month or two. Holmes was still fuming when I reached for the gate-latch. 'Do you have any money?' I asked.

His expression was guarded. 'Some.'

'For cab fare, I mean.'

'Oh. Yes. Certainly.'

Across from the lodgings in Midhope Street, I considered how best to approach the landlady. The driver tugged the reins of his impatient horse. Holmes looked at the dwelling, then at me. *Now what?* his expression said.

'I need you to go to the door and inquire after a Mrs Tory. Tell the landlady that you're a friend of her late husband's. You've just returned from the Dutch East Indies.'

He snorted. 'Look at my face. I'm white as white can be. She'll never believe I've been in the tropics.'

'You've had a bout of malaria,' I said irritably.

'Am I merely to inquire after the lady?' he asked. 'Goodness gracious, what if she is at home? Surely Mrs Tory would know her late husband's associates?'

'She's *not* at home.'

Holmes smirked, patted me on the knee, and bounded out of the cab. He handed the driver a coin and bade him wait. He was back in five minutes.

'You're right. The lady's not at home. Apparently, her grief was inconsolable. She's suffered an acute bout of nervous prostration and has been sent to an asylum in Switzerland. Her belongings were packed into a *grey* furniture van by two men this very morning.'

I groaned. No money. The driver cleared his throat impatiently while Holmes stood peering in at me, one hand on the side of the hansom. Waiting.

'I'm totally fucked,' I said, smiling hysterically.

His eyes widened, startled by the obscenity, and gave his head a little shake to erase it from his brain. The driver was less forgiving. 'What's tha' she said?'

'The lady's afraid the horse will buck,' Holmes replied suavely, hopping in beside me.

'Bless ye, missus, no need to worry 'bout ol' Bess, 'ere. She's anxious to be at 'er feed, that's all. She'll not go kicking her traces.'

My companion adjusted the lap rug over our knees again and called out: 'Then we'd best be off so old Bess can eat.'

He gave the driver an address in St John's Wood, which proved to be the newly-acquired townhouse of Mr Harry Hughes.

Chapter 21

I dreamed I was home again in my mother's kitchen, standing at the sink and looking out onto her tiny backyard garden with its flurry of flowers and lack of vegetables. Bright yellows and pinks and purples were awash with sunlight, the greens impossibly green. A feeling of happiness and contentment, the sort I'd never appreciated or, perhaps, recognised in waking life. It was the peace that came from knowing I was home.

I awakened disoriented, the way I often had when I'd first arrived. Back then there'd been excitement in the waking too. Now, just the dull ache of knowing I was so far from home that the distance could only be travelled in dreams. I was in the guestroom of Sherlock Holmes's erstwhile friend Harry, and I might never go home again.

I rose, wrapped myself in a man's dressing gown hanging in the wardrobe, and proceeded to wander the house like the victim of disaster I was. In the drawing room I found tea and biscuits. The maid Alice informed me that Master Hughes was out and that my 'cousin, Mr Holmes' would return early evening with my belongings. She was quite casual about my appearance in dishabille. Too embarrassed to ask for anything more substantial, I munched the biscuits and drank the tepid tea. As soon as she left the room, I grabbed a decanter of brandy from the sideboard and returned to the guestroom.

It was possible that I'd live out my life and die here in nineteenth-century London. A few searing gulps of brandy had me wondering what the hell I was doing here in the first place.

Jimmy Moriarty had recruited me with all the verve and enthusiasm of a true history geek, dangling all my academic obsessions before me like shiny charms on a bracelet: the waves of opposition to colonial imperialism across the world during the 1880's, the rise of militant Islam in Indonesia, the effects of aniline dyes on the fashion industry, mesmers and physiognomy, and of course, the budding art of scientific criminal investigation. My speciality.

The energy requirements for my return trip had necessitated the choice of a year in which a major volcanic eruption had occurred. Krakatoa had erupted in August 1883. This had determined a locus for the research, which met specific criteria: the personal history of Sherlock Holmes, heretofore unknown, was to be harvested from the very people who'd wiped his butt when he was a baby, taught him his sums, been to school with him... or worked in his house.

I filled my glass again and sipped at it more slowly.

Opportunity of a lifetime. Career ace-in-the-hole. Of course, the only thing I could see now was Corkle's video noir.

He'd been setting up an outré scenario with that little girl in the warehouse, hadn't he? Something designed to draw Holmes in. But Holmes had refused to be drawn. So another case had been choreographed into existence. Corkle producing and directing. Moriarty making a cameo appearance in anagrams. Of course, my other persona, the grieving widow Mrs Maria Tory, had already borne his mark. The joke had amused me way-back-when.

I could easily believe that Corkle enjoyed what he was doing, but what could Moriarty possibly get out of it? He had no need to manipulate the world powers of the nineteenth century, because in the twenty-first he had everything he wanted. Perhaps it was simply a science fair project on a grand scale. For some reason, that scared me. It was a motivation I could actually understand.

I drained the decanter into my glass and laid myself out like a corpse on the bed. The light deepened from afternoon into evening. I excused myself from tea, refused supper. I was ashamed to be waited on and couldn't will myself to get up, even when I heard Alice let Holmes in the front door.

'Master's not t'home sir,' I heard her say, 'but the lady's upstairs. She's feelin' poorly.'

'Thank you,' his voice replied, an automatic civility, projected before him like trumpets heralding the king. My saviour. My responsibility.

The door opened, spilling a flood of gaslight over the foot of the bed. I heard him gasp: 'Dear God.'

Bundles dropped to the floor, then quick steps to my side, lifting my wrist as it lay over my breast. He peered at my face, sniffed at the alcoholic waft rising from me, and let my hand plop back onto my chest. Eyes flicked to the empty brandy decanter, then me. Of course, I couldn't look away. I also had nothing to offer. After a moment he sat on the edge of the bed with his back to me, shoulders hunched, head bowed.

'Did you drop my guitar?' I asked, voice raspy, words slurred.

'I left it downstairs in the entry hall.'

'What about my books? My... music books.' I struggled to one elbow. 'Did you find them?'

He stomped across the room to the heap of my worldly possessions piled in the hallway. 'Those books which are as much music books as a banker's ledgers? No, I didn't find them.' He pushed the pile into the bedroom with his foot. 'Your code is not so difficult to decipher if one has the vaguest understanding of musical notation. Roman numerals representing the triad qualities of chords, for instance.' A sharp kick shut the door behind him.

'It must be a little more complicated than that or you'd be telling me all about myself right now.'

'Oh, that's clever, Gillian. Or may I call you "Gillian" here in the boudoir?'

I didn't answer. The room was spinning and I couldn't even shrug my acquiescence. He turned up the jet on the wall-sconce, and I moaned at the assault of light.

'Whoever has them now may be far more adept at transcribing them. But I rather suspect you know that.' He folded his arms over his chest and examined the floor. 'I had managed to decipher some of it.'

I wondered when. How long we'd been dancing this dance. He continued to avoid my eyes, which gave me the impression that whatever he'd deciphered wasn't terribly illuminating.

'I hope it wasn't about our sexual frolics. That would be really embarrassing.'

'Don't mock me!'

'I'm not mocking you, Sherlock -'

'I've had a very trying day, Gillian, very trying.' He took a deep breath and looked me in the eye. 'I was robbed.'

'Robbed?' I repeated dully. 'At the house?'

The detective laughed; a hot, bitter sound. 'No. A first class tooler picked my pocket.' He banged his fist against the wall. 'Me! Plucked like a chicken right on the street!'

Even through the leaden effects of alcohol, the irony struck deep. It was one of the first things I'd witnessed him doing, picking a man's pocket, long ago in Petticoat Lane. Why should that make me sorry? It was his karma, not mine.

'And do you know what he got for all his efforts?' he continued. 'Can you guess?'

I started to get nervous. He expected me to know. It was evident in his body language. 'What?' I whispered.

'An envelope containing useless broken shards!'

Oh, Christ. Holmes had lost the disc to a pickpocket, probably one of Corkle's people. A giggle welled up. Oh my God. Corkle had "people".

I noticed Holmes staring at me, but I was too drunk to interpret the look.

'He took my watch as well,' he said, then thrust a hand in his waistcoat pocket and pulled out a mangled case swinging from the chain. 'He dropped the watch.'

I gulped hard and heard it echoing over and over inside my head.

'It's a relief to you, isn't it?' The bitterness in his voice was like salt on a slug.

'I don't... I'm not sure what you mean.'

'The object which frightened you so badly when you saw it, there in the cell. It's gone now, and you're relieved.'

It was true. I was relieved. He'd seen this in me before I'd even made note of the feeling. If Corkle had it, then at least it wasn't being subjected to Holmes's chemical experiments. And if the pickpocket were an ordinary thief, not in the employ of Corkle, he'd see it as useless, something to be tossed in the river.

But my relief was a kind of betrayal. And more, something else that Holmes was only now acknowledging to himself: *This mystery is beyond my abilities to unravel. The answers are too strange for me to bear. This woman will drive me to madness.*

In three quick strides he was at the bed, his fingers digging into my shoulders, lifting my listless body and shaking me so hard that I bit my tongue.

'You knew it would be stolen, didn't you?' he cried. *'Didn't you!'*

'No!'

'You did! You wicked, lying whore!' Shaking me, shaking me until my brain rattled. 'What was it? Why was it taken from me?' His eyes stabbed at me over and over again, at my head, my heart. 'Who are you working for?'

'Stop it!'

'Who are you? Why are you doing this to me?'

'Leave. Me. Alone!'

He gave one last shake, and tossed me away from him with a growl of disgust. With himself or me, it no longer mattered.

I sank into the downy mattress, feeling the numb weight of the past few hours leave my body like air from a balloon, replaced by an influx of adrenaline and the intense power of outrage. I'd had enough. Of him, of Corkle, Moriarty, the whole business.

I sprang from the bed, my fists like hammers on his retreating back. 'I didn't know, you bastard!' I screamed. 'I don't know anything!' If the statement lacked verisimilitude, it rang with emotional truth.

He spun, dodging the hammer aimed at his face. His fingers closed around my left forearm, while his other hand locked over the fist falling inexorably toward his heart. My own fingers splayed and curled, trying to claw into his chest while I called him every name in my twenty-first-century lexicon of filth.

I'll never forget his expression just before he shoved me. A man facing a treacherous beast.

I probably wouldn't have flown so far, or fallen so hard, if I hadn't been clumsy from the alcohol. But my feet left the floor, my arms wheeling frantically, trying to stop my momentum. I fell against the wardrobe, right elbow impacting with a heavy brass pull.

Like most reasonable men with a modicum of self-control, the raw pulse of energy that made it possible for him to knock me on my butt dissipated as soon as he realised he'd actually done it.

A weird silence followed, punctuated by my hissing gasps and his ragged breathing.

'Oh God, Rose!' Rose, he called me, a poignant and pointed distinction of which he was barely aware. His hands fluttered like moths around my head and shoulders. 'I never meant... never intended... '

The door was flung open, revealing an outraged Harry in evening clothes, with Alice cringing behind him.

'Sherlock! Stop this at once!'

He pushed Holmes aside and knelt to wrap a cape-enshrouded arm about my shoulders. 'What in the name of God do you think you're doing? You've quite terrified your... your cousin, and worse, you've frightened the help!'

Holmes and I exchanged mortified glances before we both lowered our heads in shame. Apparently, my shame closely resembled victimisation. Harry clucked, tightening his arm around my shoulder, and then got a good whiff of my breath.

'Grief! A certain young lady has been tipping the bottle, hasn't she? I hope you haven't given her cause, old man, because I shall be -' Holmes had no opportunity to answer this charge, however, for when Harry went to pull me to my feet, my injured elbow refused to straighten out. I sat back on the floor, whimpering through my teeth. 'Good lord,' he whispered, staring at Holmes as if seeing the monster beneath the mask. 'You've actually hurt her. Have you lost your mind?'

Holmes voice was thick and painfully quiet. 'I apologise for the upset, but if you would kindly leave us a moment -'

'I think perhaps it's you who'd best be leaving, Sherlock,' Harry said.

I stiffened, my eyes wide enough to take in oceans.

Holmes stared at his shoes. 'You don't understand the situation.'

'No. I didn't understand when my father knocked my mother about either. But it will not happen here. Please *go*.'

The detective gazed at Harry, whose quiet authority in his own house couldn't be questioned, and I saw the mortar in his solid wall begin to crumble. I heard it in the sound of him swallowing, in the butterfly whisper of his eyes blinking. 'Yes. Forgive me. I've behaved... abominably.' But he looked at me, not at Harry. And I could see that he didn't seek my forgiveness, only answers to questions he could no longer ask.

My body leaned toward his, pulled by the need for resolution, closure, or a way to start anew. He took an involuntary step back, then another, shaking his head. He inclined a tense bow in Harry's direction and left.

His exit had all the appearance of humble dignity. But considering how his steps faltered on the landing, then quickened on the way down, it was obvious he was in danger of losing any scrap of dignity he had left. The front door was thrown open and banged against the wall.

'Sir!' Alice called after him. 'Your hat, sir! You've forgot your hat!'

Afterwards, Harry examined my arm. He wanted to send for a doctor.

'I'm all right,' I kept insisting, and then proceeded to heap all the blame on myself. Harry forced a few crackers and a pint of tonic water down me, and left me to sleep it off. At some point during the night, I fell off the bed and crawled under it. With my cheek on the cool floor, I hugged the piss-pot and made one of those tomorrow-I'm-turning-my-life-around commitments that come after the vomiting and before the hangover. I got back into bed and slept hard.

Alice roused me from my slumber the next morning. She said there was a boy outside, with a letter he'd give into no hand but mine. I wrapped myself in the dressing gown and made my way with slow caution down the stairs, trying to keep my head from falling off and rolling down before the rest of me.

An urchin with filthy bare feet stood boldly at the front door, his breath puffing in the morning air. He wiped his nose on a tattered coat-sleeve, the fabric and colour of which had long since surrendered to layers of snot. The blue of his eyes seemed to leap out of his dirty face as he examined the mess of me.

'Miz Paytra?'

'Yes.'

The eyes narrowed suspiciously. 'Yer's suppose to 'ave chestnut curls an' dimples in yer cheeks.' I lifted my matted hair and waved it at him as I flashed a tight smile, forcing the dimples to cut their way into my puffy face.

He held out a letter on heavy cream-coloured stock, folded and sealed with a dollop of candle-wax. As I reached for it, he drew his hand back with a wink. 'Been at the gin, 'ave ye, miss?'

Snatching it from his dirty little fingers, I said in my most regal tone: 'I'm afraid I've no money to give you.'

He leaned in close, whispering dramatically. ''E promise me 'alf-crown t'bring t'yer 'and.'

My eyes matched his for wonder at this huge sum. 'Who did?'

'Mister Sherlock 'Olmes, o'course.' The boy touched the brim of his cap. 'Pleasant day t'ye, Miss.'

Something in my gut told me this letter would not be the precursor to a pleasant day.

It began with the cold social formality of "Madam".

Madam,

The heart is incapable of reason in the best of circumstances, so I need not waste time repudiating it here. I have never trusted my heart to give me the facts. How stunned I was to find you had betrayed me. Until that moment, I had not thought I could be such a fool, and a brutish one at that. I deeply regret my actions and the injuries you suffered as a result. But one can only pour ashes over one's head for so long before it becomes mere self-indulgence.

Thus, after a long night spent wandering dark paths of despair, the prodigal has returned to himself at last. It seems I have done my mind a great disservice to abandon it for you, for it has ever been a stalwart companion. I will need this companion now more than ever. Strange events and dangerous circumstances have come to light which will demand of me quick thinking and quicker action.

A trap is being laid for me, and I must spring the trap without taking up the bait. Therefore, I will never take you in my arms again, nor meet with you, nor speak with you. Please, make no attempts to contact me. I will return any correspondence unopened, and you will be refused admittance should you come in person. In any guise.

Believe that I harbour no ill-feelings toward you, or any sort of feelings save those true and honest wishes for your continued well-being. To that end, permit me to offer this suggestion: the Salvation Army Mission. I understand that prayer and good works bring

respite from the demon drink.
 Your humble,
 Sherlock Holmes.

The body of the letter was written in ink. The postscripts were in pencil, in a hasty hand.

P.S. Have just received a lead concerning two roles portrayed by the same actor. I do not know how to interpret your assistance in this matter, but gave the messenger a five-pound note, and he will be a useful friend to me in future, I think.
 P.P.S. A lady has every right to do as she wishes with a letter such as this, but I would consider it good of you if you would burn it after reading it.

I read it several times. The first time in shock, but the second time committed it to memory, and after that I was merely trying to change the meaning of the words, to find a code with the real message between the lines, like "Gillyflower - Sorry - Coffee Tomorrow?" or "don't let the spider eat me".

I moved back to the bedroom as if I were walking underwater. The bed had been made up, the room tidied, and the chamber-pot emptied. All traces of my folly had been neatly excised. My case sat empty on the floor of the wardrobe. What little clothing I had hung from hooks; the rest folded neatly into the drawers of the bureau or removed for laundering. I had gone from maid to mistress in the blink of an eye.

On the floor next to the bed was a knapsack. Which was strange, because I didn't own one. Inside, another mystery: a bundle of familiar old clothes, the very clothes I'd worn to follow Holmes through Spitalfields. They were clean now, the discarded boots wrapped in the trousers.

Had he actually been following me that rainy day back in October, when I suspected the wrong man, the more obvious man? Or had Corkle's flunky retrieved my parcel from the alley where I'd tossed it, and these incriminating items been placed in my room to further implicate me as the rooftop robber? I hadn't noticed the clothes when the police had been searching, but I'd barely been able to breathe, let alone notice everything.

I stared down at the boots, seeing all my ignorance and arrogance written on the heels, tied up in the laces. That I'd found the boots and used them had been pure chance. And it was only because of them that Holmes had noticed me at all.

I'm not the bait, you big dope. I'm what kept you from taking the bait in the first place.

It made no sense to cut off communications with me now. If he'd truly been thinking clearly, he would have acknowledged that he still had uses for me: dangerous ones, but uses nonetheless. I had to find a way through Holmes's re-fortified armour. Give him the facts and let him choose what he could use. To that end, I had to take action. Any action would do at the moment.

After gazing long and hard at my image in the dressing mirror, I steeled myself and reached for the bell that would summon the maid.

PART THREE

Chapter 22

The Belvedere Club was named after a founder whom none of its members could quite recall having met. It was not a club with a permanent address, but, rather, a guerrilla happening which swarmed upon its ever-changing venues, made a huge mess, and left its participants reeling and insensible for days afterwards.

The current venue was located in the Borough, a three-storey firetrap waiting for the right cigarette butt. What it *did* have going for it was a dance-floor that covered the entire first storey, and this evening the Belvedere was packed to the rafters with drinking, dancing, flirting fellows whose sleek coifs and nearly-identical outfits made the task of finding Holmes even more daunting.

Harry Hughes was convinced that we were going to score on the Holmes-spotting front. For nearly two weeks we'd been making the rounds - bars mostly, some cafes, and a few private salons - hoping to catch Holmes at one of these places, but he'd been playing his itinerary close to the vest, which probably had something to do with the telegram I'd sent the day after we'd parted ways.

Sherlock Holmes. Desperate to consult. Please meet Mrs Maria Tory. Saturday. Three o'clock. Zoological Gardens. Reptile Enclosure.

I thought he'd jump on the quasi-anagram. I waited two hours, wearing the veils of a widow's sorrow, watching snakes that seemed too listless even to die. Harry received a telegram that evening:

Please advise Mrs Tory to keep her distance. S.H.

Harry had taken me under his wing after Sherlock had kicked me to the curb. I think he felt sort of responsible. Also, he liked dressing me up and trotting me out, like a terrier in a tartan coat. Though tonight was strictly tails and top hats.

There were other women at the Belvedere, although solidarity in sisterhood did not appear to be in their interests. I'd been approached by six of them already. I'd expected women dressed like me, or maybe in riding habits, so these bustled belles were a surprise. Evening gowns notwithstanding, the competition for fresh blood was getting pretty brutal. One young lady, who'd introduced herself as Iris, was stalking me still.

It was close to midnight and still, no sign of Holmes. Harry waved boisterously as he worked his way toward me through the waltzing male couples.

'There you are,' he exclaimed, as if he'd been frantically looking everywhere for me. Flushed, obviously way past tipsy, he proceeded to fan himself with the gag dance-card that had been provided at the door.

'Are you positive he's going to be here?' I asked.

He sipped his champagne, eyes roaming the room restlessly. 'Absolutely. I cunningly hinted to him that it was a very big soiree. A sodomite's paradise. He's bound to make an appearance if he's keen on defending the weak from the wicked.'

'How will he be able to tell the difference?'

He was paying very little attention to my bad humour, however. Across the room, a gentleman lifted fingers to a heavy moustache and blew a kiss. Harry mouthed something to the man, then turned to me with a pretty-please smile. 'Sweetness? Would you mind terribly if I left you to your own devices for a couple of hours?' He gulped down his champagne, eyes still locked on the object of his current affection. 'Gosh. He quite fills his trousers, doesn't he?'

On the other side of the musician's dais, rubbernecking over a sea of manheads, was that Iris woman in her mauve evening gown. I ducked into the corridor and headed downstairs, glass in hand.

Outside, the intermittent horn blast from a tug cut through the muffled cacophony behind me. There were men outside as well, but mostly smoking and talking. Somewhere to my left I heard a laugh that sounded familiar, but all men's voices had started to sound the same to me by then.

I took a few deep breaths, sipped guiltily at what remained of my beverage, and considered that it was probably time to go back to St John's Wood.

Then that laugh again, throaty, sexual, a laugh I knew intimately.

I squeezed my lips together lest a squeal escape, and inched closer, my back pressed to the worm-eaten wood of the building.

'My dear Evelyn,' Holmes was saying, 'photographs are so static.'

Evelyn? Who's this bitch?

'But to capture a moment... *the* moment...' a man's voice responded. Ah, Evelyn.

In a bored voice, Holmes countered: 'You can see boys taking it up the arse anytime you wish, live and in the flesh in Cleveland Street. It'll cost you two bob -'

'They're faking it, Cecil, you silly goose. It's a trick with the stage-lights. Most times the fellows can't even get to half-mast, they're so bored.'

'Yes, I imagine it would become wretchedly dull,' the detective replied, 'rather like playing hoops with one's sister.' The other man giggled. Holmes went on, his voice silky-smooth. 'It must be dreadful for an actor of your stature to see chaps not giving their all on stage.'

'I... I haven't been on stage for some time, my dear.' There was a heavy pause. 'By God, you have a... a... lovely mouth.'

'And you have beautiful hands, Evelyn, the hands of an artist or a surgeon. Have you ever played the role of a doctor? I imagine you'd play a doctor with great... *authority*.'

God in Heaven. That voice. I leaned back, rolling my head toward the sound, nearly as bewitched as his target.

'I... I have portrayed a doctor, in fact,' the man whispered then gave a little gasp.

'I knew it. These hands could do no less. The role involved some delicate, probing examination no doubt.'

Evelyn laughed a wordless acknowledgement.

'I wish I could have seen it,' Holmes continued. 'Will you be performing the role again soon?'

'Ah, no. Alas, it was a one-off performance. Private audience. Not to be repeated I'm afraid.'

'Oh,' Holmes said, his voice full of pouting disappointment. 'Not even for me, Evelyn? I would love to play the patient in your surgery. Prostrate upon the table and so desperately in need of your ministrations.'

'Oh, dearest, lovely Cecil, let me -' The sounds of grappling against the wall.

'Ah, ah, ah, Doctor. Not yet. If I am to be examined, I should like it to be in private.' Then in a voice huskier, redolent with sensual promises: 'Your rooms, Evelyn. Take me there.'

The other man shuddered a sigh of anguish and longing. 'I can't. My wife -'

'But I'm a shy flower. There must be some place you can take me. Some secret place.'

Then, I swear to God, I heard the wet smack and slide of lips against lips. I turned away from it, thinking, *this would be a really good time to leave, Gillian -*

Evelyn's breath stuttered from his throat. 'Yes, yes. I think I...'

'Shh,' Holmes said suddenly.

His attention had shifted. I could feel it.

I spun in the gravel and sprinted for the back door. The champagne glass slipped from my hand. Shoes crunched over the broken shards in quick pursuit.

He caught hold of my arm as I reached the landing at the top of the stairs. I had no chance to turn and explain myself before he'd twisted my arm and thrust up on my elbow hard, his body pressed close, so no-one in the crowded corridor would suspect what he was doing.

'Cry out and I'll break it.' The breath from his words parted the hair at the back of my head. He pushed my arm farther up my back by way of illustration and I bit down on a cry, nodding my compliance.

Holmes guided me ahead of him, marching me down a narrow hallway to the other set of stairs that lead to the lower level. A pale greenish light illuminated the passage at the bottom of the steps. When we reached it, he whipped me around, shoved me against the wall and hid his forearm to my throat in one swift motion.

I nearly peed my pants.

'Gillian.' His voice was a dry whisper of shock. 'Dear Jesus. Jesus Christ.' He pulled his arm from my throat, turned from me and then back again, slapping the wall next to my head. 'Are you mad? I could have killed you.'

My legs started shaking, quickly followed by the rest of me. 'I'm sorry, I'm sorry, I'm really, really sorry, I was looking for you, but you weren't here, and... and so I went outside to get some air. I wasn't... I didn't... but then you... and I just... and I should have, but...'

He squeezed my lips together. 'Hush.' Then, seeming to realise he was further terrorising me, he let go. 'You're not very good at this spying business, are you?'

'I wasn't spying on you!'

'Then why did you run?'

'I was... embarrassed.'

'By my conversation, or the fact I discovered you listening?'

That did it. Back on the solid footing of sarcasm. 'Well, actually, Sherlock, it wasn't the conversation so much as the kissy-face noises.'

He looked away, choking on his own embarrassment. 'Look,' he said. 'I'm very close to my goal now, and if you cause me to lose sight of it I'll -'

'You'll what?' I asked, jerking my chin up. 'Take a strap to me? Break my arm?'

'For God's sake!' he shouted, causing a brief lull in the buzz upstairs. He dropped his voice to rough whisper. 'In spite of the impression you've received of late, I'm not in the habit of threatening women with physical harm.'

'Maids aren't women to you, apparently,' I hissed. 'Anyway, you knew I was here. That's why you didn't come inside.'

'Don't be so full of yourself, my girl. Your presence would not have stopped me entering the building, had that been my intention. Now, what do you want?'

His body was a yard away from me, propped by his arm, but I could feel it vibrating, the muscles still battle-ready, pumped full of adrenaline. His cool was all a sham. Something very intense was going down, and it wasn't between him and me.

'We need to talk,' I replied.

He stared at me, then gave a soft, derisive laugh. 'Not a good time to chat.' He pulled away and headed up the stairs.

I lurched forward, the words coming out in a breathless rush. 'I have information you need and I'm prepared to give it to you.'

'What?'

'I have information you -'

'Yes, I heard you.' He took a step down, then another. 'Why?'

'Because... my conscience demands it. Because people have died and more may follow. Including you.'

He studied me, taking in everything that was different and everything that was the same. 'If this is one of your games, Gillian...'

'Believe me, if this were a game I'd've taken my ball and gone home a long, long time ago.'

He pressed his lips tight together with his fingers, then: 'That coffee shop in Soho. Three o'clock tomorrow.' His dark form moved up the staircase, framed by the pixilated motion of bodies from the corridor above. 'And wear a frock, for pity's sake,' he called over his shoulder.

'I'll wear what I bloody well like, arsehole!' I yelled after him, but my words were swallowed by crude laughter and drunken arguments.

After he'd been absorbed by the crowd, I sat on the steps deconstructing our brief encounter, with an eye toward finding hidden meanings in a muscular twitch or a vocal inflection. This was nothing more than superficial, dumb-girl vanity on my part. I wanted to see regret in his eyes for dumping me. But, in careful analysis of the details, the only regret he'd shown had been for nearly crushing my windpipe. I clutched this to my breast and moved on to more pressing matters.

I was pretty sure he hadn't known it was me until he'd had his arm to my throat. He thought he was chasing someone else. Therefore, he suspected someone else was after him.

I got to my feet, waited for my legs to stop shaking, then made my way back to the dance floor.

A tall, elegant blond caught my eye and dismissed me coolly. Not his type, apparently. An older fellow, sporting a shaggy goatee, scanned the room through the lens of his monocle, pausing briefly at the sight of me, then moving on to a scattering of young men, tricked out like monkeys looking for meal tickets, which, sadly, they were.

The orchestra's cellist stepped onto the dais and righted a bow that had fallen to the floor. Our eyes met. He grinned and gave a little shrug as if to say, "hey, a gig's a gig, right?".

I smiled back... then whirled away from him, shoulders cramping into hard knots. He could have been Corkle's spy for all I knew. I couldn't even trust a simple smile.

'Good evening, Miss Gillian.'

I nearly jumped out of my skin. Then I laughed. She'd finally cornered me. 'Good evening, Miss Iris,' I replied.

Any hopes of fashionable elegance to which Iris aspired that evening had been defeated the day she was born. Drab hair sought to escape from dozens of hairpins, and strands reached out like the arms of prisoners between the teeth of her fancy silver combs. Although mauve suited her colouring, the puffs, draperies, ruffles, and rosettes festooning her gown did not. She looked like any jeans-and-T-shirt lesbian forced to be a bridesmaid at her sister's wedding.

'Lovely party,' she said, 'if one is fond of sausage.'

I snorted.

'Poor thing.' She put a hand on my shoulder, a casual show of sympathy with a lingering squeeze. 'You aren't enjoying yourself in the least, are you?'

'I'm a bit fagged-out,' I said.

'Yes, men are such bores, aren't they? Always one hand on the giggle-stick and the other groping for a hole to put it in.' She raised an arm to wave down more champagne. A waft of amber-scented perfume drifted across my nostrils from the tuft of her armpit hair.

'Still, they have their uses,' I said, trying to remember what those were.

'Indeed.' She took a glass and sipped, peering anxiously about the room. 'When one needs an escort home, for instance.'

Victorian convention popped up at the oddest times and in the strangest places.

'My cousin refuses to be rousted from his fun,' she explained, pointing out the icy blond who'd been eyeing me a few minutes before. 'And he won't allow me to take the brougham.'

'I'm ready to call it an evening myself,' I said, and immediately regretted it.

Iris let out a squeal of enthusiasm that could have stopped a train. 'Oh, do let's share a cab!' She gulped down her drink and set the glass on the table behind her. 'We'll fetch our wraps and get away from all this manly musk.'

I searched the thinning crowd desperately, but saw no sign of Harry. Iris grabbed my hand and manoeuvred me to the ballroom's staircase, then down to the cloakroom. There, I stopped short and jerked my arm from her clutches.

Dr Watson was standing just outside the open doors of the main entrance, a black cigar clenched in his teeth. He was trying to avoid any and all eye-contact whilst maintaining a dour grimace.

'Dearest?' Iris asked. 'What's the matter?'

I grabbed her by her freckled arm and started to pull her towards a side-door.

She dug in her heels. 'I need to get my wrap!'

Like a cat at the sound of a can opener, Watson's head shot around.

'Rose? Rose Donnelly?'

Iris looked at him, then me. 'Is he talking to you?'

He'd already stepped inside the vestibule, as if drawn into the world by sheer disbelief at my presence in it. 'It *is* you,' he said breathlessly. I approached him with Iris clinging to my arm like leech. 'Good lord! What have you done to yourself?'

'I think she looks charming,' said Iris.

I reached into my trouser pocket, searching for my claim check.

'Here,' I said, handing it to her. 'Be a darling and fetch our things from the cloak room. Ta.' I patted her ruddy cheek with a trifle more force than intended.

She drew back, eyes narrowing fractionally a moment. Then she flashed a grin, dipped a mock curtsy at Watson, and sashayed off.

His mouth twitched in thinly disguised distaste. 'Strange company you're keeping.'

'You as well, sir.'

He coloured slightly, but his expression bespoke the cold comprehension of a man who knew he'd been used. 'You seem to have lost your homely speech, Rose. Holmes told me something of your true nature, but I didn't credit much of what he said.' *Until now*, his eyes finished.

'He doesn't have all the facts, Doctor, in spite of what he believes.'

'Does he know you're here?'

'We ran into each other. He was chatting up some chap named Evelyn.'

Watson drew in a sharp breath, and looked away lest his face betray something. Finding nothing to focus on that didn't distress him further, he finally settled on his cigar, twisting it between his fingers as if it were some strange artefact. 'I would advise you to stay out of his way this evening.'

I wondered how Watson's presence fit into Holmes's plans this night. There was a tricky enterprise going on: Holmes's seduction of this Evelyn person, all those carefully-phrased leading questions. The old Badger Game, if I weren't mistaken. One to bait the mark, and the other to spring out and say "corrupter of youth, unhand my brother!", or words to that affect. Only, instead of money, Holmes would want information. Evelyn was an actor and had played the role of a doctor recently. An Austrian doctor with an unusual name, perhaps?

Iris returned with our wraps.

'I shall make myself scarce then,' I said. 'Come along, my dear.' I draped her mantle across her shoulders, threw on my opera cape and screwed the top hat onto my head. 'I do hope the rest of the evening proves rewarding, sir.'

He swallowed, cleared his throat. 'I'll walk you out.'

'Can you be away that long?' I asked carefully. He caught my look, acknowledging this insight into his post at the door. Then his mouth quirked in a resigned smile.

'My duty as a gentleman will ever come first, Rose.'

'Well, we don't need you,' Iris exclaimed. Considering she'd been hoping for just such an escort only minutes before, this struck me as plain stupid. I had no plans of letting her tickle my pudendum or vice versa.

I said, 'I would be grateful for the company under the circumstances, Doctor, thank you.'

With his right hand over a heavy revolver-shaped object in the pocket, Watson escorted us through an area known for its high ratio of criminals to working-class types.

Chapter 23

The streets weren't empty at that late hour, nor were they teeming with humanity. Here and there a light flickered in a window high above us, while lone men, hands deep in empty pockets, walked with an eye toward opportunity. Those not lucky enough to have the pennies for a doss warmed their hands over a trash fire, passing bottles and coarse witticisms.

Iris kept up a nervous conversational chatter between us, to which I responded in equally nervous grunts of 'uh-huh' and 'you don't say?', all the while wondering why the hell this stupid bitch thought I was sufficient escort for her through *this* neighborhood.

As we came to the intersection before the bridge, she relaxed her grip on my arm. Watson pointed out the hack-stand. There were no cabs in sight, but I could see lanterns swinging from likely-looking vehicles passing each other across the bridge proper.

'I think we'll be all right waiting.' I didn't want to keep him too long from Holmes.

His fingers shifted over the item in his coat pocket. Reluctantly, he touched the brim of his hat. 'Take care, Rose.'

'Thank you. I will.' I reached out and squeezed his hand quickly. 'Perhaps we'll meet again soon under better circumstances.'

'I should like that.' He gave a small, polite bow to Iris. 'Good evening, Miss.'

I watched him for a moment, his steps picking up speed the farther away he got, until he was practically trotting. I turned to my companion, prepared to set her straight about the nature of our relationship.

Iris was removing a glove, jerking on each finger with tense, swift movements. She put the glove into her handbag. I looked at her. She smiled, then positioned her thumb and forefinger at the corners of her mouth and blew. It was an ear-piercing, high-pitched squeal of a whistle, the kind I'd spent hours trying to duplicate as a child.

My confusion over it was momentary. A horse-drawn van shot out of the side-street and turned towards me. Up top was the man Iris had pointed out as her cousin.

Oh, an ambush, I thought dully, my brain taking entirely too long to process this information. My feet were way ahead of my thoughts, however, and I was running before I even realised it, feeling my coat-sleeve slip free from Iris's quick effort to grab it.

I threw off the cape as I ran, tripping someone coming up behind me. The beautiful silk top hat went sailing off my head. I wasted no breath in shouting for help, but pumped my legs like crazy, aiming for the street-corner Watson had rounded some thirty yards away. The clatter of hooves and iron tires was deafening. I made a sudden, wild dash for an alley. It was a dead end.

The whip whistled through the air, precipitating the snap on the horse's flank. I couldn't imagine the connection of that sound to my own body. The shock of it was so intense that I was writhing in agony on the ground before the scream came out. Arms like tree-trunks swept me up, crushing the air out of me as the van pulled up. Another man came round from behind it, approaching with a dirty flannel in his hand. It was soaked in chloroform. Adrenaline rallied, and I fought with the wild strength of complete abject terror.

'Hold the bitch, for Christ's sake!' the man with the cloth said, trying to dodge my legs.

'Yeah,' my assailant sputtered, 'an' what am I doin', then?'

That voice. It was *him*, the same man who'd followed Holmes and me. 'Be still, ye little cunt,' he hissed. He gave me a hard squeeze and a harder shake. The crunch of my ribs was followed by tidal-wave of nausea. My shoes stuttered over the paving as he dragged me to the back of the van.

'Unhand that woman at once!'

Watson. Oh my God, oh my God. Thank you. Watson, with service revolver in hand, aimed at the big man holding me.

'Put her down! *Now!*' He fired into the sky.

At the sound of the discharge, the guy dropped me, right on the pavement, sending all the air from my lungs again. The startled horse took off in a dead run with the van teetering behind it.

'Rose. Come here to me. Quickly.'

I crawled partway, limped the rest, until he was close enough to take me under one arm and push me behind him.

At the far end of the street, the van's driver had got the horse under control again and was coaxing the animal to back up.

'Police!' Watson shouted to no-one. 'Someone fetch the police!' His voice was strained, and fear was tickling the edges of it. Still, he eyed the hooligans menacingly. 'What have you done with the other young lady?'

'Nothing,' Iris said, coming out of the shadows to the right of us, dainty pistol aimed at his chest.

Watson drew in a sharp breath, his eyes glancing obliquely on her advancing form, while his weapon stayed trained on the men.

'Get into the van, Miss Gillian,' she said.

The barrels of Watson's enormous service revolver were now pointed at the silk frogs that fastened her mantle. 'One more step,' he said, 'and I'll fire.'

She smiled a mockery of gentle indulgence. 'You're not the type.' She looked at me again. 'I'd advise you to co-operate, or there beside you stands a dead man. You understand?'

I saw the small man on the ground looking anxiously about. For cops, I thought. This was taking too long. The guy up top slipped his hand into the front of his jacket

'Doctor -'

Watson spun me round and shoved hard between my shoulder blades. 'Run!' he cried. I tripped forward, my legs moving automatically.

Two gunshots rang out behind me, the first one cracking loud as thunder, and the other like the bark of a dog. A man cried out. I slowed, hesitated, stopped, turned -

China Crow snatched me up in one arm and clapped a hand over my mouth. I bit down hard on the flesh between his thumb and forefinger. He roared, but didn't let go. Instead, nearly twisting my head from my neck, he proceeded to drag me backwards toward the ride to oblivion.

'Jesus!' I heard the other man cry. 'Is 'e dead?'

'Leave him!' the driver cried.

''E's seen us!'

'Then send him to Hell -'

'Not on yer say-so, tosser. Throw 'im in back. Boss'll decide.'

The chloroform-soaked rag was pressed over my nose and mouth as they hauled me through the van's doors. Kidnappers tumbled in behind me. The doors banged shut, the whip cracked, and the horse leapt forward. After a few moments, the drug did its work on me and I remembered nothing of what must have been a very harrowing ride.

***

I awakened, if it could be called that, with a headache that defied description. My lips and tongue were swollen. I was horribly thirsty, not even spit to swallow.

'Here,' a voice said. Water trickled between my lips. 'Careful. Not too much at first.'

'Doctor?' I tried to say. I blinked my eyes a couple of times to make certain they were actually open. I was looking at nothing but black. 'Am I blind?'

'No.' His breath was warm, but the moisture from it cooled quickly on my cheek. 'It's just very dark.'

Slowly my senses began to identify sounds and odours. The smell of concrete and damp wool, urine, sweat... blood? Stale, cold air. I could hear the slap of water in a pail or basin, and then the water dribbled into my mouth again, squeezed from a rag or a sponge.

After a few moments, I began to make out his shape in the darkness. The act of rationing my water was exhausting him. I could hear it in his breathing.

'Oh God!' I cried, trying to sit up. 'She shot you, didn't she? You've been shot...' The movement was more than my poisoned body could handle. I turned my head to vomit, but not much came out and soon I was hunched over, my injured ribs protesting spasms I couldn't control. I was barely aware of Watson's hands rubbing the muscles in my neck and shoulders until the fit passed. I fell onto my back again, moaning.

His voice cut through the darkness, full of quiet rage. 'Those villains could have killed you.'

'It hurts. When I take a... a deep breath.'

'You may have a cracked rib or two. Lie there and don't move if you can help it.'

I tried, but after a moment I became aware of a cold burning sensation on the skin of my inner thighs, my knees, and under my bottom. It was then that I connected the smell of urine to myself. I forgot his advice and struggled to get my trousers off.

'No, Rose. Stop. It's too cold to disrobe. There aren't any blankets.'

'I don't care!' I cried. 'I want them off. Take them off!' I thrashed on the floor, helpless, angry and mortified. I felt sick, so sick. My head throbbed, the welts from the whip throbbed, my ribs ached, and I'd soiled myself.

'Stop it, Rose! I'm a doctor for pity's sake. I've seen much worse.'

For a moment I thought he was angry with me, then realised the harsh tone in his voice was from a losing battle with the pain of his injury. He eased himself back on the floor beside me, panting.

I forced a calm I didn't feel. 'How badly are you hurt?'

'The bullet passed through the back of my leg. I shan't die from it.'

'How long have we been here?'

'Eight or nine hours, I should think. I was blindfolded when they brought us here. But I'm certain we're underground. There's a door about ten feet to our left, bolted from the outside. The walls seem thick, very solid. I believe there are vents cut high on opposing walls, though the air doesn't circulate much. I doubt they're large enough to provide an escape route. No way to reach them in any case. Though we'll try when... when we're stronger, yes?'

I almost screamed then, but the darkness pressed it down, a heavy weight on my chest. I was the one meant to be here. Watson was a liability they hadn't expected.

His head scraped softly against the floor. 'Please don't go mad on me, Rose.'

'I'm sorry,' I said. 'I'm frightened.'

'I know,' he whispered. *So am I,* the subtext said. 'It's all right. Holmes will find us. You know he will.'

Then I started to cry. Again.

'Hush, hush now. A little more water...' He held the cloth to my lips. I sucked the water from it, tasting the cotton, feeling the fibres on my thickened tongue.

I heard him drinking as well, and afterwards he said: 'The water tastes clean at least.'

We measured time in the dark by heartbeats and blinking eyelids. Finally, he dozed fitfully beside me while I counted each painful breath I took and leeched warmth from his feverish body.

Chapter 24

The throbbing in my head had subsided by the time the men came.

A heavy door scraped across the floor of our prison. Beside me, Watson started at the sound and bolted up, moaning from the agony of his own sudden movements. Conical beams of light pierced the dark and bounced about the room. I threw an arm over my face protectively, as if the light were a beloved missing pet that had returned home and suddenly gone for my jugular. But I needed to see where I was.

Lanterns illuminated a large, empty box of a room. Whitewashed walls and a door six inches thick at least, faced with lead.

China Crow and his pal flanked the door, aiming their lanterns at us like weapons. But when Corkle entered, I could see no-one else, think of nothing else. I inched closer to Watson, hardly aware I was doing it.

Dressed in his solicitor's suit, with the black felt bowler atop his fresh-from-the-barber head, Corkle seemed much taller than he actually was. The stark, inky black of his costume made his flesh seem garish: eyes like blue dots in the middle of a crayon-scribbled face. He turned to the big man with the Oriental eyes.

'The point of this was to keep her from being harmed, Mr Crow. I thought you understood that.'

'She's not been 'armed, sir.'

'Look at the greyness of her skin, the shadows under her eyes. You could have killed her.' He locked his gaze on the man, who faltered back a step, lantern swinging light and shadows across Watson and me.

'That was Ben's doin', sir,' China said.

'I just done what Davies and 'is woman told me -' the other man protested.

'I said it don't go in 'er mouf -'

'Shut it,' Corkle said quietly. There was no inflection in his voice at all. 'I was given to understand that you wished to explore new horizons, that you were bored with your work and desired the chance to prove you could handle matters which required more finesse. I have given you this opportunity and, frankly, I'm not sure you're up to it.'

'Sir,' Crow said. 'Ye said she weren't to be broke nowhere's and I didn't -'

'Her ribs may be broken,' Watson interjected.

'I done what ye asked, sir!' China protested. 'I coulda 'ad 'er afore if I wasn't under orders not to give 'er a little cosh -'

Corkle held up his hand, disregarding the excuses and shutting him up with one cool gesture. Instead, he focused his attention on Watson, mouth pursed in the mildest annoyance, as if considering what was to be done with an old rug that didn't go with the new furniture.

Watson had removed his shoe and sock, and tied the stocking around his wound. His toes were bluish-white. I hoped it was from the chill air and not something worse.

Politely, Corkle asked: 'How is your injury, sir?'

Watson gaped at him, but his voice when he spoke was strangely calm. 'If I could have flushed the wound properly and stitched it up, it would likely heal well enough. Unfortunately, it's well past the point that sutures would hold, and I am concerned about infection.'

Corkle nodded a vague acknowledgement, and turned to Crow. 'You demonstrated sound judgement in bringing him here, I'll grant you that. Anything else would have been disastrous.' He gnawed his lower lip. 'But he does present a problem.'

'Easily taken care of now, sir, if ye like.'

Corkle shook his head, and eyed Watson again, with a rubbery twitch of his lips. 'I may have use for you, Doctor. Time will tell. I can, however, provide antiseptic and bandages. If you feel this will help.'

I drew my knees up, and hid my face in my lap, whimpering.

'Calm down, Gillian. *Your* continued good health is uppermost in my mind.'

I looked up at him in dull shock. 'Since when?'

'Since always.'

'Sure. Right. All this was for my own good.' I rocked back and forth compulsively, my arms locked around my knees.

'I need you alive, Gillian.' At my incredulous expression, he chuckled. 'You're my homing-pigeon. The... ahh, implant in your left arm. Very important.'

'It's a contraceptive implant, you dumb fuck!'

He stared at me, his mouth hanging open. Then he started to laugh. He laughed for a really long time.

'Well, for your sake,' he said, lifting his spectacles to wipe away tears of mirth, 'I hope you have that as well. But for my sake, you have another sort, one that won't operate if it's removed from your body in the wrong manner. I needed you out of the way, yes. You made that necessary with all the pillow-talk. But I also needed to keep you safe. I was going to secure you in a lovely asylum in Uppingham, but the goons screwed up. Prison was the next-best solution. I did give you an opportunity to avoid this, if you'll recall...' He broke off, emitting something between a raspberry and a sigh. 'If Holmes had been decent enough to attend his father's funeral, *this*,' he gestured at the room, 'would never have been necessary.'

'Jesus,' I whispered. 'Tell me you're not responsible for that.'

'For what?' Watson asked, his eyes darting from me to Corkle and back to me again.

Corkle ignored him, his expression one of mild embarrassment. 'Look, the old fellow had a bad heart, clogged arteries. It was only a matter of months before he kicked anyway.'

'What about Liza Murray? Carolina Lopenski? Did *they* have bad hearts? What about Stewart Ronaldson? His blood seemed to leave his body pretty easily. No clogged arteries there.'

Corkle shot a glance at his associates and said mildly: 'This is not the time or place to discuss the particulars of the mission, Gillian.'

Sudden rage overwhelmed both fear and pain. 'What *mission*, Tom? What fucking mission is that? Because I don't remember signing up for the snuff film mission.'

'What the devil is going on?' Watson demanded.

Corkle kept his eyes on me, though his words appeared to be for Watson. 'Something in the nature of a scientific experiment. Being a scientist himself, Mr Holmes would be able to appreciate the elegance of its design, though not, perhaps, its intent.'

I sank to the floor next to Watson, every breath now an agony. Corkle made a grand, sweeping gesture. 'Not exactly a suite at Claridge's, but the next best thing to a penitentiary. You'll be safe here.'

Blank walls, heavy door, stark, cold emptiness. I'd be safe like a diamond or an important document.

'You can't possibly mean to lock her in this mausoleum,' Watson cried. 'It's inhuman!'

'It's not forever,' Corkle assured him. 'She'll be provided everything she needs to survive. Including your company, for a while.' The very-blue eyes blinked once, twice. 'If you're lucky, perhaps she'll give you a taste of what your good friend finds so intriguing about her. I understand she likes a good gamahauche now and again.'

Red blossomed high on Watson's cheeks, though his jaw was tight with outrage. 'You are a foul, evil-minded man, Mr Corkle!'

'Ouch, I'm bleeding,' Corkle said. He took out his watch and flipped opened the case. 'Oh goodness, look at the time. Gotta run.'

'Let him go, Tom,' I pleaded.

'Can't do that, Gillian.' The watch snapped shut and he slipped it back into his waistcoat pocket.

'I won't eat,' I whispered. 'I'll starve myself to death. You'll never get home then.'

'Starvation is a very slow method of suicide. There's always force-feeding, threats to your companion and so forth. Besides, you don't have the guts to commit suicide just to thwart little old me. Face it, darling. The Great Detective abandoned you to fate as soon as you became an emotional liability. I'm the only sure thing you have left.'

Next to me, Watson struggled to rise, as if he'd have actual power in the situation once standing. 'My friend abandons no-one! No-one! He will hunt you to the ends of the earth, Mr Corkle! Hunt you like the animal you are, and when he catches you - and he *will* - you shall pay the price of your villainy, sir, *with your life!*'

I knew Corkle would ridicule the melodrama of it, even as the words left Watson's mouth. I was embarrassed for him and ashamed of my embarrassment.

But strangely enough, Corkle merely cocked his head, clinically studying the classic specimen of Victorian manhood before him.

'He'll have to go much farther than the ends of the Earth, sir,' he said. And with that, he departed, leaving China Crow and Ben to haul in the needs for our survival.

It was the commode that set the unbearably cosy nature of confinement with Watson firmly in my mind: rather throne-like in appearance, a baroque antique. One could command armies from such a chair; plot invasions, bestow knighthoods. It was huge. It was ridiculous. The only piece of furniture in the room, and it was a toilet.

When I saw it, panic bubbled up and I made a scrambled dash for the open door; no thought of Watson, no thought of anything but me and getting *me* out of there. My mind made plans at the speed of light, excusing my abandonment of the man who'd tried to rescue me, and putting myself far into the future where I'd saved him and the world just by shutting that door and throwing the bolt.

I jerked on the handle. The stab of pain in my side killed any further effort. I was on my knees instantly, and the door hadn't budged an inch. China Crow scooped me up and deposited me on the floor next to Watson. 'Make me chase ye again -'

His boot shot out. I curled up instinctively, but the kick wasn't aimed at me. Watson's body arched like a bow, Crow's heavy boot targeting the gunshot wound in his leg.

After that, I was a model prisoner.

We had food and water. We had clean linens and warm, dry clothes. A cot, blankets, pillows, soap, toothbrushes, flannels, a basin, a barrel of water for washing, and another barrel for refuse. No razor for Watson, naturally enough, but antiseptic and bandages were provided, and laudanum for the pain. Not enough to kill myself even if I had the guts. We had everything we needed to survive but light.

My attempt to abandon Watson haunted me, but he seemed not to attach much significance to it. In fact, he insisted that the very first order of business be to wrap my ribs. I thought his injury more pressing, but he said: 'You won't be much help if you puncture a lung in the process, Rose.'

'My name is Gillian.'

'I'm fonder of roses,' he said. I didn't press the issue. I needed him to like me.

After I'd stripped out of my soiled clothing, I washed and dressed in the clothes provided, and then, with my chemise pulled up under my arms, I knelt on the concrete as he wound the strips of linen tightly about my ribcage. I felt strangely shy and vulnerable in the dark. The backs of his hands kept brushing the underside of my breasts as he wound the bandaging. His body was feverish, unbearably close.

All I could think was, *Jesus, I'm never going to be able to take a shit with this man in here.*

'How's that?' he murmured. 'Not too tight?'

'Nope,' I said. He tore the linen and knotted it with the quick efficiency of battlefield surgeon. 'Let me examine where the whip struck you -'

'No.' I pulled the chemise down, and smoothed the flannel petticoat over my legs. 'It's all right.'

'If the flesh was cut...'

'Just bruises, really.'

Sensing my discomfort, he let the matter drop.

I had to soak the blood-caked stocking with water just to peel it away from his leg. Unable to see it, I could still feel that the wound had been left too long without tending: torn edges, stiff flesh, violated tissues swollen and hot to the touch. His involuntary grunts of pain were intimidating enough, but when I unstoppered the bottle of antiseptic and caught a whiff of what was inside, I became queasy just anticipating his reaction.

'It's hydrogen peroxide.'

He took the bottle from my hand, sniffed at it, and gave it back. 'Dilute it with a little water.'

'It's not supposed to be poured into an open wound. You could die from the cure, for Christ's sake.'

'I doubt that. And I do wish you'd stop cursing. It's dreadful to hear from a woman's lips, truly it is.'

This had the hardening effect on my compassion that he must've been hoping for. I poured it over his leg, the hiss and bubble of the liquid complimenting the sound of his gargled cries. After he'd settled down into a kind of faint, I sluiced some of our drinking-water over his ankle and bandaged it as best I could without being able to see. I mopped up the water, covered us both with a blanket, and we slept.

But we couldn't avoid each other forever. There was only so long one could go without using that overlarge piece of furniture. By the time we were down to the last two bottles of artesian well-water, and the barrel we washed in was mostly soap scum, Watson was physically stronger and I could breathe without whimpering. But the air in the room was thick with the odours of our own bodily wastes and all the things we weren't talking about. He must have had questions. Why didn't he demand answers?

The next time they brought supplies, the brightness of the lantern was nearly deterrent enough to keep me from making a break for it, even without the threat of Crow's revolver. The moment for stupid bravery had not yet arrived.

During that second stretch, we were like people meeting for the first time after answering a posting in the Personals; talking around the big issues, trying to discover each other through small revelations. Yet every subject that seemed important on the outside seemed ludicrous here. Politics? Who cared? Career ambitions? What difference did those make? The nonsense of food, childhood reminiscences and family took on tremendous significance.

His childhood was all Tom Sawyer stuff; swinging from ropes tied to trees, stealing apples and skinny-dipping, playing Robin Hood in a tattered quilt cape with sticks for arrows that would never fly farther than two feet. My childhood stories involved name-brands, superheroes, and far too many explanations.

'Nike? The goddess of victory?' he'd laugh. Or: 'I understand why he'd wish to hide his identity, Rose. I simply don't see how dressing as a giant bat would help him fight criminals.'

We never spoke of Holmes. It was as if we were hiding him in our hearts and minds like a talisman against hopelessness. So we ate the crackers and mouldy cheese, plotted the practical hows and whens of our escape, and kept our secret, childish hopes to ourselves. More and more often, we woke up next to each other and didn't think twice about it.

A blind person could at least feel sunlight or the absence of it. Eventually, without a lot of warning, reality got swallowed by the dark. Dreaming with our eyes open; lying side by side, trying to see sunlight inside our heads, or fix a colour to the word "blue".

I had a dream that my head was being screwed into a painting by a guy dressed in workman's coveralls. I suppose he resembled Jimmy Moriarty in some vague way, a nerd of advancing age with a smile that could strike like a flash of summer lightning. He twisted my head around and around until it was embedded in the painting, and only my eye looked out of it.

The perspective shifted and suddenly I could see the painting on exhibit in a gallery and there was my little eye looking out of it. Diffuse-but-sunny lighting filled the room. A tall, thin young man in a top hat was leaning in close to the painting, his hands on the silvery knob of his walking-stick. He peered at some detail, then pulled back and grinned. 'Ah, there you are,' he said, 'and there's the pen I lost.'

I opened my eyes on perpetual night, and felt myself curled against Watson's back.

My first thought was "wow, weird dream, gotta tell him about this". My second thought was that he had one hell of an erection, and my third thought was "oh my God, that's my hand there, isn't it?".

The sound of his unconscious moan as I withdrew my hand caused a soft, liquid heat to well up between my legs.

I edged my hand over him again. His cock pounded against the taut fabric of his trousers like a fist at the door. His sighs were of a dream in progress. He rolled onto his back. I moved out of the way, prepared to pretend that I'd never been lying close, hadn't been touching him at all, but then he rolled again and threw an arm over me. His beard scraped into my shoulder for a moment. A little trickle of his saliva rolled down the side of my neck, and then he climbed on top of me.

Anxious to get to the buttoned flap of my drawers, my frantic movements awakened him. 'Dear God,' he rasped. 'Forgive me, I'm, I'm -'

I clenched my fingers in the front of his wool jumper, wrapped my legs around him and pulled him down to kiss his startled, open mouth. That's pretty much when he freaked out.

Over and over, his breathless apologies, and all the while he was trying to break free. Wool tore away in my hands as he scooted back from me, and back, and back, hissing through his teeth as his injured leg protested. Then - thud - right into the wall.

For a while I just lay there, confused and curiously detached, listening to his muttered prayers for help and guidance. I started to laugh.

'You must think I'm hideous,' I said.

He cleared the gravel from his throat. 'We hardly know what we're doing anymore, either of us. If any deserves rebuke it's me.'

I laughed again, bitterly this time. 'Oh, Christ, John. I was practically raping you.'

'But you knew I was...' He broke off. 'It was an unguarded moment on my part. I shall be more diligent in future.'

'What else have we got in here but each other?'

'Were I to take advantage of our desperate circumstances, it would only wrong you and make a scoundrel of me.'

'Who cares?' I screamed at him. 'What will virtue mean to anyone when we're both dead?'

'Enough of that! You're not going to die. Mr Corkle made it very clear that he needs you alive.'

'He doesn't need you, though,' I spat out. He sat alone with that truth, and I hated myself for having said it.

'Be that as it may, I shan't compromise you - or *myself* - simply because I fear I may die soon. What would be the point of living by my honour, if I can't die with honour intact?'

'What utter bullshit.' I slapped at tears on my face. 'You pay whores for the same thing and that seems to do you no dishonour.'

I heard him suck in a breath: hot shame, embarrassment, and a little that's-none-of-your-goddamned-business in one quick inhalation. When he spoke again, his voice was admirably controlled.

'Even if you were such a woman, I would not take advantage of it.'

'What's wrong with me, then? Why won't you? Why?' I wanted him to answer to all the painful questions. Why was this happening to me? Why had Holmes abandoned me? Why was I alone in a world where no one loved me?

'*Because* -' he shouted. Then stopped. In his next breath was the whisper of a secret betrayed. 'Because you are loved by another, you fool woman. What kind of man would I be - what kind of *friend* - if I could take my pleasure with you knowing that?'

'Oh,' I whispered. 'Oh. Ow.'

Chapter 25

I'd wanted the simple, mindless comfort of sex, and instead, this bomb dropped on me.

As Holmes had so aptly put it in his letter, the heart could not be trusted to give the facts. He did not trust his and I could not trust mine. It fluttered in my chest like that pathetic butterfly emerging from Pandora's box. A tiny thing. So fragile. My voice was like a fist crushing the life out of it.

'I doubt Mr Sherlock Holmes shared such a gushing sentiment with you.'

'No. But, neither have I known him to weep over a troubling case.'

Holmes weeping? Because of me? Not likely.

'Well, then clearly you haven't been paying attention, John. Corkle has a whole network of resources. And what does Holmes have? A knack for solving riddles and a few unsavoury contacts. It must gall him something awful.'

'Nonsense. He thrives on this sort of challenge. And how dare you speak to me like that? I'm not a fool. I know full well the danger he's in. Yes, I'll grant he has little experience with the softer passions. Love is the stuff of grand opera to him, motivations for murder or suicide. But I know what I saw. He wept. Over you.'

'He has no feelings for me other than the physical sort. He made that clear in his letter.' God, how I hated the sound of my own whinging voice.

'Ah, yes. The letter.' He gave a rueful laugh. 'When he burst into our rooms that night, I thought he was ready for Bedlam. My God, Rose, he had no hat!' Apparently the lack of a hat was enough for Watson to suspect Holmes's sanity.

'He left in a hurry,' I offered sullenly.

'I rather got that impression. But no sooner had he entered the sitting room than he began to search it. Not a methodical search, no meticulousness at all. He tore the pictures from their hooks, ran his hands over the walls and frames, tossed papers and books from the shelves. Tables were upended, sofa cushions thrown aside, every object in the room lifted and discarded until the place was a shambles. Thank goodness Mrs Hudson was tending the sickbed of a friend, or I'm certain we would've had the police banging down the door. Finally I took hold of him and demanded to know what it was he sought in such a manner. "God help me, Watson," he replied, "I've no idea!" He began to laugh, and then in the next moment he was sobbing, his face in his hands. "I am betrayed. The woman has betrayed me." That's all he would say. His distress was such that I could only assume he had found you with another.'

My protest tangled in the embarrassing truth of what had transpired between the doctor and me only minutes before.

'We fought,' I muttered miserably. 'But not because... didn't he tell you what happened?'

'He wouldn't. Waved aside my questions and begged me not to speak at all. I could offer no comfort he would accept, and I thought I should have to sedate him. I actually went to fetch my bag. When I returned, something had changed. An epiphany, so he claimed.' Watson paused, and I heard the scrape of his fingernails in the scruff of his beard, a sound as familiar to me as his breathing. 'I must tell you, Rose, the calm that followed concerned me far more than his prior misery. He sat on the floor staring into dead space, his eyes moving the way a cat's will do when it sees something we cannot. When he got to his feet again, he was far too subdued for my comfort. He proceeded to fill his pipe, then gathered pen and paper, and locked himself in his bedchamber.'

He gave raspy chuckle. 'I feared he was composing a suicide note. Just as I was about to break down his door, he opened it and looked at me as if *I* had taken leave of my senses. He announced in a very firm voice that he was breaking off with you. I told him I thought it the wisest course under the circumstances. Of course, I believed you a wicked woman who'd broken his heart.'

I contemplated my wickedness for a moment. Something Watson had said struck me as curious.

'He came out into the sitting room to make this announcement?'

'Yes.'

I rocked forward, hugging myself, overcome with an emotion that felt foreign, almost painful. Something close to delight, I think.

'What is it, Rose? What's the matter?' He crawled back over to me and placed a compassionate hand on my shoulder, before grunting his disapproval. 'What can you find amusing in this?'

'Sherlock's mind! It's so deliciously devious I could eat it with a spoon.'

'He was genuinely devastated, Rose!'

'He *hoped* his declaration would be overheard.'

'By whom? I was the only one present.'

'John... it's not been safe to speak in the sitting room for a few months now. I told him that when he came to see me at the jail.' I leapt up, pacing the confines of our prison in feverish excitement. 'Holmes *wanted* Corkle to know he was breaking off with me.'

'He knew Corkle was involved?'

'He suspected it. And he knew someone was listening, making use of his private conversations. He just didn't know how. He was trying to draw the bastard out in the open!' I flopped onto the seat of the royal privy, wriggling my bottom and making the hinges on the lid groan in protest. 'I'll bet Holmes was having me watched the night you and I were abducted. Oh shit! I hope he wasn't counting on Harry...'

I heard Watson rise. 'Rose,' he said, with an intensity I paid not the least attention to. 'Be quiet, please.'

'Sorry, sorry. If you knew how much more I used to curse, John, you'd be proud of my restraint.' My mind was on fire with possibilities. 'I'll bet it was that fellow with the monocle. The goatee was so fake. I mean, geez, a monocle? Did he think it made him look more gay?'

Watson grasped me by the shoulders, shaking me. 'Will you be quiet, for God's sake,' he whispered. 'Someone's coming.'

It was too early for Crow and Ben to return. We had food and half a crate of bottled water left. Therefore, my mind reasoned, we were about to be rescued.

Annoyed that he'd failed to recognise salvation when he heard it, I jerked out of Watson's grasp and ran in the direction of the door. But before I could start shouting "hey, you stupid police, we're in here!", Watson threw an arm about my chest and covered my mouth with a damp palm. His voice licked my eardrum. 'Be ready to run.'

The muffled sigh of the bolt sliding back sent the thrill of a shiver through me. The door roughed across concrete, and Watson set me away from him, as he might a glass of sherry.

Light, burning light, seared my retinas.

'It's the gent's lucky da-'

Bam. A cannonball plowed into China Crow's stomach, knocking him through the doorway to impact the wall behind him.

My eyes watched, blinking and blinking, stubbornly refusing to accept the blur of light and shadow as separate bodies. Sounds emerged from the lumpy forms: animal roars, and grunts of pain, curses, demands and decrees.

I squinted and the shapes separated.

Watson straddled the thick body of China Crow, one hand squeezing the man's throat and the other bashing into his temple. Crow's cheeks were puffed out, his face red and white, then greyish-blue. His legs jerked, his hands beat the air.

I set my mark and burst forward.

Abruptly, Ben stepped into the picture, his hands clasped and falling hard between Watson's shoulder-blades. Watson fell sideways as I leapt over Crow's feet, and we tumbled all together, Ben and me and Watson, a kitten's ball of yarn unwinding down the corridor and rolling to a stop.

With a cry of pain, Watson stumbled to his feet, clasped me under my arm, and we ran.

'Stop!' Crow rasped 'I'll blow a hole through yer soddin' -' I could feel the revolver aimed at my back, the only barrier between a bullet and Watson's body as Crow's curses faded into the distance.

We ran as best we could; him with a kind of limping, hopping motion, but fast, and me slipping and sliding in thick wool socks as he pulled me along. Watson's injury made the wearing of shoes painful, and I never bothered with them in the vault. Now I wished I was wearing the Goddess of Victory's sporting gear.

We went left at the first juncture, and left again at the second: for no other reason, I think, then because it was dark that way and dark was familiar. But darkness was a treacherous friend.

At the end of a too-short corridor was another door, just like the one to our prison, only with a big padlock looped through the hasp. Watson jerked on it, banged the door with his fist, and spun about, slapping the walls.

'God damn it to hell.' It was the softest curse I'd ever heard, more like a prayer. I took his hand, trying to tug him back the way we'd come, only to see a glow of light filling the passage. Crow rounded the corner and skidded to a halt. I placed myself between them.

'Get out the way, girl!'

'No!'

'Get out the way,' he said. 'I'll not shoot him.'

'Put the gun down!' I snarled.

'I'm puttin' it down. See?' He placed the weapon on the floor and kicked it behind him, the fucker. His hands went up, the lantern blinding me as it swung to and fro. I heard the gun slide and spin to a stop, but I couldn't see where. 'No one's gonna die. I'm to take 'im to the boss, tha's all.'

I could make out the swelling knot at his temple, and the red marks on his face and throat. My gut told me he would not easily forgive the doctor those injuries. 'You're not taking him anywhere.'

He laughed low in his throat. 'Well, what'll ye 'ave us do, girl? 'Ow long y'think the gent's gonna cower behind yer skirts, eh? Makes a man feel less than a man, don't it, sir?'

'Step aside, Rose,' Watson said softly.

'No, John, don't, please -'

Watson took me firmly by the shoulders and pushed me aside. I skidded across the floor in my stocking feet.

'I'll be all right,' he said.

'No, you won't.' *No, I won't.* That was what I really meant. As soon as his grip eased, I whirled, flinging my arms around him. I wanted to press him into my flesh and absorb his every cell. I wanted to hide him inside me forever, my last and only friend.

He plucked my fingers from the torn, moth-eaten jumper he was wearing - something a wife had knitted for her sea-faring man, perhaps - and lifted them to his lips, a farewell kiss that would haunt me forever.

It took both men to peel me away. Ben spun the doctor to the wall and cuffed his hands behind his back. Ben looked grim and badly shaken up, but Crow seemed unaffected, immune to the venom of my curses, or my feet and fists. Ben scooped up the revolver from the floor. At some silent signal, he scooped me up as well, while Crow took charge of Watson.

The walls of the corridors were thick plaster with a recent layer of whitewash. We passed sconces on the walls set at regular intervals, the sort used with oil, not gas. This wasn't an ancient place, wherever it was, but certainly not newly-built. The door to my cell was still open, a gaping black hole in the wall on my right. Ten yards beyond, the corridor ended in another door, padlocked like the one that had prevented our escape. I wondered if there might be another woman like me locked behind that door. I shot a look over my shoulder.

Crow had his hand looped through the doctor's arm, like best pals out for a stroll. He was whispering something in Watson's ear, though I couldn't hear the words. I did hear Watson's flat reply. 'You've a rather large head to hold such a small mind.'

It was a comment worthy of Sherlock Holmes, and it cost the doctor dearly.

The first blow was a kidney-punch that sent Watson crashing to the floor with a look of stunned surprise. He seemed to have no breath to articulate his pain, and a long moment passed before the moan came stuttering out between his lips. Crow stood over him, legs planted solidly, arms akimbo. There was absolutely no expression on his features at all.

'Christ on a crutch,' Ben muttered, shaking his head. 'Here it comes.' He took me by the elbow and turned us both from what was coming.

I have some disjointed memory of breaking free of Ben and jumping on China Crow's back, then of being on the floor of my prison with Ben sitting on *my* back while I cried and roared and begged until my throat was raw and no sensible sound would come out. But the sounds of the beating didn't stop. Inflicting pain was some sort of tantric meditation to Crow. I stopped my ears and still I heard it: unending, interminable, hurting, hurting, hurting.

But so skilful was the punisher at his art that Watson was able to walk out of my life on his own two feet. The last time I saw him - ever - Crow brought him to the door to say goodbye.

'Say goodbye now,' Crow commanded the pulpy mass beside him.

Blood poured out of Watson's mouth, and out of the blood came words. Not goodbye. I think he said: 'Have faith.'

***

I can be forgiven for not recording in detail the time I spent alone. Long stretches of despair interspersed with dreams of home or nightmares of sound. I didn't eat much or often. I drank water merely to feed my tears, and after a while, I had no tears left anyway. I talked to myself. I screamed for help. Sang every song I knew. Masturbated until I was raw. Pinched and scratched myself until I couldn't feel it anymore. Cold bricks. Inky black. Madness. Toward the end, I hardly moved. I wanted to die but it was taking so long.

When Crow and Ben paid call on me again, something had changed.

The light sought me out in the darkness as it always had. I closed my eyes as I always did.

'Jeh-sus. She's a mess.'

'I done me worse.'

Silence. Then: 'Ye'd best not. Boss'll find out.'

'Won't know the difference. Look at 'er.'

Footsteps, then the crack of knees. A little poke in my shoulder. 'Oi.'

I coughed, opened my eyes onto the fat shade of Crow kneeling beside me. He smelled of gin. He smelled like he never wiped his arse. His knees cracked again as he stood. I rolled onto my back and looked up at giants.

'She's dropped a good stone.'

'Plenty o' flesh on the bone still. We could get ten, maybe fifteen from Dick Smiley just as she is.' There was a pause. 'I mean, if Moriarty don't pay us what 'e owes.'

The hands that had beaten and broken Dr Watson were sweating. He wiped them on his trousers

'Ye'd best do naught can be seen on 'er outside,' the smaller giant said.

'Shut yer 'ole, Ben.' He jerked his head in the direction of the door. 'Wait outside.'

Ben stared at him.

'Go,' Crow said.

'Leave a bit fer me then,' Ben said.

Suddenly, a dialogue that had seemed wholly unconnected to my empty world began to make horrible sense. *Not this*, I thought, *I can't go through this. It's too much. I'm tired.* But I rolled over and got to my feet anyway.

I guess I'd hoped for a burst of superhuman strength in the face of peril. An act of God would have been nice. But it was just me stumbling around, too weak, too slow. Crow let me get all the way to the door. It was part of the game.

My face kissed the concrete, the skin on my knees scraped bloody as he dragged me closer. His hands were huge, brutalising knobs, stroking and subduing simultaneously. My skirt fluttered over my back. The buttons of my drawers popped and flew. He spat on his cock and introduced it to my arse. Not even the right hole for Christ's sake.

I was exactly what he wanted me to be. A scared collection of cavities and handholds. My body's weakness had betrayed me, so I betrayed my body. I left it to suffer and debated whether or not to leave it for good. The time I'd spent alone in darkness made it so much easier to detach, and my soul seemed to float above the scene like a kite, stretching the line between life and death to the snapping-point.

But China Crow, with his torturer's instincts, knew I was attempting the ultimate escape, and he would not have me absent. He tricked me back with a soft word and gentle caress. 'Pretty, sweet thing. Such a good lass.'

When one is starving, the smell of food can cause both nausea and salivation. My flesh had a similar reaction. I ached for human contact, yearned towards any semblance of tenderness, yet bile came to my throat. I found myself firmly and painfully present inside my flesh. That was no good at all. I had to get out again.

I concentrated on the light, the sunny array of bright new things piled in the barrow in the hall, trying to separate myself from myself.

Biscuits. Biscuit tins. *Oh God.* Biscuit tins. *Help me.* Red. Blue. Green. Gold. Petticoat. White. White. *Oh my God. Stop, stop, stop it, stop it -*

Crockery jars gleamed and wavered. I blinked the sweat from my eyes. The black iron bands on a barrel leapt out in shocking relief. I blinked again and a large shadow sprouted from the light -

I screamed. The sound reverberated off the walls, shrivelled China Crow inside me and squirted him out. The shadow in the hall split suddenly in two. I screamed again.

'Bloody stupid cunt!' He flipped me onto my back and straddled me, his fingers twisting in my hair as he pulled me toward what he was frantically massaging with his other hand.

That did it. There was no way he was putting that thing in my mouth. I reached out, grabbed hold of the softest part of him and squeezed.

Then *he* screamed. His hands slapped wildly but I couldn't feel them. 'Ben! Christ! She's got me - the bitch has got me - leave off - aaww, God! Ben!' I twisted my nails into the tender bag of his scrotum and leaned back. His fingers struggled to free themselves from their tangled grip in my hair. His fist pounded my temple. Flashes of light exploded behind my eyes, but I wouldn't let go. I couldn't.

Then - rapture - the metallic click-click as a hammer drew back and a shell rolled into place. I laughed. *Come on, Ben. Pull the trigger.*

'Ben is indisposed,' said the voice.

I opened my eyes. The barrel of a revolver was stuck in Crow's right ear, turning his whimpers to the breathlessness of terror. I felt a brief flash of disappointment. I would have to go on living. I poured over every surface of that weapon as if the weapon itself were part of the hand that held it, a thing of muscle, blood and sinew.

The gaunt face of Holmes seemed suspended in the darkness above Crow's head, glazed by the yellowish light from the corridor. His face moved near the criminal's rough cheek, mouth so close they could have been lovers.

'You're between a rock and a hard place, Mr Crow,' he said in his scary quiet voice. 'Shall I have her tear them off, or shall I blow your brains out?'

Crow made a gargling sound. Holmes's finger twitched.

'Do know how close I am to killing you?' The barrel of the revolver dug its way into the man's bulbous head. '*Do you?*'

The big man keened.

'You can let go now.' Crow's eyes rolled in their sockets. 'It's all right. I have him.'

Holmes was talking to me.

'Let go, Gillian.'

My brain struggled to make my hand obey.

'Let go, sweetheart.'

Ah. He'd found the key. My fingers unlocked. Crow made a horrible, horrible noise, then fell to one side and curled up.

'On your belly,' Holmes told him. 'Face down.'

'Don't kill me, for the love of God -'

Holmes snarled, kicking him hard in the tailbone. 'Perhaps I should do what you're best at. Break a few of your bones, eh? On your belly. Now!' The man rolled onto his stomach, gagging. Holmes's knee dug between the man's shoulder-blades. 'Hands behind your head, just so. Good. Don't move, or I'll scatter your tiny brain around the room. You understand?' Crow grunted an affirmative.

Holmes said nothing to me, didn't look at me, even as he pulled me to my feet. He wrapped my fingers around the grip, my arms sagging from the weight of the weapon.

'If he moves, pull the trigger,' he said.

'OK' I stared at the broad back of Crow, concentrating hard on the sign of a twitch. Holmes stepped outside the door.

The sudden ache that filled me was so intense, like a little kid coming out of service-station to discover her parents driving away. I'm holding my Popsicle (only it's a gun) and I see the back of the car speeding down the highway (only it's *his* back) and... oh God! He left me. He left me here.

'Don't leave me! Please, please don't -'

The light was blocked again as Holmes, huffing a little, pulled Ben's body into the room. 'I've no intention of leaving without you,' he said between his teeth. 'Point the gun at Mr Crow, if you would.'

I turned the weapon from Holmes to the intended target. Holmes let Ben's upper body drop, the head hitting the stone floor with a thud. He retrieved the gun from my stiff fingers and proceeded to circle the room, keeping the revolver trained on them as he gathered up a blanket here, a piece of clothing there, a shoe...

'Where's the other one?' he murmured, kicking at stuff on the floor. I watched, afraid that if I took my eyes from him he'd disappear, but when he finally looked at me, really looked at me, I had to throw an arm up to shield my face. His eyes were incandescent. They hurt more the light.

'Oh, Gillian,' he whispered. I peered over my arm. *What kind of voice was this?* 'I tried to get here sooner. I tried. You must believe me.'

I couldn't decipher the meaning of glistening eyes and down-turned mouth, the moving frown between his brows, the angle of his head. I'd forgotten how. After a moment, his shoulders slumped and he resumed his search. For what, I didn't know.

'Here it is,' he said thickly. A shoe.

He took my elbow gently and guided me, shuffling, into the bright corridor.

Crow's voice behind us was screechy as a cartoon mouse, but soon became a scream, pleading to Holmes, who was God then.

God pulled the door closed and threw the bolt.

Chapter 26

The blanket Holmes wrapped around me smelled of camphor. He knelt at my feet like Prince Charming, shoe in hand. I thought, *this is just another dream where I get rescued.* My hand slapped against solid wall to steady myself when the shoe did not slip on gracefully to proclaim that I was the woman he sought.

'We have a journey ahead of us,' Holmes said, trying to force a twisted, dirty wool sock into a man's dance pump. 'Do you think you can walk?'

'Walk, dance, fly...'

'You're not dreaming, Gillian.'

'You always say that in my dreams.'

The other shoe went on more easily. 'You're not dreaming. I fear your injuries will make that all too clear soon enough.' He picked up the revolver and thrust it into the waistband of his trousers. 'I should have been here sooner if I hadn't panicked like a damnable fool.' He rolled the barrel off the cart and banged it on the floor, liquid sloshing inside. 'Crow thought he heard someone following and sent the little fellow back for a look. Stupid, *stupid* lack of concentration on my part. Of course, I couldn't use the lantern for fear of it being seen. I'd been following theirs, you see.' He jerked his head at the lantern, hanging from a hook on the wall. 'Some of these passages are pitch-black. Retracing my steps took forever. I couldn't hear their voices and thought I'd lost them...'

My brain stopped following the swift, nervous flight of his words. If I were dreaming, he certainly didn't look the way I saw him in dreams. In my dreams he glowed like Krishna.

He kicked at the wheels of the barrow, mouth moving, nonsense coming out '- well-oiled, bounded in rubber, so not much hope there -'

I suppose it was his clothing that finally convinced me I was awake. He was dressed like a merchant seaman in a boiled wool jacket and jumper, trousers well-worn at the seat and knees. The wooden grip of the gun poked out of the waistband in front, the barrel aimed at a rather precious part of his anatomy.

'- I heard you cry out but I couldn't risk Ben sounding an alarm, you see. I feared Crow might -'

'Why do men do that?' I wondered aloud.

His mouth stopped moving. He shook his head. The words were so soft, I cocked my head to catch the sound. 'It makes a weak man feel powerful, I suppose.'

'Aren't you afraid it might misfire?' I asked.

'I'm sorry?'

'In your trousers like that? What if it goes off?'

A breathy laugh of comprehension, not amusement. 'Oh.' He jiggled the grip of the pistol. 'The safety-catch is in place.'

'It could still go off.'

'Yes. All right.' He put the revolver in the back of his trousers.

After a few moments, a prize was held up: a tin red-cross box. He removed a brown bottle, tucked it into his pocket and began making a nest of blankets and clothes within the barrow.

'You haven't asked me,' I said, clutching the blanket over a shudder.

'Asked you what, bijou?'

The endearment brought another shudder. 'About Watson.'

He tensed, bent to retrieve a rucksack from the floor.

'You thought he'd be with me, didn't you?'

'No. I knew he'd been taken. The news came to me in cardboard box. A message wrapped around the little finger of a man's right hand.'

I slid down the wall, knees drawn up, staring at the bolted door.

'It wasn't his finger, Gillian.'

'You're sure?' I whispered.

'Quite.'

'I don't know where he was taken, or how long ago,' I offered.

He looked at his shoes. 'I estimate you've been alone here for five or six weeks.'

'Six weeks?' I couldn't believe it. 'That's all?'

He gazed at the padlocked door at the end of the corridor, then at me.

'Strange that your door had no similar lock upon it.'

'They weren't worried about someone getting in,' I said through chattering teeth.

'Still, I wonder...'

He went over and rattled the lock, then pressed his ear to the door. If it were anything like mine - six inches thick and lined with lead - he couldn't have heard much. He dropped the rucksack to the floor and started digging around in it. 'There could be a passage, or steps leading up.' He withdrew a large leather wallet and opened it flat on the floor, to display an impressive assortment of lockpicks and keys. The tools of the master cracksman. I watched as he probed the secrets of the lock.

'Where'd you learn that handy skill?' I asked. My voice so chipper it startled me.

It startled him too. He shot a worried glance over his shoulder before turning back to his task. 'A burglar by the name of Moole. He'd been arrested for a sloppy break-and-enter that ended in the death of a shopkeeper. I proved he'd been carrying out another robbery in a different part of town at the time. He was sent to Dartmoor, poor old bugger. Shortly before he passed on, he bequeathed me his kit.' I heard the clank of the lock surrendering to Holmes's ministrations. 'Ah. A willing woman,' he chuckled softly.

- knees burning, thick thumbs pressed into my flesh -

His hand touched my shoulder and I swallowed a scream.

'Are you in pain?'

'It's the light,' I snapped, shading my eyes. 'It's giving me a headache.'

He unstoppered the brown bottle and put its mouth to my own. 'The light,' he repeated. 'Of course. Nothing to do with being struck repeatedly on the side of the head. Here now, not too much.' My mouth followed the bottle like greedy baby. He reached out, wiping the traces of medicine from my chin, his hand lingering, cool knuckles dragging over my cheek.

Across the hall, almost on cue, came a muffled pounding from behind the door. Too late, I reached for his hand.

'Don't,' I said. His left hand trembled over the sliding bolt. 'Don't do it.'

He whirled on me. 'Mercy? You plead mercy for him after what he's done?'

'No!' I screamed. 'I want him to suffer! Suffer in the dark, wondering if he'll ever see sky, or stars, or streetlamps or anything, ever, *ever* again!'

He looked at me, and the language of his body I'd thought lost and forgotten came back. I understood what was etched so deeply in his face, written in his every gesture: guilt, rage, exhaustion, frustration and terrible grief.

My head felt suddenly very heavy, and I laid it on my knees. 'He's not the one you're after, Sherlock. He's just a little, *little* player in a much bigger production.'

He sucked in a breath, leaned back against the door and sank down. The revolver dangled between his knees and he dragged a hand over his face, erasing whatever I'd seen. 'But what is the play about, Gillian?'

'I'm not sure. I thought I knew, but... I'm having trouble thinking right now.'

Holmes sighed and got to his feet. He folded up Moole's tool kit, returned it to his pack, and shrugged into the straps again. His voice was subdued, gruff, as he removed the padlock from the hasp. 'Wait here. I'll have a look.'

'I'll go with you.' I started to get to my feet, but I couldn't seem to find them.

'Save your strength. I'll have a quick look and be back for you.'

I continued to paw my way up the wall, stood leaning against it, waiting for my legs to solidify. He lit the bull's-eye lantern, opened the shutter, and grasped the door's handle. It groaned its way by inches across the floor of the hallway. Light played over stairs that led down, not up. Fetid air drifted from the blackness below, and he took a step back.

'There's something dead down there, Sherlock.'

'A rat most likely. I shan't be long.' Yet he hesitated.

'It's not a way out,' I told him.

'We don't know that yet.'

'I'm going with you.'

'Very well! If you should faint, don't expect me to –' He bit off the angry retort, fully aware that to finish it would make him a liar. I had him over a barrel of guilt. 'Stay close behind me and mind your step.'

We proceeded down uneven stairs, roughed out of the earth itself. Walls grew increasingly damp and slimy to the touch. Unfortunately, so did the steps.

Holmes slipped from my grasp and skidded down several feet ahead of me, circles of light from his lantern bouncing over the walls and ceiling in a Tinkerbell dance.

'No, no,' he cautioned me as I made my way to him. 'I'm all right. I've reached the bottom, though I don't recommend the method.'

He caught my hand at the base of the stairs. We found ourselves in a tunnel of claustrophobic proportions. The air was close, sticky, and the smell got stronger as we moved through it; sickening sweet, yeasty, mingled with decaying blood and a waft of carbolic. Other chemicals I couldn't identify. The scent reeked of *perfume de Corkle*.

Holmes's sweaty fingers slid out of mine. 'Wait here,' he grunted, and then he was gone. Quick steps faded with the light he'd taken with him.

After a moment of hyperventilating panic in a pitch-black tunnel, I began patting my way along the wall, shoes scuffling along until I could track a glow. The tunnel grew perceptibly wider, and I was almost breathing normally again when I emerged into a large room cut out of the earth and shored up with bricks and timber.

Holmes stood with his back to me in the centre of the space, the lantern held out in his stiff fingers, arm crooked and immobile as a statue's.

He had stumbled onto a movie set, a snuff-film chamber of horrors, complete with camera, adjustable lighting umbrellas, spots, drops, and props.

The central image in this macabre installation was the body on the stone slab. It was in the same position I'd seen in the video, only now the body was wrapped in layers of gauze, coated with a pale yellow substance; amateur embalming followed by an amateur attempt at mummification.

There were worse things in the room, which my eyes saw and my mind refused to translate.

Holmes whirled on me, gasping like a baby taking its very first breath. His expression was a perfect mixture of gut-sick dread and terrible confusion.

'What *is* this?' he shouted. I couldn't respond, couldn't stop my eyes bouncing from one grotesque image to another. Male genitalia in jars of preserving fluid; scalpels in a gleaming row; a little girl's bloody dress; tin pails stained with rust or blood; an enema bag suspended from a meat-hook. A head in a hermetically-sealed glass case, eyes and mouth sewn shut.

Locked steamer trunks stood like sentinels flanking the entrance, flanking me as I stood there, seeming all the more sinister by the mere fact of their presence in such a room. They could contain anything. Suddenly, the images were blocked by Holmes's chest.

'Don't look, don't look, don't look,' he murmured, lips pressed to my hair as he forced me to step back and back again. My butt kissed the hard-packed earth, and he whipped the blanket completely over my head. His clammy palms, squeezing my numb hands, were no comfort at all.

'Don't look,' he repeated firmly, and moved away.

But I was compelled to look. I couldn't *not* look, any more than Holmes could *not* investigate.

Tending to my terror had enabled him to recover from his own, it seemed. He examined the contents of the room with a sweep of the bull's-eye lantern, spotted an oil lamp on a shelf and lighted it. Turning quickly from the horrors it illuminated, he carried it to the white-draped table next to the body on the stone slab.

Surgical instruments were lined up in a gleaming row, and he traced his fingertips dangerously over razor-sharp edges and smooth bone handles. Next to that, a smaller table held a washbasin and a spirit lamp over which a white enamelled pot rested on a trivet. Holmes brushed the hair from his forehead, picked up one the scalpels, hand posed over the face of the mummy.

'I thought I told you not to look,' he said.

'What are you going to do?'

'I'm going to find out if this is real, or some sort of dummy.'

A dummy! Yes, that's what it was. Beneath the gauze wrappings would be a body filled with sand.

The blade was so sharp, it hardly made a sound as he drew a fine line over the forehead, and down over the mouth. After this vertical slice, he made two horizontal cuts, one over the brow and another at the chin. He set the scalpel aside. Long fingers dug into the slit and pried the wrappings from the face. There was a slight hissing sound and the detective reeled back, hand over his mouth. He turned away. He turned back again.

'Oh,' he moaned softly, chin sinking into his chest. 'Dear God...'

I thought, *no, no, no, please don't let it be John, please -*

'It's Harry's friend,' he whispered.

My relief was quickly followed by self-reproach. I'd known it would be Stewart Ronaldson, not a prop filled with sawdust. Yet, the entire display seemed designed to make Corkle somehow greater than the sum of his parts. With this tongue-in-cheek nod to the horror genre, he'd failed to see the obvious about himself: If one cuts off penises and puts them in jars then one is certifiably insane.

A strange, uncomfortable bubble of laughter tickled the back of my throat. I swallowed it.

Holmes moved from Stewart's body to the head in the glass case, comparing it to a photograph he held. Poor head, with its jagged bit of bone, covered in dried and shrivelled viscera, poking out from the raggedy edges of the neck. Only the pale hair, still curled into a modish wave back from the brow, made me think of Merrill Holbrook. Holmes grunted and thrust the photograph into a back pocket of his trousers, free to turn his attention to what intrigued him most. Now that I noticed, the cameras and lighting equipment were in the stages of being broken down for storage. Probably what the trunks were for. Perhaps Corkle had never meant the detective to see that part of the installation.

Holmes ran his fingers tentatively over metal and plastic, fiddling with the screws that made the light-stands and adjustable shades go up and down, back and forth, seeing how everything worked on a practical level. The camera fascinated him: how could it not, with all those buttons and things that whirred and beeped and lit up?

I took a breath. Couldn't feel myself breathing.

He turned the camera over and over in his hands. 'Parts of this appear to be composed of similar material as the broken plate from Corkle's room. Was it a photographic plate, then? How does it record the images? Who designed it? Where is it from?'

'Another time,' I whispered.

Holmes sighed, misinterpreting my reply. 'Sooner or later I will know the truth, Gillian.' He placed the camera on a table and picked up his lantern to survey the room again. A full circle brought him around to face me. 'This is Moriarty's laboratory, yes?'

So. Holmes had discovered Moriarty in concept if not in person.

'This is Thomas Peerson Corkle's little shop of horrors. He's not Moriarty. At least, he's not the one I met.'

'Whatever he's calling himself... he created this place, did he not?'

'I can only assume as much.'

'It's a hideous joke.'

'Yes.'

'Why?' he asked. 'What's it for? Why go to the trouble of using real bodies? Why light the stage for a performance if all the actors are dead?'

'Let's get out of here. Please.' I tried to get to my feet. My muscles were jelly. 'Please, Sherlock.'

Perhaps I hadn't spoken out loud. His back was to me, hiding the fairy-light of his lantern. But when he turned around, he held something else, cradled like an aborted foetus in his palm. His fingers spread. Long, silky strands of red hair glittered as they fell through the light.

I felt the scream well up, but it never came out. A black shapeless thing seemed to gather form before my eyes, rising from the floor to fill my mouth and nostrils. I heard myself gasping and gasping for air as I beat at the thing that threatened to devour the last tiny spark of light in my soul.

Chapter 27

I spent a week in Middlesex Hospital, the benevolence of the institution owing more to Harry Hughes's money than the tenor of Holmes's overwrought demands.

A sister of mercy scrubbed my flesh raw in an effort to rid me of the filth of my experiences, layer by subcutaneous layer. Mewling, but otherwise too weak to protest, I accepted this fresh pain. The water was warm at least, and the soap smelled nice. She dragged a fat comb through matted curls, even trimmed my nails short so I wouldn't scratch myself. She assumed that if I weren't mad already, I soon would be.

As a woman who'd been held captive in a dark room for several weeks was something of a novelty, I saw a parade of medics. Serious young men, trying not to look as uncomfortable as they felt.

'Ah,' a doctor commented, 'I have seen this before in such cases. Gentlemen, you will note the unresponsive, glazed expression. Her mind is gone. Her body ruined.' I laughed, which only confirmed the learned man's diagnosis. 'What sort of life can she hope for now?' he commented sadly.

'Get out,' said Holmes. 'All of you. Get out.'

My eyes were weakened from my time in darkness. I was curtained off from sunlight and gaslight and moonlight. They gave me dark spectacles to wear should any other form of light somehow penetrate the shadows.

One day, over the protests of the nurses, Harry brought a five-course meal from Previtali's, packed lovingly by the master chef himself into wicker baskets. China, silver, sparkling wine glasses and wine to accompany each course.

It was a gesture born of guilt. He'd been berating himself constantly since his first visit and he'd become something of a bore. But the food was so much more appealing than the beef broth and gruel I'd been swallowing for days that I made an effort to eat it. The doctor on the ward, pleased to see me trying, told the nurses to let me eat what I would, but that I was to have no more than a sip or two of wine.

I gnawed the squid in thoughtful silence. Harry kept checking his watch.

'What's going on?' I asked suspiciously.

'All sorts of things, but I don't think Sherlock wants you to know about them.' He darted a glance around the curtain dividing me from the woman and her gallstone in the bed next to mine, then drew a chair close to me. 'Apparently, withholding evidence in a robbery case is something quite dreadful. And then yesterday he was served with legal papers.'

'You think he'll be prosecuted?'

'Don't know. This has to do with something else. Something worse.' He plucked a tiny sauce-covered tentacle off my plate, his voice dropping to a whisper. 'A horrid woman is divorcing her equally horrid husband and has named

Sherlock as correspondent. That idiot actor he was chatting up the night you were... you know, when it all happened. T. Evelyn Wickford. Holmes left that night with Wickford in a rented carriage. Dr Watson was supposed to follow them.'

At the mention of Watson's name, I pushed the plate away.

'It seems the man's wife was also having her husband followed by a private inquiry agent. He spied on them, got it all down on paper.' I gulped. 'Oh, nothing *physical*,' he hastened to add. 'Sherlock was trying to trick some sort of confession from the man. He didn't tell me what about. Anyway, now the hag's suing for divorce. She'll get it under the circumstances. Irksome, isn't it? After all the lovers that fat old man's had, it's Sherlock gets marked for it.'

Holmes came in a short while later. He looked strained and tired, but when he saw the china plate in front of me emptied of food, he smiled. Harry had eaten most of it, though we chose not to share that information with him.

'Forgive my late arrival. I had to detour to Pall Mall, and it took longer than I expected.' Pall Mall. His brother lived near there. 'How are we today, Miss Petra?'

'We're better, but... we don't look very happy.'

'We're not,' he replied. Harry shot him a furtive, questioning gaze. Holmes flicked a glance in my direction and gave his head a small shake.

Harry leapt to his feet. 'Well, I'd best be off. I'll send a couple of boys round to pick up the remains.' He gave me a quick kiss on the not-bruised side of my face and hurried out of the door.

Holmes took the vacated chair and crossed his legs, foot bouncing nervously as he beat the crown of his top hat with one spotless glove. I poured a glass of wine and handed it to him.

'Divorce, eh?'

He threw his head back with a groan. 'I knew I should never have told him.'

'What are you going to do?'

'Well, if I must appear in court, and it seems I must, I'll simply tell the truth. I was pursuing an investigation.' He drained the glass, and then leaned forward, squeezing my hand tightly. 'A trivial matter. You mustn't concern yourself. Here's good news. You're being released tomorrow. Harry's agreed to put you up. Seems he missed your company.'

'Where will you be?'

He averted his eyes, and his mouth was already framing an avoidance when the door to the room opened and a nurse's voice said in that hushed way of nurses: 'Over there, sir, the last bed on the left. Please take care not to disturb the others.'

'Thank you, Sister,' Lestrade's voice replied. He poked his nose around the curtain. 'There you are, Mr Holmes.' The rest of his wiry little body followed, and he stood uncomfortably at the foot of the bed, turning his hat by the brim.

'Sorry to disturb you at your sickbed, ma'am, but I needs must speak with Mr Holmes on a matter of some urgency.' He looked at Holmes and jerked his head in the direction of the corridor. 'Privately.'

Holmes's eyes widened, and he scrambled out of his chair.

'If this is about China Crow,' I cried, 'you two will stay right here.'

Lestrade squinted at me. He gave a little gasp of recognition, and his face flushed. 'Er, yes, miss. It's to do with them that were keeping you locked away.'

'If you tell me they have escaped, Inspector -' Holmes began, his jaw tight.

'Well, in a manner of speaking, that's just what they have done, though they shan't find Hell a pleasant way to spend eternity. We found 'em in the room just as you said, only, well, they were dead. Asphyxiated with poison through the vents. We don't know what sort, as yet.'

'And what of the other room?'

Lestrade met the detective's eyes sympathetically. 'There weren't nothing in it, Mr Holmes. The dirt was marked up and heavy objects had clearly been moved quick-like, but no evidence of what you claimed to've seen.'

Holmes growled and slammed the top hat on his head. Walking-stick in hand, he swept from the room, crying: 'No evidence! We'll just see about that!'

This incident was the talk of the ward for the rest of my short stay.

Three days later, tired of waiting and filled with a creeping anxiety that time was running out, literally, I paid a call to the house in Baker Street.

'I've come to see Mr Holmes,' I told Mrs Hudson.

'He's consulting with a gentleman at present, ma'am,' she replied.

'May I wait?' I asked. 'I've walked some distance and I'm not well.'

The guitar case in my hand seemed to trigger the memory of a strapping girl once in her employ, but she didn't recognise that girl in the gaunt woman standing on her doorstep. My face was hidden beneath a widow's veils, my speech the mannered dialect of a lady. After a moment's uncertainty, she drew me in, clucking in sympathy for my sorrowful plight - whatever it was - and bade me be seated in the foyer.

'Whom may I say is calling, ma'am?' she asked.

'Mrs Maria Tory,' I replied.

I heard her rap lightly on his door. Barely two seconds passed and he popped out of the doorway, peering over the railing.

'Mrs Tory,' he said, hurrying down the stairs. 'Forgive me. I had intended to visit you but my schedule is somewhat hectic of late -'

'I forgive you,' I whispered.

In the sitting room was Lady Holbrook's solicitor, Mr Maitland. He bowed, though it was clear he didn't welcome the intrusion.

I sat in the basket chair, trying to appear too involved in my own concerns to care what they were talking about. All around me were the telltale signs of preparations for a journey. A long one. A medium-sized trunk was already half-full.

'If we could continue this discussion at your offices, Mr Maitland...' Holmes began.

'And what more is there to discuss, sir? The purpose of hiring you was to avoid a scandal. Scandal is now imminent.' Maitland looked pointedly at the trunk on the floor, then back to Holmes. 'You will not be able to run from the consequences, I warn you.'

The detective's jaw clenched. 'I am not running from any consequences, Mr Maitland.'

'Indeed? It is my understanding that you spent a good deal of your retainer on liquor, clothes and various indiscretions. One of which has come back to haunt you, if my sources are correct.'

'As I recall from that first interview, my willingness to play the part was what led you to retain my services in the first place.'

'You said you could find him!'

'And I did,' Holmes replied coldly. 'That his head was no longer attached to his body in no way alters that fact.'

'Where is the proof?'

Holmes went to the mantel and withdrew a photograph from an envelope. He thrust it in the solicitor's face. 'Is this Lord Merrill?'

From Maitland's reaction of distaste, I knew it must be the photograph Holmes had taken from Santelli's studio on the day of our outing. Maitland drew his eyes away and nodded.

'This is the face I saw,' Holmes finished.

'But... even so, there is nothing to bury, for Heaven's sake!'

'I will gladly sign an affidavit to the effect that I know him to be dead. The bride is a widow. The family keeps her wealth. Where is the problem?'

'An affidavit from a man named in divorce proceedings involving infidelities with sodomites is not particularly useful.'

'There is a lady present, sir, in case you have forgotten,' Holmes said coolly.

Maitland bowed in my direction again. 'Forgive me, Madam, I do not wish to seem rude, but my business with Mr Holmes is -'

'Finished,' Holmes said.

'Far from it. As there is no proof that Lord Merrill is dead and not simply run away from his wife, her father has begun annulment proceedings on her behalf. My client's family may be left destitute as a result, in which case I personally will file charges against you.'

'For what, may I ask?'

'Fraud.' The solicitor turned to me. 'Madam, I would advise you find yourself another agent to deal with your difficulties, for this man will never again practice his questionable craft in this city - or in the civilised world for that matter - when I have done with him. Good day!'

No sooner had Maitland left the house than there was a scuffle in the foyer.

'Sir, you can't go up there!'

'Let me by, woman! He's put me off long enough, I say. Let me pass!'

The detective took a deep breath and drew himself to his full six feet three inches. He stepped into the hall and called down. 'Let him pass, Mrs Hudson. Oh, and Mrs Hudson? Would you be so kind as to make tea for my guests? Do come up, Mr Murray.'

The droopy basset-hound eyes were more pronounced in him, but the vivid red hair identified him perfectly as Liza's father. He whipped the hat from his head and bowed, first to me, then, more tersely, to Holmes. 'I've come to inquire about my girl, Mr Holmes.'

'Won't you sit down, sir?'

Murray was too agitated to take the offer. 'Look you now, Mr Holmes, I gave you money in good faith to find the murderin' fiend that killed my Liza. Money taken up by friends and neighbours could little afford it. I want to know what you done for your pay.'

'Surely you can take refreshments before assaulting my skills and character.'

This calm response caused the man to blink in confusion. 'I've not come to assault you, Mr Holmes. I want answers, is all. Was it the pie man? Have you found him out?'

Holmes looked miserable. 'Yes. And no.'

'Like all your answers, no answer at all. I want back the five quid I give you or I'll go to the papers! Don't think I won't. You'll be shown for a fraud, a fraud that takes advantage of a poor man's grief!'

At Murray's initial request, Holmes had gone immediately to his desk, but when the final words left the man's mouth, the detective paused. I saw a shudder pass through him, that somebody-walking-over-your-grave kind of shudder. Twice in one day he'd been called a fraud.

He jerked open the top drawer of the desk, shuffled papers, and withdrew a wrinkled brown envelope, fat with coins.

Seeing that envelope gave me the strangest feeling of hope. This whole time I hadn't known he'd been investigating Liza's death. I couldn't get into the man's head. And neither could Corkle.

Holmes handed Murray the packet. 'Here is what you gave me in December. A different man will do no better for you, I fear. I have reason to believe the person responsible for your daughter's death has left the country.'

No. Impossible. Corkle was the person responsible, and he needed me to get home. He couldn't have left without me. He couldn't have...

Through a cloud of crepe, I saw Holmes and Murray bending over me.

'She's fainted.'

'Fetch a glass of water from the sideboard. Quickly, man!'

I didn't feel like I'd fainted. I was fully conscious of far too much.

Holmes threw back my veils and removed the dark spectacles. I turned my head from the light.

Mrs Hudson chose that moment to bring tea. I heard the rattle of the tray, and her gasp. 'Dear lord. Is it Rose? What's *she* doing here, Mr Holmes?'

'She's a client,' he replied. Then: 'Thank you, Mr Murray.'

'Poor woman,' Murray murmured. 'She's suffered at someone's hand, that's sure. Was her child one of them?'

'A different crime executed by the same evil man. I don't wish to be rude, sir, but -'

'I'm real sorry, Mr Holmes. I had no right to come bustin' in your door. I suppose you done your best.'

'My best will have to get much better, I'm afraid.' He clasped the man's hand.

'But I will find the devil and bring him to justice no matter how long it takes. That much I promise you.'

Murray nodded, not trusting his voice. Then he was gone.

I opened my eyes. The shades had been drawn again, softening the edges of everything. Holmes leaned against the door, arms crossed over his chest.

'You should not have come,' he chided. 'You've not yet recovered your strength.'

I looked about at the disarray of an anticipated hurried departure. 'Where are you going?'

'Wherever Corkle has gone.'

'You know where that is?'

'Singapore, the East Indies...' He blew out a noisy sigh, and then deposited his lean body on the sofa across from me. 'How is it the devil is a step ahead of me all the way?'

'He knows your tricks. He knows too much about your life, even the parts you haven't lived yet.' I rose and went to the fireplace. 'May I use your magnifying glass, please?'

Holmes came up behind me and handed me the glass. I wasn't sure the transmitter would still be there. Surprisingly, it took me only a moment to find it. With the detective peering over my shoulder, I pried the thing loose, using one of his pipe-cleaning tools. It lay in my palm, a wafer-thin piece of plastic, mocking the colour of my flesh. He plucked it greedily from my hand before I could close my fist.

'And this is... what?'

'It's how he... how we listened to your conversations.'

'This? Has Mr Bell done something astonishing with his articulated telephone?' He turned it over and over, looking for markings, and watching the colours blur and shift.

'There's another on the underside of that table.'

I'd barely finished the sentence before he was on his back beneath it, hands doing a shadow-puppet dance of excitement from behind the table scarf. After he'd retrieved the transmitter, I held out my hand and he reluctantly dropped the pair of them into my palm. Before he could scramble up again, I went to his chemical table and dropped them into the jar of sulfuric acid. When I turned back to him he was all glower.

'You didn't have to do that.'

'There are things a clever man like you shouldn't be messing with. I would have destroyed the disk too, if it hadn't been stolen from you. Which I had nothing to do with, by the way.'

'I know.'

'Do you want to hear the truth of me now?'

He swallowed. 'God help me, Gillian. I don't think I do.' Then he whispered: 'Yes.'

Chapter 28

I ate a sandwich, drank the tea, and recreated my world for him.

Sherlock Holmes smoked pipe after pipe, long legs crossed, eyes closed, exactly the pose Watson had described in his writings. Though I knew the picture I painted plagued his mind with a million questions, he didn't ask a single one that didn't pertain to the issues at hand. And to credit his remarkable genius, he didn't dismiss my tale outright.

'It fits the facts, I suppose,' he said tentatively. 'But the idea that I should be singled out for such a curious experiment is not nearly as flattering as I would have imagined.'

'I think you were chosen because you're interesting without being terribly important to major world events. A few sensitive documents recovered for the government, but -'

'Ah. Thank you. That puts a lid on any drop of vanity I had remaining.' He took the pipe stem from his mouth and stared at it, then reached to tap the dottle into the ashtray with a pile of others. 'So... you have a device that tells you what o'clock it is in any part of the world, allows you to speak to anyone in the world, shows you pictures of major world events as they happen, and yet you say you never carry it.'

'One can become a slave to information, Sherlock. Spend so much time trying to save time that all your precious time is wasted.'

'A strange commodity, time.'

'It's all relative,' I said. But it was a joke he couldn't get.

He looked at me, dark brows drawn together in a troubled frown. 'If what you say is true -

that Watson will chronicle my life's work for public consumption - then wouldn't the simplest, most effective way to end my career be to kill the man who will make me so well known?'

I let out a shaky breath. 'It may have been considered. I don't know. If Watson doesn't write about you, someone else could. I don't think Moriarty wanted to challenge fate. He only wanted to see if it existed.'

'I don't believe in fate,' he said.

I leaned toward him. 'Prove it.'

'How? Clearly I haven't the tools.'

'This is *your* world, Sherlock Holmes. The Professor is operating on your turf by remote control, relying on Corkle to achieve his objectives.'

'Ah,' he said. 'I suppose one cannot be an effective puppet-master if the strings are too long.' He gazed at the pipe in his hand for a moment, then asked: 'And why do you suppose you're here, Gillian?'

'Corkle said I have something in my arm, a kind of beacon that'll make sure we get back where we belong.' I shrugged. 'Other than that, I don't see how my presence was required at all.'

'I do,' he said softly. My indulgent, sceptical smile caused him to redden. 'I mean, I think I do. For one, if the Professor is as clever as you say, he'd know full well his agent could not be trusted. How else could Moriarty ensure that you returned safely unless Corkle's own return depended upon it?'

'Why should Moriarty care if I return, Sherlock? Anyway, my usefulness as a spy ended that night in the linen cupboard.'

His blush deepened. 'Perhaps I've misunderstood, then. You *are* some sort of an expert in your field, are you not? As such, you would have a wide range of knowledge about British society in the nineteenth century, ameliorated by personal experience. You have also acquired a knowledge of me, which can be considered... unique. It would be vital to his experiment that you, of all people, return safely. If there are changes in my life as recorded in your history books, who else will be able to tell what has changed, if anything?'

That hit me hard. Very hard. Mostly the fact that he'd seen so clearly what hadn't occurred to me. I was the king in this game of chess: no real power, and yet, the very piece without which the game would mean nothing.

'I didn't know,' I choked out. 'I'm sorry. I'm *so* sorry I've been a party to this.'

'What difference does that make?' he snapped. 'You're sorry. Apology accepted. Can we move on?' He reached over and gripped my hands tight between his own. 'I don't give a damn about the reasons for all this. I don't even know that I believe them. I know Thomas Corkle has Watson, and that is more important than whether I am perceived as great in some future I shall never live to see.'

'You *know* he has Watson? You're certain?'

He brought out a bit of brown paper from a pocket inside his jacket; wrinkled, stained, folded and refolded countless times. 'This was delivered to my hand in the wee hours of Friday last.'

The writing was the doctor's. I'd seen it dozens of times when I'd been their maid. But this wasn't the usual physician's scrawl. It was the shaky hand of a desperate last chance. "22 May. Live pool. Hope. And jeer."

'Hope and jeer?' I looked up. '*Anjer!* Anjer is a port of call in Java. The relay station for the send-forward is on a mountain south of there.'

'Java,' he whispered. 'Of course. The *Hope* is a barkentine out of Liverpool. It left for the Dutch East Indies two weeks ago.'

'And you just received this on Friday?'

'It had to pass through many hands. It's remarkable it found me at all.' He took the paper back from me and stared at it. 'Or perhaps not...'

I gazed about at the hurried preparations. 'You weren't thinking of leaving without me, were you?'

'Obviously.'

'Well, you can't.'

He smiled. 'Obviously.'

***

Our ship arrived at Java on the 16th of August, skirting the smaller islands through the Sunda Straights. Krakatoa put on a dazzling pre-show for free, belching plumes of steam and ash into a deep blue sky.

In my time, Krakatoa no longer jutted majestically from the ocean. With the force of more than ten-thousand atomic bombs, it had erupted and collapsed into the sea a century before I was born, taking the lives of countless living creatures with it. As I looked about, I wondered how many of the people watching would be alive after the volcano's epic. Hot showers of glass would pummel the earth. Airwaves with amplitudes greater than those of the largest nuclear weapons tests would make four journeys around the globe. Ash would circle the world for years to come, changing the weather, the economy, and the colour of sunsets in Surrey.

One hell of a power-source.

With fake papers obtained from Shinwell Johnson, we travelled as husband and wife. The times we spent on that journey were the only truly happy times we had together, for all that they were doomed. The day we stepped on shore at Anjer, we both knew it. It was in the air, in the heat of the dry monsoon pressing on our lungs. The land rolled beneath our unsteady sea legs and sweat burst from our pores. Our clothes were damp in less than a minute.

Holmes arranged for our baggage to be sent on to the hotel, and returned from this task hat off, wiping the perspiration from his brow with an already-soggy handkerchief. He pointed to one of the small ships anchored off shore.

'There it is,' he said. 'The *Hope.*'

A time-bomb started ticking in my head. *Ten days until send-forward.*

'Well, *I* feel somewhat hopeful now that I've seen it,' he said, as he helped me into the carriage.

I settled into the seat, smoothed my skirt, and turned to assure him that I was also brimming over with hope, that we'd soon find Watson and everything would be peachy. But as I looked down, the glare of sun on the water erased his features for a moment. I must have made some sound. Anguish, perhaps. Startled, he paused, one foot on the carriage-wheel.

'What is it?' he whispered anxiously. I stroked the sharp edge of his jaw, felt the slight bristle of whiskers beneath.

'Nothing,' I said, shading my eyes. My gaze drifted to the boats rocking gently in the bay, then back to him. His gaze was dubious and slightly vexed. 'Really,' I insisted. 'It's nothing.'

Climbing in next to me, he muttered: 'I hate it when you do that.'

I snapped open my parasol. With a low grumble to me and a sharp word to the driver, the carriage jerked forward and we trotted off to our shady room at the Imperial Hotel.

Chapter 29

The air was perfumed with the tangy aroma of tamarinds. Orchids grew within the dappled light and shadow of foliage girding winding paths, wickedly sensual flowers that seemed to yearn for the tickle of a dragonfly on a throbbing stamen. Spider-webs pulsed and glittered. Insects hummed. Tiny Javanese sparrows shot from tree to tree like darts from blow-guns.

Paradise with the Sword of Damocles hanging over it.

Most of the natives were Muslims, but as in any port city there were sections devoted to sailors and their fun. Dressed in nothing but my underpinnings and a silk shawl, I became one of the mixed-breed whores plying her trade in bars frequented by European seamen. I left with a different sailor each night. He just happened to be the same man.

By the fourth night I was beginning to think I'd be sitting on some sailor's lap for the rest of my life, while all the time the bomb kept ticking. *Six*-tick-*days*-tick-*left*. Holmes nursed a drink at a solitary table, while I chatted up the boys. Being the consummate actor, his Gallic sailor was a study in dark thoughts. Perhaps he'd lost his woman to another; perhaps he'd killed someone as a result; perhaps he was just a naturally mean individual. I avoided him myself, though a couple of the other girls didn't. To my annoyance, he accepted their company at his table. Sometimes I'd venture a glance and notice a girl's chair much too close to his, her hand beneath the table as she leaned into him. I tried not to let it affect my mission.

But finally, we got the break we'd been looking for. A very drunk, very young seaman from the *Hope*, one Kenneth Dalby, told me a curious tale of how he'd earned a sizeable sum shipside. He showed me a pearl necklace he'd probably purchased for his mother or sister, promising it to me if I'd step outside with him. I nibbled his earlobe, hoping Holmes was watching, and whispered that I needed to go 'make water chop-chop'. I gave the French sailor a wink on my way out of the back door.

The moon was high, ringed by a greenish hue, caused by the particles Krakatoa was throwing into the atmosphere. I stared up at it nervously.

Holmes's voice startled me.

'Well?' he said. He struck a match and the bowl of his pipe glowed, illuminating his face in skeletal fashion.

'Mr Dalby has offered me a string of pearls to adorn my lovely throat.'

'To what great good fortune does Mr Dalby owe his largesse?'

'It seems that some scientist chap they had on board – little man, spectacles – paid Mr Dalby and a fellow crewman five thick 'uns each to haul a couple of trunks from below deck and throw them overboard after they'd left Singapore. They were godawful heavy, he says.'

'Two trunks?'

'Probably the video equipment.'

The moonlight shone down on his troubled face. 'From what I've seen, all of that could easily fit into one trunk.'

'He might have had stuff I didn't know about.'

'Gillian, we must face the possibility.'

'No. Watson is his bargaining chip to assure my co-operation.'

'He doesn't need to assure your co-operation. You're here now.'

'But he couldn't have known that when he had those men throw the trunks overboard.'

He jerked his shoulders in a tense shrug. 'As you say.' Smoke from his pipe billowed softly into the moon-bright sky. 'I think we've discovered all we can for the moment. Let's get you back to the hotel. You need to rest.'

The careful use of pronouns set off an alarm. 'What will you be doing while I rest?'

'Making inquiries of my own. No...' He drew me close to stop my protest, face nuzzling behind my ear and jostling the orchid there. 'I shall never be able to concentrate with you underfoot.'

Young Dalby, wondering if I'd fallen in, leaned out the back door of the bar and saw the two of us strolling away arm in arm. 'Oi! Why're you going off with that bloke? I got pearls in my pocket, you daft whore!'

Holmes snorted. 'He won't have them long if he keeps announcing it like that.'

'Frenchie's got something better in his,' I threw over my shoulder.

The boy ducked back into the building, and we could hear his cries inciting shipmates to join him in beating the 'frog what stole my girl'. Laughing like fools, Holmes and I took off running.

He left me at the hotel. I went to bed, got up late, washed, put on the bloody uncomfortable corset and proper lady's clothes, and had breakfast alone. He didn't return that day or that night. I knew he sometimes disappeared for long stretches when he was hot on the trail. But after another day with no word from him, I knew something was wrong.

I paced the balcony outside our room, cooled by the breeze through the sugar palms. Beetles the size of small mice, and moths of *every* size, dive-bombed the citron candles burning in pots of sand along the balustrade. Mosquitoes feasted on me, but I refused to seek escape under the screen of netting over the bed. I was dressed only in drawers and camisole, pacing and scratching the bites bloody, when I heard the door opening inside the room.

I turned in relief, but it was short-lived.

'The lady was expecting her husband, it seems,' the tall, blond gentleman in spotless white linen said. It was the driver of the van on the night I was kidnapped, the one Iris had pointed out as her cousin. He looked the quintessential landowner now, straw hat upon his head, holster on his hip. Stepping in behind him was the bitch herself. She grinned.

'How's married life treating you, Miss Gillian?' she asked.

They both had guns, of course.

***

Corkle had taken residence in a manor house on a small coffee plantation about five miles east of Serang, an inland town between Anjer and Bantam Bay, conveniently located in the foothills of the mountain where the relay station was to be set up.

Iris and Nigel had allowed me to pull some clothes over my underwear before escorting me to the wagon waiting outside: trousers, and one of Holmes's shirts. I wasn't too afraid they'd use the guns, but they made me go barefoot lest I take off into the jungle en route. To make extra sure I didn't, they secured my wrists to the cords that lashed the wagon's canvas to the wooden clapboards.

Oxen pulled us over roads that narrowed and inclined gently upwards. The farther inland we went, the closer the jungle, until it was so close that a frond poked me in the eye through my peephole.

It was sweltering by the time we reached our destination the next morning. Iris hared off to freshen up while Nigel led me into the main room of the house, and went to stand guard on the veranda.

I glared at Corkle, dressed in silk and linen, seated in a high-backed rattan chair. All he needed was a Persian cat to stroke and the picture would be complete.

He smiled, coolly beneficent. 'Gillian, darling. So glad you could join me.'

'The Doctor Evil routine is wearing a bit thin, don't you think?' The next words rasped out of a very dry throat. 'What have you done with Holmes?'

'He's safe. You can see him after you've refreshed.' He gestured to a Javanese servant, just beyond an arched doorway. A tall, cool glass of mango juice and black tea was placed in my hand. Corkle took a glass for himself and the servant folded back into the woodwork. 'I was beginning to worry,' he said, then pinched the air between his fingers, 'just a tad.'

I downed my drink and wiped Holmes's shirtsleeve across my mouth. 'I was surprised you left without me, considering I'm your passport back to the twenty-first.'

'Well, shit happens, you know? Some crime boss out of Docklands got a territorial wild hair up his arse. I had to leave sooner than anticipated. No matter. I knew I could trust the great detective to bring you to me.'

'Christ, Tom. Dumb luck is what that was. He didn't even find me until June. And if I hadn't gone to see him on the tenth, he would have been long gone without me.'

He actually seemed a little shaken by this, but then shrugged it off. 'Oh well. Dumb luck. Kismet. Incredible karma. What matters is that you're here.'

I eyed him over my glass. 'Is Watson here as well?'

'I left him in Telok Betong. In the care of some friends of mine.'

'Most of the population of Telok Betong will be gone after the twenty-eighth!'

'Yes, but if you're a good girl then we'll trot over to Serang and wire my friends to have him moved to high ground before the first tsunami hits.'

I shook my head wearily. Even the disgust and horror I felt for him had lost its bite. I was going home soon. Nothing left but the victory dance. 'Does Holmes know he's alive?' I asked.

'No. He believes his friend perished at sea. Which is how it's going to stay. You say anything to him, and John Watson dies with ten-thousand others.'

'Fine. I'd like to see Holmes now.'

'He's all right -'

'*Now!* Now, Tom!'

Nigel appeared at the door, his hand on the grip of his pistol. 'It seems Miss Petra wants assurance that our other guest is well-provided for,' Corkle said.

***

The hut where Sherlock was secured sat on a mound of earth overlooking rolling hills full of coffee trees. A squat, round building, twenty feet in diameter, almost palatial as huts went, with a thick, solid beam supporting the peak of the thatched roof.

Corkle thought if I came with the food, Holmes might be more inclined to eat it.

Sat with his back to the door, spine resting against the beam, he had his legs drawn up and his head down. When I entered, he jerked, as if startled from a daydream. I heard the rattle of metal before I actually saw it.

My sweetie, my honey, my darling dear was chained to the support beam like a dog. Naturally, I dropped everything and flung myself upon him with exclamations of horror.

'Ow,' he said.

'What have they done? Where are you hurt?'

'You're kneeling on the chain.'

I leapt up to rant at Nigel, pace, and curse Thomas Corkle to hell, then fell to my knees again at Holmes's side in an anxious examination of his person. Except for a couple of mosquito bites on his forehead, the chafed skin beneath the collar and a lump at the back of his head, he seemed none the worse for wear.

'Mostly dirt, Gillian,' he said wearily. His eyes widened as they took in my appearance. 'You're wearing my shirt!'

'I'll wash it with my own hands, all right?'

He almost smiled, but the emotion was fleeting. 'Have they mistreated you?'

'I'll live,' I said, as I surveyed his prison. The length of chain suspended from his collar was maybe eight feet. He could pace the room in a full circle, but couldn't climb out the window or step outside the door. There was a covered wooden pail positioned as far from him as possible. I perched myself in front of him on the dirt floor.

'They tell me you're not eating,' I said, laying out the fare before him.

'I'm on spiritual fast.' He grabbed the water-bag and took several huge gulps. The noise from the chain punctuated his every movement. 'I've asked for nothing,' he said, stoppering the bottle. A moment of silence, then: 'Nothing but a *sodding cigarette!*'

Nigel, who'd just lit up, exhaled ostentatiously.

Holmes tossed the heavy chain aside. It snaked away, pulling the collar at his throat before slithering to a halt on the floor to his left. The rims of his eyes filled, startling me. Liquid splashed over his bound hands.

'Watson is dead,' he whispered.

Nigel tensed. I clung to my promise like a life-buoy.

I took his hands in mine, rubbing my thumbs under the metal cuffs. 'What happened? How did you end up here?'

'After I left you at the hotel, I hired a native to take me across to the *Hope*. I climbed the anchor chain and had a look around.' He pulled his hands away and angrily palmed the tears from his face. 'She'd picked up convicts in Singapore, chain labour to work on the new lighthouse just south of Anjer. They'd been shackled in the bowels, knee-deep in bilgewater half the time.' His head drooped and his words were barely above a whisper. 'I found a scrap of wool tweed. Not common cloth for a Chinese convict to be wearing. I slipped off ship and swam back to shore. An opium den and three houses of ill-repute later, I located Dalby's shipmate in the Chinese quarter, the one who'd helped him throw the -' Air rattled from his chest. '- the trunks overboard. We had a chat about the funny little scientist chap and his two assistants, a Mr Davies and his sister...'

'I thought they were cousins.'

'Apparently, they're both.' My mind made the obligatory *ew* sound. 'Of course,' Holmes continued, 'had *I* come from the same womb as that woman, I'd be inclined to distance the relationship myself...'

Nigel threw the cigarette to the floor. 'I've had just about enough of your mouth.'

Holmes leapt to his feet, looping the chain about his wrist with a couple of quick twists. I scrambled out of the way as he stretched the heavy links between his hands, leaving just enough slack to wrap around Nigel's throat.

'Do step closer, Mr Davies,' he said, his teeth clenched in a smile.

The other man did not accept the invitation, choosing instead to pull the gun from the holster on his hip.

'No!' I shouted. 'Knock it off. Both of you.'

'Don't fret, Gillian. Mr Davies is too much the coward to venture within striking distance.'

'I managed to cosh you over the head easy enough when we brought you here!'

'I *let* you do it, you idiot! You think I didn't know you were following me?'

Nigel's chiselled jaw worked back and forth in futile outrage. The detective's anger cooled considerably at the sight of it. He dropped the chain, an almost dismissive gesture, as if it were too good a weapon to waste on someone so stupid. 'If Corkle cannot leave without you, Gillian, then I assumed he would find a way to bring you to him, though not when we were together. I'd hoped they might take you at the hotel that night -'

'Oh! Thanks a lot!'

He shrugged. The convict's collar bit into already-raw skin below his Adam's apple. 'I assumed Mr Davies job was to inconvenience me. A clout over the head, bound and gagged in a warehouse... nothing I couldn't get out of. It never occurred that he'd use me to assure your co-operation in the same manner he had with -' He broke off, shying from thoughts of Watson. 'I was a fool not to see his game.'

If Holmes knew Corkle's game, he was one up on me. I rubbed my chapped lips, thinking hard.

'Go,' I said to Nigel. His chin jerked up, teeth gnashing inside his jaw. I pointed to the door. 'Take your little gun and get out.'

'Don't take orders from creatures like you.'

Holmes fists got tighter. He took two steps. I blocked his path. 'Nigel. Get out or I'll tell your boss that you threatened to shoot me and thereby ruin all his plans.'

A quick flash of panic distorted his features. The gun inched its way beneath his coat, as if hiding it would change the facts. 'I didn't threaten you!'

'*Get out!*'

The flap of a door lifted and fell back again. 'I'm still listening!'

I sat down and started slapping foodstuffs onto a platter. 'This all from Corkle's kitchen. The water's sterilised and the fruit's been washed in it. None of this is poisoned, nor will it have any adverse effects on your digestive tract.' I thrust the woven platter toward his feet. 'Now eat it.'

He looked at the food, then me. 'Tyrannical little hen, aren't you?' Wrapping smoked fish and a handful of rice in the flatbread, he leaned back against the pole.

'I'll try to come tomorrow, but it might be late,' I said, taking a swallow of water from the bag. 'I have to go into Serang in the morning with the arsehole.'

'Which one?' he asked around a mouthful of fish taco.

'Corkle. It's to do with the trip home,' I lied. I lied for Nigel's benefit. I didn't realise until the words were out of my mouth that the lie was also a truth Holmes and I had chosen not to deal with, except in the abstract.

The thrum of insects, the susurration of wind through the trees, the cry of a bird, Nigel's boot-heels turning in the dirt outside... small sounds, amplified by the shared illusion that if we didn't breathe then time would stop. But time was a hardened bitch who stopped for nobody.

Holmes set the half-eaten food on the platter. 'That's it, then.' My hands hovered over him like gulls seeking refuge on a barren rock. He turned his head, his eyes, his entire being away from me. 'Don't.'

I sat on my knees before him, knowing that this black-and-blue moment might be the last we shared. Once Corkle sent the telegram to Telok Betong, he'd be an idiot to let me see Holmes again.

Holmes heaved a sigh, a windstorm blowing the hair back from my face. He banged his head against the pole. A raw sound emerged from him: rage, anguish, resignation. Then, before I could react, he'd dug his heels into the dirt and shoved his shoulders hard against the beam. The roof creaked. I shot a panicked look up. Bits of falling debris littered my face.

Spitting and blinking, I turned back to see him rescuing his fish taco from the sprinkling of dust. He took a bite. Chewed. Swallowed. The support beam listed ever so slightly. Earth had been worked loose around the base. He'd been hiding most of the damage with his backside.

I stared at him, mouth hanging. 'Are you out of your mind?' I hissed. 'This beam must weigh a ton.'

He scoffed. 'Not even close.'

Nigel's body blocked the sunlight. 'He's had enough. Pack it up and let's go.'

Shaking with anxiety and hope, I obeyed.

Chapter 30

August 24th.

In the morning, we rode into Serang to send the telegram and assure Watson's life. I read the message over before he sent it.

He'd signed it "Moriarty".

When we were outside again, Corkle cleaned the dust from his spectacles with a handkerchief. He looped the curved wires over his ears and settled the creamy straw hat upon his head.

'When will they receive the message?' I asked.

'He'll be in the prison this afternoon.'

The prison in Telok Betong was on a hill not far from the Resident's house. It was one of the few buildings that survived the devastation. Watson would be safe there. But under what conditions? And for how long?

'Of course, this means I can't allow you to see Holmes again.'

Big surprise there.

'Why, Tom?' I heard myself say.

'Oh, Gillian! You really need to ask?'

'No, I mean, why... *everything*. The horror-show. The basement room. The video-cameras. Because I don't believe for a moment that it was part of any program. And I find it *really* hard to believe the S&M child-sex was Moriarty's idea.'

'Hmm.' The blue of his eyes gazed into the blue of the sky. Dark clouds dimmed the sun for a moment, then drifted past. 'Think a lot of the Professor, don't you?'

'He's a genius. That doesn't mean I think a lot of him.'

He dragged his eyes away from the heavens to look at me. 'Gillian, dear. Did you really, seriously believe that anyone - even Jimmy Moriarty - could have single-handedly come up with a way of sending people back to the nineteenth century? His last technological breakthrough was a way of copyright-protecting MP3s, for Christ's sake.'

It had been a long time since that thought had bothered me. 'Yeah, but if it needs something the size of Krakatoa to make it work -'

'And what good's the power, without the method? No, darling. Suffice to say that the technique... and it *is* a technique, not a technology... required inspiration from elsewhere. Divine inspiration, if you like. Although his patrons aren't exactly rosy-faced little cherubs.'

My patron had patrons? Divine ones?

Seeing my expression, Corkle huffed in annoyance. 'It's enough to say he made a deal with a higher authority. Call it the Host Celestial if you like. Or gods in need of followers. In fact, I get the impression that if they don't have an audience then they don't exist at all.'

'What the hell are you talking about? *What* higher authority?'

Corkle tutted, as if he'd just decided to condemn me to the slow-reader group for life. 'Think of them as an idea rather than an entity. A cultural trend, if that's any easier for your pretty academic mind to cling onto. Horror, mutilation, and other hi-jinx seem to bring the idea into clearer focus, for some reason.' He took up the reins of his horse and mounted, then proceeded to look down on me in every way possible. 'You really do have to stop thinking of the time-travel process as if it's all done with machines. It's more of a lifestyle. One I've reluctantly had to embrace to make this project such a success.'

Reluctantly. Uh huh. A nine-year-old girl on a slab, with Corkle's hand between her legs. Genitals pickled in jars. A head with its eyelids lovingly sewn shut. I realised, then, that to ask whether Corkle was working with Moriarty's approval was missing the point.

Moriarty was doing this for a reason. For Corkle, the method had become an end in itself.

Which raised one more question.

'Tom?' I asked. 'Why have you been using Moriarty's name through all this?'

He laughed. 'Well, if something *should* go wrong - I mean, seriously wrong - I want his tag on the wall, not mine. Don't see why his hands should stay clean, while you and I are knee-deep in the shit.'

I experienced a moment of grudging admiration. Indeed, why should Moriarty be safe? I squinted up at Corkle's squat little body, with the sun reflecting off his plantation garb, and the admiration evaporated like the sweat in my armpits. *He*'d been the cause of Watson's suffering, not Moriarty. He'd been the cause of mine.

Thomas Peerson Corkle wasn't going to get home. Ever. I'd decided that long ago in a darkened room.

As our mounts neared the plantation, their pace quickened, necks stretched out toward the promise of a currycomb and feedbag. I could just make out the top of the huge banyan tree that stood guard next to the house, when shouts and frenzied activity caused Corkle to spur his horse to a trot.

Nigel was doing most of the shouting. We dismounted and walked our horses through the chaos. A look of anxiety glazed his face upon spotting us. 'He's gone!' he shouted. 'The bastard's gone!'

Corkle's hands gripped the reins so tightly that he nearly toppled, pulled on by the horse's momentum, before he thought to let go.

'When?'

'About an hour after you left. Iris took him food and water and saw the hut had collapsed. She thought he might be buried underneath, but all the coolies found in the debris were the manacles, blood all over them.' He shot a glance at me. 'Had help I imagine.'

Corkle turned. 'Does he know about Watson?'

'Not from me.' I was unable to keep the smile off my face -

The slap was swift, delivered with the flat of his hand. Tears burst from my eyes and blood trickled down the back of my throat.

'Where's he's headed?'

'You fucker!'

'Is he headed for Telok Betong?'

'You fucking son-of-a-bitch!'

'Have you any idea how many ways he could end up dead in the jungle, Gillian? Is that what you want?'

'You've ruined his life! What's the difference?'

He turned to Nigel. 'I want every man available on the search. Pull the coolies from the fields. Any servant that knows the area. Tell them there's twenty guilders in it for the man who finds him.'

'The Van der Vermers keep dogs...'

'Half a day's ride, Nigel. He can't have got far, and there's no way in hell he could lose the collar and chain without a key or a bloody hacksaw.'

Nigel nodded, and strode off to organize the search parties.

Corkle dragged me around to the front of the house. Iris was sitting dejectedly on the steps of the veranda. She leapt to her feet when she saw us approaching.

He threw me at her. 'Keep an eye on her. Tie her to a chair if you must.' Which she did, with pleasure.

They didn't find Holmes that day or the next.

***

August 25th. 11:30.

A few of the villagers from surrounding campongs, enticed by the promise of twenty guilders, added their knowledge of the area to the search.

'He's not to be harmed,' Corkle kept reiterating. Which made me glad, though I couldn't understand why it was so important to him.

Everyone was out there with torches and machetes, tearing the jungle asunder. Everyone but Corkle. He was at his desk in the study with my journals in front of him.

I'd been tied to one chair or another since two o'clock the previous day, and now sat tied to a somewhat more comfortable chair in Corkle's study. My butt ached, my legs and arms ached, and my bladder was truly full to bursting when I announced my need.

'Again?'

'I'm nervous about the send-forward.' It was partially true. 'You know you can just scan those in and run the decryption program when we get back, right?'

He glanced at me with a cheery smile. 'This is more fun. Like a Sudoku puzzle.'

'I really have to pee.'

'In a minute. I'm thinking we should get an early start. Be at the relay station around ten.'

'Uh-huh. Tom? What if Holmes *has* died accidentally? You know, fallen off a ledge or drowned or something? How would Moriarty be able to tell if he died *before* the send-forward?'

'I imagine you'd tell him.'

I imagine you'd find a way to prevent that, I thought. 'But what if we get back and something *has* changed?'

He looked up suddenly, nostrils twitching. 'Do you smell something?'

'I mean, Sherlock's really smart. He might become the greatest criminal mastermind ever known, or discover plastic polymers fifteen years ahead of time, or -'

'For God's sake, shut it, will you?'

'It's a pretty problem she presents, don't you think, Mr Corkle?'

For the third time in my life, the voice of Sherlock Holmes came from shadowy recesses in a dark hour. This time, however, I knew he was there before he uttered a word. He looked awful, smelled worse. But he glowed like Krishna.

The collar was still locked about his throat, the chain looped around his chest, Road Warrior fashion. He held a gun in one grimy, scraped-up hand, and a really big knife in the other. Corkle's pen tapped a nervous rhythm on the top of my journals.

'Sherlock,' I said, 'I really have to pee this time and he won't let me out of the chair.'

'The naughty fellow,' he replied. Behind me, the knife cut swiftly through the ropes. I stood up, shaking my arms and stamping my feet to get the blood circulating again.

'Do you have the key to this collar, Mr Corkle?'

'Yes.'

'I do hope it's on your person, because I'm in a dreadful mood and a long search might incite me to hurt you.'

Corkle reached for his watch-chain. The key dangled from the fob.

I snatched it from his trembling fingers, turned it in the padlock, and removed the lock from the hasp. Hinges protested as Holmes pulled it from his throat. Bits of mud and other less pleasant detritus flaked off him.

Corkle leaned back in his chair casually, straining for the right element of adversarial admiration, but it didn't wash. He was extremely nervous. 'The privy, eh? I must say you are the most audacious individual I've ever met. So we've all been doing our business on you for the past two days?'

'Not quite,' Holmes said. We grinned at each other.

I'd made the discovery of Holmes's whereabouts while finishing my business the previous night. Squishy sounds of movement from the unpleasant contents below caused me to peer into the hole like a co-ed in a slasher film. Naturally, a *thing* thrust out of it. Naturally, I screamed.

Iris rounded the outhouse just as a whisper from the fetid darkness said '-snake I would have bit your -'

'What's going on in there?' The hook-and-eye latch on the door rattled. 'Unlock the door!'

I released a shattered breath. 'A snake! A snake!'

She screamed even louder than I had, her feet pounding in the other direction.

I could just make out the whites of his eyes and two dark projections that might have been knees.

'You're insane!' I hissed at him.

'Is Corkle here?' he whispered back.

I pounded on the wooden bench with my fists. 'Take that you beast! No, he's out searching for you. Oh my God it's huge!'

'Help! Help!' Iris screamed. 'For the love of God, someone help us!'

Us, she said, as if we were best girlfriends or something. Servants came running to her cries, but I knew there were only women on the grounds. There would be no man hitching up his trousers to challenge the dragon in the shithole.

'Oh my god! It's horrible! Watson's alive.'

'Good. When Corkle's alone, let me know it.'

'Don't just stand there!' Iris screeched. 'Fetch my revolver!'

'Oh! Oh goodness, I'm such a goose,' I called. 'It's just a vine.'

Iris wouldn't use the privy after that, and the servants weren't allowed to use it anyway. I developed a convenient intestinal bug.

Corkle's eyes flicked to Holmes, his mouth pursed in distaste. 'You're tracking shit all over my floor.' The knife was at Corkle's throat before he'd finished the sentence. Any protest I intended to utter refused to come out of my mouth. But instead of gutting the pig, Holmes slapped the knife onto the desk, reached over and wiped his hand on Corkle's spotless linen jacket. Corkle sat paralysed, afraid to look at the knife lest a glance be mistaken for a challenge.

'That appears to be Nigel's revolver,' Corkle commented, jarring me from my thoughts.

'Yes,' Holmes said. 'He didn't need it anymore.' Over his shoulder: 'Bring me the chain and collar.' I did, alarmed at how heavy they were.

'You're not going to do me up in those, are you?' Corkle squeaked.

I tossed Holmes the padlock. 'I'll grab supplies and we'll get the hell out of here,' I said. He grunted his acknowledgement, pulling Corkle from his chair.

'Gillian,' Corkle called after me, his voice high with panic, 'we have a rather pressing engagement tomorrow that I shouldn't like to miss!'

'You will not be attending that engagement, Tom.'

'You can't go without me!'

'I believe it's you that can't go without her,' Holmes replied.

I ran through the house, gathering up whatever I thought he'd need that I could find in a hurry, soap being at the top of my list. In the room that Nigel and Iris shared, I took clean clothes and boots for Holmes, pausing only long enough to relieve myself in the piss-pot, which I left in the middle of the room for Iris to stumble over in the dark. When I returned a few minutes later, rucksack loaded, Corkle was trussed like a pig for roasting. I crammed my journals into the pack.

Corkle struggled with the bindings, trying to get in a position to look me in the face. 'Gillian. Don't be stupid. You have the implant, but only I know how to operate the system.' My mind stuttered to a halt. 'The implant was Moriarty's guarantee that I'd get you home. The system was my guarantee that I'd get home.'

I stared at him, desperate to see a lie. His face gave me nothing. My own face must have been a beacon.

'Ah,' he murmured, 'now it's getting through your wee brain -'

In that instant, everything that had happened, everything he'd done to me and to innocent others crushed together inside my skull until the pressure exploded my last bit of reason. I snatched up the revolver to empty every chamber into *his* wee brain -

'No!' Holmes cried. 'The sound will carry for miles!' But I didn't care. His fist closed around my hand that held the gun. A battle of the sensible and insane followed until he'd wrestled me to the floor and pressed his knee into my wrist. Nerves jerked and fingers loosened. The barrel of the weapon bumped against the floor. He scooped it up and tucked it into the back of his trousers.

I lay there panting, tears burning a trail down the sides of my face. What was the point of going on now? Why should I even try?

Holmes stood over me, breathing hard, his forehead furrowed, mouth a thin grim line. 'Don't accept it, Gillian,' he said. 'Don't you dare consign yourself to his version of the facts.'

I scrubbed the tears from my cheeks, took a few deep breaths. He reached down and pulled me to my feet. I picked up the rucksack and hooked it over my shoulder.

Holmes retrieved the knife from the desk and tested its sharpness against his thumb. The glint of the blade caused sweat to burst on Corkle's forehead and upper lip.

'The search-parties will be returning in a few hours,' Holmes said. His grip on the weapon was almost casual. 'He's the only one who knows where you're going.'

'Jesus,' Corkle whispered.

I'd wanted the man dead only moments before. But what I would have done out of righteous rage, I seemed unwilling to sanction when executed with cool, well-reasoned efficiency. I wondered if Holmes had made the same careful decision with Nigel Davies. Of course, it made perfect sense in this case. Slit Corkle's throat and escape with no chance of pursuit. But in the end, the thought of that act being my last memory of Holmes seemed the greater risk and burden.

'We could knock him out or something.'

'Hitting a man over the head does not guarantee unconsciousness for any length of time.'

'Gag him then. We'll put him in the cupboard. It'll buy us a few hours, anyway.'

Holmes acquiesced with a shrug, but I saw a flicker of relief in his eyes. He tore off his shirtsleeve, wadded it up and stuffed the reeking fabric into Corkle's mouth. Together we rolled him into the closet. His grunts of pain gave me small satisfaction.

Outside, the moon was just cresting the top of the creepy banyan tree.

'There are at least twenty people out there searching for you,' I said, as we marched quickly across the yard toward the cover of brush and jungle.

'Ten at most. The promise of money loses its appeal after so long a time in fruitless pursuit.' I glanced at the house, the glow of the lamp in Corkle's study illuminating a small patch of grass outside the window. 'You should have done it anyway.'

'Shall I go back?'

I shook my head. On the brink of agonising loss, I sucked in a breath and instantly regretted it. He really stank. I thrust the rucksack at him. 'There's soap in here. You need to clean those wounds really thoroughly.'

'Yes, Gillian, I am aware of that.'

'Crap. I should have grabbed another water flask.' I dug the clothes and boots out of the rucksack, and pushed them at him along with a flask, a lantern, and a box of matches.

'It's a good twenty miles back to Anjer,' I said, pointing through the thickets. 'But don't leave high ground for at least three days.' I nipped into the overgrown path that led toward the foothills. Holmes moved swiftly up behind me, batting a low-hanging branch out of his face with a snarl.

'I know which way to head if want to go to Anjer. Even if Corkle told the truth on the matter of Watson - and that's a very big if - the straights will be nearly impassable for another week. I couldn't possibly get to Telok Betong before that. You've said as much yourself.' He grabbed my arm and jerked me around to face him. 'What are you doing?'

I forced a steely resolve into my voice because it sure as hell wasn't anywhere else in my body.

'I'm going home,' I said. His grip faltered and I pulled from his grasp.

Arrows dipped in sarcasm shot at my back. 'Just like that? No goodbye kiss?'

'I have to try. You know it. There are people who have to be made accountable for what they've done.'

'You can't just expect -'

'What? You think you're the only one who can bring a rich and powerful man to justice?'

He fell back a step, blinking at the vehemence in my voice. 'I... I don't believe I've done so as yet. I was going to say, you can't walk blindly through a jungle in the middle of the night. You have no weapons. No machete. Did you even think to bring a compass?'

A compass. Damn. 'Sherlock. Turn and walk the other way, please. Please.'

'No. This is idiotic!'

'Fine. I'm an idiot. I'm not like you, all right? I'm not as smart as I thought. I'm not a brave person! This is a huge leap into a big, terrifying void. No guarantees, no way of knowing if anyone will even know they're supposed to be waiting on the other side. What if he's right? If you're with me, I don't know if I can... damn it! Damn it, this is hard enough -'

'Then why make it harder?' His voice was so tender I thought it'd kill me. 'At least, at the very least, Gillian, let me see you home.'

I wiped my eyes and dripping nose on my shirtsleeve. *His* shirt sleeve, actually, as his barely-disguised grimace reminded me. Considering the state he was in, his reaction made me laugh in spite of myself.

'I'll let you see me as far as the gate,' I conceded.

Chapter 31

We had only one near-miss with a search-party. Though I couldn't understand what they were saying, from their body-language Holmes appeared to be correct. The promise of money wasn't enough to keep them from their homes another night.

After about three miles we decided to chance lighting the lantern. Moving through mountainous jungle terrain at night is a tense experience at best, and without a machete it was just stupid. Holmes was kind enough not to say so. More than once, anyway. He did his best with the knife, but tree-roots and thick vines conspired to trip us all the way. By the time he veered off toward the sound of rushing water, I was huffing hard, my legs a-tremble and my nerves a-jangle. I only wanted to sit down for a few blessed moments, and he could do whatever the hell he had to.

But we stepped into something out of a fairy-tale. There were two small waterfalls with a clear, shallow pool between. The larger of the falls tumbled from a ledge of rocks into the pool. The overflow from the pool formed the second fall, with a ring of spongy moss around it. Doubtless a popular watering-hole for the animals, but as none were about, we boldly claimed the space.

Holmes began stripping immediately. Filthy garments were balled up and flung as far as he could fling them. Soap in hand, he stepped into the pool. I collapsed gratefully onto a mossy rock, rolled onto my back, and stared at the sky.

Even with a full moon, the sky was filled with stars. Before electricity lit up every city on the planet, one could lie on a rock, look at the stars and *know* the universe was a huge, wondrous thing.

Except that after tomorrow there'd be no sunlight, no starlight, no moonlight... nothing, for two whole days. It would seem like the end of the world. It would *be* the end of the world for many. I looked at my companion. A good, long look. Perhaps the last.

Under the noisy rush of the falls stood some sort of elemental; dark head thrown back, eyes closed as water tumbled, bounced, and beat hard on his head and shoulders. A froth of soap bubbles danced at the edges of the pool before falling into the stream below. Trails of bubbles streaming over his pale face, throat, chest, between his shoulder-blades and down and down -

I stepped into the pool, fingers reaching to trace the ridge of his spine.

He whipped around with a gasp, a spray of water from his sopping hair flinging across my face.

'I was just going to wash your back,' I lied.

'Oh.' He handed me the soap. 'Sorry. Lost in thought.'

'What were you thinking about?' I asked, rubbing the shrinking cake of soap across his shoulders. The shoulders tensed.

'Gillian,' he said with an exasperated sigh. 'You promised never to ask me that.'

'When?'

'On ship. You said it was a sign of a woman's insecurity and that *you would never do it.* What if I were merely thinking about my toes, or how much I'd like a cigarette? I'd have to invent a thought simply to impress you with my brilliance. It's a horrible burden.'

'Your toes?' I replied, scrubbing vigorously. 'Why would you be thinking about your toes?'

'You promised, Gillian!'

'I don't remember promising any such thing.' I patted him between the shoulder-blades. 'There you are. You can rinse now.'

He turned to face me, water spilling over his back. He cocked one eye beneath a streaming lock of hair. 'You also promised to wash the shirt you're wearing.'

'I was merely humouring you.'

His expression remained sternly resolute.

I stared at him. 'What? Now?'

'Never mind,' he said, taking me by the arm and pulling me closer. 'I shall do it myself.'

And a very thorough job he did of it. Not only the shirt, but underneath it and down the back of my trousers where the tiny sliver of soap got lost. His valiant efforts to retrieve it were all for naught. I was forced to remove the trousers, and, well... everything.

I awakened with a numb hand under my head, and Holmes nowhere in sight. The position of the sun was not encouraging. Nine or ten in morning. Two, maybe, three hours up to the relay station, putting us there around one o'clock. Cutting it pretty damned close.

Behind me, the morning conversation of monkeys carried a note of high annoyance, as if they were wondering when the strange creature was going to get the hell away from their watering-hole. The mossy bed beside the stream was matted where we'd crushed insects in our passion. My clothes lay in an untidy heap near the edge of the pool. They weren't dry: in fact, they were slightly steaming. I brushed the plant-matter and dead bugs from my butt, stepped into the trousers, pulled on the shirt, slipped on the sandals, and put my hands on my hips.

Where the hell was he?

The sound of the falls, symphonic by moonlight, was now an annoying pounding in my head. I opened my mouth to call his name. And shut it tight.

Beneath the music of the falls was a rhythmic back-beat. A thunk, crack, and crashing rhythm, quite methodical, almost angry, moving ever-closer. My first thought was a wild beast. My second thought was that no beast of any kind needed machetes to get through the jungle.

I ran for the pool and leapt in, my feet dragging, my arms like propellers trying to get to the dense brush on the other side.

A crack of gunfire crumpled my legs, and I fell to my knees in the water: not hit, just completely terrified. I put my hands high in the air. It seemed the proper thing to do.

'Turn around,' Iris shouted. I did, stirring up the silt, pebbles gouging my kneecaps.

She held a machete in one hand and a revolver in the other, as if uncertain which to use on me first. Rivulets of sweat poured down her splotchy face through layers of grime. She was panting. She looked ridiculous. I repressed a hysterical giggle.

'Where is he?' she cried. 'Where's the bastard that killed my brother?' The machete lopped off the head of a fern, and she took a step towards me. *'Where is he?'*

'I don't know!' My raised arms began to shake violently.

She gestured with the gun. 'Get over here.'

I slogged through the water on my knees. Holmes was nearby, I was certain. I gripped the moss on the bank and began pulling myself out. Iris tossed the machete aside, and grabbed a fistful of my hair to assist me in my efforts.

'Up,' she said, fingers still locked in my hair. I scrambled to my knees again. 'Hands behind your head.'

The barrel pressed to the back of my skull. Sound came bubbling out of me: not a cry, not a sob, not a whimper. I knew it was a sound I'd never make again.

'Here's a noise ought to bring him running,' she said. A strange, prolonged moment of silence followed. No chatter of birds. No rustle of branches. Even the noisy water seemed muted, as if all the jungle were waiting expectantly for the noise she promised.

The hammer went *click-click*...

A shove sent me sideways just as the gun went off. A whistling rush of air past my temple, sulfurous odour, smoke; and then a thump, thump, thumping sound, my own heartbeat in the chamber of my ear. I tumbled into the pool and came up coughing, hair streaming into my eyes. I pushed it back, turning round and round, churning the water in my terror. I couldn't hear anything but that muffled thump.

Iris was on the ground, rolling out of reach of the butt of Corkle's shotgun. He was shouting something at her, his face florid from exertion or fury, or both. She came up in crouch, and fired, but

not at him. A ripple in the tall grass of the clearing was bowling a line toward fern fronds and the twisting puzzles of tree-trunks.

Her mouth was moving, distorted with rage and grief. She'd lost her brother. Her cousin. Lover. Whatever. Oh, I thought, bad people have feelings too. Interesting.

Corkle was still shouting at her. I couldn't hear the words, couldn't have paid attention to them anyway. Holmes rose from the grass, gripping the machete. I scrambled out of the water.

There were powder-burns on his hand, but Nigel's revolver was nowhere to be seen. Blood slipped down his face along his right temple, dripping onto his shirt. He looked stunned, possibly in shock as he swayed and lurched forward, trying to raise the machete, surprised that his arm wouldn't obey.

He'd been shot. In the head!

I ran towards him. I didn't think about Iris with her gun cocked and ready, didn't realise I was about to be shot in the back until I saw the panic in Holmes's eyes. His hand went up and out, to grab me or push or -

A muted crack. Another one, a little louder. I collapsed against him, knocking him into the ferns. I could feel his chest heaving beneath me, then his hands patting me all over. Through the dull ringing in my ears rose a mantra: 'Oh God, oh God, Gillian, Gillian...'

'Stupid bitch! You had to rush ahead, didn't you?' It was Corkle's high-pitched tirade that finally popped my ears.

Holmes was still pawing me, looking for holes. 'Please, dear God, please, Gillian, if you love me, say you're not hurt...'

What a curious request that was. *I love you. It hurts. It's all been for nothing. I'll just lie here on your chest if you don't mind.*

'Well, that's just bloody grand, isn't it?' Corkle cried.

'I'm all right, you moron!' I yelled. A deep sigh shook Holmes's entire body and rattled my own, as I lay sprawled over him.

He eased me from him slowly, and rose on haunches and fingertips. Corkle's boot was busy punishing the lifeless form of Iris. Smoke drifted lazily from the tip of his shotgun. Spent, but still mightily pissed off, he discharged it again. I gagged back bile.

Corkle turned, squinting against the sunlight, swinging the shotgun in our direction. Holmes wriggled in anticipation, as if he could now out-race a bullet. The slice across his temple poured little rivulets of gore down the sides of his face, but his teeth were bared in an animal grin. Men were such fucking idiots sometimes.

I sprang up from the grass, arms in the air. 'I'm here! Don't shoot him!'

Corkle gazed at me with his mouth open. His eyes flicked to something over my left shoulder, and he gave a little start. His expression confused me. It was one of profound panic. I turned to see Holmes rising from the thicket.

'What are you doing?' I cried.

Muttering incoherently, Corkle fumbled with the gun, hands shaking hard as the detective strolled leisurely toward him.

'Sherlock, Jesus Christ, just get away! Get out of here!'

Corkle broke the shotgun in half. The barrels dangled down between his legs. He struggled to get something out of his pocket, and by the time I realised they were shells, Holmes had jerked the gun from the man's stiff, fumbling hands.

Apparently, my lack of knowledge in the gun department could fill a book. Both barrels had been discharged and would have to be reloaded, a fact of which Holmes was perfectly aware.

Corkle opened his mouth, but before any sound came out, Holmes belted him.

Spectacles hung twisted and broken from the wire over his left ear, and his face glowed an angry red. Holmes slapped him again, calmly, coldly, very hard. The shells fell from the little man's fingers. Holmes picked them up and proceeded to load the gun.

'Mr Corkle,' he said, 'I'm going to ask you a few questions and I would appreciate your honest replies.' With a snap of his wrist, he locked the barrels.

Corkle swallowed convulsively a few times before his mouth reformed into its bland smile. 'Honesty has few rewards, Mr Holmes.'

'For you. Why else would Professor Moriarty have so many stipulations attached to your mission? That Gillian was to be protected from harm, for instance. A matter you failed to assure, by the way. But for my intervention, you might have been stranded here forever.'

Corkle hooked the twisted wire of his glasses over his ear again. 'I left ample clues as to her whereabouts. Clearly, I overestimated your abilities.'

Holmes pulled the gun's hammers back and peered down the sights, then eased the hammers forward again. 'You may well have done so. But no matter, she is here now.'

'Yes. And I shall be stranded forever.' Corkle looked at the gun. 'One way or another.'

'That all depends on your willingness to give an honest answer.'

'An honest answer buys me life?' Tom laughed. 'I doubt that very much.'

'Not merely life, Mr Corkle, but your ticket home.'

'*What?*' I cried. 'You have no right to offer him that!'

Holmes rested the shotgun in the crook of his arm, with the stock against his chest. His finger stayed curled over one trigger, thumb upon the hammer. 'If this man is responsible for the crimes you say he's committed, I will not suffer him to live in my world. We have our share of evil already. Mr Corkle? The truth if you please. Did you throw John Watson's dead body into the ocean, or is he alive in Telok Betong?'

Corkle pressed his lips together, eyes searching for a trick. Whatever he saw in Holmes's face apparently convinced him. 'He was alive when I left him there.'

'Did you have him removed to the prison as Gillian has told me?'

'I sent the telegram. I can't guarantee the response to my request.'

Holmes nodded grimly. 'That seems an honest reply. One final question.'

Corkle peered up at the sun's position. His eye twitched spasmodically, ticking off the seconds until our departure. He rolled his neck and tugged at his collar. 'Could you make it quick, Mr Holmes? We are rather pressed for time.'

I could see the detective's back tense beneath of fabric of his shirt. He rolled his shoulders, looked at his feet as he asked: 'Did you murder my father?'

For a long moment, only the jungle gave reply; the whine of insects, squawking birds, the cacophony of water, and the rustle of plant-life moved by unseen creatures.

Corkle's tongue darted out, wetting his lips. His eyes moved from me, to Holmes, to the gun, back to Holmes again. 'You seem to feel you already know the answer to that, Mr Holmes.'

'I know that shortly before Gillian and I left London, my brother informed me that the heart tonic our father was administered on the morning of his passing was poisoned.'

'I did not administer the tonic.'

'Did you pay someone to administer it?'

'I don't believe I'm going to answer.'

Holmes raised the shotgun and aimed both barrels at Corkle's chest. 'Then I shall kill you where you stand.'

Sweat rolled down the sides of the little man's face, but his words were amazingly cool. 'Without proof? No. You must have proof for everything. It's your worst failing, I believe.' There was a hint of truth in what he said, enough to make Holmes falter. 'And now, you want to hear the truth from my lips in order to justify doing what you've wanted to do all along. Well, I shan't grant you dispensation. You shall have to play judge and executioner without a confession from me.'

Holmes drew back one hammer. His voice was slightly shrill. 'You've murdered enough others to justify pulling this trigger.'

'You have no personal stake in those others. No guilt or remorse to assuage. You believe that if I confess to killing your dear papa, you can purge your soul of a lifetime of –' The rest of his words were swallowed by a distant, thunderous rumble that beat the air above our heads.

'We're too late,' I whispered, looking at the sky.

'Merely the noon detonations,' Corkle said, squashing the strange sense of relief I'd felt. 'We still have time. However, you, Mr Holmes? Not so much.'

'I'm confident I'll survive.'

'Yes, well, pity about your sister though. Sweet girl, Genevieve.' All the air seemed to leave Holmes's body. 'Red hair, hasn't she? Like your father's?'

'*What have you done?*' Holmes whispered hoarsely.

'Me? Nothing. But I do have an acquaintance. You may be familiar with him. Francis Black? The Pie-Man.'

'Pie-man? You mean there really *was* a pie-man?' I looked at Corkle, trying and failing to keep the smug off his face. 'But... I *saw* you. You killed them. I saw it on the disc.'

'Francis killed the girls,' he said, then chuckled softly as he delivered the punch-line. '*God* told him to. All I did was make a performance of it.'

'Yeah, that... really doesn't make it OK.'

'Francis Black didn't kill Stewart Ronaldson,' Holmes said. 'Or Merrill Holbrook.' His face was much too pale beneath the brush-strokes of gore.

'No.' Corkle scratched his cheek, looking contrite. 'But, well, you see, the girls weren't attention-grabbing enough, were they? Seems I had to be willing to get my hands dirty. Regretable, but necessary.'

'And all this talk of Francis Black? Is that designed to "grab my attention"?'

Corkle didn't bother to correct Holmes misapprehension. 'Ah. Yes. Well, it seems Francis recently found himself a good post. A man who should, by all rights, be confined to an asylum is now employed at one in the West Country.' My fists clenched painfully, wanting to rip the fat smiling lips off his face. The barrels of the shotgun sunk towards the ground, Holmes's eyes transfixed by those same lips cheerfully hammering the final nails into his soul. 'Say, didn't your brother mention he'd found a rather fine institution to care for your sister?'

A breath shuddered out. Holmes was shaking, shaking so hard I could hear the rattle of his teeth.

'I don't know that Francis will find Genevieve evocative.' Corkle continued. 'A child's mind in a woman's body might not elicit those voices that torment the poor sod. But then again, it might. You know... I think if you turn around right now and run like hell down this mountain, there's still a chance you'll be able to get a wire through to your brother.'

'Why?' Holmes cried. 'Why would you do this to me? Why?' It was a question asked of the universe. Reasons demanded from the God of Reason that had abandoned him here.

'To see what would happen.'

'That's not a reason!'

The smaller man shrugged. 'It's a reason you've used often enough. What happens if one applies pressure just so? Adds a drop of this to that? Pokes the creature here or there?'

Holmes went utterly still. 'That's not *your* reason.'

'It's his *lifestyle*,' I spat out.

'That's rather personal, darling,' Corkle said. He picked up his hat from the ground and dusted it off smartly. 'But let's speculate. What if a certain dynamic individual's life, as recorded for posterity and future generations, could be...oh, erased, let's say, through the manipulation of situations and events early on in the subject's career? The introduction of a devastating public failure, humiliating scandals, unexpected hardships. Would such an individual overcome adversity to build his life and reputation anew? Would he still find his small place in the history books? That's what Jimmy Moriarty wanted to find out. He felt death would be cheating, and I agreed.'

'You still haven't answered my question,' Holmes said.

'Why I would do this to you? Let's see. Money? Power?' Corkle put the hat upon his head and tipped the brim in a polite bow. 'Or simply because, Mr Sherlock Holmes, I *can*.'

The detective blinked. That's all. Just blinked. He looked at me, a question in his eyes I didn't realise I'd answered until he'd turned back, swung the shotgun up and fired both barrels.

My eyes would focus only on the hat sailing through the air, and not the scattered mass of organic debris that went with it. No head for his hat, Corkle's body wobbled, and instead of following his brain, fell forward.

I think I must've passed out, because the next thing I knew I was rising to my elbows, spitting mud from my mouth. The air sparkled and buzzed. Water from the falls drummed to the rhythm of my slow-beating heart.

Holmes was sitting in the grass. His knees were up, feet planted wide around the shotgun on the ground. Grey eyes stared dully at a crumpled heap of limbs a few yards away from him.

'I don't feel... right,' he said.

'Jesus. Oh God. Jesus.'

He looked at the waterfall. 'I don't *feel* right.'

The emphasis he placed on that word stunned my mind into focus.

'This is not how my life is. I can feel the wrongness of it in here -' His fingers were rigid, pounding into his chest as if her were trying to dig something out of it. 'In here. Deep inside me. I've become a void. Nothing. Nothing at all.'

And I knew he *wanted* to believe that, wanted to see himself as a specimen in a killing jar, because it was easier. Better to be nothing, than to be someone facing the end of the world as he knew it.

But he wasn't a nothing. He was Sherlock Holmes.

I sat down beside him, forcing myself to look at the body of Tom Corkle. 'Sherlock,' I began tentatively. 'You didn't kill Nigel, did you? You've never killed anyone before now, have you?"

'I found him. Thrown from his horse. His neck was broken. I took his gun...'

Suddenly, he turned his head aside and quietly vomited. Barely noticed he'd done it, merely drew his sleeve across his mouth.

'What's to become of me? How shall I ever -?' He kicked the gun away suddenly, and locked his arms tight around his knees.

'You'll save Watson. You'll get your sister out of that place. You'll make sure Mr Pie-Man can't hurt anyone else.'

But his eyes couldn't stay averted forever, drawn to the bloody meat in the grass that had once been a man. A strange little noise came out of him, and though he tried to stuff it back in, there seemed no stopping it. His shoulders pitched and rocked like a boat in choppy waters as he wept.

I could offer little comfort but my silence and my hand, until I noticed that our sleeves were dotted with flecks of grey. Ash had begun to drift over the forest, falling on the leaves and the water and us. I leaned against his shoulder and whispered: 'I have to go.'

He squeezed my hand so hard that the bones made little popping noises. Then he looked into my eyes, for once not searching out lies or truths. Perhaps merely to assure himself that he knew me well, however briefly.

***

The shelter was a yellow dome amongst the greens and browns in the clearing near the peak. Holmes came to a dead stop when he saw it, all remaining scepticism flying in the face of its presence. But as we approached, I could see the garish colour dulled by a fine layer of ash.

When we stepped into the perimeter of the sonic field, Holmes's face screwed up in pain. He touched the wound at his temple, wondering if his injury had brought on the sudden headache.

'It's the zapper,' I explained. 'Keeps the curious away. Wait here. I'll shut it off.'

He didn't wait, but waded through the pain to follow me into the tent. I would have made an issue of it, except that the dead monkey in the ring of monitors had kind of distracted me. I located the zapper and turned it off. Holmes seemed too busy gawping at the sleek, wafer-thin monitors to find a dead monkey remarkable. Clearly lusting to touch, he drawled nevertheless: 'Is this going to be a trick with mirrors? Because I should be terribly disappointed.'

'What kind of crazy monkey would put itself through the zapper to get in here?'

Holmes glanced at it. 'I don't think it came willingly. Someone stuck it with a sharp object and bled it out. Blood's over there.' He pointed at bowl pushed up against the side of the tent, set in a half-circle of candles burned down to stubs. There was only a congealed smear in the bottom of it. Jesus. Was this what Corkle meant by "operating system"?

The Styrofoam cartons were empty, having contained the equipment around me. But several plastic storage containers held an assortment of pilfered treasures from the basement of the British museum. Skulls, tusks, and other oddments.

'This *is* a trick with mirrors, isn't it?' Holmes was saying. 'Like scrying? Occult science rather than empirical.'

Near the monkey I spotted a small medical case. Inside was a knife with a curved blade, its bone handle covered with faint, intricate markings. With it, the incongruity of a twenty-first century hypodermic syringe, and a bottle labelled "d-tubocurarine".

Holmes's startled exhalation was hot on the back of my neck. I shivered, turned. His face had that mind-a-whirl expression, though his body was still as stone. 'It would appear your fate was to follow that poor little creature.' He poked a finger at the bottle. 'Curare. At least you were to be mercifully relaxed when he killed you.'

I dropped to my knees, gazing dully around me at the screens, the keyboards, the single tower that linked them together and couldn't possibly be enough. I picked up the wand, aimed, and clicked. Every screen popped alight with the soft whirr of fans, the blinking, blinding rush of numbers tripping over their surfaces, faster and faster until I couldn't bear to look at them anymore.

'That's supposed to be the pre-launch sequence.' My voice sounded weird, as if I were already far away.

'Gillian, please, don't do this.'

I stared at my hands as they clenched the fabric of my trousers, forcing myself to *believe*. Believe that Corkle intended to extract the implant from my arm and use it to return without me. Believe that there was an implant at all. Believe that *he* believed some ritual sacrifice was required to make it happen, and not that it was true. I had to believe he was insane and that I would go forward without him, even as another part of my mind was mocking me for magical thinking, for all this desperate faith and hope.

Then I saw it. The camera bag. The mini-discs were in a pocket. I held them up 'See? My proof. Justice will out.' Holmes was trying hard to maintain his cool, but his eyes gave him away. 'Look,' I said, 'you'll do exactly as I've told you?'

He gave a terse nod. 'Stay here until tomorrow. Drink only the water in the flask. Keep to the high ground for at least two days. Wait for the rescue ships in Anjer.' He ventured a grin, strained around the edges. 'Then I'm off to Telok Betong to rescue Watson.'

I tried to grin back, but my mouth wouldn't do it. I fumbled in my rucksack and thrust my notebooks at him. He blinked at me, stunned. His proof.

'You can't be in here when it happens. It creates a null-time bubble, and if you're caught in it -'

'Don't do this,' he said. 'Please, I beg you. I have a dreadful foreboding - '

I'm not sure if I threw myself into his arms then, or if he grabbed me and lifted me off the ground, but suddenly we were wrapped around each other - touching, touching, touching - as if fixing the scent and texture and taste of each other into the cells of our bodies.

A pop. A crack. I thought it was my heart. But the next sound was so loud that we fell in a heap of limps. Hell's mouth had finally opened up to swallow the world.

'Go,' I shouted over the noise, as we stumbled to our feet.

'Go,' I screamed again, pushing him through the slit in the dome.

I saw him trip, arms wheeling, books flying. Then he was simply standing with his back to me, gazing into the maw of the sky. He turned. He shouted some final, desperate message before the hand of God swept over the landscape and knocked every living thing flat to the ground. Inside the bubble, all was silent.

The monkey twitched.

EPILOGUE

It was raining mud.

Even the monkeys had ceased to protest this assault from the sky. Only Krakatoa spoke, a series of cracks and rumbles some thirty miles away. The jungle hunched like a child waiting out a parental tirade.

Within the shelter, the young man huddled.

The major detonation had occurred at three o'clock, just as she'd said. A crashing wave of wind had followed the detonation, seemingly rushing ahead of it, flattening the smaller trees and sending him sprawling, as if the wind itself were fleeing a monster and Lord help anyone that got in its way. When he'd risen to his feet again, he'd whirled about, seen the shelter, and experienced relief. Round as an Eskimo's igloo and swept clean by the wind, the shelter remained a solid reality. He thought, for some reason, that the dome itself was the bubble she spoke of, so he rushed towards it, overjoyed. He would open the slit in the centre and find her alive within; face smeared with soot, chestnut curls in disarray, the dimples at the corners of her mouth announcing a smile about to happen, though she wouldn't be at all happy. Not nearly so happy as he -

But there was nothing in the shelter.

No dark mirrors with bright numerical symbols marching boldly across their surfaces. No boxes, no discs. No Gillian. Nothing to scrye an uncertain future for him. And while the shelter remained solid enough, protecting him from the mud and the pellets of pumice raining down from the heavens, he knew somehow that it would not stand as proof should he return someday.

Still, he had her journals. He was young. He was clever. He had places to go and people to rescue. And he'd heard it said that every calamity brought with it fresh opportunity. If the past proved not to be writ in stone, then neither was his future.

Another series of explosions shook the shelter.

Sherlock Holmes held his breath, hope rising, even as stones beat a threatening tattoo over his head. Perhaps one of these detonations would be the one that brought her back to him, though common sense and reason told him otherwise.

Reason - that cool, disdainful god - looked upon hope as a grain of sand in a delicate instrument.

by Lawrence Miles
starring JULIAN GLOVER, ISLA BLAIR,
PETER MILES, WANDA OPALINSKA and
JANE LESLEY
with GABRIEL WOOLF as SUTEKH

Time-travellers, crusaders and evil from ancient Egypt - follow the audio adventures of Faction Paradox from Magic Bullet!

KALDOR CITY

An ultraviolent tale of power and intrigue set in the universe of
Chris Boucher's **Doctor Who: The Robots of Death,**
starring Paul Darrow, Russell Hunter, Trevor Cooper,
Tracy Russell and Philip Madoc

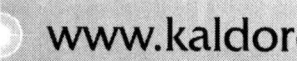 www.kaldorcity.com

REDEEMED

THE UNAUTHORIZED GUIDE TO ANGEL

Drunken Irish lout. Mass murderer. Broody, guilt-stricken recluse. Lover of the Vampire Slayer. Heroic champion for the helpless. C.E.O. of a hellishly powerful law firm. Fated player in the Apocalypse.

The more one tries to discern the vampire Angel, the harder it becomes. Working from a disused hotel in Los Angeles, Angel and his valiant allies experience triumph and tragedy... only to, in the finest L.A. fashion, fall prey to the most seductive and corrupting influence of all: their own insidious greed.

More than two years in the making, this highly enthusiastic yet unofficial guide serves as one of the biggest advocates of the *Angel* series. In particular, this book analyzes the entire show in berserk detail, with an eye toward reconciling the features of the *Angel*-verse against themselves, and dissecting the formidable vision of *Angel* producers Joss Whedon, Tim Minear, Jeffrey Bell and more. Among other concerns, this book seeks to answer such vitally important questions as "How Does the Invitation Rule Work?", "Who is Angel's True Love?" and "Why Do Catholic Objects Harm Vampires?"

OUT NOW ISBN: 0-9725959-3-7
Pages: 352 Retail Price: $24.95

www.madnorwegian.com

mad norwegian press

1150 46th St . Des Moines, IA 50311 . info@madnorwegian,.com

introducing the all-new novel...

Faction Paradox
WARLORDS OF UTOPIA

Adolf Hitler, the Gaol.

In the exact centre of the island was a tower. It was an ugly concrete stump four storeys high, a brutalist version of a medieval keep. There were tiny slits for windows. There wasn't a door. Around the tower, thorns and weeds had grown into a jungle. The tower held one prisoner.

Surrounding it was an electric fence. And the guards. Millions of strong men and women with the bodies they should have had, unmarked by armband or tattoo, allowed to grow up and grow old. Proud people, many with names like Goldberg, Cohen and Weinstein. Men and women who would never forgive. Men and women who lived in the vast, beautiful community that surrounded the tower, keeping him awake with their laughter, their music, the smell of their food, the sight of their clothes, the sound of their language and their prayers and the cries of their babies. They felt they had a duty to be here. They had always been free to leave, but few had.

On Resurrection Day itself, some had realised that as everyone who had ever lived was in the City, then *he* was here. It had taken longer to hunt him down. Few knew where he'd been found, how he'd been leading his life. Had he tried to disguise himself? Had he proclaimed his name and tried to rally supporters? It didn't matter. He had been brought here, his identity had been confirmed and he had been thrown in the tower that had been prepared for him.

Some of those living in sight of the tower had wondered if they were protecting him from the people of the City, not protecting the City from him. And it was true: the City - the glorious, colourful, polymorphous, diverse City, with uncounted races of people living side by side - was the ultimate negation of the prisoner's creed. The vast, vast majority people of the City didn't care who he was and couldn't comprehend his beliefs, let alone be swayed by his rhetoric. Individuals who'd killed, or wanted to kill, many more people than he had remained at liberty and found themselves powerless. Had imprisoning him marked out as special? Such things were argued about, but the prisoner remained in his tower.

Every day bought requests from individuals, organisations and national groupings who had come up with some way to harm him within the protocols of the City. There were also representations from his supporters, or from civil liberties groups, concerned that his imprisonment was vigilante justice or that no attempt was being made to rehabilitate him. There were historians and psychologists and journalists who wanted to interview him. There were those that just wanted to gawp at or prod the man they'd heard so much about. All of them were turned away.

One man had come here in person. An old Roman, in light armour.
The clerk, a pretty girl with dark hair and eyes, greeted him.
'Your name?'
'Marcus Americanius Scriptor.'
While she dialled up his records and waited for them to appear on her screen, she asked: 'He's after your time. You're a historian?'
'I was,' the old man said. 'May I see him?'
'The prisoner isn't allowed visitors, or to communicate with the outside world. He is allowed to read, but not to write. Oh, that's odd. Your record isn't coming up.'
'It wouldn't.' The Roman didn't elaborate.
He looked out over the city to the tower. The young woman was struck by how solemn his face was. Most people who came all the way out here were sightseers, sensation seekers. Even some of the gaolers treated the prisoner with levity. Mocking him, belittling him.
'Don't you ever want to let him loose?' he asked, finally. 'Let him wander the streets, let his words be drowned out. On another world he was an indifferent, anonymous painter.'
'It sounds like you know that for certain,' she said, before checking herself. 'To answer the question: no. He stays here.'
'I met him,' the Roman told her. 'On a number of occasions.'
She frowned.
'A long story,' he told her. 'I suppose I'm concerned that you torture yourselves by having that monster in your midst.'
The woman had heard many people say such a thing.
'Not a monster. A human being.'
'But the only human being you've locked away for all eternity.'
'The wardens have ruled that he will be freed,' she told him.
Americanius Scriptor seemed surprised. 'When?'
'First he must serve his sentence, then he will be released.'
'When?' he asked again.
'In six million lifetimes,' she told him.
Marcus Americanius Scriptor smiled.
'I'll be waiting for him,' he told her. He turned and headed back to the docks.

Release Date: OUT NOW

info@madnorwegian.com
www.madnorwegian.com

ABOUT THE AUTHOR

KELLY HALE lives in the beautiful Pacific Northwest of the USA, a magical kingdom filled with Voodoo doughnuts, espresso houses, and independent booksellers that take up entire city blocks. A version of this novel (yes, this very one you hold in your hand) won Grand Prize in the North American Fiction Contest, January 2000. All that money is long gone. She also co-authored a novel, *Grimm Reality*, with Simon Bucher-Jones (BBC Worldwide October 2001.) After 30 years of writing short stories, two have been published (Go, Kelly!) "Blood, Pith, Crux" (Aeon Speculative Fiction 4) and "Peter I Am Lost" (Modern Magic, Tales of Fantasy and Horror, Fanstasist Enterprises, April 2006.) Her play, *Mogo Mansion*, enjoyed a brief but successful run in Seattle way back in '93. She's currently hard at work on another novel. Hard, *hard* at work. Yeah, that's the ticket.

ACKNOWLEDGEMENTS

Thanks to my family for lifelong support: Mom, Dad, Mitch, Scott, Tracey, Stephanie, Annikke, Rose, Devon Tuvalu, their spouses and offspring. Many thanks to all the keen eyes of helpful readers over the last eight years: My writer's group, who sat through this book, and others, from inception to grand prizes. Brenda, Sally, Erin, Dwight, SBJ, PDS, Sheahan, Liz (two or three times), and anyone who downloaded the first version (bless your hearts.) To the beautiful people on my LJflist who made big dreams come true, especially Mags for martinis at Harry's Bar in Paris, LAW for the pasties of Penzance, LM for pizza and Cassanova in the posh cave. And most of all to my son, Simon, who grew up with writers, actors, and musicians and still thinks he's led a charmed life. May it continue to be charming.

This book is dedicated in memory
of Al Shartner and Dwight Peterson.

EDITORIAL STAFF

Series Creator / Editor
Lawrence Miles

Publisher
Lars Pearson

Cover Art
Sandy Gardner
(www.sandygardner.co.uk)

Interior Design
Christa Dickson

VISIT US ON THE WEB

www.madnorwegian.com
www.faction-paradox.com